Kilworth, G.

014.

THE ROOF OF VOYAGING

By the same author

IN SOLITARY
THE NIGHT OF KADAR
SPLIT SECOND
GEMINI GOD
THEATRE OF TIMESMITHS
THE SONGBIRDS OF PAIN (*short stories*)
WITCHWATER COUNTRY
TREE MESSIAH (*poems*)
CLOUDROCK
SPIRAL WINDS
ABANDONATI
HIGHLANDER (*as Garry Douglas*)
IN THE HOLLOW OF THE DEEP-SEA WAVE
HUNTER'S MOON
MIDNIGHT'S SUN
IN THE COUNTRY OF TATTOOED MEN (*short stories*)
FROST DANCERS
HOGFOOT RIGHT AND BIRD-HANDS (*short stories*)
ANGEL
ARCHANGEL
HOUSE OF TRIBES

Books for children and young adults

THE WIZARD OF WOODWORLD
THE VOYAGE OF THE VIGILANCE
THE RAIN GHOST
THE THIRD DRAGON
DARK HILLS, HOLLOW CLOCKS (*short stories*)
THE DROWNERS
THE ELECTRIC KID
BILLY PINK'S PRIVATE DETECTIVE AGENCY
THE PHANTOM PIPER
THE BRONTË GIRLS
CYBERCATS
THE RAIDERS
THE GARGOYLE

THE ROOF OF VOYAGING

Book I of
The Navigator Kings

Garry Kilworth

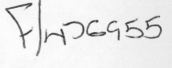

ORBIT

An *Orbit* Book

First published in Great Britain by Orbit in 1996

Copyright © Garry Kilworth 1996

The moral right of the author has been asserted.

Map and illustrations by Wendy Leigh-James

A CIP catalogue record for this book
is available from the British Library.

ISBN 1 85723 422 7

Typeset in Sabon by M Rules
Printed and bound in Great Britain by
Clays Ltd, St Ives plc

Orbit
A Division of
Little, Brown and Company (UK)
Brettenham House
Lancaster Place
London WC2E 7EN

To Lisa and Bill Fedden

Contents

Author's Note

This is a work of fantasy fiction, based on the myths and legends of the Polynesian peoples and not an attempt to faithfully re-create the magnificent migrational voyages of those peoples. Other authors have done that, will do it again, far more accurately than I am able to do. This particular set of tales, within these pages, alters a piece of known geography, while hopefully retaining the internal logic of the story: my apologies to the country of New Zealand, which has changed places with Britain. (New Zealand and the Maori are not forgotten and appear in Book II of The Navigator Kings.) The gods of the Pacific region are many and diverse, some shared among many groups of islands, others specific to one set of islands or even to a single island. Their exact roles are confused and confusing, and no writer has yet managed to classify them to absolute clarity, though Jan Knappert's book is the best. Where possible I have used the universal Polynesian deities, but on rare occasion have used a god from a specific island or group for purposes of the story. Since the spelling of Polynesian gods and the Polynesian names for such ranks as 'priest' varies between island groups, I have had to make a choice, for example *Tangaroa* (Maori) for the god of the sea and *Kahuna* (Hawaiian) for priest. In short, for purposes of homogeneity I have taken liberties with the names of gods and with language.

For the facts behind the fiction I am indebted to the following works: *The Polynesians* by Peter Bellwood (Thames and Hudson); *Nomads of the Wind* by Peter Crawford (BBC Books); *Polynesian Seafaring and Navigation* by Richard Feinberg (The Kent State University Press); *Ancient Tahitian Canoes* by Commandant P. Jourdain (Société des Oceanistes Paris Dossier); *Pacific Mythology* by Jan Knappert (HarperCollins); that inspiring work, *Polynesian Seafaring* by Edward Dodd (Nautical Publishing Company Limited); *Aristocrats of the South Seas* by Alexander Russell (Robert Hale); the brilliant *Myths and Legends of the Polynesians* by Johannes C. Andersen (Harrap); and, finally, the two articles published back to back that sparked my imagination and began the story for me way back before I had even published my first novel, *The Isles of the Pacific* by Kenneth P. Emory, and *Wind, Wave, Star and Bird* by David Lewis (National Geographic Vol. 146 No. 6, December 1974). Thanks to P. Jourdain for the invocation to Tane. I am unable to acknowledge sources on one or two myths due to the anonymous form of the papers in which I found them. My apologies and thanks to the authors, from whom I would be pleased to hear, should they wish to contact me.

My grateful thanks to Wendy Leigh-James, the design artist who provided me with a map of Oceania decorated with Polynesian symbols and motifs.

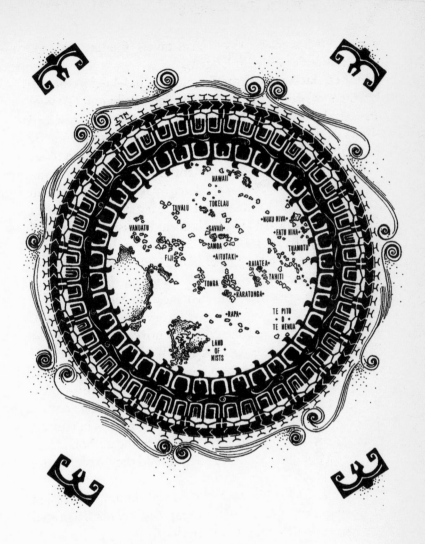

Oceania

Pantheon of the Gods

Amai-te-rangi: A deity of the sky who angles for mortals on earth, pulling them up in baskets to devour them.

Apu Hau: A god of storms, God of the Fierce Squall.

Apu Matangi: A god of storms, God of the Howling Rain.

Ara Tiotio: God of the Whirlwind and Tornado.

Aremata-rorua and Aremata-popoa: 'Long-wave' and 'Short-wave', two demons of the sea who destroy mariners.

Atua: An ancestor's spirit revered as a god.

Dakuwanga: The Shark-God, eater of lost souls.

Dengei: The Serpent-God, a judge in the Land of the Dead.

Hau Maringi: God of Mists and Fog.

Hine-nui-te-po: Goddess of the Night, of Darkness and Death. Hine is actually a universal goddess with many functions. She is represented with two heads, night and day. One of her functions is as patroness of arts and crafts. She loved *Tuna* the fish-man, out of whose head grew the first coconut.

Hine-te-ngaru-moana: The Lady of the Ocean Waves. Hine in her fish form.

Hine-tu-whenua: A benevolent goddess of the wind who blows vessels to their destination.

Hua-hega: The mother of the trickster atua, Maui.

Hine-keha, Hine-uri: The Moon-Goddess, wife of Marama the Moon-God, whose forms are Hine-keha (bright moon) and Hine-uri (dark moon).

Io: The Supreme Being, the 'Old One', greatest of the gods who dwells in the sky above the sky, in the highest of the 12 upper worlds.

Kuku Lau: Goddess of Mirages.

Lingadua: The One-armed God of Drums.

Magantu: The Great White Shark, a monster fish able to swallow a pahi canoe whole.

Maomao: The Great Wind-God, father of the many storm-gods, including 'Howling Rainfall' and 'Fierce Squall'.

Marama: God of the Moon, husband of Hine-keha, Hine-uri.

Marikoriko: First woman and divine ancestor, wife of Tiki. She was fashioned by the Goddess of Mirages out of the noonday heatwaves.

Matuku: A demi-god, kite-flyer, son of Tawhaki.

Maui: The great Oceanian trickster hero and demi-god. Maui was born to Taranga, who wrapped the child in her hair and gave him to the sea-fairies. Maui is responsible for many things, including the birth of the myriad of islands in Oceania, the coconut, and the length of the day, which was once too short until Maui beat Ra with a stick and forced him to travel across the sky more slowly.

Milu: Ruler of the Underworld.

Moko: The Lizard-God.

Nangananga: Goddess of Punishment, who waits at the entrance to the Land of the Dead for bachelors.

Nganga: The God of Sleet.

Oro: God of War, commander of the warrior hordes of the spirit world.

Papa: Mother Earth, wife of Rangi, first woman.

Ra: Tama Nui-te-ra, the Sun-god.

Rangi: God of the Upper Sky, originally coupled to his wife

Papa, the Goddess of the Earth, but separated by their children, mainly Tane the God of Forests whose trees push the couple apart and provide a space between the brown earth and blue sky, to make room for creatures to walk and fly.

Rongo: God of Agriculture, Fruits and Cultivated Plants. Along with Tane and Tu he forms the creative unity, the Trinity, equal in essence but each with distinctly different attributes. They are responsible for making Man, in the image of Tane, out of pieces of earth fetched by Rongo and shaped, using his spittle as mortar, by Tu the Constructor. When they breathed over him, Man came to life.

Rongo-ma-tane: God of the Sweet Potato, staple diet of Oceanians.

Rongo-mai: God of Comets and Whales.

Ruau-moko: Unborn God of Earthquakes, trapped in Papa's womb.

Samulayo: God of Death in Battle.

Tane: Son of Rangi the Sky God, and himself the God of artisans and boat builders. He is also the God of Light (especially to underwater swimmers because to skin divers light is where life is), the God of Artistic Beauty, the God of the Forest, and Lord of the Fairies. As Creator in one of his minor forms he is the God of Hope.

Tangaroa: God of the Ocean, who breathes only twice in 24 hours, thus creating the tides.

Tawhaki: God of Thunder and Lightning. Tawhaki gives birth to Uira (lightning) out of his armpits. Tawhaki is also the God of Good Health, an artisan god particularly adept at building houses and plaiting decorative mats.

Te Tuna: 'Long eel', a fish-god and vegetation-god. Tuna lived in a tidal pool near the beach and one day Hine went down to the pool to bathe. Tuna made love to her while she did so and they lived for some time on the ocean bed.

Tiki: The divine ancestor of all Oceanians who led his people in their fleet to the first islands of Oceania.

Ua: The Rain God, whose many sons and daughters, such as 'long rains' and 'short rains' are responsible for providing the earth with water.

Uira: Lightning (see Tawhaki).

Ulupoka: A minor god of evil, decapitated in a battle amongst the gods and whose head now rolls along beaches looking for victims.

Whatu: The God of Hail.

PART ONE

'Sail to the left of the setting sun'

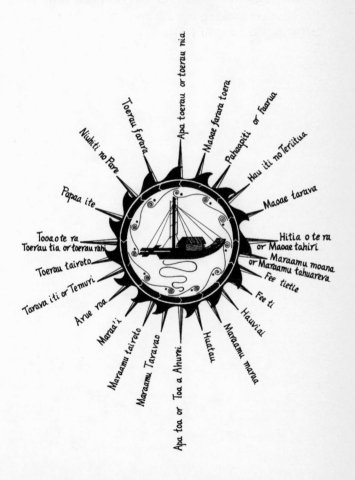

1

The giant Head rolled along the beach, driven forward by a strong, cold sea-breeze.

Leaves rustled in the frangipani trees and white blossoms drifted down to the earth as the wind swept the Head beneath their branches. Fruit bats like prehistoric birds soared through the thickening dusk. Palm-rats, sensing the presence of evil, stiffened in their climb, panted quickly, and stared with small fearful eyes at the strange tracks left upon the coral sands.

On the face of the Head, twice the size of that of a mortal, was a look of intense purposefulness. The Head had smelled the presence of seafaring men on its shore. Mingling with the sea-bottom odour of drying weed, shell-fish and crustaceans coming from the exposed reef, the thick cloying perfume of trumpet blooms, the sometimes unbelievable stench of rotting mud in the mango swamp, was the smell of groin sweat, oiled skin and hair, and stale breath.

There were exhausted seafarers, potential victims, who had fallen asleep in the land of the Head. One of these newcomers to the island was close to death and very ripe.

The Head's long black hair whipped the coral sand with its flails as it sped along.

Crabs scattered in panic out of its path.

The Head's lips were curled back in an expression of contempt, to reveal two rows of neat, even teeth. Its smoky eyes were smouldering with the desire for blood and flesh. The two broad nostrils were flared and cavernous.

The Head belonged to the god Ulupoka, severed in a great battle with the sky god, Rangi. Now it roamed the sands of certain islands, bringing disaster and disease to the earth, looking for men near to death to bite in their sleep to make certain of their demise. Once bitten by Ulupoka, either around the neck or the feet, the wound was fatal.

There was a beached double-hulled canoe above the waterline. Its Tiki, impotent on the shore, stared fixedly at the sky above the distant horizon. The pandanus sail was spread to dry between two chestnut trees near by. Perched on the prow of the boat, its feathers powdered with the pollen of orchids, was a barking pigeon, a bird whose call was not unlike the sound of a dog. The dust of dried lichens greyed the sides of the vessel, where it had been dragged over rocks to the top of the beach.

Not far from this boat the rolling Head of Ulupoka found Kupe and his six companions asleep in a make-shift hut beneath some giant ferns. Since they had fallen asleep a giant spider had woven a web with strands thick enough to catch a small bird in its nets across the entrance to their hut.

The Head bounced into the encampment and jumped into the hut, breaking the web and releasing its victim. It flew away, its high note waking the dying man. The sailor opened his eyes just as Ulupoka landed heavily on his chest. The Head bit the dying man deeply in the throat, swallowing his larynx so that he could not cry out. The only sound the mariner made was that similar to the single *gulp* of a tree frog.

It was enough to awaken the youngest member of the party, a boy of seven by the name of Kieto.

'Who's there?' cried the boy, in terror.

Ulupoka's Head, unwilling to be seen by a mortal, bounced out of the hut and into the swiftly descending night. When it was some distance from the Oceanians it let out a sound like that of a parrot burned by fire: a hideous laugh. The forest echoed with the noise and souls were chilled. Ulupoka rolled on, into the waters of the ocean, to cross the reefs to another island where there might be more dying men.

The spirit of the bitten man left his body and began the long walk along the path across the sea to the land of Milu, ruler of the dead. The dead man was rather resentful. Although he knew he had been dying, of heatstroke and exhaustion, he had been thinking very hard in his sleep about the meaning of life. Gradually, as he slept, the answer had come to him. He felt now it was bitterly ironic that he should come to know the meaning of life just at the point of his death.

'Just before Ulupoka bit me, I realised what it was all about,' he complained to Milu, who was waiting for him at the end of the purple path. 'And I died before I could tell anyone.'

Milu smiled. 'It's always the way,' he said.

After the boy's cry woke Kupe and his men, they found the dead mariner. In the light of torches lit from the embers of their small fire they saw he had torn open his own throat, with the nails of his fingers, in his terrible fever. The man had drunk seawater just before they had sighted land and they concluded this had driven him out of his mind. They took him out of the palm-leaf hut and laid his tattooed corpse on the mosses under a nokonoko tree.

'We'll bury him tomorrow,' said Kupe. 'Rest now, my brave fishermen.'

'I had a nightmare,' complained the boy, Kieto. 'I dreamed a monster came into the hut. A great head without a body. Its eyes were like embers and its tongue was a giant centipede. Its hair was long and thick, like black weed. It grinned at me – a grisly grin, like a dead man's smile.'

'A monster?' cried one of the other seafarers, shuddering. 'Listen to the boy . . .'

Kupe knew that his men would not stay on the island and get their much-needed rest if they believed a monster was on the loose. It was necessary that they replenished their store of drinking coconuts at least. Even if the boy was right – and young people were often more sensitive to these things than older men – it would be courting death by thirst to leave the island immediately.

'It was a *dream*,' he told Kieto and the others, 'nothing more. Since we have no kahuna with us to interpret the dream, then we can't be sure whether the omens are good or bad. Let's sleep on it tonight and discuss it in the morning. All dreams are clearer in the light from Ra's benevolent rays.'

There was a grumble of dissent from the fishermen, but they were very tired too and gradually sank back down onto their mats and into fitful sleeps. Kupe placed the torches around the hut, keeping his men within their circle. The gods, ancestor spirits and demons who shared the known world with men, there being no other place to inhabit, were all wary of fire.

The boy was still awake when Kupe went back into the hut.

'Are we safe?' asked the trembling Kieto.

'Yes, safe, safe,' replied Kupe.

The boy then fell instantly asleep, reassured absolutely by the leader of the expedition, the great navigator, Kupe.

It was a strange expedition, completely spontaneous, and one that would soon catch the imagination of all men and enter the legends of the Oceanians even as it was being carried out. Kupe had been fishing off the shore of his home island, Raiatea, when a giant octopus had stolen the bait from his hooks with its many arms. Enraged, Kupe had leapt from his small fishing canoe into an ocean-going vessel cruising near by. He had turned the crab-claw sail and given chase, at that time encouraged by the men already in the large canoe.

Following the ripples of the giant octopus they had been taken far away from Raiatea, until some of the men were concerned that they would never see their homeland again.

'Where's your seafaring spirit?' cried Kupe. 'Who knows what new islands we shall discover under the roof of voyaging? This octopus is obviously some kind of sea demon, sent by one of the gods, intent on leading us somewhere beyond our knowledge, for it never completely submerges and loses itself. Perhaps the Great Sea-God, Tangaroa, wishes to show us some new land we have never seen or heard of before? When I trap this great octopus and kill it, *then* I shall return to Raiatea and not before.'

Since they were ordinary fishermen and Kupe was of noble birth they did not argue, though one or two would have killed him if they thought they could get away with it. However, Kupe always kept his lei-o-mano, his dagger of kauila wood rimmed with sharks' teeth, stuck in his waistband. Kupe was a great warrior and the oportunities for catching him unawares were almost non-existent. Finally, his mana was almost as great as that of a king, so the fishermen did as they were told, day by day, night by night, ever sailing on into the unknown reaches of the Great Ocean ruled over by the god Tangaroa.

Kupe was confident in himself, for though Oceanian navigators might not know where they are going, they *always* know where they have been. He had memorised the way across the roof of the heavens, and across the many-islanded sea, to where they were now. His mariners would have done likewise. Even the boy, were he the last to survive, could find his way back home again. It was in their nature, in their instinct, to memory-map their path as they voyaged. What was more, on returning home they would describe their journeys so accurately to those who had never made the trip, the voyages could be repeated without them.

Kupe knew where he was from the shape of the waves, the star paths, the Long Shark At Dawn which was the rash of white stars across the roof of voyaging, the underwater volcanoes, the sea birds, the swell and the drift, the passing islands, the trade winds, and a thousand other things that were like signposts to him and his men. He could follow these markers back to Raiatea, possibly even *blind* when the breezes carrying the aromatic blends of islands and sea were in the right direction.

He could *smell* his way home.

At the same time he kept a record of his voyage on a piece of cord in the form of knots. The size, type and distances between the knots enabled him to recall certain sightings as well as to mark the distances between islands. This device was used by many Oceanic navigators and would be inherited by a named chosen legatee on the death of the navigator.

Tonight, the giant octopus had gone into an ocean trench, at least a league deep, and out of Kupe's reach. Kupe was sure however that they were not at the end of their journey, where he expected a battle with the ocean beast. He was being led to the creature's home waters, where the fight would be to the octopus' advantage.

Kupe had asked himself many times – *why*? Why was he following this creature at a whim? Kupe had suffered stolen bait before, from crabs and cuttlefish, lobsters and crowns-of-thorns. Why had he taken it into his head to chase after this particular beast?

It had to be the work of the gods. His fate was at the end of this voyage, one way or another. It would either be Kupe's destruction, or he was being given a precious gift.

He had no idea what shape or form that gift would take. Perhaps the gods were leading him to a heavenly island?

The only other explanation was that Maui, the ancient trickster hero, was leading him on a fruitless voyage to nowhere. This was of course possible, but if the slight but powerful Maui had decided to play a game with you, you went along with it or you were destroyed. Kupe knew it was best to ignore that possibility and hope for a better.

When morning came, and the roof of voyaging with its islands of stars had gone from the sky, Kupe leapt to his feet.

As always he was first up. The torches had burned to the ground and were charred and cold. He used wood from a kaikomako tree to produce fire by friction, making a nest of coconut fibre to catch the smouldering sawdust. This he whirled about his head on a cord until it burst into flames. Soon he was cooking yams and bananas over the heat of a fire made with white driftwood from along the shoreline.

The parrots, fruit doves and parakeets were already shouting at one another. The frigate birds, bandits of the air, were wheeling above the ocean, ready to steal from more successful feathered anglers and each other. Shoals of tiny fish, like thousands of silver splinters, were arcing across the surface of the lagoon. It was a new and brilliant morning, with a softness to the puffed clouds lying on their blue bedding.

'Up, up,' he cried, allowing the smell of the food to waft over the sleeping men, to stupify them. 'Eat, my brave sailors, we must be on our way. The great octopus stirs out in the deeps, beyond the lagoon. The dark waters bubble. We must sail when he comes to the surface.'

The men rose, grumbling, rubbing the fine, white sand from their creased faces. Some of them went immediately to a pool to drink, while others simply sat and stared bleakly at the still blue surface of the lagoon, finding it difficult to suppress the desire to fish its bountiful waters.

The boy, Kieto, assisted Kupe with the cooking, eager to be of service. His nightmare was now forgotten in the brightness of the sunshine, when the fears of night had left with the departure of Hine, Goddess of Darkness and Death.

'Will we be going home soon?' Kieto asked of Kupe. 'Shall I see my father?'

For all his eagerness to follow the giant octopus, Kupe regretted one thing: that he had not cast the boy into the sea before leaving Raiatea, so that Kieto could have swum back to the reef or shore and would not now be on a dangerous voyage into the unknown. The octopus had left the scene so quickly though, there had been little time to think of such things.

'Soon,' he told the boy. 'I feel it in my bones. The journey will be over soon.'

Leaves rustled in the trees and the boy Kieto stared up at them.

'We have no ancestors here,' he remarked in a hushed voice. 'These ghosts are all strange to us, Kupe. They play in the trees and bushes like our own spirits, but we cannot offer them worship, for we do not know them.'

Kupe nodded. 'True, Kieto, but there are powerful gods with us on this voyage. The great Tangaroa will not let any harm come to you.'

'You are beloved of Tangaroa, are you not, Kupe?' said Kieto, his face shining with admiration.

'Perhaps I am,' smiled Kupe, touching the boy's hair. 'But I would rather have Maui for a friend than any other ancient hero, for he plays such mischief with those he does not love. Now let us eat, quickly, for the octopus stirs.'

The pandanus mat sail filled with wind and the light double-hulled canoe sped through the chopped waves. The seafarers were on a platform between hulls made from te itai trees, lashed together with hand-rolled fibres from the coconut husk. On this platform sat a palm-leaf hut for shade. A bailer worked almost constantly on the hulls, as canoes always leaked water where the wood was sewn together and caulked with breadfruit sap.

'We are heading towards Apa toa,' cried Kupe. 'Keep the ocean swell to starboard.'

Apa toa was the name of a wind, not a place, for though they had no instruments or charts to follow, there was a wind-flower carved in the bows. The tattoo signs for twenty-three major and minor winds, with arrows pointing at the direction of their sources, were etched deeply into the wood, making the shape of a many-petalled circular bloom. The wind-flower was both aesthetic and practical; an artistic decoration which had a functional purpose.

Ahead of them, below the surface of the sea, swam the great dark shadow which was the octopus. The beast was languid in movement, but not slow. It took all Kupe's skill to keep up with the creature. Po, the man at the helm, struggled with the steering oar to keep the craft on a true course.

Kupe, as the navigator, was constantly searching the surface of the ocean and the skyline, even the clouds, for signs to remember. A light green colour on a cloudbase to one direction meant an island or even atoll, where the waters of a lagoon were reflecting on the sky. Frigate birds meant there was land somewhere near. He listened for the sound of reefs and watched the colour of the water change through many shades.

The double-hulled canoe Kupe was sailing belonged to the fisherman Po and it was Po's Tiki which stood on the deck of the vessel. The carved wooden idol was the eyes and ears of the crew. Since Po had hewn this Tiki it was to Po it spoke, inside his head, and it irritated Kupe that he was not directly in control of the entire boat. Po, however, did his best to please Kupe on all occasions, knowing that once the voyage was over he would be rewarded for his part in the expedition.

There was a bird cry from inside the deck hut and Kieto went in to feed their latest captive: a kula parrot from the islands they had just left. Kupe would have liked to have taken a breeding pair, since the bird had a breast of scarlet feathers. It would have made them all rich men, for red feathers were the currency of exchange on Raiatea and Borabora. However, the octopus had left just as they had caught their first kula and there had been a scramble to get on board the boat and head out to sea, leaving the riches behind them.

When the night came down again, Kupe was able to watch for the kaveinga, the path of stars which rose one after the other over the dark horizon. He knew their secret names, and those of the slower-wheeling fanakenga, or zenith stars which pointed down to particular islands in their wake.

When he had to sleep, Po took over the watch and the oar both, keeping the gleaming phosphorescent ripples made by the fleeing octopus in his sight.

After many weeks there came a time when the sea darkened quickly and large waves reared before them. The craft bravely fought through these, the men using their heavy oars rather than trusting to the sail. Eventually they came upon some high cliffs of an island too large to hold in the eye. It swept away on both sides of the craft to somewhere deep in the mists.

They followed the octopus down the length of this land, to its bottom, where the shore was wild and untamed. Here the wind was cold, the sea was cold, the skies grey. Sharp, hissing rain joined with stinging spray to rob the seafarers of energy, to fill them with a bleakness of spirit. The waves grew mountainous, with rushing peaks of white which touched the swirling greyness above, and sky and sea seemed one.

The sea and scouring rain had hewn the rocks of the

coast into grotesque shapes and tall stacks. The wind had cut fissures in the rockface deep enough to swallow a man. There were pinnacles that towered like giant spears over the small craft and great boulders loomed suddenly as if vomited from coves just a few moments ago. It was a dark, forbidding place with ancient secrets moaning for release from a hundred-thousand caverns; with cryptic silences locked in fathomless caves.

'The giant beast has led us to a giant land,' said Kupe, in wonder. 'It is here we shall do battle.'

Indeed, as if the octopus had heard his words, it rose frothing to the surface and turned, coming towards the canoe at a monstrous speed. Its massive tentacles were pumping behind it, shooting it through the spume like a racing canoe powered by a hundred men. Its great eyes were wide with hatred. Its beak chopped at the surface of the sea, in anticipation of crunching the bones of its determined adversary.

Po let out a cry and pulled hard on the steering oar, while the rowers beat the waves with their rowing oars. The hero Kupe stood on the front of the craft, awaiting the onslaught, his lei-o-mano in his strong right hand.

Po, with the help of the brave little Kieto, managed to turn the canoe at the last moment, and the octopus swept by the stern. A single tentacle flashed over the deck of the craft, snatching at the beast's enemy. Kupe's tattooed body was hauled over the side, caught in the suckers on that terrible limb.

'He's gone!' cried Po, to the other sailors, who let out a moan and started paddling away from the scene.

Kieto yelled, 'Don't leave him!'

They ignored the boy in their desperation to escape the giant. Their terror would not allow them to accept the thought that Kupe might win. All they wanted to do was put a great distance between themselves and the octopus, fearful that the creature might wreak more revenge upon the craft.

Kupe and the octopus were lost behind a huge wave thrown back by the high cliffs of the land.

'Stop,' screamed the boy. 'He'll be left to drown in these grey seas . . .'

Still the wide-eyed mariners, nightmares running like shadows over their faces, through their eyes, would not stop paddling. Kieto raced to the sail and heaved upon the line, half raising the pandanus mat in the full force of the wind. The craft lurched sideways, spilling one of the rowers into the sea. Luckily the man overboard clung to one of the trailing lines and managed to keep with the craft.

A mariner rushed for the boy, wielding a paddle club.

'You stupid young idiot!' shrieked the man. 'Don't make me kill you.'

Kieto stood his ground and would have been felled by the man, had not Po cried, 'Look!'

All eyes turned to where he was pointing and they saw a thrashing and foaming on the surface of the water. Tentacles were waving, whipping the waves, causing a boiling of the ocean. When the spray fell hissing around the craft and their vision was clear, they saw Kupe sitting astride the octopus' head, his legs wrapped around the enormous beak keeping it locked shut, his arm plunging repeatedly into the bulbous form. Once, twice, thrice . . . then the hardwood dagger snapped, its shark-toothed point buried deep in the flesh of the octopus.

Po groaned, 'He's done for. The beast will take him down now, pulp him and feed on his rotting flesh.'

But even as Po spoke, and the creature began to dive, Kupe bit the octopus, sinking his teeth between the creature's eyes. He bit deep, seeking a vulnerable spot in the beast's brain. The pair of them disappeared down into the depths, leaving a trail of small bubbles in their wake.

This time the mariners waited in silence, not attempting to flee, their strength gone and their will tied securely to the man who had slipped down towards the home of

Tangaroa. Mists were drifting over the edge of the nearby cliffs, spilling like slow liquid into the leaping waters of the ocean. They filled the cracks and caves along the high walls of rock with cold smoke and rolled over the colder surface of the sea.

Suddenly, up came the great Kupe, like a coconut released from submarine weeds, bobbing on the waves.

Kieto cheered. 'There he is! There he is! Kupe has won!'

Po let out a whoop, and was joined by his fellow mariners; it was the sound of relief rather than joy, yet the dripping Kupe, as he was hauled aboard, did not blame them. This was a selfish act he had carried out, this act of revenge. Yet he acknowledged to himself, if not to them, that he had no choice in the matter. He had been compelled by some inner spirit to make this journey and fight this fight. Now it was over. They could return to Raiatea, having found an immense island, perhaps more than an island, far beyond their own waters.

'I shall call this place "Land-of-Mists",' he told his mariners. 'If ever you are asked how to reach it, you must tell the inquirers to sail a little to the left of the setting sun at this time of the year. That will lead them to the Land-of-Mists as surely as the octopus led us.'

2

'We shall fashion a new sail when we reach one of the smaller islands,' Kupe told his crew, pointing to the crab-claw. 'In the weave shall be the shape of an octopus – a symbol of my triumph over the creature. But first, I wish to explore these coasts just a little before we begin to return to our homeland.'

Aware that they had entered a new ocean, new seas, the Oceanians felt insecure and a little afraid. This eerie, tall world was far removed from their own. It seemed less civilised, less understandable. Here there were strange winds, from unusual corners. Here the weather was ruled by unpredictable gods with moods sometimes savage, sometimes sullen, but rarely joyous. Here currents and tidal eddies seemed erratic and impetuous, changing at whim, following some mad god's directions.

At every turn the Raiateans expected horrible monsters to lurch from the caves, or rise dripping with seaweed from the depths. They sensed the area's differentness in their souls, knowing it to be a place quite unlike any Oceanian island. This was a piece of the earth which *should* have dropped away, into the chasm of nothingness beyond, but had somehow remained attached to the true world of the myriad islands of Oceania.

They sailed the waters for a few days, touching land once or twice, but warily. There were the lights of fires on the cliff tops at night, and on some of the smaller islands which were scattered some way up from the main body of land. In places the fires were so numerous Kupe felt there was a strong presence, a great many inhabitants, on that rugged coast. He and his men would stand no chance in open battle against such a number.

'I wonder what dark gods they pray to here?' he murmured to his crew. 'This is indeed a place fit for demons.'

The Oceanians heard the beat of drums on the night air and the wailing of diabolical voices on the breeze.

The skies over the main island seemed always grey, with thick cloud blocking out the face of Ra. There was a great deal of rain, which washed down its own pathways on the cliffs, into the restless ocean. It was a brooding land, seeming to nurse resentment in its breast for some unknown ills perpetrated upon its crags and buttresses. A wild nature it had, with a savage spirit. Its warriors, Kupe was certain, would be just as fierce, just as brutal as the landscape on which they lived.

Then finally, as the crew were about to set off towards home, Kupe asked them to wait. He pointed to a cliff face.

'Look there,' said Kupe. 'A white figure.'

The men, on following his arm, saw a creature on the vertical granite, working its way from crevice to crevice.

'A demon, more like,' cried Po.

If it was a demon it was in the shape of a white-skinned, barefoot man in sea-washed ragged garments, a cloth bag slung over his shoulder. He was collecting birds from their cliffside nests as he went, fulmars which he first strangled then placed carefully in the bag. The man seemed strong and nimble as he swung from crack to crack on the sheer face of the grey rock, at a height of some fifty men. Sometimes he hung by only one hand, his feet dangling, his other hand engaged snatching the fulmars from their nests.

Sometimes the birds wheeled about him, shrieking in his ears, furious at his murder and theft of their comrades. He was a white and grey ghost mobbed by smaller white and grey ghosts.

Kupe concluded that the man was very strong, to be able to bear his own weight so frequently with a single arm.

'See how he clings to the rock,' he murmured. 'And his movements are so dexterous.'

Still, the figure seemed confident, uncaring of the attacks by the birds, unimpressed by the drop into the deep ocean. If he fell, the sea would be sure to swallow him whole; Tangaroa would eat him. Even as they watched the waves clawed at the stone face, eager to rip the man from his perch. What amazed Kieto about the man was his long, flailing hair. Surely he was not a demon, but a hero from the past?

Po suddenly shouted, 'See – at the top of the cliff.'

They all stared upwards, to witness another figure, this one with black hair flying in the wind. The face was again of a whiteness they had never seen before, except in albino children, and this new figure was slight, less muscled. The arms were slim, the shoulders lean. Kupe thought it to be either a woman or a youth in a ragged shift.

When the wind blew the shift hard against the figure, emphasising the shape beneath, Kupe concluded it was a woman; the breasts were large, the waist slim, the hips wide.

This person screamed something down to the man collecting fulmars, her face contorted. There was either distress, or anger, or some other violent emotion evident in her gestures. Her hands seemed to claw at the air. Her body contorted as if she were struggling with an unseen assailant. At times her mouth opened to scream words incomprehensible to the Raiateans, while the high wind lashed at her, screaming back.

She disappeared for a moment, then reappeared with a

large rock in her hands. She purposely threw the stone down on the man. It struck and bounced from crag to crag, knocking off further chunks of stone. The man managed to swing one-handed out of the path of the falling rocks, though the acrobatics left him dangling dangerously for a moment.

'A husband and wife battle, I think,' joked one of the mariners. 'Perhaps he has not been in her bed recently, but wandering a little amongst the beds of others?'

The men laughed at this, pleased to have some release from the tension.

The woman was railing at the man again, clawing at her breast as she did so. Spitting ugly words down upon the lone climber. She was clearly very distraught, as if the man were stealing her babies from those nests, rather than seabirds. Every so often she threw her arms high and shrieked at the dark, grey clouds, as if requesting assistance from the gods.

'This is no matrimonial dispute,' said Kupe. 'I really think she means to kill him.'

Indeed, as if to prove him right, the woman disappeared again and returned with a rock larger than the one she had thrown down on the man before. So heavy was this stone she appeared to have difficulty in lifting it. Buffeted by the strong winds at the top of the cliff, the woman heaved the massive stone over the edge, the effort pulling her forward.

The stone plunged through space, completely missing the bird-nester, to splash only half a man's length from the Oceanians' bows.

'Look out!' cried Po. 'The bitch nearly sank us.'

'See, she falls!' Kieto yelled.

The winds and the weight of the rock had caused her to overbalance and she followed in the wake of the stone she had cast down on the head of the man. She made no sound, but turned once in mid-air on her descent, her arms and legs stretched wide to form the shape of a star. The climber reached out for her as she passed, to grasp and save her, but her weight ripped him from the rock face too. Together they plummeted the whole way into the waters of the ocean, not far from the craft. It would only take a short while for the cold waters to drag them down, where they would be smashed by the waves against the cliff.

'Take them,' said Kupe.

The Raiateans paddled the canoe to where the two figures were struggling in the waves. The man was dragged aboard first. Po struck him with a paddle to keep him quiet. Then the woman was hauled over the deck. She was only semi-conscious, from her great fall, and they tossed her in the palm-leaf hut.

'Now, let us be on our way,' Kupe ordered. 'Steer to the right of the sun.'

When the man came round they were in calmer waters. Kupe had bound the man, hands and feet, so he would be no trouble to them. The woman was also bound with sennit cord, to stop her from jumping into the ocean, something she had already tried. So far the woman had remained silent, sullen and brooding, simply staring bleakly out over the passing waters at some unseeable thing in the middle distance.

The man woke on his side, coughed seawater on to the deck, and then tried to lift his head to see his captors. Now that the sun had dried him, they saw his hair was thick and red upon his head, not dark as they had first thought. His face too was covered in coarse, reddish hair, so that only his eyes and nose were visible. His pale, freckled arms were also hairy.

Po said, 'He's got more hair than a hog.'

'*Is e Dia mo bhuachaill*,' he yelled into the face of Po.

Po leapt back with alacrity, his face taut.

'It's true, he *is* a demon,' Po cried. 'We must chop him into small pieces and throw him into the water before he

FWD6955

chants again. Who knows what magic he can conjure with those strange speakings?'

Kieto said, 'I think he has the head of Ra. See how the red hair circles his white face . . .'

The man then proceeded to pour such dark language forth from his lips, all of it seemingly directed at Po, who was in his line of sight. Po looked around frantically for a weapon, seized on a wahaika club, and was about to dash the man's brains out, when Kupe took hold of his arm.

'No! This man is my prisoner.'

'But he's not a man,' wailed Po. 'He's a creature of the darkness.'

'Then why hasn't he set himself free?' Kupe reasoned. 'If he's such a powerful demon, why does he allow himself to be trussed like a chicken? No, this is a man, a very *strange* one, I'll grant you, but a man just the same. Look how bruised his white skin is – this is ordinary flesh.'

'*Cha ghabh mi tuille,*' shrieked the man.

Po shuddered, remembering the land where the mist dropped like veils from high stone walls and drifted over the cold face of the sea as if it were shrouding a monster beneath.

Kupe had not admitted it to his fellow seafarers but he was fascinated by the creatures they had caught. The woman seemed quite wild, like a creature born of a storm, and the man too was not civilised or refined in any way. Kupe had already formed a certain respect for the man, for though like Kupe the man had no tattoos on his face, there were several on his body. They were of a design Kupe did not understand – in fact the longer he stared at them the more they confused him, making him feel giddy and a little ill with their complex interweavings – but they were definitely a body decoration of some kind.

There were, unlike those tattoos on his own body, pictures of strange creatures on the man's skin. A shiver of fear went through the normally phlegmatic navigator when he

looked at these illustrations. They were like no other animals he had ever seen before and he did not want to ask their names in case they were beasts from some damned place, some taboo land in an Otherworld, the names of which might turn an ordinary man's mind to dust.

In a calm moment, when the man was no longer frantically fighting his bonds, nor screaming at Po and trying to bite the terrified mariner's legs as he passed, Kupe sat by the sickly-pale creature and tried for information.

Kupe pointed to himself. 'Kupe,' he said.

The man's washed-blue eyes stared hard at Kupe and he shook his red mane petulantly.

Kupe repeated the gesture and the word several times. Then he pointed to his prisoner.

'Who are you?' he asked.

The man blinked those strange eyes, the colour of the sky near the horizon after rain.

Finally, the man said, 'Pict.'

Kupe pointed to the woman, who glared back.

'Who is she?'

The man gave the woman a tight, bitter little smile, before saying to Kupe, '*Is i so a' Scot bhean.*'

Kupe shook his head, indicating that he did not understand so many words strung together.

'Scot,' the man repeated. 'Scot *bhean.*'

The woman spat at him and turned her head away.

So it appeared their names were Pict and Scot, and that they hated each other with a terrible venom. Or at least the woman loathed the man. Kupe was not so sure that Pict hated Scot, for there was something wistful in the way that Pict's eyes rested on the form of the woman sometimes; almost as if the man deeply regretted the antipathy. Some secret lay between these two creatures which would not be resolved until Kupe and his crew taught them to speak properly, in the way real people should. He gave the task of teaching them to young Kieto, since they both appeared to prefer the child's company to that of any of the men.

'Will you teach them to talk?' asked Kupe of Kieto. 'I would appreciate your help.'

Kieto, who was afraid of the two white demons they had dragged from the sea, hesitated, but finally said, 'I can try, Prince Kupe.'

'Good,' Kupe smiled at the boy and ruffled his hair. 'One day I think you will become a great hero, Kieto.'

'Like you?' said the boy, in great pleasure. 'Just like you?'

'Perhaps greater,' laughed Kupe. 'I have only discovered a new land – you, I think, will conquer it.'

It was Kupe's intention to revisit the island where they had picked up the kula parrot, but on the way back a storm blew them off course and he understood that the gods did not wish him to become wealthy.

'Wealth spoils a man, in any case,' he told Po. 'It makes him suspicious of other men and it makes him mean and pointed. Don't you agree?'

'Yes,' said Po, sighing, 'but I think I would have enjoyed being spoiled.'

Kupe smiled and shook his head.

'You think you would.'

'I *know* I would,' said Po, refusing to be shaken.

At first, the deadly chill of the wind and evaporation of the seawater from the skin of the captives took their toll on the newcomers' strength. It was conditions such as these which had shaped the physical and mental nature of the hardy Oceanians over the centuries. Spray from the bows drenched every part of the canoe and drying a wet skin in a cold wind was an accepted fact of a mariner's life. Kupe's seamen were provided with a layer of insulating fat and stamina to help them.

The captives however were not used to being sodden much of the time. They sat miserably shivering and hugging themselves on the deck of the canoe, even on hot days, until their bodies readjusted a little and they were able to cope. Both were hardy individuals, used to a cold, wet climate, even if they usually spent much of their time in stone-and-turf crofts. They were not the kind of people to die in such circumstances, though many others might. They were too obstinately angry with each other, and with life in general, to allow the wet and cold to carry them off. A fatal blow to the head with a club wielded by one or the other, yes, but not a thing like exposure.

Kieto began teaching the man to speak like a real person, instead of a demon or ghost.

The man learned quickly, over the many weeks, there being all the time in the world and no distractions. The woman refused to learn at all, simply glowering every time Kieto tried to engage her attention. So it was that they spoke with the man first and took his side of the story as the truth.

His name was not Pict – that was his people – he was called Seumas, and the woman the Pict told them, from a different people called the Scots, was named Dorcha. Seumas had killed Gealach, the husband of Dorcha, in a fair fight over the possession of a weapon called a 'sword', which once the deed had been done and bitterly regretted by Seumas, he had flung into the sea in an attempt to expunge his guilt.

'A man's life is not worth a *sword*,' he told Kieto. 'I have wished Gealach back to life again a thousand times.'

'What is a sword?' asked Kieta.

'A long knife,' replied Seumas.

Kieto knew what a knife was: a lei-o-mano, or a spike of sharpened obsidian, or a sliver of shell with a wooden handle.

'How did you kill him?' asked Kieto, fascinated by tales of single combat.

The pale, faded eyes stared at the boy for a moment before replying, 'We fought on a hill at dawn, just as the world was waking. It was a long fight, for though Gealach was small, he was heavy-set and strong. Twice he almost broke my spine when he had me in a bear grip. On the third time I plunged a blade into his throat seven times. The blood spurted forth like a burn from a mountainside, staining the heather. He cursed me with his last gargled scream . . . that's why I'm here today, I suppose – the result of Gealach's curse.'

Kupe, who had been listening, said, 'If that's so, why is the woman here? Was she cursed too?'

Seumas conceded that this was a mystery. He stared at the woman, sulking as usual under the deck hut.

'Perhaps she was unfaithful to him, at some time? Perhaps she was barren and could not bear him children? Perhaps she was cold in bed and kept her thighs tightly together when the passion was on him? Who knows. If I am here because I was cursed, then she too must have done something to displease a dying man whose oaths the gods take seriously.'

Kupe said, 'If a woman wishes to go with another man, then that is a matter for the priests to decide. If a woman cannot bear children, then another will bear them in her place and make a gift of them to her. If a woman has no wish to be penetrated, that is her right, and the man must either seek his gratification elsewhere, or find a cold stream to rid himself of his desire.'

Seumas stared at Kupe and a grim expression came over his face.

'Your people must be very different to mine. It is our right to kill the woman if she goes into another's bed. A barren woman, we believe, must have sinned and upset the gods at some time to be so cursed, and therefore it is *her* fault there are no offspring. If a husband wants his wife, she must give herself to him, or be taken in anger.'

'Indeed,' said Kupe, shaking his head sadly, 'we are from different worlds.'

That night the vessel passed the 'island with the stink of ghosts' putting fear into the hearts of the men as they passed on the outside of the reef, their eyes on the moonlit bleached bones of the dead, like broken coral, which were the beaches on the island with the stink of ghosts. Po asked the Tiki to take them away as quickly as possible, before the smell of the unhappy, dead spirits overwhelmed the crew and they were forced against their will to land on the island.

'What is that foul odour?' asked Seumas, but no one answered him for fear of arousing the rage of the island's castaway ghosts, and they slipped on under the stars to happier waters.

Next morning, on a calm sea, the Pict was being rubbed down with vegetable oil by Kieto. The Pict's pale complexion had turned a nasty red colour under the sun, even though he spent much of his time in the shade of the deck hut. The oil would help protect his delicate skin.

The woman too was beginning to darken a little, though she had been much more careful than the man to keep herself covered from the sun.

Seumas stared at the wooden statue on the deck as he was being massaged and asked Kieto, 'Who is that ugly brute Po seems to love so much?'

He nodded at the roughly hewn idol strapped to the front of the deck.

'That is Tiki,' whispered the boy. 'You must not call him ugly or he will take us out onto false waters, where we'll lose ourselves in darkness and all drown.'

'Really?' said Seumas. 'But what is it, this Tiki?'

'Tiki was our first ancestor, who led us out of the darkness into the light. Now he is still with us, in our wooden statues of him.'

Seumas stared at the idol. 'Well, he was surely an ugly bastard . . .'

'Bastard?'

Seumas hesitated and then replied wryly, 'Someone born out of wedlock – if Tiki was the first, then he couldn't have had married parents could he? So, in a manner of speaking, he was a bastard orphan – with all due respect.'

Dorcha stirred in the hut. There were two men on the back of the craft, fishing for the day's meal. A small turtle already lay on the deck. The woman had been watching these two, but she turned now and stared at Seumas.

'I know of another bastard,' she said, darkly in the language of the Oceanians.

'Meaning me, I suppose?' said Seumas. 'I thought you couldn't speak their words.'

'I only had to listen while they were teaching you,' she sneered. 'You think you're so clever? I got it while you were still stumbling over that thick tongue of yours.'

She then ignored Seumas and turned to Kieto.

'Boy,' she said, her dark-stone eyes flashing, 'who is this Tiki? Is he the Adam of your people?'

Kieto was frightened of this savage woman who looked like a witch in her ragged dress, with her curly, matted, dark hair piled wild and thick about her head. Her face, beneath the tangle of hair, was pretty enough, though a little sharp and often quite dirty. And she ringed her eyes with the black of charcoal from the fire, making them look like deep pits within which were two glintering black jewels.

As the Pict had done before they made him bathe, she stank strongly of body odour and the peat turf of her homeland, with a few other unidentifiable smells besides. The toes of her feet, bound in leather strips, poked filthy and odorous from between the hide cladding. She resisted all attempts to wash her body, scratching and clawing at any man who laid a hand on her, as if cleanliness would weaken her in some way. Since the dirt was thick beneath her nails, not unnaturally the men were frightened of getting an infection from the wounds she inflicted.

'The Adam?' asked Kieto, nervously. 'What is the Adam?'

'Adam and Eve,' said the woman. 'Are you heathens too, like that bastard there?'

Seumas laughed. 'She's heard about a new religion,' he said. 'The worship of a man who was pegged through his hands and feet – nailed against a tree.'

'What's that?' asked Kupe, who had been busy with the sail, 'a man was pegged up on a tree? Surely, it must be the tree they worship then, not the man? The man was obviously a sacrifice to the tree, wasn't he?'

'That's my thinking, certainly,' said Seumas. 'This new religion has come from somewhere south of our land of Albainn, from the country of the Angles and Jutes. It started on one of the islands, so they tell me – a place called Lindisfarne – and there are people known as monks and priests involved. I would hang the lot.'

Dorcha gave Seumas a disgusted look and turned away, as if he were not worth the effort of an argument.

Kupe asked, 'What is your thinking then? About the gods?'

'Me? I might make a prayer to the sun for coming up in the morning, or to the moon for giving me a good hunt – perhaps to the mossy rock where I took my first girl, or a sacred tree from which I cut my first spear? – but I would not pray to a crucified man hanging from a tree. Let the flesh rot on him, and the corbies pick at his bones, he wouldn't get *my* words sprinkled on his spirit.'

'Heathen,' muttered Dorcha. 'Murdering heathen bastard – I hope *you* rot on a tree some day.'

'Heathen am I?' snarled Seumas. 'Don't I ask the Owl-god to watch over me at night and warn me of the coming of my enemies? Don't I call to the Hare-god or the Stag-god for speed when I run? Don't I yell for the Eagle-god when I fall on the kill? How can I be a heathen? I pray to more gods than you have fingers and toes. More than *one*, at any rate.

'And if I do hang on a tree, I don't want them to pray over *me* like they do to that creature of yours.'

'Don't worry, they won't – they'll just spit on the corpse.'

'Good. Make sure you're the first.'

'I want to be the one who puts you up there!' she said, whirling on him, her eyes flashing.

Kupe was steering the canoe in the direction of the wind Maoae farara toerau, which on the wind-flower was the first to the right of the top petal of the bloom. There was a thin layer of light grey ambergris on the surface of the sea, which had a pleasant smell in the noonday sun. Kupe had been explaining to Seumas that the waves had points in this part of the ocean and its colour was a deep grey-green, which put them in the region of an island known as the Conch.

'We are nearing our home island of Raiatea and will soon be amongst our people.'

Seumas nodded. It meant nothing to him. He was, now that the initial shock of his capture and his interest in his captors had waned a little, feeling very homesick. He wanted to be in the mountains and glens of Albainn, smelling the sweet turf, chasing the deer, feeling a chill wind on his skin and the dew beneath his feet. The ocean around him seemed endless, surely *was* infinite, and his life ahead of him eternal.

There was a woman he loved back there in Albainn, with a lithe pale body and a temper to match a wildcat's. Seumas had been about to be joined with her in tribal marriage when he had killed the Scot, thus delaying the wedding. The two spiral tattoos on his neck were symbols that he was betrothed and unavailable to other women. Po had told him that on Raiatea the men wore a flower called a frangipani bloom behind their left ear when they were similarly betrothed, but even Seumas could see that the flower could be switched to behind the bachelor ear in a sexual emergency. Now he had betrothal tattoos and yet he was still unmarried. No woman would take him seriously.

He stared gloomily out over the desert of water wondering if he would ever see his homeland again. Kupe had taken him, so the man himself had said, in order to familiarise the Oceanians with the ways of the Albannachs. Did Kupe really believe that Seumas was a traitor, that he would betray his people? Seumas had said as much to the great navigator.

'Not yet,' Kupe admitted, 'but by the time we need your help, you will be one of us.'

'I shall never be one of you,' replied Seumas, fiercely. 'I am a Pict first and an Albannach last, and there is no room for any other loyalties between those two.'

'So you say now,' smiled Kupe, infuriatingly. 'In any case, just by studying you and the woman, we can get a certain amount of information about your people – useful facts.'

Seumas had nodded grimly. 'If you're thinking of trying to conquer Albainn, forget it. The tribes there are full of fierce and brutal warriors, who would rather kill outsiders than each other, and they're quite fond of murder and pillage amongst their own kind, believe me. Scots, and my own people, the Picts. Clans who hate each other will join to fight a common enemy. In the land above us the Angles and Jutes have found that to their cost. They too are more than a match for you, being more advanced in the science of warfare than us. They have weapons the likes of which you have not even dreamed.'

'We shall conquer Albainn *and* the land of the Angles – what do you call it?'

'*They* call it Englaland. We call it *Cú-Tir*.'

'What does that mean?'

Seumas smiled. 'Land of Dogs.'

Kupe nodded. 'We shall conquer that land – and yours.'

Seumas laughed. 'They are too many – and there are Irish on an island near Englaland.'

'We shall still conquer them also,' said Kupe, with remarkable if infuriating confidence.

Dorcha spoke now, from the shadows of the hut, where she was drinking coconut juice and eating sweet potato and breadfruit.

'The Pict is right – you will never conquer our tribes, nor those above us, the tribes of Englaland.'

'And why is that?'

'Iron,' she said, simply.

She had used the Gaelic word, not knowing the Oceanian equivalent.

Seumas saw what she meant and had to give her credit for her intelligence. Not until now had he actually realised that there was no metal on the boat, in the boat or about the Oceanian seafarers who crewed the craft. Their weapons were made of wood, teeth, shells and bone. There were wooden pegs and binding cord keeping the canoe together. They wore no copper amulets, nor bronze torcs, nor golden earrings. It had been obvious to Dorcha and was now clear to Seumas, that the Oceanians did not know metal. It was outside their experience.

'The woman is right,' he said. 'You can't fight a war against the Albannachs and English tribes without iron weapons. You'd be cut down like wild wheat under sickles.'

'This *iron* is a superior material?' questioned Kupe.

'It is harder, tougher and more resilient than the hardest stone or flint, and you can sharpen it so finely you can cut a hog's hair in two lengthways.'

'It sounds lethal.'

'It makes a man ten times more powerful.'

'Well,' smiled Kupe, 'so at least we know about this iron, before we go into battle against it.'

Seumas's face fell. He knew that he and Dorcha had been duped by the smooth tongue of Kupe. It was exactly

as the great navigator had told him just a short time ago –
the Oceanians would learn much just from talking casually
with their captives, without the full co-operation of the
Pict and the Scot.

'Perhaps,' continued Kupe, 'you can show us how to
make this iron prior to our departure for the Land-of-
Mists, which is the name I have given your country.'

Seumas looked quickly at Dorcha, then said to Kupe,
'I wouldn't and I couldn't – you can't make iron out of
nothing – you have to have ore.'

'You think we haven't got this ore?'

'I'm certain, or you would have found it and used it by
now, just as we have. Anyway, it's as I say, we wouldn't
show you how to use it, even if we could. You're talking
about invading our land, our people. How can you expect
us to assist you in that endeavour?'

'We're not going yet. Perhaps not in my lifetime. One
day, when the time is right, when the gods decide we must
go to the Land-of-Mists and conquer it. Then we shall go.
But that's in the future. By then you will have children by
one or more of our women, and Dorcha will have for a
husband one of our men . . .'

'A very brave one,' muttered Po, sitting sewing
nearby. Kupe ignored this remark, while Dorcha glared
at the mariner with black-rimmed eyes, causing him to
twitch in embarrassment – and not a little fear of witch-
craft.

'. . . and you will be Raiateans, both of you.'

'It still won't help you defeat men of iron,' Dorcha told
Kupe. 'Even if we fall down and kiss your feet.'

'There are ways,' replied Kupe, his casual confidence
confounding both the Albannachs. 'Alliances can be made,
friends can be bought. The time will come.'

Kupe suddenly turned and sniffed the breeze.

'I smell land,' he said. 'The swell is taking us closer to an
island. Look.'

He pointed to a far distant cloud on the base of which was a light green tinge.

'That's the reflection of a lagoon,' he told the two Albannachs. 'An atoll or an island. We shall soon be in Raiatean waters. Tiki has seen us home.'

'God bless him,' muttered Dorcha, but even Seumas didn't know whether or not she was being sarcastic.

3

Once he had become used to the idea of
captivity, a condition which would have been abhorrent to
him several weeks ago, Seumas was able to turn his mind to
studying his captors.

There was much to admire in them. They seemed
civilised and appeared to have a higher standard of living
than his own people. There was a harmony between them
which Seumas did not recognise at first, coming from a
clan where discord was the prime mover and motivater of
deeds.

The Picts lived in caves and hovels, while Kieto had
described to him houses made of hardwood with elabo-
rately carved doorposts and pillars, good thatched roofs
which kept out the rain, and solid walls. Inside these houses
it was neat and clean. There were no half-gnawed bones
scattered over the bedspaces, as there were in Pict dwellings,
nor the ashes of a dozen previous fires littering floors.

For food the Raiateans had a vast array of fruits and vegetables. Even on board the canoe there were taro roots,
yams, coconuts, pandanus fruit, dried bananas, sweet potatoes and breadfruit. In separate gourds there were
breadfruit paste, hard poi and fresh water. There was no
meat on board, but Kieto had told him that back on the

island there were pigs, dogs and something called a chicken which was apparently a flightless domestic bird.

Most of the flesh the islanders ate however came from fish in the sea; a dozen varieties of reef fish, dorado, shark, barracuda and turtle kebabs.

In turn hundreds of varieties of shellfish were gathered from the coral, along with crabs, lobsters, cuttlefish and squid.

The Raiateans seemed to eat like kings.

The climate on Raiatea, and its near neighbour Borabora, was kinder than that of Albainn, being hot and sunny most of the time, with much rain at certain times of year.

Yet, there were things Seumas did not like about his captors.

They seemed arrogant beyond their measure, which to him was a great sin. A Pict was modest about his achievements and his prowess. Po would brag for hours about a shark he had caught with a magic stone. The bailers would laughingly challenge Seumas to keep up with their rhythmic bailing with half-coconut shells and laugh at him again when he had to stop because his arm felt like it was being wrenched from its socket. Even Kupe, the aloof navigator prince, informed Seumas proudly of his achievements as a warrior, saying he had never been beaten in single combat and describing how he had chased and killed the great octopus which had led him to Albainn.

They are too full of themselves, he thought. *They make too much of their skills and talents.*

Again, their physical appearance and manners were too feminine for a Pict. Even though they were a stocky race of creatures, their faces were too pretty, too unblemished. Seumas could not help feeling superior to them in manliness, though he was at a loss to explain how. Certainly their seamanship was second to none, their navigating skills nothing short of magical, their individual strengths astonishing. Yet, they were not *masculine* in the Pict sense. They moved too fluidly, walked too lightly on their feet, had too ready a smile and too soft a touch.

A Pict, or indeed Angle and Scot, held himself inside, did not reveal easily his ability at anything. A Pict had fortitude without display. A Pict hid his endurance and grit, his mettle, beneath a gruff but indifferent exterior. A Pict did not smile overmuch, nor fuss with foodstuffs, nor care very much where he shat. A Pict was stern and hard, hitting a man first then offering hospitality to the cripple later, after the man was disabled and pathetic. A Pict was a rock of a man, walking heavily on the earth, stepping aside for no one, bludgeoning those who dared to block his path.

A Pict was, in Seumas's opinion, more of a *man*.

Finally, he was contemptuous of the way they treated Dorcha, most of them being afraid of her, and others, Kupe especially, treating her like some kind of a *lady*. None of them seemed to smell or see the *womanliness* about her. None of them seemed in the least interested in bedding her. The smell of her drove Seumas crazy with sexual desire. He could not understand how his captors could stay away from such a woman. Once, her loose shift blew up above her waist, under which she had nothing, and Seumas almost choked on his passion.

If Dorcha had been a captive of *his* he would have taken her long before now (though almost certainly against her will). Seumas found the widow of the man he had killed immensely desirable. Seumas was glad his breeks were loose and full, for they often hid a penis stiffened to the point of being painful. His lust for her haunted his every waking moment, as he often caught sight of her white thighs while she slept under the deck hut on a windy afternoon, or the shape of her breasts disclosed by a wet shift that stuck to her skin. Sometimes he felt he would go mad because he knew he could not have her.

*

After the death of her husband Dorcha had only one thought in mind: to kill her husband's murderer. The desire for revenge flooded her every moment. She was desperate to see the Pict's blood splashing on the earth. She had pictures in her head, of him begging her for mercy, of her laughing at him, reminding him of how little mercy he had shown her husband, and then dashing out his brains with the laugh still ringing in his ears. These were wild thoughts, wild pictures, but they had sustained her through her grief and through the realisation of her poverty.

It was true she had loved her husband and desired the death of the Pict for emotional reasons, but she also had to avenge her husband's death in order to be accepted back once more into Scots society. The other women of the clan would not speak to her until she had righted the wrong, retrieved her family honour, shown the Picts that the Scots were a people with whom to be reckoned. Until that time she would have been an outcast, eating the roots of trees, begging for scraps from strangers, perhaps selling her body to wayfarers and travellers.

Had there been a man in the family, a father or brother, who could have carried out this deed on her behalf, she could have stepped back and been a spectator. But the clan had been massacred the previous year in a battle with a clan in the next glen and many of the menfolk were already dead. A murder was a murder, however, and a stain on a clan's honour.

On being captured by the Raiateans, something bad inside her had died. She still wanted to kill the Pict, but there was an indifference settling next to her desire for revenge. The world of Albainn seemed far away now, another life, and it was clear to her that the Oceanians were not going to harm her in any way. She had no doubt they could be ferocious in war, indeed whenever the necessity arose, but they did not seem to feel the need for constant aggression like her own people. They were not belligerent for the sake of it, had little scorn in them, and there was a gentleness about their spirit which she felt was a power of good.

In these waters she sensed the presence of strange gods, quite unlike those she had known in Albainn, or the new religion which was creeping into her homeland. More psychic than her fellow Albannach her spirit quickly tuned to the supernature of her new environment and she believed the stories Kieto told of ancestor ghosts, the spirits of ancient heroes and the tales of the creator gods of the sea, earth and sky.

Here, under this clear sky, the stars were brighter and more numerous. Recently, having come out of her sulks, Kieto had shown her the major constellations: The Bird's Body, The North Wing, The Bamboo, Small Face with Small Eyes, Adze, The Carrying Stick, Double Man, White Squirrelfish Stars, The Net, The Path Of Three and The Tongs. Her people had no names for these sets of stars, but a monk passing through her village from Lindisfarne, the same man who had brought the message of the new religion, had told her another list of names, like Sirius, Aries, Alpha and Beta Centauri, Southern Cross and Taurus. It was all so fascinating, so magical, and she wept for the knowledge that could be hers if someone would only pass it to her.

There was little homesickness in her, for the peat-fire hearth she had left behind, for the damp, stinking croft where her blankets rotted and her husband's empty stool stood ready to remind her of her widow status.

From what she had heard she was going to an island in the sun, whose name was Raiatea. A *heaven*. That sounded better than the place whence she had come, which once she had lost her man might be called 'Near Hell'. She was going to a place where food was in plenty; where there were hot, white sands and gentle breakers on beaches protected by something called a coral reef; where the women were held almost equal to the men; where colours were bright and days were long and warm with delicate breezes caressing the skin, where fruit could be picked from trees all year round and the only thing to fear was a tropical storm.

That sounded like a heaven to her.

As for the Pict, she now felt a little sorry for him, though this feeling was heavily diluted by her hate for him. He looked miserable and forlorn as he sat on the front of the canoe's deck, the spray flicking over his salt-stained ragged vest and breeks. Occasionally he would turn and look at her and she would see the lust in his eyes and feel contempt for him. He wanted her, she believed, not because he desired her for herself, but because she was the wife of his victim. He wanted complete victory, to conquer all. That was why he wanted her, though she doubted he understood that himself.

The Pict himself, she also realised, unlike her was longing for his home. But then the Pict had more back there than she had herself. He was a man, for one thing, and had a much higher status in life. He could do as he wished: beat his wife when he felt unhappy, kick his dog, hunt, kill a man for a sword or any other possession. He could get out of the hovel whenever he wanted to, and leave his woman to wash his filthy clothes, to cook his meals, to make his bed, to wait in patience with open legs ready for him to bury himself inside her. He was master back there, and she much the slave, and all that had changed when the two of them had been swept away into this other world of darker men with brighter souls.

Kieto was no longer so afraid of the woman with the strange smell and fish-belly skin. Kupe had instructed him to teach the woman and the man the legends and stories of real people, tales of larger-than-life heroes of the ancient world, like Maui; of great ancestors like Tiki; and of Great Gods like Tangaroa. Kieto began with the story of how the coconut came into being.

*

The goddess Hine, who has always been known for her appetite for men, fell in love with the gigantic Eel-man, Te Tuna. She lived at the bottom of the sea with him amongst the waving fronds of the sea bed plants. Eventually, however, Hine became bored with Te Tuna despite his great size in the region of passion, and she made an excuse to leave him.

'I need a new raiment,' she said. 'I shall visit the Neka-neka tribe, who are superb weavers.'

'As you wish, my dear,' said Te Tuna, not suspecting that she intended to stay away forever, 'but come back to your sea bed soon.'

With that, Hine left, but not to seek garments, for she could spin her own with great skill, but rather to look for a new man to satisfy her. She called first at the atoll of the Raru-vai-i-o, the Deep-penetrating-men, who were known throughout Oceania for their sexual prowess. Arriving in the early evening, when the skies were blood-red, at a time when the men were seeking their partners for the night, she stepped naked onto the coral shores. They asked her who she was, and she told them. She said she was a woman seeking a new great shaft of desire to fulfil her needs.

'Look to my dark triangle, you men of these fair isles, for it has a need to be cloven asunder!'

Now Hine is a goddess of amazing beauty, but her presence on the atoll terrified the tribesmen.

'You must not stop here, Hine,' they cried in fear, 'for we know the monster Eel-man to be a ferocious warrior. He will come here with his intimates and slay every one of us. You must look for your new lover elsewhere, for our fear makes us hang limp like a palm leaf in the rain.'

Feeling nothing but contempt for the Deep-penetrating tribe, she continued on her way to arrive at some islands where lived the men of the Peka tribe, or Loving-hug people, who were famous for their lingering embraces and sexual stamina.

'Will one of you take me to his bed?' cried Hine, in frustration, 'or are you frightened little men, like the Raru-vai-i-o tribe?'

'Let your desire carry you further,' shouted the Peka men, hiding in the bushes, 'otherwise Te Tuna will thrust himself amongst us as a blunt-nosed shark and cause us untold misery.'

Angrily, Hine left the Peka men and sought out the men of the Ever-erect tribe, whose sturdy staves were known throughout the watery world, but on hearing Hine's request they scuttled away and hid in damp caves, where for the first time in their lives they became flaccid and useless to women.

Fuming with discontent now, Hine went on her way, to arrive at last on the shores of the island where the demi-god Maui lived with his mother.

Now Maui's mother wanted grandchildren and she knew Hine to be a fertile goddess, so when she heard Hine's plaintive call, she encouraged her son to go out and invite the goddess to his home. Maui did as his mother bid and fell in love with Hine immediately, taking her to his bed that very night. Hine's sighs could be heard over half the ocean and all the other tribesmen emerged from their hiding places knowing she had at last found a lover who could satisfy her carnal needs.

The trouble was, the tribesmen were so relieved they took to mocking Te Tuna, telling him he was a cuckold. The great Eel-man, whose penis everyone believed to be the largest in the world, was at first unconcerned by their taunting, since he was not a creature who liked to roam far from his nest. He satisfied himself by sullying Hine's name, calling her a woman of no virtue. He told everyone she was hopeless as a paramour and had never satisfied him anyway and that he was glad to be rid of her.

Still they jeered at him, cried that what lay under his skirt was a small insignificant thing compared to that which was under Maui's, until finally he lost his temper and threatened to visit Maui's island to teach him a lesson.

'We'll see who has the biggest,' he cried. 'Mine is so large the elements go mad when they see it!'

Te Tuna then began a karakia chant, to assist him in his endeavour to destroy Maui, for nothing now would satisfy his fury but the total destruction of the little demi-god.

The tribesmen listened to the chant and then went to tell tales on the Eel-man, calling at Maui's island and informing him that Te Tuna was going to meet him in mortal combat, and that he should make himself ready for a contest.

'Pooh, I am not afraid of an *eel*,' said Maui. 'How big is he anyway?'

'Big?' the tribesmen cried, delightedly, 'he is *immense*.'

'Is he as erect and massive as that stone stack over there?' asked Maui, pointing to a tall needle of rock.

Fearing that Maui would shy away from the fight, they replied, 'More like a soft-wood tree.'

'What about the shape,' asked Maui. 'Is it straight?'

'More like a curved fern tree,' they answered.

'Ha!' sneered Maui. 'Then he'd better beware, because if I reveal what I have underneath my tapa bark skirt it will turn the weather insane.'

Nothing happened for a while, however, because Te Tuna was busy with his chants. As his power grew the skies became darker and darker, lightning flashed, and thunder rolled. The waves on the ocean grew large and crashed on the beaches of Maui's island and the other people of his tribe began to grow frightened.

'What if Te Tuna is not satisfied with destroying Maui,' they whispered amongst themselves, 'but wants to demolish the whole of our nation?'

They grumbled that men should not steal the wives of others, even if those wives should come to them first.

One terrible day, when the sky was black with worry, the Eel-man finally arrived on the shores of Maui's island and called him to come out and fight. Te Tuna had brought with him four very dangerous friends: Pup-vae-noa, or Mound-with-a-target; Porporo-tu-a-huaga, or Massive-testicles; Toke-a-kura, or Swollen-clitoris; and Maga-vai-i-e-rire, or Loop-that-strangles-man's-penis.

Te Tuna stood on the reef of Maui's island and took off his tapa bark kilt, revealing his monstrous eel. The ocean reeled at the sight and produced a tidal wave, which swept towards Maui's island and threatened to engulf it.

'Ha!' cried Maui, in triumph. 'I knew I was larger!'

With a sweeping gesture he tore off his own skirt and exposed a small man's most mighty weapon. It was twice the size of the Eel-man's and the sky gasped and swallowed the wind, the land shuddered and shrank, and the giant wave reversed itself immediately, rushing back and carrying off Te Tuna's friends.

The Eel-man himself was left at the mercy of Maui.

Now Maui is not a vindictive demi-god, but simply a cocky young half-deity. He is magnanimous in victory. He is always full of himself, but with good reason, having a thousand tricks at his fingertips. Once the two were clothed he extended a welcome to Te Tuna and asked him to spend the night on the island.

'Just because we have fought, and you have lost, does not mean that I should not offer you hospitality,' said Maui.

However, though the Eel-man accepted the invitation he had to spend several sleepless hours behind thin walls, listening to the moaning of Hine in the throes of ecstasy. Maui made love to Hine the whole night long. It was more than Te Tuna could stand.

'We must fight again,' he said savagely to Maui. 'This time the contest must be a little more fair.'

'What do you suggest?' asked the trickster god.

'We must each go inside the other's body, one at a time, and try to defeat one another.'

Maui agreed to this and said Te Tuna could go first.
The Eel-man began by chanting his karakia.

The enormous eel swims through the sea,
His strength is superlative,
His boldness and courage unbeatable.
The moray is majestic muscle, it fills the coral hole
    with its menacing form.

With that he disappeared into Maui's body and tried to
destroy Maui from within, seeking out his heart to squeeze
it until it burst. But the tricky Maui kept his heart on the
move, changing it now with his liver, now with his kidneys,
now with his pancreas, all of which slipped from Te Tuna's
fingers, they being so slithery. Finally, Te Tuna's time was
up and he had to emerge.

'Now it is my turn,' said Maui.

Now the feisty man begins to fight,
Entering with no fear or fright.
He is disdainful of the other's deed
Being sure to fulfil his own creed,
    To win at any cost!

With that, Maui entered the body of Te Tuna, who immediately began moving his heart around so that Maui could
not grasp and crush it. Maui did not bother doing this
because the tricky demi-god had swallowed a stem of
mohio fern which made him expand to four times his normal size. Maui grew rapidly until he caused the mighty
Eel-man to burst asunder. Te Tuna exploded like a plugged
volcano, his flesh flying everywhere. Only his head
remained intact, which Maui severed from his shoulders.

Maui threw the head on a rubbish tip, but his mother got
hold of it and told Maui to bury it beside the house. Maui
did so, underneath the window, then forgot all about it.

After the annual rains had been he noticed a shoot coming up from the ground where he had buried Te Tuna's head.

'That's a new one,' he murmured. 'What kind of plant is that?'

The shoot grew into a sapling, then a tall tree with feathery fronds at the top. At the point where the leaves grew, some sea-green oval shapes appeared. Maui's mother called them coconuts.

When Maui first picked one he found the juice very sweet. Later there was meat inside the kernel. Maui planted some more coconut palms. He took the leaves from the palms and used them to make a roof for his house. The trunks he employed as corner posts. Soon other men were doing the same, putting to use every part of the coconut palm. The gigantic Eel-man had become one of the most useful plants in the whole of Oceania. Maui sang:

This is the way we favour our foes:
We do not throw them on the offal heap,
Nor cast them into the ocean:
We let them ripen anew
In some more useful form to men.

I am the trickster demi-god Maui
Who swallowed a leaf, destroyed my foe:
The dolt Te Tuna tried to undo me
But cunning and cleverness overcomes
*   anger, strength and boastful oaths.*

Such a dunce, Te Tuna, pompous eel!

When the story was over, Seumas raised his eyebrows and looked at Dorcha. She ignored his attempt at conspiracy, so he said to Kieto with some prudishness, 'I don't think it's fitting that you should tell such stories in front of a woman.'

'And why not?' asked Dorcha, turning on him. 'You think women don't talk of such things?'

'I don't think they should,' he said, primly.

She snorted at him. 'You are a poor man, Seumas.'

He didn't know what she meant by that, but it left him feeling wretched.

At that moment the mariners on board the ocean-going canoe started yelling and jumping up and down. Seumas looked up to see what was the matter and discerned a white line of breakers in the distance. Beyond this were the still waters of a light-green lagoon, and from the middle of this placid lake rose an island, green and lush, with ragged peaks and crags veiled in mist.

The shape of the rocks was quite unlike those of Seumas's homeland, where the boulders and ridges had been worn smooth by the passing of time. The natural architecture here rose narrow and sinister out of deep clefts in the mountain and some twisted into hideous shapes as if clawing at passing clouds. Seumas was quite willing to believe there were gods amongst those ugly mizzle-shrouded peaks.

On the beach, from which the sail with the black octopus had been sighted, were laughing, waving people with flowers in their hair, around their necks, and even around their ankles and wrists.

'Raiatea,' cried Po in Seumas's ear. 'My homeland.'

Seumas nodded. 'Your homeland – but not mine.'

Po's Tiki received the crew's thanks for leading them homewards. Kupe reserved his main worship for Tangaroa, the god of the ocean. Tangaroa was greatly pleased with Kupe, who had followed the octopus sent by Tangaroa to lead the navigator prince to the shores of the Land-of-Mists. He received the sacrifice of turtles and sharks which Kupe cooked and ate in his honour, with due gratification. The god of the sea slept green and peaceful that night, in the knowledge of his success.

PART TWO

Most Sacred, Most Feared

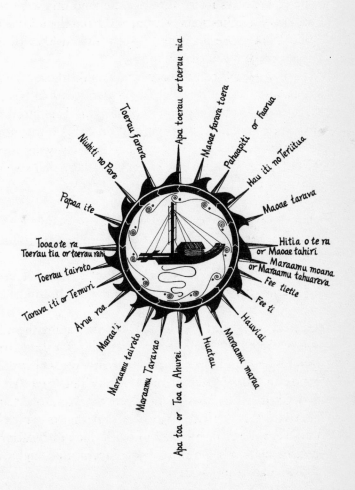

Toerau farava

Niuhiti no Pare

Apa toerau or toerau nia

Maoae farara toera

Pahaapiti or Fuarua

Hau iti no Teriitua

Papaa ite

Maoae tarava

Tooao te ra
Toerau tia or toerau rahi

Hitia o te ra
or Maoae tahiri

Maraamu moana
or Maraamu tahuareva

Toerau tairoto

Fee tietle

Tarava iti or Temuri

Fee ti

Arue roa

Hauviai

Maraa'i

Maraamu maraa

Maraamu tairoto

Huatau

Maraamu Taravao

Apa toa or Toa a Ahurei

1

The place is Tapu-tapu atia, 'Most Sacred, Most Feared', beneath the shadow of the ancient mountain. Low, tenebrous clouds seem to gather here, during the wet season, around high walls of rock dressed in old lichen and ancient mosses, coloured a darker green where they have absorbed the cold shadows into their damp garments. These clouds, with the forest behind and the clothed rock face in front, effectively enclose the area, making it a kind of capped glade rejected by the creatures of the island because of its isolation and lack of sunlight.

At the centre of Tapu-tapu atia stands the massive Investiture Stone, the four corners of which were once supported by the corpses of four men, the sacrificed guardians of the stone, though these are now dust and their spirits stand in their stead. Youths beloved of the tribe were brought godlike here, in earlier virtuous times, to the throb of drums and the chant of sacred fangu, and their skulls cloven with the edge of a priest's paddle club. Their goodness was shared among the living, went into the fertile land, the deep stone. Only the most beautiful, the most adored, deserved such an end.

'Most sacred, most feared' still has the smell of death clinging to the great stone, whose face is bare of any moss or lichen, and whose coldness emanates from within its heart to chill the air within the glade.

It was here, in this place – taboo when no ceremony was taking place and the priests were absent – where young men were given their adulthood, that the spy Manopa met with Prince Tangiia to impart his information.

Ra was just coming out of the night sea, into the sky god Rangi's territory, overpowering the 'Long Shark at Dawn', that flush of stars which sweeps across the roof of voyaging in a great rash of brilliant white.

Manopa stared around him at the whispering leaves; there were unseen ghosts abroad. There was only one world, shared by the quick and the dead alike. The spirits of the dead had to live on the same landscape as people of flesh and blood. Each did their best not to trespass on the domain of the other. Sometimes a clash was inevitable and ghosts, being the more sensitive of the two, were angered.

A wickerwork shark hung from the branch of breadfruit tree above Manopa's head, telling all that the fruit from these boughs belonged to the gods. Such fruit was mashed and stored in stone vaults, underground by priests. In time of famine this stored food might be blessed and distributed amongst the people. A king could eat it at any time, his mana being great.

The shark, hanging by a single thread, turned this way and that, as the wind changed direction. Manopa stared at this spinning, hollow fish and shivered. This silent valley was a gathering place for the sau of his ancestors. There would be malevolent demons as well as dark gods, in this place of blood. Manopa gripped a magic whalebone club in his right hand, hoping this would be enough to ward off any malignant spirits that might want to enter his body.

Tangiia, on the other hand, was more concerned with the living. His brother Tutapu's men were everywhere and while it was doubtful his brother would have him wilfully assassinated while their father was alive, there might be an overzealous warrior willing to take the law into his own hands, hoping for eventual favours from the future king.

'What news is there?' asked Tangiia. 'Is my brother still plotting against me?'

'The moment your father dies,' said Manopa, 'Tutapu intends to kill you and eat your roasted heart. He will not share the island with you, nor give you any part of what he considers to be his rightful inheritance – not Borabora, nor any of the smaller isles which come under your father's rule.'

Tangiia sighed. 'I would be quite willing to take a small piece of what my older brother considers to be all his own, but it seems the gods don't want me to remain on my home isle. If I'm to avoid bloodshed I must make preparations to leave Raiatea for good. Will you and your men come with me, Manopa?'

The broad-faced Manopa grinned. 'If I stay here your brother will eat *me* instead.' He became serious once more as a dark shadow fluttered through the forest near by; perhaps a bat returning to a cave; perhaps an ancestor-spirit looking for a live soul to devour. 'We must build some canoes, Prince Tangiia – at least three great pahi canoes – enough for two hundred people. I shall see to their secret construction on the far side of Raiatea. Your brother at present resides on Borabora, since he cannot stand to be near you, and we must hope he stays there until after we've gone.'

The young and handsome Tangiia, still only eighteen years of age, nodded his head.

'He's afraid I will attempt to assassinate him in his sleep. He's even had a wooden floor constructed around his bed which makes twittering sounds when someone walks on it. I'm told that when one treads on the planks the sound of birds warn him that someone is in the room. He's sure to remain on Borabora until he feels ready to attack me with his warriors. Now for our part, we must recruit others for a voyage into the unknown,' he said to Manopa. 'Perhaps Kupe will come with us?'

Manopa shook his head. 'Prince Kupe remains aloof from politics. He's a lone adventurer. His expeditions are spontaneous voyages, made on the spur of the moment without any real preparation. He would become bored with all the intrigue, the boat building, the provisioning of craft, the selection of greater and lesser navigators. Ask him to jump into a dugout and go within the moment, and you're more likely to get him as an ally – but he won't join a mass exodus. He hates crowds.'

'You're right, I wasn't thinking. What about his young protégé, Kieto? The boy is almost fourteen now. He went on the voyage which brought the other people to us.'

'Seumas and Dorcha? Yes, but Kieto was a child on that voyage – not more than seven or eight years.'

'Still, he learned much from Kupe, and has hardly been separated from the navigator since that time.'

Manopa nodded. 'True – and speaking of the goblin, why not take him too? He longs to leave this island.'

'Seumas wants to go home to this Land-of-Mists which Kupe found, not to another island, but you're right, he's a restless soul and he might be useful to us, if we meet some of his kind by accident.' The young prince hesitated, then said, 'I want to take Nau Ariki with me.'

Something cold, like an invisible clam shell, seemed to razor into Manopa's soul. He had been dreading these words from his young prince and friend. It was not enough that the youth was restless and ambitious, but he had to want the very female destined to marry his older brother.

'Nau Ariki is to be Tutapu's *wife*. You would be foolish to abduct her. The anger –'

'Perhaps she would come of her own accord?' interrupted Tangiia a little waspishly. 'Have you thought of that?'

'She is promised to your *brother*,' said Manopa. 'Hard as

that may seem. Look, we share the same basket of food, you and I – we have done since children – I would not lie to you, Tangiia. The girl must go to your brother. She wouldn't thank you for taking her with you. It would make both of you unhappy.'

Tangiia was young and headstrong, deeply in love with Nau Ariki, and would not listen to good advice. He spoke almost feverishly of the young maiden, his eyes burning.

'I *must* have her with me – she is part of it all – don't you understand? Without her I would rather stay here and have my brains dashed out by my brother's club.'

Nothing Manopa said would alter Tangiia's mind about Nau Ariki. The youth was completely infatuated by the seventeen-year-old girl, who, Manopa admitted, was something of a rare beauty. Not only that, she had a spirit to match. There was that which was bright and open about her, which caught a man's attention the moment she spoke to him. This candid and unguarded disposition often hid the fact that Nau Atiki was highly intelligent. It was no wonder Tangiia was in love with the maiden: half the men on the island loved her.

'I must –' began Tangiia, but then both men heard the single *clack* and whirled towards the rainforest.

Manopa turned pale and gripped his whalebone club.

'Is it one of the Peerless Ones?' he whispered, meaning the forest fairies who often disguised themselves as birds and wrapped their forms in sunlight and moonlight to confuse mortals.

The sound came again, this time unmistakably seashells being rattled together. It was not fairies but some man or woman spying on the pair as they stood near the Great Stone.

Manopa was first to move, with Tangiia close behind him. The pair of them ran straight towards an area of thick bushes. A startled, frightened creature ran from the shrubs, like a deer, through the shafts of sunlight penetrating the canopy. The two men would never have caught up, so fast was their quarry on its feet, had the runner not tripped over a buttress root and gone sprawling, the shells tied in the long locks rattling.

The two men, one large and bole-chested, the other broad-shouldered and strong, caught up and stood over an exceptionally tall Raiatean with a pretty face.

'I didn't hear anything,' cried Boy-girl, hands out to ward off the blows. 'I heard nothing at all.'

Boy-girl curled up like a leech, making herself look very small and pathetic. Manopa's club was on the descent, when Tangiia caught his arm.

'No,' said the prince.

'But he *heard*,' hissed Manopa. 'He'll betray us. You can't trust a creature like this.'

'I won't tell anyone,' sobbed Boy-girl. 'Don't hurt me, please, Manopa. I'll be as silent as the sacred rock.'

'Stand up, Boy-girl,' said Tangiia.

Boy-girl climbed slowly to her feet. She stood in a bright pillar of sunlight and was at least a head taller than Tangiia, who was no dwarf himself. Boy-girl's body was extremely lean and supple, though not *thin* in the sense that no bones protruded. Her hair was decorated with dozens of pretty seashells, the bounty of the ocean, and it was these which had made the noise that gave her away. There were ribbons and flowers hanging from her locks too, and from her wrists and ankles. The colours.of her bark-cloth skirt were brighter than those of the two men who confronted her and she had make-up around her eyes to enhance their beauty.

'Please don't hurt me,' she said, calmer now. 'I want to be one of you – go away with you.'

From an early age Boy-girl had shown a preference for feminine ways and once this had been seen to be a permanent part of his personality it had been encouraged, and he became *she* to all those except men like Manopa who was secretly afraid of her special powers. From time to time there were men who wanted to live their lives like women and Oceanians in general saw no harm in this behaviour; in fact the Boy-girls of the clans performed a special social function. There were warriors of the tribe who had no desire to be feminine, but who preferred sleeping with another man to lying with a woman. Boy-girls took these warriors to their breast and gave them comfort.

'We need people who are *useful* to us,' said Manopa with some contempt. 'Not silly-headed creatures.'

Boy-girl turned on the stocky, bluff warrior. 'I am so *useful* it would make your head *spin* to know the ways, you tragic man,' she cried. 'I can sing songs you've never heard before – I can make such music as you would think the sea was coursing through your veins –' Boy-girl was indeed very creative. '– but better than that, I can steal a man's mind.' She stared directly at the bulky warrior.

Manopa shuddered. He had witnessed this feat. Boy-girl could look into a man's eyes, whisper in his ear, and the man would start barking like a dog, believe he *was* a dog, and eat scraps from around the fire, yap at passers-by, and cock his leg up at a tree for a piss. Boy-girl had done this to a man who had insulted her. She had made a woman who had cast a slur on her act like a cockerel for many hours. Later, when Boy-girl had called the magic off, the dog-man and rooster-woman wondered why people were laughing at them when they passed, having no recollection of their time spent as animal and bird.

Manopa considered this a very dangerous skill, this magic passed down from some mischievous god, and he wanted no demonstration of it here.

'Take your eyes off me, damn you,' cried Manopa, turning his head away. 'You turn me into a dog and I'll tear your throat out, whatever Prince Tangiia says.'

Boy-girl giggled and rattled her shells.

Tangiia said seriously, 'Do you understand what a position you've put yourself in here, Boy-girl? If my brother gets to know of my plans, I am dead where I stand. It would be safer for us to kill you now.'

'Safer, but not wiser, my prince,' said Boy-girl. 'You wish to build some pahi canoes without Tutapu's knowledge, yet if he goes out on the waters in his canoe he may hear the hammering and chiselling, the adze's hewing out the trunks. I could whisper in his ear, get him and his basket-sharers to ignore such noises. No outsider can reach Tutapu without going through his bodyguards or his priests – he isolates himself from the rest of the people for fear of assassination.'

Tangiia looked up at Boy-girl doubtfully. 'Can you do that? Can you beguile a whole counsel of men? It doesn't seem possible.'

'If I can get them all together, I can do it.'

Manopa, who had been listening with some interest now, moved next to Boy-girl, trying to ignore the sweet smell of the oil with which she bathed her body, saying, 'How can *you* get close to Tutapu?' he asked. 'How can you get access to the inner circle of his basket-sharers?'

Boy-girl smiled one of those smiles which normally infuriated Manopa.

'He likes me,' she said. 'He calls me to his bed.'

Manopa grunted and shook his head at Tangiia. 'This creature will betray us,' he warned. 'With pillow-talk.'

Before Tangiia could reply, Boy-girl snapped, '*Creature* yourself, hog's-body. If I could kill Tutapu now, I would – I *hate* the vile man. He's nasty to me, pinches me, hurts me and makes bruises after he's finished with me and starts feeling ugly with himself. He's a despicable man. But I'm not strong enough to murder him with my bare hands and I have to go to him naked. They even inspect my mouth before they let me in his hut, to make sure I have no needle to use as a weapon under my tongue. I wish I *could* kill him for you.'

'Why can't you do something with this magic of yours?' asked Manopa, grunting out the words.

'It's not that powerful,' admitted Boy-girl. 'I can't make a man kill himself or put himself in deadly danger. Believe me, I would have him dancing and singing over the clifftops if I could, onto the rocks below.'

'I wouldn't want you to,' Tangiia interrupted. 'I have no wish to kill my own brother, no matter how he feels about me. Show me the bruises, Boy-girl, where you've been hurt by my brother.'

Boy-girl let her skirt drop to her ankles and revealed her thighs. The smooth, silky skin was covered in ugly wheals. Even Manopa winced.

'He uses a piece of sharp bamboo sometimes,' said Boy-girl, 'in places I *can't* show you.'

'I believe you,' said Tangiia, sighing.

Though it was said he would make a good king over a nation, Tutapu had a reputation for cruelty towards individuals. There was something in his make-up, a vicious streak, which came out at odd times. Tutapu could also be extraordinarily generous and warmhearted when the mood was on him. While they had been growing up together, Tutapu had been a good older brother, teaching the younger Tangiia how to hunt and use weapons of war. Tutapu had also sung many songs to his sibling, patiently teaching Tangiia the words. It was only once they had reached manhood that the canker had entered Tutapu's heart.

'What do you want me to do?' asked Boy-girl, covering her male genitals, though not without a sly look at Manopa, to make sure he had been looking at her.

'If you can beguile my brother's basket-sharers, then I wish you to do so. Since you are committed to our cause you can also recruit one of the other people, Seumas. Your success in this will prove to me your loyalty and your worth, for if my brother finds out you have helped me in any way, he'll skewer your kidneys and barbecue them over a charcoal fire.'

'If he doesn't, I *will*,' grunted Manopa.

'You great hog,' giggled Boy-girl, 'you're so *strong*.'

On a remote beach on Raiatea the boat-building began some seven days later. The heavy work was to be carried out using almost exclusively one tool – the adze. The Raiatean adzes were mainly of basalt, though some of those for lighter work were fashioned out of a clam shell fixed to a haft. There were also stone axes, drills of sharks' teeth and bone needles. There were large scissors and chisels of human upper-arm bones, graters of coral and sanders of sting-ray skin. These tools were first placed in an open-air temple dedicated to Tangaroa, constructed near the building site, in order that the Great Sea-God, the creator, might impregnate them with his divine presence.

A priest invoked Tane with this fangu chant:

> *Go and take hold of the adze,*
> *In the niche of the holy place.*
> *Hold, that it be taken out enchanted*
> *Made light that it may produce sparks*
> *In doing its many tasks.*
>
> *The awakening of the adze!*
> *Let it travel a little seaward,*
> *Present it, let it fight and attack:*
> *Let the axe go against the spray*
> *Inaugurating its flying girdle,*
> *Awake for Tane*
> *Great god of artisans!*

Along with extraordinary ability the boat builders required a profound religious mentality to assist them in their task.

Then the work began with the cutting of the chosen trees. Ati wood for the keel and the planks of the hull.

CHAPTER TEN

Ranunculus to Veronica

For some, gardening is a case of filling space with what is easiest to grow, if they bother at all. This method may involve one or more specialities from roses to rock plants or from annuals to shrubs according to preference or suitability for soil and situation. Hardy plants, however, embrace such a wide diversity that a selection could be made that would grow in any given soil or situation found in English gardens. When enthusiasm reaches the pitch of wanting to grow plants not fully adaptable to one's particular soil then gardening becomes a challenge, and when this challenge is accepted, successes bring the savour of triumph along with mounting interest and widening knowledge. To reach that happy state, one has to have both a love and a 'feeling' for plants and experience may have been gained partly by trial and error. Losses as well as successes with rare or uncommon plants may well have occurred, but this is an integral part of one's gardening life.

My own experiences include a fair number of failures, in spite of having unusually favourable conditions since I went all-out to collect and grow uncommon plants. The vast majority of them grew well, just as they would in most gardens, but what I find especially satisfying is the ease with which so many choice plants grow once their basic needs are met. An example is *Ranunculus aconitifolius flore-pleno*, the double, white Fair Maids of France. This has been in sparse cultivation for generations, but for years I shied away from trying it again, having lost it the first time. The Dell garden, with places for both moisture and shade lovers, led me to try it once more in moist, sandy loam in full sun and there it has flourished ever since. Double white flowers do not appeal to everyone, but this, somehow, is different for in each there is perfection of form and composition and in May and June a group becomes a 2-foot mound of dark green foliage studded by countless numbers of these intensely white buttony flowers $\frac{1}{2}$-inch or so across. The

roots are fingery, from a quite small central crown, and dormancy
during autumn and winter is complete. As for adaptability, this is
wider than I had imagined and it seems fairly safe to say that where
its relative the trollius will thrive, so will this charming ranunculus.

Another double, but bright yellow in this case, will grow in any
sunny situation, but it is by no means choice. This is *R. acris
flore-pleno*, flowering at about the same time and with much more
resemblance to the Buttercup. This grows quite erectly to 2½ feet.
R. gramineus, as its name denotes, is grassy leaved, the glaucous
green leaves radiating from a neatly growing plant. Stems 9 to 12
inches high carry glistening yellow flowers for several weeks and
make this an attractive little plant for the front of a sunny bed or
border.

Rhazya (and Amsonia)
One of the seeming anomalies in plant nomenclature is to place
Amsonia and *Rhazya* as separate genera. I have heard some people
aver that *Amsonia tabernaemontana* and *Rhazya orientalis* are
identical but though there is a difference, the two may just as well
come together here. *A. tabernaemontana salicifolia* has slender
willow-leaved stems 2 feet or so tall borne in great profusion from a
tough, sturdy but compact root. For several weeks, small light blue
flowers of periwinkle form make a pleasingly graceful plant, but no
bright display. *R. orientalis* grows more compactly, with smaller
darker leaves and the deeper blue flowers are more closely clustered. Both plants are easy to grow in any sunny or half shady
place, yet in spite of having considerable charm, both remain
uncommon.

Rheum
Just as the culinary rhubarb is of easy culture, so is the rarely seen
ornamental species *Rheum palmatum*. Its fault is that of being too
massive for most gardens, and because its leaf spread is vast, there
is a considerable gap when these die back in late summer. Where
space permits, however, the magnificence of its early summer display, with statuesque spikes up to 8 feet high in May and June, is a
sight to behold. The type is pink flowered, but deeper, almost red
shades come in the *atrosanguineum* and *rubrum* forms. An early

Hutu wood for the masts. Mara, from the breadfruit tree, for the oars.

There was a special hut constructed for the building of each pahi canoe, so that work on polishing the keel, the sides, and other pieces could take place while continuing the preparation of the rigging and sails, the former braided from nape fibres of the coconut shell, and the latter from dried pandanus leaves cut into ribbons and whipped together to form matting.

Once the parts had been shaped and smoothed the wood was covered with a protective coat of red clay and charcoal, then assembled: pegged and glued with utu sap, and lashed with sennit. Breadfruit sap and shark oil provided the caulking material, smeared over every part of the great canoe.

Fitted to the prow of each vessel was a small part taken from an ancient sacred canoe, to introduce the new canoe to Tangaroa and the minor gods of the ocean.

'*O what have I, O Tane,*' sang the boat builders while they worked, '*but sennit, the cord of the coconut, to hold thy cane, that she might go over long waves, and over short waves, to the near horizon, even to the far-off horizon, this sennit of thine, O Tane. Let it hold! Let it hold!*'

There would be more rituals once the boat was complete, for the launching and the consecrating of the boat once it stood in the water, drinking the waves.

On the deck of each vessel, once they were complete, would stand two masts and a couple of bamboo huts. The canoes would hold 60 to 70 passengers and a crew of 20, plus supplies for a month and baggage necessary to start a new life.

Io, the Old One, Father of the Gods, watched this activity below with some interest. He had heard Papa, the Earth-Goddess, and Rangi, the Sky-God, speaking about the coming events. There was already conflict between certain gods, not necessarily between Papa and her husband Rangi, but others who were concerned with the rights and wrongs of Tutapu's threat to kill his half-brother. These were Tangaroa, Maomao, Hine, Hau Maringi. Any friction on earth always had its counterpart amongst the gods. The truth was, the gods loved distractions, and mortals were always providing them with new amusements. They were bound to take sides in such issues. Io saw it as his task to maintain some sort of balance, a fairness, in these times.

Seumas, lying in the shade of the doorway of his hut, saw Boy-girl coming. He wondered whether to remain where he was, or walk down to the lagoon. Boy-girl always made him feel uncomfortable. He wanted to shake her by her shoulders and tell her to wipe her face, comb the shells out of her hair, and walk like a man. Boy-girl had always had a crush on Seumas which she did little to disguise in front of him. She even followed him up the cliffs sometimes, where he collected eggs, the frigate birds whirling about his head the way fulmars had done on the cliffs of his homeland of Albainn.

When she reached the hut, Boy-girl stared down at the bronzed, tattooed man and looked lovingly into his sea-washed blue eyes.

'I love your tattoos,' she murmured, reaching out to trace one with an elegant finger, 'all those swirls and circles.'

'What do you want?' growled Seumas, testily, knocking her hand away. 'I'm not in any mood for idle chat.'

Boy-girl squatted down and played with the hem of her bark-cloth skirt. Seumas was wearing a similar wrap-around, made from the paper mulberry tree, his woollen garments having long since rotted away in the humidity of the tropics.

'I have to talk to you,' she said, 'about something important.'

'If it's about the fairies again, forget it – I'm not interested in meeting any of them.'

The last time Boy-girl had been to see Seumas, she had told him she had a fairy trapped in a cage of twigs in the forest, and would show it to him if he went with her. Seumas, quite rightly, believed it to be a ruse to get him into a solitary place where Boy-girl hoped to work her charms and not inconsiderable enchantments on the 'other person' to make him her lover, if only for a short while.

The temptation to see one of the Peerless Ones he had heard so much about was strong with Seumas, but not so strong that he was fool enough to accept Boy-girl's invitation on trust.

'It's not about my games, it's about Tangiia.' She lowered her voice. 'He's planning to leave the islands forever, along with his people. His brother, you know, is scheming to kill him once their father dies. Tangiia doesn't want to fight his brother – he would rather seek a Faraway Heaven.'

Seumas was vaguely aware of these affairs, from the whispers of the shell gatherers, when they combed the shallows of the lagoon at low tide looking for edible molluscs.

'What's all this to do with me?' he asked. 'I don't want to get mixed up in politics – it's more than my life's worth.'

'You could come with us. I'm going. So are Po, Keito and a number of others. It might take you closer to your homelands.'

Seumas glanced quickly into Boy-girl's brown eyes.

'You're going to the Land-of-Mists?'

Boy-girl shrugged. 'Possibly in that direction.'

'Too vague,' growled Seumas.

Seumas stared across at the hut where Dorcha lived with her two husbands, twin brothers who could not bear to be parted, even by marriage. One of the husbands, Ti-ti, was cooking some fish in an earth-oven. There were stones in the umu pit around which firewood had been burned, thus bringing the stones to a high heat. Fish wrapped in damp pandanus leaves had been laid on the stones to cook. The belly of each fish had been slit, the innards removed, and hot pebbles put in their place to ensure cooking right through the flesh. Ti-ti suddenly realised he was being observed and looked up, to scowl at Seumas.

'Don't look at me like that, man, or I'll stuff one of your hot cooking stones down your throat,' growled Seumas, under his breath.

Boy-girl giggled, aware like everyone else that Dorcha's husbands hated Seumas, and that the feeling was mutual. Everyone knew that Seumas was in love with Dorcha, and that Dorcha hated Seumas so much that she was not above flaunting herself in front of him to let him know what he was missing, thus infuriating her jealous husbands and rousing Seumas to such a pitch of choler he almost choked on his frustration.

When the two Albannachs had arrived on Raiatea Seumas had been stunned by the comeliness of the local women. What was more he was unusual enough to find himself much in demand amongst these lovely females. One after the other came to him in his hut over the first two or three years and he sated himself on sex that would have been unthinkable back in his homeland. A man *there* was lucky if he had one woman who remained passably pretty for a few years before the ague, fire smoke and childbirth in bad conditions took its toll on her looks.

Here there were astonishingly graceful and captivating beauties who actually enjoyed going with a man, seeming to get as much pleasure from it as he himself.

Yet, once he had been to bed with a dozen of them, it all began to pall. They were ravishing, exciting, but he was not in love with any of them. For the first time in his life he realised that to get the most out of the sexual act, there had to be a spiritual union, as well as a carnal one. His head had been full of fantasies before but when the fantasies became reality he came to the knowledge that it was necessary to love the person you were making love to, if there was to be a flight into absolute ecstasy.

So he had taken a wife, after Dorcha had taken in her husbands, the two brothers who fussed over her like mother hens. Mary, as he had called her, not liking many of the names they gave themselves, over which his tongue continually tripped, had been a sweet woman with a happy disposition six years younger than himself. She was not the most beautiful woman he could have chosen, but she was enough like the girl he had left behind in Albainn to make her interesting to him. In his way he had been very fond of her and they had been reasonably content, until she died in pain when some organ in the region of her stomach turned rotten and poisoned her blood.

Dorcha had visited him then, for the first time without rancour, and offered her sympathy.

However, her bitterness went so deep she could not help herself throwing a parting shot at him as she left him by the grave, saying, 'Now you know how it feels.'

Boy-girl, seeing how intently the glum Seumas was staring at Dorcha's hut, whispered, 'I can make her come with us.'

His head swivelled round and he stared into Boy-girl's eyes, then back again at Ti-ti.

'And,' added Boy-girl, 'we can leave those two behind.'

Seumas said nothing. He stared again at Boy-girl, then rose to his feet without a word and strolled slowly down to the lagoon, past the magnificent house of the father of Tangiia and Tutapu, with its carved wooden doorposts and its totems.

Inside the house an old man lay sick and dying. Seumas knew that once the king was dead, which could only be a matter of weeks, there would be civil war on the islands. He might try to remain aloof from the disturbance, but it was unlikely he would be allowed to. One or the other side would eventually demand his loyalty and he would have to choose between them.

If Tangiia left Raiatea and sought a new home, this

would avert the immediate crisis it was true, but Seumas did not trust the self-indulgent and paranoid Tutapu, who saw a plot against his life under every leaf of the forest. There were good rulers and there were despots, and Seumas had no doubt which one Tutapu would turn out to be, when he took over.

Once on the white coral sands, which burned his feet in the noon sun, Seumas walked into the shallow waters of the lagoon, followed for a while by his pet dog, Dirk. When Dirk saw that his master was deep in thought and paying no attention to him, the hound left him and went back to sleep in the shade.

Seumas waded slowly out to the edge of the reef, keeping to the smooth coral paths winding amongst the many-coloured stags-horn and fan corals with their sharp edges and points.

There was much beauty in the waters of the lagoon, from the hundreds of gaudy and graceful reef fish and anemones, with lacy scarves for fins, to the hermit crabs in their stolen homes – fragile combs, polished cowries, frilled murexes – scuttling out of his way.

There was also a sinister side, with thick-bodied moray eels poking their narrow heads out of holes, octopuses dancing away like fleshy spiders, and the odd barracuda trapped inside the reef when the tide went out. There were stone fish, ugly as a heinous sin manifest, the dorsal fin of which was deadly poison and if trodden upon took your life within a day. There were whip-tailed sting-rays and huge, tentacled jellyfish as delicate and monstrous as the wedding veils of an ogre's bride.

The lagoon, the reef, was thriving with life and colour though, and Seumas never ceased to marvel at it. It helped him think, to walk through this wonderland of grotesque fish and many-hued coral with its fantastic forms.

He reached the edge of the reef where the waves reared high above his head, becoming thin and translucent green for a moment, before crashing down on the coral barrier and magically melting into the placid waters of the lagoon, though they were only a body-length away from where he stood.

Out there, in the deep ocean, were monsters. Sharks that could swallow boats, giant squids that could crush canoes to pulp, swarms of deadly stinging translucent bells more numerous than wasps, killer whales, sea snakes more venomous than any serpent found on land. There was one type of tawny jellyfish that weighed as much as thirty men together and spread its filaments as wide as an island.

Did he really want to travel where there was the possibility of meeting such company?

'Well?' shrieked a voice over the boom of the surf. 'Are you coming?'

Seumas turned to see that the tall, willowy Boy-girl had followed him out to the foaming gulleys where he liked to stand and meditate. She looked unhappy. Boy-girl was not at home in the water, unlike most Raiateans, preferring dry land beneath her feet.

'I'm *thinking*,' he roared at her.

Miserably, Boy-girl found an exposed head of brain coral, the earthly symbol of Tangaroa himself, and stood upon it while Seumas made up his mind. Eventually he turned to her and smiled.

'Why not? It'll be a great adventure, won't it? What have I got to lose?'

She smiled at him and clapped her hands. 'Wonderful – I shall tell Tangiia today.'

'When is it to be – the departure?'

'When the pahi canoes are ready and the weather is right – we must have a diversion – a storm or something.'

'We're going to leave in a *storm*?'

'Perhaps,' she smiled, wagging a long finger at him. 'We'll see. A big brave man like you shouldn't be worried about such things. Shame on you. Are you afraid of death?'

'I'm not afraid of dying, I'm afraid of the *boredom* of being dead,' he confessed. 'I'm afraid that there'll be nothing to do but lie in my grave staring into an endless future. I hate being bored. It's agony for me to do nothing, or to do something which makes the time drag and makes me wish it was over. Some journeys are like that you know. Death must be like that.'

'Shame on you,' she said again, laughing.

Boy-girl then began wading back to the beach as if she were walking through raw sewage.

Seumas turned to face the great expanse of ocean again, upon which once more he was about to embark. There were small crab-claw sails out there now: fishermen in their canoes. The sea was as much their home as the island; they spent almost an equal amount of time on both. Yet there was something about a major voyage which captured the imagination of everyone, even a landsman, a climber, an egg-gatherer and bird-strangler like Seumas, who was more at ease on a sheer cliff than he was on the water.

He felt heroic at first and his spirit expanded inside him. Then he remembered what had been promised him and to what he had agreed, and his swollen soul shrank within his body again.

'Yes,' said Seumas to himself in Gaelic, thinking of his planned abduction of Dorcha, 'shame on me.'

After speaking with Seumas, Boy-girl went to where Kieto was fishing from the beach. Boy-girl and Kieto were friends, brought closer together by their mutual interest in the goblin, Seumas. When Seumas and Dorcha were first on the island there were few Oceanians who would engage them in conversation, or even pass them with a greeting. Most were afraid of the white-skinned savages who some-times spoke with the tongues of demons, and others thought it best not to risk contamination.

Kieto, however, had come to regard Seumas and Dorcha

with some affection, after their voyage over the great ocean together, and Boy-girl was obsessed with the strange beauty of the man. Sometimes the two Raiateans met to discuss the pair, though Boy-girl's interest was more with Seumas than with Dorcha.

'I have persuaded Seumas to come with us on the voyage,' said Boy-girl, sitting on the sands and watching the young Kieto whirl his net.

Kieto gave up his fishing and came and sat by Boy-girl.

'That's good,' said the boy. 'Is he pleased to come?'

Boy-girl shrugged. 'Not so pleased, but I think he will be, once we are out on the ocean.'

Kieto nodded, looking out at the toothed waves rearing and crashing on the reef. The ocean was like a wild beast, caged by the coral reef. Its great mouth was ever foaming; its jaws opening wide in its attempts to swallow the island; it rushed and gnashed and bit at the reef, trying to break through. The ocean, with its hard-edged light and big, brittle skies, was a beast which would never be tamed. You rode on its back and hoped you would survive the experience.

Kieto said, 'Yes – here he is just idling away his time, not really living. Seumas is a man made for adventure. He is like one of our heroes, waiting to prove himself. I think that out on the ocean he will wake, as if from a long sleep, and begin living the life he was meant to live.'

Boy-girl nodded. 'I remember how he was when he first came to us – angry at everyone, at everything. You could see the cruelty in him. He can be a cruel man. You could see the hardness like flint, in those blue eyes. And he hated us all then, especially me,' Boy-girl giggled. 'He hated my lovely decorations, my nice slim hands, my pretty face. He once yelled at me, "Is there a man underneath?" and I told him, "A bit of one – enough for *you*." He could be so confused. He didn't know how to treat me – or others. But there was a *fire* in him, which seems to have died now.

'The bitterness, and his idea of what a man should show of himself, conduct himself – how a man should act – has changed. He's mellowed. Now the fire is just a few glowing embers. It needs the ocean winds to make those embers flare into flame. Seumas will come alive again.'

Kieto nodded. 'Yes, much of the old Seumas is good – but not the Seumas who's afraid to show compassion or kindness. We don't want the unfeeling Seumas to return.'

Boy-girl nodded and smiled at Kieto. 'Don't worry, you and I will never let him become that silly man he once was, completely – we will draw out the bravehearted adventurer in him, direct him along a straighter path, and then he will not need those jaggedy edges he thought were so necessary to him when he first came to us.'

'He is not a man to control,' warned Kieto. 'If you try that, he'll kick against it.'

'I don't mean we shall control him, just steer him gently towards those things which make a man brave and hon-ourable – once he knows the way, he will go there himself,' replied Boy-girl.

'I think there will be no need for us to do anything, once we get out there on the ocean's back,' said Kieto. 'I think Tangaroa's world will shape him into what he can be.'

Boy-girl nodded and replied, 'Perhaps you're right.'

2

'The king once went on a voyage himself,' explained Kieto, to Dorcha, 'as a young man. He was not much older than I am now when he left the island. There were two brothers older than him when he left and he thought he stood little chance of becoming king once his father died, so he believed he had nothing to lose.'

'But he must have come back,' Dorcha said, 'to be here now.'

'He was away on his travels for twenty years. By the time he returned his father and both his elder brothers were dead. The two young men had killed each other in battle, leaving the kingdom without a chief. As he stepped ashore there were warring factions, each claiming one of their own as the future king. He stated his own claim to the first people he met, proved he was the rightful heir, and demanded the kingdom.'

Dorcha was sitting inside the entrance to her hut, weaving some mats from dried grasses and strips of bark. She was almost as deft as the Raiatean woman at this particular craft and had added some artistic designs of her own to their decorative patterns. Kieto often came to teach her the history of his peoples, she being eager to learn.

'Had he not changed in twenty years?' she asked. 'Did they recognise him straight away?'

'Indeed, the ravages of his travels had taken its toll on his features. He had left Raiatea a young and handsome man, without a blemish on his body. Since that time he had been burned by the sun, bitten by a shark, had hungered and thirsted, all of which did much to change his appearance, as well as age filling out his body and stealing his youth.'

'I know,' cried Dorcha, 'they identified him by his tattoos!'

'No, he was too young to have tattoos when he left the island.'

Dorcha grumbled, 'Oh, come on then, you'll have to tell me how he proved his name – I can't guess.'

'What is it that we have, which you admire so much?' smiled Kieto.

Dorcha stopped her weaving and looked across at the youth.

'Why,' she said, 'your memory, of course. It's something you people have kept which we in Albainn have lost over the centuries. And the way you see things. I'm told you can remember every part of the journey to my old island, Kieto. It all looked the same to me – the waves, the sea, the stars . . . every part of it. How did memory help the king?'

'He was able to recite the genealogy of his family, without a flaw, going back to the first ancestor.'

'And they accepted this as proof of his identity?'

'Of course,' said Kieto, 'any other man would have recited a *different* genealogy.'

'Of *course*,' she smiled, but she knew Kieto missed the irony in her tone.

Kieto said, his voice much lower, 'Will you not come with us, with Tangiia, when he leaves the island?'

Dorcha shook her head. 'No, Kieto. I've found my home and here I'm staying, whoever is in charge. I've found a contentment here I never thought existed. You may all perish out there on the waves – or even before, if Tutapu discovers what you're up to. Everyone seems to know you're leaving except him – I don't understand why.'

'Boy-girl has bewitched him,' whispered Kieto.

'Well, it only takes one person disgruntled with Tangiia or any of you, to betray you.'

'No one can get near Tutapu except his basket-sharers, and they have had their ears shut by Boy-girl.'

Dorcha shook her head as she weaved. 'It's a very dangerous game and you'll be lucky to get away.'

Suddenly, the doorway darkened, and both the occupants of the hut looked up, startled to see a figure blocking it. Then Kieto heaved a sigh of relief, as he recognised who it was. Dorcha, however, snarled, 'Get out – you haven't been invited.'

Seumas remained where he was. 'I saw your two little flowers go off gathering molluscs for you, chattering like young girls. I need to talk to you.'

'Well, I don't wish to speak with you,' she said, turning over her weave and inspecting the back of it. 'Get out of my light.'

'Dorcha, for the sake of the gods,' he pleaded, 'it's been nearly eight years since I killed your husband in a fair fight – will you never forgive me?'

'*Never*,' she said, her eyes flashing hatred.

'It was a fair fight,' he repeated wearily, looking at Kieto, as if hoping for some support. 'If it had been me that had been killed, she would have forgotten it had ever taken place by now. I never took advantage, I never cheated. It was right under all the rules of single combat.'

'It left my husband dead,' Dorcha said, 'you can't expect me to forget that, ever.'

Seumas squatted down, still in the doorway, and stared at the mats on the floor beneath his feet.

'What can I do?' he asked, very quietly. 'How can I make you forgive me? I will do anything.'

'Go away,' she said.

'I am going away,' he replied, 'with Tangiia's fleet, when it sets sail. I want you to come with us. You may be in danger here, when Tutapu becomes king. He's not the most stable of men, and you're a foreigner here.'

'I'm staying,' she said, attentive to her work.

Seumas sat there for a very long time while Kieto stared at him, unwilling to get involved himself in this long-running feud between two people he both loved.

Finally, Seumas said, 'Boy-girl offered to make you come on the voyage . . .'

Dorcha, dark and lovely in her twenty-seventh year, looked up sharply.

'You what? Why are you telling me this? You must have asked her to do it for you.'

He nodded. 'I can't do it. I've hurt you enough already. I thought I could do anything to get you, but I can't. I'm ashamed I even accepted Boy-girl's offer in the first place. I want you to come, but I want you to come *willingly*, without any magic from Boy-girl. It would be wrong . . .'

'It would not only be wrong,' she said, her voice low and hoarse with fury, 'it would be your last unholy act against my person. Seumas, you must see this is best for both of us – you go, I stay, and when I'm out of your sight I'll go out of your mind, and we can forget each other for good.' She paused for a moment, then added, 'I promise, once you've gone, I'll think well of you again – I'll forgive you for murdering my man.'

'Very magnanimous of you,' he said, dully. 'You're prepared to forgive me, if I'm prepared to lose everything I ever wanted in life.'

She stared at him, feeling some pity in her heart for him at last.

'I'm not your *everything*, Seumas, believe me. If I gave myself to you now, you would be tired of me within a week. This is a great opportunity for both of us. We can start to live again, properly, without the constant reminder of each other. I think I shall be able to breathe easily once more.'

Seumas groaned and got to his feet. He left the hut without another word. Dorcha continued to stare at the place where he had crouched and finally shook herself.

'It's best this way,' she muttered, returning to her craft.

'Are you sure?' asked Kieto.

Dorcha slapped his leg playfully. 'Don't you start too, young man!'

Now the doorway darkened again, but this time it was Rian, Dorcha's other husband, standing there. In his right hand he had a basket of live shells. He put this down and reached for a patu club, propped against the doorpost.

Dorcha said sharply, 'What are you doing, Rian?'

Rian looked at her darkly. 'I saw him leave – *he*'s been here – violated my home.'

'So, you're going to fight him?' she spat at her husband. 'Are you prepared to die?'

'I'm not going to die. I'm going to kill *him*.'

Rian was the better built of the two husband-brothers, having broad shoulders and a thick chest. His arms and shoulders were muscular. He had distinguished himself in battle when the Raiateans had been at war with the people of the Huahine Islands. There was a dramatic scar on his tattooed ribcage from a lei-o-mano knife, the sharks' teeth having left the mark of lightning from his left nipple down to his naval.

'If you go out to kill someone, you must be prepared to die. Seumas has killed men in single combat too. He fought and killed my first husband over a piece of iron. You haven't seen him in battle mood. I would say he's at least your equal.'

Rian looked hesitant, but argued, 'Your first husband was a man like him – of the same land. Seumas doesn't look very strong to me –'

'If you think it's strength that wins fights, Rian,' inter-rupted the young Kieto, 'you have much to learn.'

Rian's eyes opened wide at this remark, coming from a youth who had not even been invested yet.

'A boy? Would you teach me how to fish?' cried Rian.

'Kieto's trying to make you see what you know is true yourself, Rian,' said Dorcha, 'only your pride and anger is blinding you. Seumas is a skilful warrior. It's true I didn't invite him into the hut, but he came here out of good will, and not to insult you. Please, put down your club.'

Rian stood for a moment, his jaw set, then his shoulders slumped a little and he replaced the club by the doorpost.

'If he comes here again,' said Rian, 'I'll splatter his brains on the coral. You be sure to tell him that, boy, when you see him next.'

Kieto knew when it was wise to remain silent.

Tutapu's kahuna, the priest Ragnu, was officiating at the kava-drinking ceremony. The stupefying drink was being mixed in a wooden bowl in the centre of Tupatu's council hut. Some time ago the women and children had chewed the peeled roots of the kava plant to a pulp and had spat the mush into the bowl, where it had been diluted and then put aside to ferment. Now it was ready to drink and simply required a fangu chant from the kahuna to give it full strength.

The prince himself sat cross-legged on his mat and brooded. Around the prince were gathered his basket-sharers; men who ate from the same basket as he did himself and therefore his closest companions, a small group like many other similar groups within the wider organisation of the clan. Even a lowly fisherman had his basket-sharers to assist him in times of trouble.

'Ragnu,' said Tutapu, 'how is the old man today?'

The kahuna looked up from his chanting and stirring to smile through the gaps in his teeth.

'He is well, my prince.'

Tutapu knew this was reverse news, to protect Tutapu from eavesdropping ghosts, and that he could be sure his father was sinking fast.

'Good, good,' he murmured.

His father was dying, yet the old man seemed to be hanging on to life with the tenaciousness of a limpet to a rock. Tutapu was fond of his father, in his way, but things were becoming difficult for Tutapu and until the king died nothing could be done about his brother Tangiia. The honourable thing was to wait until the king's death, then challenge Tangiia to single combat to the death. Tutapu believed his own skill as a warrior, coupled with the magic of Ragnu, would ensure his victory over his younger brother.

And if he was not victorious, well then, he would be dead and with his ancestors. One thing was certain, there could only be one king of the two islands of Borabora and Raiatea, and Tutapu meant to be that king. To leave his brother alive, even though Tangiia might swear loyalty to him, was too risky. One day Tangiia would be sure to let his ambition and jealousy rule his head and there would be insurrection. Better to sort it all out when their father died and have done with it.

It was especially difficult, because Tutapu did not hate his brother, indeed he had loved him strongly once. They had grown up together, played amongst the palms, gone fishing together, shared first experiences.

Tutapu would always recall with fondness the time they had climbed the mountain together and become lost in a labyrinth of hanging valleys. It had been Tangiia who had brought them through, with his fierce conviction that they would not die, that someone would find them. Indeed, this had spurred Tutapu into greater efforts to find a path out of the valleys, which he eventually did, and the pair of them were discovered by searchers leaving the maze of valleys.

The first cup of kava was placed in Tutapu's hands by Ragnu.

'Drink, my prince,' said the priest.

Tutapu motioned Ragnu to his side.

'Tell me what you saw today – at the marae,' he ordered the priest in a low voice.

The kahuna Ragnu was also a visionary, who had eyes in the future. Those eyes were not as clear as Tutapu would have liked them to be, for their view was foggy and vague since the mediator was Hau Maringi, the God of Mist. However, Ragnu was able to give some indication of future events. That day he had been to Most Sacred, Most Feared, to ask Hau Maringi to show him the future.

Tutapu was beloved of Hau Maringi. This was mainly because Hau Maringi hated Tangiia, the youth having slighted him once while out fishing by calling an oath because the mist descended just as the young prince had found a shoal of fish. Tangiia had lost sight of the shoal and swore violently at the mist for losing him his catch. Hau Maringi had never forgiven Tangiia for this insult.

Nevertheless, Hau Maringi had still demanded a human sacrifice, for the task of showing Ragnu what might be.

Ragnu was hesitant now that Tutapu had asked him the question. His news was not good and messengers sometimes paid a price for bad news.

'Come,' growled Tutapu to his kahuna, his eyes bloodshot. 'Tell me.'

Ragnu stared at the patterns on the prince's body, some like whirlpools on the breast, an elaborate comb-like tattoo across the upper chest, sea-wave lines around the shoulders, the backbone of a fish, running down the length of his sternum, its spines following the spread of the ribs on either side. He looked into these designs and felt himself drowning in them for a moment, felt himself gazing into the vortex of his master's body and experienced a giddy sensation. He forced out his answer.

'I saw the two islands in chaos,' murmured the priest. 'I saw people like wraiths in the mist, thin and hungry. It wasn't clear, but it seemed that there was the smell of decay in the air, the scent of death and disease.'

Tutapu sipped moodily at the intoxicating kava juice.

'What does this mean?' he asked.

Ragnu said quickly, 'Hau Maringi is showing us the future as it will be – if your brother lives.'

'You're sure of this?'

'No one can be *sure*, my prince,' said Ragnu, silkily, 'but I am *almost* certain. How else could it be? If Tangiia is dead, and you alone rule the islands, there can only be harmony.'

Tutapu thought about this for a while and finally, to Ragnu's relief, he nodded. 'It seems to me that what you have seen is the chaos of a divided kingdom.'

'Quite so,' Ragnu said.

Tutapu nodded and dismissed the priest with a wave of his hand.

'Dancing,' he ordered.

A conch horn sounded and drums began to beat, rapidly, causing the blood of those who heard them to race in their veins. The drummers' hands were a blur, as they performed their art, the sound they made filling the night air. The crickets and tree frogs ceased to be heard as their cacophony was drowned.

Soon there were maidens gyrating before the prince, causing a stirring in his loins that would soon be dampened by the kava, once it took its hold on him. Only Boy-girl could make him feel anything while he was under the influence of kava, and Boy-girl was not on Borabora that evening.

Boy-girl had excused herself and asked that she be allowed to attend another feast, on Raiatea, a celebration to appease the ocean demons Aremata-Rorua and Aremata-popoa, the 'Long-wave' and 'Short-wave', whose

immense power often took the lives of sailors and fishermen. Tutapu had reluctantly agreed to her absence, but
was now beginning to regret his decision.

The dancing, feasting and drinking went on for several
hours. To eat there was suckling pig, dog which had been
fed only on fruit and vegetables since its birth and consequently its flesh tasted sweet and succulent, ovenbaked reef
fish, all manner of spitted and roasted birds, taro, yam,
sweet potato, breadfruit and banana. The prince liked a
good show of food, even if he himself tasted its delights
with a desultory tongue.

Finally, the prince's companions were quite drunk,
though the prince himself remained coldly sober, his murderous thoughts chilling his brain and keeping the full effect
of the kava at bay. At one point in the evening he sighed
heavily and was asked by one of his friends, the man
Nanato, why he was so sad.

'My brother . . .' murmured Tutapu.

Nanato was very drunk and also very eager to please his
prince, who allowed him to share the royal basket. Nanato
was grateful for the privileges he received. Nanato unwisely
allowed his gratitude to slip into his tongue.

'Leave your brother to me,' said Nanato, placing a hand
on the prince's thigh.

Even as he spoke the words Nanato knew how foolish he
was being, but the drink had blunted his reason and his
emotion was running like a fast tide. The promise had been
made in haste and now there was nothing Nanato could do
but follow through with the deed. He experienced a sense
of helplessness, as he realised that his statement – vague as
it might have been – was eagerly grasped by the prince.

Tutapu stared at his companion hard. 'I do not wish to
know what you mean,' he said. 'If I'm without the knowledge
of your intentions, I am innocent of any deed. The gods can't
punish me for something I know nothing about. However, if
you should choose to please me in some way, there are fifty

red feathers in my treasure box which shall be yours.'

This was indeed a generous reward. Fifty red feathers would make Nanato a rich man. With ten red feathers he could buy a pig, with twenty a canoe, with thirty a beautiful woman.

'I leave you now,' he said to his prince, and climbed awkwardly to his feet, to stagger to the door.

Once outside, the cool air struck Nanato in the face, sobering him a little. There was a certain horror in his heart, for what he was about to do, but he had robbed himself of any alternative. If he failed to kill Tangiia tonight, Tutapu would have him put to death. Nanato, not surprisingly, did not want to die, not yet, not for a foolish, drunken statement.

Now that the job had to be done, Nanato gave it his full consideration.

The choice of weapon was important. A club was too messy and not sure enough. A knife was better than a club, but unless Nanato could catch Tangiia in a deep sleep there might be a struggle. Nanato was not certain he could beat Tangiia if it came to hand-to-hand fighting. A spear was too unwieldy. It would be best, he decided, if Prince Tangiia were unaware of what was happening to him, and that meant subterfuge.

The safest way to kill the prince, Nanato came to the conclusion, would be to use poison. He would poison the tip of a bone-hooked barracuda lure, fixed to a wooden shank, and prick the prince's leg in the dark. The prince would think he had been bitten by an insect, rub the spot, and go back to sleep again. In his sleep his blood would thicken and by morning he would be dead of heart seizure.

It was a good plan – for a drunkard.

The lure was found, the point poisoned, and Nanato then set out in his canoe across the sea between Borabora and Raiatea.

*

Amai-te-rangi, a god who lived in the sky, was furious to learn from one of the forest fairies of Borabora that a man was planning to kill a prince with a fish hook.

'That's *my* prerogative,' the god grumbled. 'I am the fisher who angles for men! This Nanato creature is stealing my mode of dealing out death to mortals.'

Amai-te-rangi delighted in lowering nets and lines from the sky and catching mortals, whisking them up to his home where he cooked and ate them. Small, relatively insignificant gods like Amai-te-rangi guarded their methods of catching men jealously, their techniques being all they had to make them special amongst their contemporaries. That a man was about to kill another man using a fish hook was disrespect to Amai-te-rangi.

Yet, there was little he could do about it himself, since it was night and he could not see the man in the canoe. If he dropped his lines, he might catch the man by chance, but it would be an uncertain thing. Amai-te-rangi sought the assistance of the Great Wind-God, Maomao, explaining the reason for his fury and asking for his brother's help.

Maomao said, 'I can understand your anger and would like to help, but if I blow at the moment, I might create a hurricane which would destroy more than a single man in a canoe. It would be better to ask the Great Rain-God Ua to drown the man in his canoe as he crosses the waters.'

Ua was not very sympathetic to Amai-te-rangi's request, since he had only recently created a deluge for another minor god, in another part of Oceania.

'I need some rest,' said Ua. 'Try someone else.'

Eventually, Ara Tiotio, the deity of the whirlwind, agreed to assist the injured fisher-god, and came screaming through the darkness to blow the terrified Nanato back to Borabora, shipwrecking the unfortunate man on the beach and sucking the remnants of his canoe up into the night sky, to be scattered later over a distant part of the ocean.

Honour was satisfied and Amai-te-rangi thanked Ara Tiotio, and went away to find a place to rest.

Nanato woke on the beach the next morning and staggered back to his hut. There he was found by others of Tutapu's basket-sharers and dragged before the prince. The prince, quite understandably, wanted to know if Nanato had anything of importance to tell him, now that the night was over.

'I – I was shipwrecked,' complained Nanato. 'I had no time to kill your brother.'

Tutapu raised his eyebrows. 'Kill my brother? What, before the death of our father? This is a monstrous crime you planned to commit. Have you no shame, no remorse? I ought to banish you from the islands!'

'But you *knew* I was going to murder Tangiia,' cried the hapless Nanato. 'We agreed –'

'I agreed to nothing,' said Tutapu, stiffly. 'It remains for me to pronounce your punishment.'

Tutapu, who had no wish to dispose of such a potentially willing assassin as Nanato, was about to give the man a relatively light sentence, when Ragnu whispered in his ear.

'We are in need of a good man,' murmured the priest, 'to pay Hau Maringi for his visions of the future.'

'Ah yes,' nodded Tutapu, a little disappointed by the intervention. 'Hau Maringi must be paid.'

'I must test Nanato for suitability.'

'Do so,' replied Tutapu.

This conversation took place out of the earshot of Nanato, who was taken by Ragnu to a quiet stone room in the temple.

'Now,' Ragnu said, after the terrified Nanato had been seated on the floor. 'I have a few questions.'

Nanato watched as the high priest squatted down opposite him and began chewing on a root.

After gathering his thoughts, the Ragnu asked, 'Have you ever done anything evil in your life?'

Nanato's panicking mind swept back over his past. He could, with all sincerity, deny any serious evil-doing. Had he murdered Prince Tangiia, of course, he would have been unable to give a negative answer. However, that deed had not taken place, thanks to the God of Whirlwinds.

'Not *really* bad. I – I've cheated a little when trading meat and fruit – but everyone does that, don't they?' he pleaded.

'Of course,' said Ragnu, in an understanding voice. 'No one expects you to be absolutely pure. If you were, you would be a god. Anything else?'

Happy that Ragnu was so compassionate, Nanato searched his mind for other small misdeeds.

'I once stole a canoe – but I took it back again.'

'When did you take it back?'

'Six months later. I thought the owner was going to die of an illness, but he recovered.'

'That seems to be all right. You simply *borrowed* the canoe, while he could not use it. You were actually making sure the canoe was maintained, otherwise it might have rotted away through misuse.'

'Yes – yes, that's it.'

Ragnu nodded and seemed to go off into another reverie. Nanato wanted to be told to go, to leave the temple and return to his hut. The question of banishment still hung in the air. In some ways banishment was worse than death, since a man might end up on a ghost-filled island in the middle of nowhere. He did not know what had passed between the priest and the future king, but he guessed his fate was in Ragnu's hands. He realised of course that he was being tested. Having answered all the questions to the obvious satisfaction of the high priest, he wanted now to be told he was free to leave.

'Have you – have you ever done anything *good* in your

life?' asked Ragnu. 'I mean, something above the ordinary? Remember, you are in *my* temple. The gods will tell me if you are lying. Only the truth will serve you here.'

Again Nanato scoured his memory and came up with a true and happy answer.

'I once saved a woman from a shark. She was standing in the water when a shark took off her leg and would have eaten all of her if I hadn't jumped out of my dugout and beat it with my canoe paddle. She lived for three months afterwards. Unfortunately, her stump rotted and she died.'

'Still, you performed a courageous act – was this from the same canoe of which we spoke? The *borrowed* canoe?'

'I think it was,' said Nanato, eagerly. 'I'm *sure* it was.'

'Hmmm, so because you borrowed the canoe a woman had three extra months of life – and was not carried away to sea by a shark, but buried in a family grave?'

'That's true. That's true.'

Rangu nodded thoughtfully and after a while said, 'I think you are basically a *good* man, Nanato, and therefore a fit subject for a human sacrifice to the God of Mist and Fog, Hau Maringi. Have you anything more you wish to say?'

Nanato, who believed until now he had been defending himself against banishment, realised too late what were the reasons behind him being tested.

'I am unworthy!' he cried, desperately. 'Please – I am not good enough.'

'Let me be the judge of that,' murmured Ragnu, rising.

'The prince *loves* me,' sobbed Nanato.

'We could not sacrifice you otherwise.'

The terrified Nanato was bound hand and foot to a long pole and carried out on to Ragnu's marae.

Ragnu and his priests began the chants, the sacred fangu, and gradually the kahuna weaved his way towards the platform where the unfortunate Nanato lay.

As Ragnu raised the obsidian dagger, Nanato spoke.

'I am a loyal subject,' he said, helplessly. 'I have always loved Prince Tutapu.'

'That is as well,' whispered Ragnu, 'since you are being sacrificed for your goodness, not because you are evil.'

The dagger still poised, Ragnu looked up into the trees, which stirred with a gust of wind.

'Dakuwanga is there,' said the high priest, 'I sense it. He swims through the air, waiting for your sau to leave your body, so that he might swallow it and grow strong.'

'The Shark God?' cried Nanato. 'Please wait until he goes away – I want to go to Milu's land . . .'

Ragnu was not unsympathetic to this request and waited until the leaves in the trees were still, then he plunged the ritual weapon down through Nanato's chest, the glassy-stone dagger crashing through the rib cage, to pierce the victim's heart. Blood fountained, covering the priests as well as the sacrifice. There was a shout of joy amongst them, for goodness and mercy had triumphed over evil – again.

The ritually slaughtered Nanato was left on the ahu platform decorated with skulls and carved wooden planks, just where a pig had been lying two days before.

Tutapu was made quite sad by his loss.

Hau Maringi was pleased with his gift.

3

Nau Ariki's affectionate name was 'Kula', after the bird brought back by Kupe from a strange island. She was the daughter of an ariki, or high chief, and his wife Papite who was captured in a war raid on Maupiti Island. The kula bird had a breast of red feathers, used as money, and was therefore considered very precious by the Oceanians. Nau Ariki was regarded as the most precious possession of the high chief of a fertile volcano region of Raiatea and hence her nickname.

That Kula was a healthy, beautiful woman did not make her exceptional, for there were many beautiful maidens amongst the hillside women. The air was cooler on the mountainside, the canopy of the rainforest more protective of the skin, and the water cleaner and clearer. What made her exceptional was her cleverness and her strong sense of duty. She was only seventeen, yet she saw the path of life clearly before her, which was marriage to Tutapu, once he became king.

Kula was bathing in a pool in the forest, with her companions and basket-sharers, girls of her village. They were laughing and ducking each other under the waterfall in water as green as the leaves on the bushes. They had a trick of flailing the surface with their long black hair, by flicking their heads, to keep their companions away. It was while Kula was performing this feat that she noticed a motion in the shrubs near by.

She stopped and called, 'Who's there?'

There was no answer and one of the younger girls cried, 'It's a ghost!'

A ripple of anxiety went through all the women, then a man stood up from behind the shrub and revealed himself.

'Prince Tangiia?' cried the seventeen-year-old Kula. 'What are you doing here, watching the girls bathing?'

Her voice chastised him gently. It was forbidden to gaze upon bathers, whatever their sex. Those maidens standing halfway out of the water turned their backs towards the man. Those on the banks of the pool wrapped their tapa skirts around the lower half of their bodies.

When he did not answer her question, Kula said, 'Have you come to court someone?' She looked around her at the other maidens. 'Who's the lucky girl desired by the handsome and bold Prince Tangiia? Hands up anyone who wants to marry a prince with the face and body of a young god?'

Several giggling maidens put up a hand, some of them thrusting two in the air, laughing shyly as they did so. Tangiia scowled, not pleased by this mocking, taking the frangipani flower from behind his ear and casting it to the ground. Kula realised she had gone too far.

'I'm sorry, you must expect a little teasing when there are girls all together. Did you wish to talk to anyone?'

'I – I wanted to talk to you,' said the young man.

'To *me*?' said Kula, in mock tones again, unable to help herself joshing this awkward young man. 'You need the permission of my grandfather for that.'

She was teasing him, for Kula's grandfather, like several venerated old men, was taboo to anyone outside her family. Only those directly related to him could go near and speak with the old man, his advice being a marketable commodity which could be sold by the family to others. Tangiia would have needed an intermediary to ask the grandfather's permission for anything and since the most available person to act as that go-between was Kula herself, she was creating a paradox for him.

'Do I?' he said, confused. 'How . . .'

Kula laughed and rolled her eyes. 'Tangiia, you are *slow* sometimes.'

'I'm a warrior,' he said, stiffly, 'not a priest.'

'Warrior or priest,' she said, 'you're treading on a tree I planted yesterday.'

Tangiia moved his foot, awkwardly, aware that he had crushed a tiny sapling, just sprouting from its seed. The Princess Nau Ariki was a devotee of Rongo, God of Agriculture, Fruits and Cultivated Plants. She spent much of her time planting and growing things which would later yield a harvest. Her grandfather called her affectionately 'the gardener'.

'I'm sorry,' he said, clearly frustrated. 'I came to speak to you about marriage.'

She frowned. 'Marriage to your brother? Does he need an emissary now? I thought it was all settled.'

'I came to ask you to marry me,' said Tangiia in a choked voice.

'You?' Kula said, wondering if it was a joke. Was he teasing her back now, getting even? As she stared at his face she could see by his eyes that he was serious.

Kula felt a jolt of annoyance pass through her. Without another word she left the pool and picked up her skirt, wrapping it around her waist. Then she walked off into the rainforest, with Tangiia following her. When they were beyond the hearing distance of the other maidens, she turned on him in anger.

'How dare you ask such a question in front of my companions? You know I'm promised.'

'I haven't asked any question yet,' he replied, huffily. 'I

simply told you what I came to speak to you about.'

They were in a glade where the shafts of sunlight broke through the canopy and illuminated the mosses and grasses of the forest floor. He tried to reach out to touch her, but she backed away. He sighed and plucked a leaf from a nearby bush, startling a monitor lizard resting beneath.

'You don't love me,' he stated.

Kula was a little confused by this remark. 'It's not a question of love. It's a question of *duty*. It's common knowledge that your father is on his death bed and that Tutapu is poised to become king. As king he will need a wife. He has chosen me to be that wife. My mother and father are very proud of the fact that I've been chosen. The death of an old king, one who has ruled wisely and without favour, always disturbs an island such as ours for a while. It's important that things settle down quickly – as his wife I can help Tutapu establish himself, be accepted as his father's replacement.'

By the time she had finished this speech, she had calmed a little, and was breathing more easily. The tension in the glade was high, not just because of him, but because of her too. She had feelings she did not want to admit to anyone, least of all Tangiia, and hopefully with a certain amount of effort not even to herself. She had been told, and believed, that once she was married to Tutapu she would forget all other men. Her situation would dictate her feelings to her and she would grow comfortable in her position as queen of the two islands.

'Then I am lost,' murmured Tangiia, hanging his head in despair. 'I must do what I must do.'

Thinking he meant suicide, Kula took hold of his hand for a moment.

'Oh, no,' she said, 'you must not harm yourself.'

It was traditional for young men to throw themselves off clifftops when they took their lives. Kula suddenly had a picture in her head, of Tangiia's smashed, broken body lying on the rocks, with the waves washing over it. It was an image that horrified her.

'You will find another wife, one better than me.'

'Never,' said Tangiia, his eyes burning hotly. 'I can never love another woman. How can you even think it?'

'Men do,' she replied, sadly, letting his hand fall. 'Some men can forget very easily.'

'I'm not one of those men.' He stared about him, at the rainforest. 'I'm not talking about killing myself anyway, I'm talking about going away from here, forever. These islands – I shall not be sorry to see them behind me.'

Kula nodded. 'There is a rumour you're leaving. It's a secret from your brother – to prevent war between you. I think it's very wise of you, and very noble. No good can come of a kingdom contested by two brothers.'

'And you don't care that I shall be gone,' he said, bitterly.

She wanted to tell him she cared very much, that she would weep for him, that she would always carry a special place in her heart for his memory, but she dared not.

Instead, she replied, 'I shall be sorry to see my husband's brother leave the islands where he was born.'

'Ha!' he cried and turned on his heel to stalk away, down the slopes, to his home near the shore.

Kula sighed deeply and walked slowly back to the pool where her basket-sharers, subdued by her absence, greeted her quietly. No longer did the green glade, with its sparkling waterfall and placid pool, seem beautiful to her. No longer were the waterplants and grasses fringing the bathing area a source of pleasure. The lustre had gone from the wet rocks, the glitter from the rivulets rushing downstream, the shimmer from the freshwater fish that played amongst them and nipped their toes. It was as if a storm cloud had moved over, and all fell in its dull shadow. Kula blamed Tangiia for this change in the atmosphere and tried to feel anger.

All she could feel was despair.

Her friends could tell Kula was troubled, but did not press her for the reasons. They each had their idea of what was bothering her. When Kula did not enter the water again, they began to get out and dry themselves. Finally, they were all ready, and walked with her along the paths to where their village was perched on the volcanic hillside.

Kula went to the hut of her grandfather and found him sitting outside. She took up a wooden bowl and began to serve him some banana porridge with her fingers. Since he was a tapu the old man was not allowed to touch food and had to be fed by others.

He saw that she was confused and unhappy and asked her why.

'Grandfather,' said Kula, 'why is life so complicated?'

He stared at her for a while, then said, 'You mean why are you in love with one man, yet must go to another?'

Her head came up and she stared into his rheumy but wise old eyes. 'Yes,' she said.

Her grandfather smiled at her and gave her a nose-kiss.

'Be assured,' he said, 'the gods will not let you do the wrong thing. If you are meant to marry the man you love, then the gods will ensure that happens, and if not – why then they will keep you from him. What is meant to be, will come.'

Her grandfather was a great storyteller amongst their people and to help her over her sadness she asked him to tell her a tale about love.

'Tell me a story about a love that was never meant to be,' she said, 'and so ended tragically.'

She believed a tale that reflected her own position might aid her in understanding her own situation better. At her young and emotional age, to immerse herself in the sadness of another, an even more unfortunate lover than herself, helped to eclipse her own unhappiness. It was an indulgence.

Her grandfather obliged her, as she fed his toothless mouth the cold porridge, and he spoke between swallows.

'You remember the story of the Moon-Goddess, Lona, who fell in love with a mortal, a beautiful young man named Ai Kanaka, whose tattoos were the wonder of all who saw him? He was having his latest tattoo chiselled on to his thigh when the moon came out and Lona saw him. She fell instantly in love with him and wanted him by her, even though he was a mortal. The trouble was, he was too far away for her to reach from her moon-kingdom, and since he was a fisherman he never slept on a hill, always in his palm hut close to his canoe on the shore.

'Enlisting the forest fairies, she asked them to beguile Ai Kanaka. They clustered around his hut, as he sat outside roasting a fish. He saw the fairies in the light of the dying flames of his fire, staring at him from the shadows of the forest with large, beautiful eyes. Clearly he was the object of their interest and he played with the fire, poking it with a stick, and watching the Peerless Ones out of the corners of his eyes. When they did not go away, intrigued and fearful, Ai Kanaka finally spoke to them and asked them what they wanted with him. The fairies told him if he climbed the high mountain and stayed there until the dawn he would receive a magnificent reward.

'Ai Kanaka was not only afraid of the fairies, he was eager to learn what treasure would be his, so he climbed the ancient mountain and fell asleep between the roots of a tall tree.

'Since he was now close to her, Lona had not far to fly. Descending from the roof of voyaging on her wings that very night, she carried him off while he was asleep, into the White Kingdom of the Moon. There she ruled with Ai Kanaka at her side, and they were very happy for a while, but shortly after arriving Ai Kanaka died because he was an earthling.'

Kula's deep-brown eyes were damp with sorrow.

'How terribly sad,' she said. 'If I took a lover to my breast and he died, I should want to die too.'

'So did Lona,' replied her grandfather, 'but she had a duty to do – to light the earth and ocean with her purity.'

'Of course,' nodded Kula. 'Her duty.'

In a small corner of Raiatea preparations for an exodus were moving quickly ahead.

The three pahi canoes were almost finished now and were receiving their final coating of vegetable and shark oils to keep the water out of the stitched hulls. They were magnificent craft, especially now their rigging was almost complete, and the sails of woven leaves were in place, two to each vessel. Shaped like the crab claw which gave them their name, the sails were dedicated to the Wind-God Maomao, who was pleased to bless them. A pahi was built to run before the wind, but was also extremely manoeuvrable for its size.

The pahi themselves were double-hulled canoes with a deck between, two masts – one fore, one aft – and twin huts side by side on the deck. Their length was that of fourteen men, head to toe, lying on the sand. Their speed was that of a fast-walking or trotting man along a hard-packed beach.

Most of the men who were to sail these craft had not yet been on a long voyage. Many had sailed to nearby islands in smaller boats, even as far as Tahiti, using the shunting method of changing tack: picking up the mast bodily, with the flapping sail still attached, and placing it in a different position on the deck. These great pahi sails could not be so managed, and thus the rigging and manner of changing course was completely different, a supervised operation under a deck officer who bellowed instructions to the sailors as they worked the rigging.

Moreover, this voyage across a vast tract of ocean was a venture into the unknown. Mankind has always feared the unknown and the Raiateans were no different from other peoples. There was a sense of dread in many a breast. They imagined, dreamed at night, of a multitude of disasters which might befall them, which *could* befall them.

There would be encounters, surely, with great ocean monsters. There would be storms, great winds, currents that would take them off their course, monstrous waves, fast seas, strange tides, swells, waterspouts, whirlpools, hunger, thirst, and a thousand other unforeseen catastrophes to surmount. They would, at times, be lost on a vast ocean of water, not knowing which way to go, though the old king had been a magnificent navigator worthy of his rank, and he had passed these skills on to his two sons. It did not matter, the sailors told each other, that Tangiia had never made such a voyage; memory was the key to knowledge and an Oceanian's memory was superb.

Their courage was bolstered by their faith in Prince Tangiia, who, once he left these shores, would be their new king. Tangiia, with the help of other navigators of lesser rank: the blind old man, Kaho, who used his son Po'oi as his eyes; the star watchers: those who knew the directions of the te lapa, the streaks of subsea light; the feelers of the swells that lifted the stern of the boat; the bird watchers; the good listeners who could hear reefs from a long way off; the smellers who could scent land from afar. All these, and others, would assist their king in finding a path across the sea to a Faraway Heaven where Tangiia could rule his people in peace.

Yet, it did take *immense* courage to contemplate leaving their homeland. All they had, all they had ever known, was invested in these islands. To leave them behind was to die and hope to be born again. And *only* hope, for nothing was certain.

The alternative was to stay and face a civil war, with brother killing brother, and the land polluted with bitterness and a desire for revenge which would take generations to clean.

While the pahi canoes were being finished the loading of

provisions began. Caged rats, dogs, chickens, pigs. Water in gourds. Breadfruit paste, pandanus fruit, green bananas, yam, taro, sweet potatoes, dried akule fish, arrowroot flour, dried skipjack and tuna, sugar-cane, hard poi, and most important of all, coconuts at all different stages, from hard meat coconuts, to soft meat coconuts, to drinking coconuts.

They took also seeds and roots to plant when they arrived at the new island, which were stored on the vessels, in case there was no paper mulberry there, or (Rongo forbid) no coconut palms from which to take fibres for cordage, posts for huts and bridges, leaves for roofs and basketwork, and shells for containers. Without the coconut palm they would be desperately poor and possibly even perish.

The provisions they took were enough to last the voyagers at least a month, perhaps twice as long with severe rationing.

Then there was the ceremony of the launching.

It was deemed a shame amongst the boat builders that no recent war had left the islands with enemy bodies, which could be placed between the log rollers when launching the canoes, to ensure a sacred entry into the ocean for their craft.

'In my grandfather's day,' said one master artisan, 'they put *live* captives under the keels at the launching, but people are only concerned about naval architecture these days – they care nothing for the religious side of things.'

This was not quite true, for their operations were regulated by clearly defined rites during the building of a pahi, the artisans themselves members of a caste and working under the guidance of a high priest.

Manopa hardly ever left the site, overseeing things in a nervous and upsetting way for the boat builders, who worked best when left to their own devices. No instruments or drawn plans were used; the boats like their dwellings were vernacular architecture. There were men

amongst the artisans whose job it was to measure by judgement, and whose eye was to be trusted for length, shape
and size.

Manopa constantly interfered in this exercise, by sug-
gesting that a curve was slightly out of true, or a plank a
shade too long. He was invariably wrong, there being nothing the matter with the eye of the artisan, and everything
the matter with Manopa's perception of the length, breadth
and height of sections of the craft. Still, he continued to
insist on his own judgement, which had little skill or experience behind it, and slowed the building to a point where
the artisans complained to Tangiia. Tangiia took Manopa
aside.

'Look, I know you're doing your best here, Manopa,
but you have to leave these people to do their work in their
own way.'

'Who's been complaining about me?' demanded
Manopa, glaring around him at the boat builders.

'I'm not going to tell you – it's not important. You are a
warrior, a captain, good in battle. I need you here on the
site in case it's discovered and you have to defend it, but
you must not interfere with the work.'

Manopa was hurt. 'I've built boats before. I'm as good as
the next man at building boats –'

'Small craft, like a váa or pu hoe, with an outrigger, but
not a great pahi. You are not qualified to judge in these
matters, Manopa, and I am asking you as a friend to leave
these people alone. We *must* get the canoes finished soon.'

Manopa dropped his head, feeling something of a failure. It was in him, as in many men, to wish to be good at *all*
things. He needed to be the father figure, to whom all men
of all professions came for advice. It was difficult for him to
admit to himself that there were others who knew better.

'The trouble with every one of us,' said Tangiia, 'is that
we can all build a small canoe, every man and boy amongst
us. We all have our little tool kits: the adze, augers, drills

and abrasers. Our grandfathers give them to us when we are young and we treasure them before handing them on to our grandchildren. Because of that every man thinks he can build a pahi.

'It's not true, my friend. The pahi requires special talents. It has to be exactly right. Think of the strength needed for such a voyage – the durability needed to cope with monstrous waves of great power and long days of constant movement of planks, ropes, hulls, for storms and other adverse weather conditions. A pahi doesn't just need to carry nearly a hundred people, it needs to withstand the pressures and strains of a mighty ocean, day in, day out, for months.'

'But a small canoe . . .'

'A small canoe gets beached every few hours, the binding cords tightened when necessary, the repairs done on time. A small canoe only has to cope with lagoons and coastal waters. There's no comparison between a small canoe and a pahi. A man has to be close to the gods to build a pahi – he has to be pure artisan, through and through, with no warrior or fisherman inside him to interfere with his mental calculations. Do you understand – you're not less of a man because of that, Manopa. I wouldn't try to tell them how to do it myself.'

'You wouldn't?'

'A boy of eighteen? Why should I know what has taken men more than a lifetime to learn?'

Manopa's brow furrowed at this remark. 'How can it take them more than a lifetime? They only live one life.'

'The knowledge is in their bones, in their blood, passed down to them from their forefathers. They have a natural skill we could not learn in a thousand years, you and I. Yet put them in battle beside us, and see who kills the most foe.'

Manopa's bole-chest swelled. 'Ah, yes – see then who has the skill!'

Manopa then took on the task of supervising the loading of weapons and other artifacts aboard the three pahi canoes.

Into one of the twin huts on each pahi deck went patu, kotiate and wahaika hand clubs of whalebone and stone, spears with tanged obsidian points, harpoons, lure shanks of schist and serpentine, fish hooks, adzes, knives of stone, hardwood and fishbone, and finally, slings.

The handling of weapons was a job for which the boat builders considered Manopa to be much better suited.

It was late evening and the king's house was in semi-darkness, with only a small fire to light the room. His thin, frail body lay on a bed of leaves, the eyes open and staring at the rosewood ceiling. A ceremonial cloth was draped over his loins, to hide the shrivelled remains of what had once been a man.

In his time the king had been a giant, with muscles that stood proud of his heavy frame. In those days his oiled, tattooed body had been the envy of many of his male subjects and the desire of many of the female islanders. The hands that wielded club and knife so deftly in battle had been known to crush limestone to powder. His strength had been legendary, his feet nimble, his navigating skills equal only to the great Kupe.

Now the skin that bore the tattoos was wrinkled and grey, the muscles wasted, the cheeks hollow and gaunt. Bones protruded from every part of his anatomy. There were dark rings around his eyes. His thin, grey hair was spread around his head like a fan, giving him the look of a frightened animal. Indeed he *was* frightened – by his impending death – and the gnarled fingers clawed feebly at the earth beside him.

He had almost come to believe himself immortal. Like many before him and many that would follow him he had begun to confuse absolute power amongst mortals with heavenly power. It had come to seem ridiculous to him that a man whose whole being and presence, whose nail parings, hair, dirty washing water and very shit was considered to be sacred and had to be buried with ceremony in a holy place, would take the path of a normal man and eventually die. 'Surely', he had told himself as an old but fit and healthy man, 'I shall live forever?'

There had been three queens, but now they were all dead. A sister as old as himself now cared for him, night and day, washing his body, feeding him, administering medicinal herbs and potions left by the king's personal kahuna.

Tangiia hated to see his father brought so low, this man who was so full of mana, whose very shadow was taboo to commoners. Only family, high priests and royal personages could touch the king or stand in his shade. Any food which passed the old man's lips immediately became taboo to others. There were trees which belonged only to the king, amongst them a type of banana tree which bore fruit only once in its life. There were canoes which only the king and his priests could touch. There were caves, and waterfalls, and stones which had to be avoided by all others but the king. The wicker-leaf sharks hung by cords to warn others of the taboo nature of these objects and places.

'Father?' said Tangiia, kneeling by the old man and taking his hand.

The eyes swivelled as the king looked into his son's face.

'It would have been better,' said the king in a voice like dry leaves rustling, 'to have died in battle.'

'But who would have killed you?' asked Tangiia. 'None could beat you.'

'True, true,' said the old man, with a wisp of a smile flitting across his face. 'I was too skilful for them all – none could touch me.'

He sighed, the phlegm rattling in his throat. His sister brought him a bowl into which he spat a red-green fluid. Tangiia looked away.

'Not a pleasant sight,' said the king, 'to watch an old man die.'

'You are afraid, Father?'

The old man turned bleak eyes on his son again.

'Yes – but I would say that to no one but you. Your brother would laugh at me – the Great King afraid of a thing that comes to all men and women in the end – it would amuse him. His soul is harder than your own. But he is not cruel, he simply lacks compassion. He will make a good king.'

'So will I, Father – even though I do not have the heart of a shark.'

The king tried to sit up, shaking his head, but fell back on the bed again.

His sister said, 'You are upsetting him.'

Tangiia replied, 'I have to tell him something – leave us, please.'

She hesitated but Tangiia glared at her. 'Go!'

After a few more moments she left the house, picking up an empty water gourd on the way out.

'There must be only one king of the two islands,' croaked the old man. 'You must serve your half-brother. Otherwise there will be bloodshed – a divided kingdom. The valleys will ring with the lament of the mourners, the hills with the cries of the dying. A red tide will run across the sea.'

'As the son of my father and his third wife, I would serve the son of my father and his second wife, but he would have me killed if I tried. He is too suspicious of me, knowing that some of the people prefer me to him. I shall be king, Father, but of a new land. I plan to seek a Faraway Heaven.'

The old man stared at his second son and the light of old remembrances came to his eyes.

'You are leaving? A voyage?'

'Yes, Father – I – I have come to say goodbye, for I must leave before . . .'

'I should be more willing to go to Hine-nui-te-po, the Goddess of Darkness and Death, whom even the great Maui could not defeat, if I knew my kingdom was safe from strife.'

'Be assured it will be so, Father, and when you meet the cunning, intrepid Maui, be so kind as to ask him to watch over me on my voyage across the ocean.'

Maui now dwelt in the Land of the Dead, being the first man on earth to die as he tried to pass through Hine-nui-te-po without her knowledge while she slept, when a songbird woke her and she discovered Maui's presence inside her.

'I shall do as you ask, my son,' said the king. 'A man alone on a voyage . . .'

'I'm not going alone, Father, I'm taking three pahi canoes full of people with me.'

The old man's brow furrowed again.

'Will that not anger your brother Tutapu?'

'I can't be held responsible for my brother's emotions, Father. I must do what I feel is right. And I can't make such a voyage alone – I am not *you*, I don't have your self-sufficiency – I need people around me. I should go mad on my own. In any case, what is a king of an island without people, but a lost dreamer, a man of wickerwork and leaves? My brother will have the two islands and if he is not satisfied with that, then I believe the gods will be angry with *him*, for his greed.'

The old king sighed again, the wind fluttering through his parched lips like a dry breeze through a breadfruit tree.

'I am making a lone voyage again – the voyage we all have to make alone, even you.'

'Yes, Father.'

The king rolled on to his side, the effort obviously painful for him. He reached out and touched his son's head, tracing the youth's tattoos with one of his fingers. Then he fell back again and returned to lying on his back.

'You are a handsome boy,' said the old man. 'You look like I looked when I was young.'

'Not so handsome, Father.'

The old man nodded. 'And what about the goblins, what will they do when you leave?'

The king meant Seumas and Dorcha, who were often compared to tapua, mountain goblins, not because of their size but because of their white skin. When Kupe brought back his two captives several years before, the old king had thought about sacrificing them to the gods, being convinced by his high priest that such creatures were not human and therefore had to be destroyed.

Only the fact that Seumas had tattoos had saved both him and Dorcha from ritual execution, the king being convinced that he was a mortal like any other, to have to prove his manhood by suffering the dangerous and painful operation of having tattoos chiselled into his skin.

'One is coming with me, the other is staying – the woman wishes to remain here.'

The king nodded slightly. 'Does the Seumas still have eyes in the back of his head?'

He was referring to the way in which Seumas rowed a dinghy he had once made, with his back facing the direction in which the boat was travelling. This method had so upset the people of Raiatea that Seumas had destroyed the boat, for fear someone was going to accuse him of being a supernatural fiend.

'Not any longer, Father.'

'Good, good. He might be of use to you, the goblin, if you meet any demons. He speaks with their tongue, you know, for I have heard the harsh sound myself. He talks with his dog too – I swear they understand each other. To feed a dog on meat and give it a name! I never was quite sure I had done right, to allow the goblin to survive. Once, I remember, he fashioned a living monster from a dead pig's hide, with bamboo sticks for legs. An evil, wailing thing.'

The old man shuddered even now at the thought, before continuing.

'His fingers danced down one of the creature's legs, while he blew into the hollow end, and the sound of the dead pig came out, screaming for its life back. I tell you, king or no king, it put the fear of demons into me . . .'

'I remember that time,' said Tangiia, 'when he brought the pig back to life. I was a young boy. It *terrified* me, that monster he made out of skin and twigs.'

The king coughed and spat into his wooden bowl. 'We burned the monster on a fire – the pig with no eyes, ears or mouth, which could shriek like a tortured parrot – and we nearly burned the goblin along with it. He promised not to bring back to life any more of his deviant beasts, so I allowed him to live. Now he is to go with you, on your voyage. But what of the other?'

'She has her two husbands.'

The king grunted as he tried to imagine what it would be like making love to a mountain goblin. His head became full of hillside waterfalls and dense greenery, of mossy beds, buttress-rooted trees reaching high into the roof of voyaging, and dark caves full of bats. He rather envied the twin brothers, Ti-ti and Rian, finding out what it was like between the legs of a woman whose skin was so fair. Yet, on the other hand, she had a temper like a rooster on fire. Perhaps the experience would not be as interesting as it was awful?

A cough rattled in his chest once again and the old man let his tired eyes rest once more on his younger son.

'So, we must say goodbye now?'

'Yes, Father, I leave tomorrow at dawn.'

There was a wetness in the king's eyes, which he tried to wipe away with a feeble hand.

'Take me with you?' he said, almost like a baby.

'Father, you know . . .'

At that moment the king sat up with a jerk, as if someone had kicked him in the back, and he stared around the hut.

'Sister?' he called, with fear in his voice.

The old woman came trotting back inside and on seeing the king's face let out a cry herself.

'He's going!' she said.

Tangiia took hold of the frail body and tried to force it down again on to the bed of leaves, but it was as if his father's bones were locked. It was impossible to move him. The king's eyes rolled in his head, his twitching lips let forth a hissing noise, and then he keeled over sideways.

The king's sister put a finger to the old man's lips, held it there for a moment, and then withdrew it.

'He is with Hine-nui-te-po,' she murmured, and then suddenly started to let out a mourner's wail.

Tangiia quickly reached out and staunched the sound which came from her mouth with his hand.

'NO!' he said. 'No one must know the king is dead – not before I leave the island.'

'You're leaving?' the old woman questioned.

The prince nodded, quickly. 'My brother will move against me if I stay.'

The king's sister was silent for a moment, then she said, 'We will pretend he is asleep. You must go as soon as you can – may the gods be with you.'

Tangiia left his father's body and went quickly to the house of the Farseeing-virgin, Kikamana. He quickly informed her of what had passed and asked her what were the signs. Kikamana looked through the doorway at the darkening sky.

'Maomao is coming,' she said, 'in his biggest cloak of feathers – perhaps before another dawn.'

Tangiia stared at the sky, but could see nothing un-toward. Still, Kikamana was seldom wrong about these things. Her visions were unsurpassed, even by Boy-girl. A hurricane was coming. Well, it might be a blessing in disguise. If they could beat the wind, it would prevent any early chase by Tutapu, should he feel so inclined.

'We start as soon as it gets dark,' warned Tangiia.

Next he went to one of the novice priests who had been in charge of the boat building, not running because that would have attracted attention, but strolling and calling greetings on the way to friends and neighbours.

Manopa was still at the site and he saw by Tangiia's face that something had happened.

'What is it?' he asked. 'Tutapu?'

'No, it's my father, the king . . .'

The prince told them what had happened and of his plans to leave the island that night.

He said to the priest, 'We shall need a god with us, besides the Tikis already on the vessels, to help guide us through our troubles. Many of the statues at Most Sacred, Most Feared are of hardwood and too heavy to take on board. Take some men when darkness falls and steal me an effigy of the Great God of the Sea, Tangaroa – and place it on the deck of my canoe.'

'Steal a god?' cried the priest, a little shaken. 'What if it curses me?'

'Tangaroa will not curse the priest of Tangiia,' said the prince with impressive confidence. 'Go!'

The priest waited no more, but called men to his side, then set off towards Tapu-tapu atia, where there were statues of gods sprouting from the rainforest floor as if growing from the grass and moss of that sacrosanct ground.

'Manopa, you begin gathering the people together, but be discreet. Start with Boy-girl. Tell her I need her here immediately.

'At once,' replied his lieutenant, too loyal to voice again his misgivings about the task for which he knew Boy-girl was required.

Tangiia stared at the roof of voyaging. Already the signs

of evening were moving over the sky as Ra turned the clouds to the scarlet of precious feathers. A short time later he saw Boy-girl dancing along the sands towards him.

'Now for Kula,' murmured the prince.

Tangiia's men approached the enormous Investiture Stone at Most Sacred, Most Feared with great trepidation. They were aware of the living part of the stone; the spirits of the men who belonged to the dust of the corpses beneath the four corners of the stone. They were aware that the four guardians, now themselves revered ancestors who required human sacrifices from time to time, would not approve of the removal of Tangaroa's image from the shadow of the ancient mountain.

The glade pulsed with silence, its stone heart filling the night with a dreadful, heavy stillness.

Even the priest, new to his profession, felt the terror clutch at his heart.

Around the great stone, which reached like a primordial tree towards the roof of voyaging, stood many wooden statues half-buried in the ground. They thrust themselves from the moss like rotten molars in an old man's mouth, their features covered with lichen and often crawling with insects. The eyes of the idols were not blind though, having spiritual sight, and the men who had come to steal one of them could feel those eyes boring into them, out of the darkness of this hallowed, awesome hollow.

'Go softly, go softly,' warned the priest, staring about him, unable to see very much except vague shapes in the gloom of the glade. There was a belt of human skulls around the nearest idol, which because of its height and position the priest guessed to be the Goddess of Darkness and Death. Since the priest was a young man, a neophyte, he did not know the glade as well as one of the elders amongst the kahunas, and was having difficulty in orientating himself. His unease over what he was doing did not help matters.

There was a moon, but Tapu-tapu atia was under a rock hang, beneath a canopy of vines and aged trees, and they could *feel* darkness around them. It was like being enveloped in a soft, damp blanket. The men frequently trod on the planted bones of their ancestors, or tripped over a leaf-twig effigy; they were dizzy with misgivings and apprehension.

The priest offered up prayers to the more powerful ancestors, while his four companions stumbled around in the dense gloom, feeling for the statue of Tangaroa the Great Sea-God. The priest could feel the sponginess of the moss beneath his feet and half expected the forest floor to open and take him down for violating the sanctity of this place belonging to heroes, dead spirits and gods.

One of the men placed his hands on an image. He ran his hands over the head of the carving, wanting it to be the right statue, eager to be gone from the place of Most Sacred, Most Feared.

'Here it is,' he whispered, quickly. 'This one feels like Tangaroa – this must be the idol Prince Tangiia meant –'

Then he gave out a strangled cry, like a bird caught in a noose, and fell to the floor in a fit. He thrashed around amongst the leaves and twigs, filling the hearts of his companions with horror. One of the other men ran away, gasping for breath as he did so, his feet drumming on the forest floor, his fear overcoming him.

A second man had the presence of mind to fall on his unfortunate companion having the fit, and push a stick between his jaws, to stop him from biting off or swallowing his own tongue and choking himself.

'The demons are in him,' said the priest, softly. 'He must have unclean hands. One of you take the statue . . .'

'Not me,' said a man, quickly, 'I may have unclean hands too.'

The priest knew that there was very little time, so he pushed through the group of men himself, felt around on the forest floor for the wooden statue, and eventually found it.

'Help me,' he snarled to the nearest man, and began rocking the wooden totem backwards and forwards.

There was a moment's hesitation, then someone came to his aid. They frantically pushed the statue backwards and forwards, to loosen it in the turf.

It seemed that either the totem itself had grown roots, or it was caught amongst the network of tree roots which ran beneath the rainforest floor. Even when it was as wobbly as a child's first tooth, it refused to be wrenched from the ground. Two men broke some vines from nearby trees and wrapped them round the wooden idol to pull in the dark, while a third used a broken branch to lever beneath the stubborn god. Finally, it was eased out of its hole, the smell of its rotten base filling the glade. Insects flowed from the hole and up the arms of the men, who let go of the god and brushed them away quickly.

Then the image was hoisted on to shoulders and borne off at a rapid pace through the rainforest. The man having the fit was slung across the back of another and he too was carried from the dreadful place, gibbering as he was bounced along. The one who had run away was waiting for them in some agitation on the edge of the forest and he mumbled his apologies for allowing fear to overcome him, before helping with the sick man.

The idol was taken quickly to the vessel in which Tangiia himself would sail and laid inside one of the deck huts, ready for erection once the journey began. The young priest, now feeling quite pleased with himself, rolled the idol on to its back, knowing it was irreverent to leave it face down on the deck. The mossy features of the totem were now visible to him, in a shaft of moonlight, and he recoiled in horror.

The image they had taken from the glade was not of Tangaroa after all, but some obscure god which the young priest did not even recognise, its features were so worn and pitted with the passing of time. It was obviously a great god in a minor form, whose special powers were unknown to the neophyte.

There was no time to go back to Tapu-tapu atia, and in any case the priest was too shaken to make a second journey. It was better to deal with Prince Tangiia's anger later than to repeat what had already been a terrible experience. It must be, he told himself by way of excuse, that this is the god we need on the voyage, otherwise why would it be here now?

He quickly covered the totem with palm leaves and went out of the hut into the fresh air.

This, the prince's canoe, had already been launched and was bobbing gently on the waves in the lagoon. The wind was rising steadily as men, women and children were herded on board. On the beach the other two canoes were being dragged over the log rollers towards the water, the launching parties eager to get away from the islands before the hurricane arrived.

Men and women were all helping with the launch, while others were tending to the livestock: the dogs, pigs and birds. There was a sense of quiet urgency about the exodus.

People sniffed the air as they worked, taking in the last draught of the fragrance of blossoms and the scent of vegetation they would have for a long while. This was the smell of their homeland, which they would have to leave behind. Already many of them were beginning to feel homesick. They stared into the darkness, visualising the volcanic mountainous hinterland, knowing that the next landfall they might see would not have familiar contours. They would have to memorise new maps of their surroundings, new pathways, new trees. Old friends – the pool in the forest glade, the waterfall, the great silk cotton tree by the ledge – all these would be far behind them.

More importantly, they would have to find fresh maps of

the coastal waters of their new homeland. Around Raiatea and Borabora they knew where to find hiding squid, shoals of bonito, prawns, shellfish, crabs, the whole bounty of their immediate surrounding waters. In their future island they would be lost for a while, fishing in fallow waters, running lines for a harvest that was not there, spearing flashes of light.

So their last scent of Raiatea was important to them; a moment to treasure, to be able to recall at a later time.

The wind became brisk and began blowing a coconut husk along the beach as if it were Ulupoka's Head.

4

A traitor lit a fire high on the slopes of the Raiatean mountain. The light from its flames was visible from Borabora and on seeing the glow from this particular crag, another man ran through the forests of Borabora, towards the house of Prince Tutapu. His excitement was such that on reaching the house he ran straight past the unprepared guards and into the room where the prince slept. The sound of birds filled the bed chamber and Tutapu leapt instantly to his feet, a club in one hand and a knife in the other. His face was creased in fury.

'Ha! An assassin!'

He struck out with the club, catching the runner on the shoulder, felling him to the floor. A crunch of bone had preceded the man's fall and he screamed in agony. Tutapu was about to deliver a death blow when the man shrieked, 'Prince – I'm the messenger, from the mountain!'

Tutapu's hand was stayed as he peered through the dimness of the room at the man. The two guards ran in from outside and stood over the messenger, their spears raised ready for the order to kill. Tutapu rubbed his sleepy face with his hand.

'What? Why do you come charging in here at this time? Are you insane? You deserve to die.'

'The light from the signal fire – Raiatea – your father is dead!' cried the unfortunate man.

Tutapu stood for a moment in the stillness of the room, while he absorbed this information, then he walked briskly towards the door, the twittering of songbirds following his every footstep.

'Warriors!' he yelled. 'Awake, awake! Sound the alarm! Make ready the war canoes. The king is dead.'

A moment later there was the sound of a conch horn blowing in the night air. A great hollow-logged drum which had been patiently gathering silence and dust, now released its deep sounds. Warriors leapt from their beds and ran down to the beaches. The prince himself was already donning his feathered war headdress and selecting his favourite weapons, a large spear, the head of which was made from obsidian, and a flattened club with a tapered edge which could slice the top off a man's skull at a single stroke.

Tutapu was a formidable fighter who had killed many enemies in battle and now he was going to kill his brother.

Smaller drums were sounding now, from the front of the war canoes, where stood the wooden effigies of Oro the War-God. Tonight Oro had on his war face and his spear was raised in wrath. Accompanying their fierce and brutal father on this expedition were smaller goddesses: Oro's three daughters, Axe-eye, Head-eater and Escape-from-a-Hundred-Stones. Two of the daughters faced the flanks, the other one looked behind, in the opposite direction to her father.

The daughters would help protect the warriors from sneak side and rear attacks, while Oro was in the forefront of the battle with his bloodthirsty warriors, wreaking havoc.

Five war canoes were launched and the fleet set out towards Raiatea, the drums pounding.

On Raiatea the faint sound of the distant war drums was

heard floating over the ocean. Men and women froze into statues; children began crying. There was a suppressed panic felt in every breast. Tangiia was a good young prince who would make a fine king, but none of his people believed he was a match for his older brother, who had already been tried and tested in war and was known to be a vicious but superlative warrior.

A calm voice suddenly sounded from the midst of the launching parties on the beach.

It was that of Kikamana, the Farseeing-virgin.

'Do not fear the spears of Prince Tutapu, people of Prince Tangiia – the gods are with *us* tonight. I have appealed to one of the goddesses, who has promised her help.'

This information had an immediate calming effect on the launching parties. The splendid figure of Kikamana in her robe of white feathers, her arms lifted in supplication to the night, her hair flowing like black water in the wind, was enough to fill the hearts of the people with trust. They continued in their work of moving the mighty canoes into the lagoon.

Tangiia himself was assisting with the launching when Boy-girl appeared out of the rainforest edge. She was leading a young woman gently by the hand. When she came close Tangiia was relieved and happy to see that the woman was indeed his beloved Kula. The eyes of the princess had a glazed look and with a motion of her hand, Boy-girl indicated to Tangiia that he must not speak to the maiden. He watched, as did many of his followers, as Boy-girl led the mesmerised Kula past the launching parties and on to a canoe. It was not the pahi which Tangiia himself would command. Tangiia wisely decided he would not need to confront Kula until she was used to the idea that she had been abducted against her will.

Seumas, who had witnessed this scene, was suddenly sorry he had not taken Boy-girl's offer to do the same with Dorcha.

'You've got *your* woman then,' he said to Tangiia, hardly failing to disguise the envy in his tone.

Tangiia nodded and sighed. 'Yes, I have her – but can I hold her?'

Seumas realised the prince was right. Certainly if Dorcha had been tricked on board, she would still not have submitted to him once the spell wore off. He would have been in no better a situation than the one he had experienced on Raiatea for the past several years. It was probably better to make a clean break and forget the Celt woman, put her out of his mind forever.

Seumas went back to assisting with the launching.

Finally, all three canoes were on the water.

'That way, that way!' raged Tutapu, pointing with his spear. 'Are you blind? Can't you see where Raiatea lies?'

The sailors managing the boat were at a loss. In front of them was the island of Raiatea, a dark, hunched giant rising from a darker sea, yet the prince was pointing away from this piece of land, towards an empty horizon.

'Turn the vessel, turn the vessel,' shrieked Tutapu. 'Are you all traitors? You want my brother to become king, is that it? Well, this is the way I treat traitors!'

With these words Tutapu struck the nearest man with his paddle club, cleaving his skull. The sailor flopped half over the edge of the canoe, his limp arms trailing in the water. Tutapu kicked savagely at the body, sending it over the side, where it would no doubt make a meal for the sharks and barracuda, ever active in this stretch of water.

On seeing this act, the other sailors immediately changed tack, heading in the direction towards which their prince was pointing. If Tutapu wanted them to go out into open sea, then that's where they would go, land or no land.

Ragnu, in command of another war canoe, called across the water to Prince Tutapu, asking him where he was going.

'To kill my brother,' yelled Tutapu. 'Are you against me too, high priest?'

Ragnu, who like all priests was an unrecognised half-brother to both Tutapu and Tangiia, assumed that Tutapu had seen something out of his own vision, such as a flotilla fleeing from Raiatea. The high priest ordered the other war canoes to follow that of Tutapu's, whose constant harping at his men had taken them at least seventeen boat lengths in front of the fleet. Ragnu kept his eyes open for signs of the refugees seen by his prince, so that he might be amongst the first to board their boats. Ragnu was looking forward to taking the life of his half-sister Kikamana, the Farseeing-virgin, whose powers fired his jealousy and anger.

The wind was picking out the waves now, pinching their tops and drawing them to high points. One of Maomao's sons, Howling Rainfall, came sweeping in from the Arue Roa direction on the wind flower. The rain soaked the mat sails and slowed the fleet until the rowers were ordered to increase their pace.

Ragnu looked at the sky, dark and swirling with high clouds, and knew Maomao was coming himself.

'The Big Wind,' he murmured.

It was then he began praying to Hau Maringi, the God of Mists and Fog, their ally in this battle against Tangiia.

Hau Maringi came at Ragnu's bidding and enveloped the fleet of Prince Tangiia, swallowing the canoes so they rested deep inside Hau Maringi's gullet, a place of eternal greyness, where even Tane could not penetrate with any force.

Inside the body of Hau Maringi, Prince Tangiia's people began to panic, running this way and that over the decks, trying to raise the sails by feel, telling each other they would be able to get through the Eater-of-boats, the coral reef, by sound rather than by sight. Hau Maringi thickened himself, until even sounds were muted and the crashing of the waves on the reef had strange echoes which confused the listeners, causing them more anguish.

But Hau Maringi was no match for most other gods, and one of Maomao's sons arrived, the vanguard preceding the Great Wind-God's own arrival, to blow Hau Maringi into an empty quarter of Oceania, where he fumed coldly, resting on an ocean without vessels.

Once the fog had been blown far out to sea, the great pahi canoes with all their livestock, crew and passengers on board, began to head out towards the reef. It was a scene of colour and noise that was witnessed from the beach by those who had chosen to remain behind. The hasty but brave departure was now in progress. The open ocean, with its unknown perils, its vast empty regions, awaited them.

The hindmost to leave the lagoon shore was Tangiia's vessel, now named *The Scudding Cloud*. Seumas was one of the last men aboard, accompanied by his pet hound, Dirk. The dog watched Seumas, to satisfy itself that it was all right to be on this floating island, then settled down on some bedding. Seumas stared at the shoreline, then made a decision.

Seumas cried to Kieto, 'Hold on to Dirk, for me, lad!' and leapt from the deck into the water, then he ran across the shell-covered beach towards Dorcha's hut.

Dorcha was standing beneath a palm, watching the fleet leave the island. Rian and Ti-ti were standing with her. Seumas saw her and went to her. Rian stepped forward, a heavy club bearing the war face of Oro in his hand. There were honed whales' teeth protruding from the head of the club, and carved spikes from the upper part of the haft. It was Rian's intention to see one of these sharp projections buried in Seumas's temple.

'Hine-nui-te-po has given you to me,' said Rian, triumphantly. 'Now you will go to *her* bed.'

Dorcha cried, 'No, Rian!'

The warrior turned on her. 'Be quiet, woman – this is for us to settle. You wanted him dead, now I'm going to give you your wish. Later you will thank me.'

He turned back to Seumas and began swinging his club, aiming first for Seumas's head. The Pict ducked and weaved, as skilful in his footwork as any Raiatean warrior. Rian then began attacking his body, hoping for a blow which would put paid to the lithe movements of his adversary, so that he could then step in and crush his skull.

Seumas arched his body as the club swept past his midriff. Out of his waistband the Pict finally drew a knife made from a sliver of a large clamshell with a hardwood handle. The blade had been whetted, sharpened to a fine edge. When Rian moved in again, the wide sweep of the club exposing his body, Seumas threw the knife.

Rian gave a grunt as the shell-blade pierced his abdomen and dangled there, like a fish that sunk its teeth into his belly-fat and refused to let go. When he looked down at his wound, Seumas launched a drop-kick at his opponent. Struck in the throat by the Pict's heels, Rian went flying backwards and lay on the ground gargling, his club abandoned.

'Seumas!' yelled Tangiia from the craft. 'We're casting off – *now*.'

The blood was roaring in the Pict's ears. He snatched up the club and stood over the wounded Rian, making ready to deal a death blow to the man's head. The club went up.

A shout came from Dorcha. 'Seumas – no!'

Seumas paused. He had already killed a husband of this woman and she hated him for it. Now he was about to repeat what was in her eyes a terrible crime. The knife wound in Rian's stomach was not mortal, the shell-blade being too light to throw effectively. It had not penetrated deeply. Seumas let the club fall to the ground. Ti-ti rushed forward with a cry and fell on his knees, to cradle his twin brother's head in his arms.

Seumas looked towards the lagoon and saw that *The Scudding Cloud* was halfway to the inner reef.

'Dorcha?' he said, in a pleading tone. 'Come with me – please?'

She seemed about to move towards him, just a slight gesture, then her mouth set firmly.

'No – get out of here, go away. I shall be happy never to see you again.'

'Dorcha?'

There was another shout from the canoe as it picked up speed, heading for the gap in the reef.

'Go!' she screamed, her black eyes glistening.

Seumas sighed heavily and turned to run down the sands to the water. He dived into the lagoon and swam swiftly towards the canoe. He could see Kieto, straining to hold back an anxious Dirk, who stood on the back of the canoe's platform deck, barking across the lagoon.

A line was dropped overboard, which trailed the boat, and eventually, just as the craft was passing through the gap in the reef, he caught hold of the end of this cord. He was dragged over a patch of coral, which scratched him severely, then they hauled him on board. His hound, Dirk, came to him and licked his face and shoulders, wagging its tail, pleased that it had not been abandoned as it had feared.

Seumas just lay on the deck, gasping.

Tangiia said, 'Kieto, find some herbs to put on these scratches before they fester.' Then to Seumas, 'You were nearly left behind – and all because of a goblin.'

Seumas went up on to his elbows. 'I'm a goblin too,' he said.

'Yes, a very foolish one,' Kieto intervened. 'Now hold still while I staunch the blood . . .'

Seumas did as he was told, his eyes on the beach. The dawn was just coming up. Ra was shaking his fiery head, getting rid of the sleep, before rising from his bed. In the first few rays to penetrate the morning air Seumas could see Dorcha standing on the sands. She was perfectly still, illuminated by a ray of light that had cut through the rain clouds. Her ferocious beauty tore a hole in his heart. He watched her until she became a small, cloaked figure, like a dark fairy, then saw her raise a pale hand and give a single wave.

He waved back, solemnly, wondering if he had finally been forgiven for his trespasses.

By the time Tutapu finally realised he had been tricked by Kuku Lau, the Goddess of Mirages, the war flotilla was far out at sea, in the opposite direction to that taken by Tangiia's fleet. So real had Kuku Lau's false 'Raiatea' seemed, that Tutapu had almost stepped ashore, on to what was most certainly a wave of water. Only a change in the light had stopped him from leaping on to a non-existent beach.

'A mirage!' he cried in anguish. 'I should have listened to you, Ragnu.'

By now the rest of the flotilla had caught up with the leading war canoe and they were all locked together with their paddles, waiting for the king's orders.

The wind was becoming dangerously high now, the waves rearing and crashing into each other, churning the ocean to a milky white. Spume from the tops of the combers lashed the bodies and faces of the warriors, soaking and chilling them as the temperature dropped. The spray was so fine, it was like mist that blew constantly into their eyes, stinging them, blinding them with its salt. A strange sky with a hard light at its core had grown around the flotilla and almost every man there was aware that calamity would befall them if they did not get to some safe haven before Maomao swept down upon them from his faraway country.

Tutapu ordered his rowers to turn towards the real

Raiatea, knowing they would be lucky to make the lagoon without loss of life. A Big Wind was most certainly coming and Maomao could not be appeased with mere words. A sacrifice was necessary, of a pig or dog; something to show Maomao that he was not taken for granted. It needed to be a temple ceremony in a marae, not just a quick effort out here on the ocean, or even on a beach.

They rode the whitecaps back towards Raiatea, with Tutapu constantly asking his men if they could see the island too. His confidence had been severely shaken by Kuku Lau's tricks. He realised how easily even a minor goddess could toy with an ordinary man, even if that man was a king.

By the time the flotilla reached the outer reef, the waves were giant rollers with high twisting peaks. War canoes were not fashioned for bad weather conditions, like the great ocean-going canoes, but for the quick strike. A 'long wave' from Aremata-rorua caught one of the war canoes broadside and capsized it, sending men tumbling into the mountainous waters. Several were swept away, their cries for help lost on the wind. Others struggled to hold on to the rest of the canoes, or managed to ride over the reef on a high wave of surf, and then strike out across the lagoon for the shore. Stone weapons sank to the bottom of the sea; wooden ones floated away into the lashing waves.

When the canoes reached the beach they were hastily drawn up the sands and then men ran for the safety of some caves. There was no time for sacrifices to Maomao, only to crawl away into a rock hole, where the wind could not reach.

Tutapu's precious headdress was torn from him and whisked away by Maomao to some trove where the Wind-God kept all the treasures he robbed from mortals.

However, the king managed to reach the caves before the full force of the hurricane began to sideswipe Raiatea. One of the last men to reach the caves was almost inside when a whole palm tree snapped at the root and flew through the air to hit him like a mighty spear full in the chest, carrying his corpse away on its point, its haft flighted with feathery palm leaves.

Inside the caves were huddled other inhabitants of the island, bemoaning the loss of the old king and pondering on the damage the hurricane would cause to crops, houses, canoes and livestock. Also inside the cave were the most precious of the last of these: pigs, fowl and packs of dogs, all sitting quietly, stunned into immobility and silence by the awesome furore of the god who had deigned to pay them a visit.

'When this is over,' growled Tutapu, 'I shall seek out my half-brother and slay him.'

One of the Raiateans shook her head. 'They're gone,' she said.

Tutapu was perplexed. 'Gone? Who's gone? Where?'

'Prince Tangiia and over two hundred people. They left in the dawn. There were three pahi, each carrying about seventy passengers.'

Tutapu's eyes narrowed. 'Run away, has he? Am I the only one here who did not know he was planning this escape? How has he managed to build canoes without me being told? These people who have gone were your neighbours. You must have seen them gathering stores together, making preparations.'

One old man said, 'We tried to tell you – at least we tried to tell your basket-sharers. They listened, told us they would inform you, but obviously never did. Even Ragnu was told many times of the planned exodus by our spies –'

'Liar!' hissed Ragnu, gripping a club. 'I was told nothing.'

The old creature, who was a fisherman and whose salt-encrusted skin had white wrinkles, chuckled offensively. It seemed that this aged but sagacious servant of the king was too elderly to be afraid of death, which was extremely close at hand, and continued divulging previous secrets.

'You *were* told, but you didn't *hear*,' said the old man, his face crinkling with a wry smile. 'Boy-girl put a spell on all Prince Tutapu's basket-sharers, so they would nod their heads when being told of the escape, then immediately forget what had been imparted to them. Even when you were told what Boy-girl was doing, you still didn't hear what was being said.'

Ragnu stared at the old savant and searched his own mind for fragments of the truth.

In the end he nodded. He said to Tutapu, 'I think he's right – we were bewitched by Boy-girl.'

Tutapu spat into a corner of the cave. 'So, my brother has fled? So be it. No blood need be shed. He has more good sense than I gave him credit for, and less ambition than I believed he was nurturing. I hope he finds a home somewhere a long way from Raiatea and Borabora, so we may never need to meet again. I can no longer stand the sight of him.'

The high priest added, 'These islands were becoming too crowded as well. Taking two hundred or so islanders with him has done us a favour, my king. Fewer mouths to feed, more land to occupy. And the old king's house is yours at last.'

Tutapu felt a warm satisfaction spread through his limbs and torso.

'Yes, good. I shall live in my father's house with Nau Ariki as my bride . . .'

'Ah,' said the old man, who seemed suspiciously close to enjoying himself, 'I don't think so.'

Tutapu frowned. 'What don't you think?'

'That Nau Ariki, the one they call Kula, will be your bride.'

Ragnu snorted and said imperiously, 'You foolish old man – have you not heard that the princess has already agreed to marry King Tutapu?'

'I heard that, yes,' the old man's throat rattled with catarrh, 'but it won't happen.'

'Why won't it happen?' asked Tutapu, gradually coming to the realisation that others knew more about everything than he did himself.

'Because Princess Kula has gone with Tangiia.'

Tutapu leapt instantly to his feet and was about to rush out through the cave doorway, where the storm howled and screamed, calling for further victims.

Ragnu clutched his king's ankle and forced him to sit down, at the risk of having his own head caved by a club.

'You can't go out there now, my king. Wait until the storm dies down. Then we'll catch up with Tangiia.'

Tutapu's impatience to get at his half-brother and throttle him with his own loin cloth held for the moment.

The hurricane actually took three days to subside, by which time Tangiia and his canoes could have been anywhere in the world. Just because he had set off in a certain direction, did not mean he was keeping to it. Tutapu left the cave with a terrible fervour in his breast. Not only had he been robbed of his brother's death, but of his own bride! Eventually, someone would have to pay for those crimes. Now was not the time though, for there was much work to be done, an island kingdom to restore to its former glory. A prince might go flitting off after his dreams, but a king had responsibilities.

'One day,' he told Ragnu, 'I shall find that brother of mine and make him swallow dirt by the handful.'

'I shall be the one to force his mouth open, with my dagger,' snarled Ragnu. 'You must know too that our spy has gone with Tangiia's fleet.'

'For our purposes, or for his?'

'Our man is still for you, my king. A bird arrived back at its nest today, flying from the Hitia ote ra direction on the wind flower – when Tangiia finds a new home, I expect our spy will return to us and tell us where your brother has gone.'

'In the meantime,' mused Tutapu, 'we shall know my brother's whereabouts from the birds?'

'His direction, at least. And there will be signs left by our spy, on the route they take. It will not be difficult to follow him, if we ever wish it.'

King Tutapu said, 'But not at this time. Now is the time to make the islands my own. They still have my father's colours running through them. I need to concentrate on this.'

The high priest, who also had no desire to be riding the waves while there were islands to rule, quickly agreed that this was the time to rebuild, not chase after errant princes.

Raiatea had been devastated by the hurricane and Maomao had left nothing but a broken land in his wake. They could not curse Maomao, for he might return and make them pay, so they went about clearing the mess with heavy hearts. There were huts to restore, canoes to carve, crops to replant, shattered trees to clear, totems of gods to right.

For food they used the coconuts that had been blown from the palms and the shellfish cast up on the beaches by the storm. The work began, with King Tutapu presiding over his people.

A royal funeral took place after the initial clearance had been completed, since ancestors had to be given due cere-mony.

The former king was given a magnificent burial on a sand-bar at the mouth of a small river, thus on land but close to water, and in his grave were placed water-gourds, necklaces, sharks' teeth, adzes, tattooing needles of dogs' teeth, candle-nut soot for tattoo pigment in bone contain-ers, harpoons, drilled eggshells of many colours and tanged spear heads. These gifts to his father from Tutapu were greatly appreciated by the spirit of the old man, who went to his rest clutching a carving of a canoe in one bony hand and a model house in the other.

There were many songs sung in praise of the old king, which echoed through the high green valleys.

He had been a great warrior and would be a loss to his people, the songs said, but now he was with his ancestors who feasted on the flesh of sacrificed men and turtles, and was happy to take his place in the world of spirits.

There was one huge feast in which pigs were roasted, sharks were baked, and for which many kinds of fruits and nuts were gathered.

There was dancing and singing, the shadows of ancestors joining the living at the fires. Each family's atua was present at the feast and treated with great awe and respect. Heroic deeds were re-enacted, the masked dancers *becoming* the heroes of yesteryear, slaying sea monsters, defeating powerful enemies and eating their hearts and livers, hunting the great wild boar-like creature, Puata, who walks on hind legs, talks like a human, is incredibly strong and eats people.

When the feasting and dancing was over, the people crawled away exhausted. The new king had not failed in his duties towards them or to his father and ancestors and they felt grateful for that. It seemed that now Tutapu's half-brother had gone from the islands, he was a changed man, and destined to become one of the great chieftains of the kingdom.

Dorcha had for the first time, like many of the islanders, witnessed the funeral of a dead king and the inauguration of a new king, and was fascinated by both. Tutapu sent for her the day after his father's funeral and thanked her for not joining in the exodus.

'They told me you would have me executed,' she said, 'in their efforts to make me go with them.'

'Why should I do that? You have proved to be a loyal and trustworthy subject. You will be rewarded for that.'

She stepped forward to take his hands, to thank him, but he recoiled from her quickly.

'I'm king now,' he warned her. 'I've moved closer to the gods – one step away from divine. My person is sacred. I am – taboo. If you touch me you may die from the divine power which fills my body. Even now my mana is filling the void in this room.'

'Oh,' she faltered, 'of course.'

His face took on an expression of petulance.

'It's very awkward. I used to be surrounded by basket-sharers, but they can no longer touch my basket. If a fruit I eat has lain next to one they eat, then they become sick. Only the priests can come close to me now, since their own sacredness protects them from my mana – only they can prepare the food for me. It's very troublesome.'

'One of the hazards of being king, I suppose.'

He sighed as if he bore the burdens of the world upon his shoulders.

He sent her a small pig and a necklace of rare shells, which she in turn thanked him for graciously, pleasing him the more. Dorcha felt valued once again and had Seumas returned to the islands at that moment she might have spat in his eye and told him what she thought of him and his Prince Tangiia, who had taken little notice of her except to call her a goblin.

With her two husbands fawning on her, and the new king pleased with her, Dorcha was almost a princess in her own right. In her old land of Albainn she had been a drudge and a skivvy, valued it had to be admitted, by her husband in his way, in the way of Celt males, but treated as less worthy than a good hunting dog. Had she borne her husband a son, the son would have been her superior in the household. If she had not died in childbirth she would have faded into an early old age, creased and dried by constant cooking over a peat fire, disregarded by her son and gradually rejected by her husband in bed.

Here, she was loved and cherished.

It was true there was little *passion* in her life, but was passion a necessary ingredient to happiness? When she really thought about it, passion was a destructive thing in itself, creating tension and cravings that were not always fulfilled. She was, she decided, better off without passion. She only had to think about Seumas to remember how passion could eat away at a soul and destroy a person from within.

King Tutapu oversaw the rebuilding of his kingdom, sparing little thought for his younger brother, now out on the ocean somewhere, trying to find a new home. There was, strangely, little rancour in his breast either, which even he found surprising, given how much he had hated his brother.

One day, however, King Tutapu discovered a small imperfection, a defect in his new kingdom. He was lying on his mat with one of his many cousin-concubines. She had stroked him with her soft hands until his penis was a budded, hardwood shoot. He was just gently prising her knees apart, to find the garden of his pleasure in which to plant his ripe cutting, when Ragnu came running to him, to tell him that a god had been stolen from Tapu-tapu atia, probably by Tangiia's men.

'Which god?' asked Tutapu, the anger building in his breast again. 'One of the Great Gods?'

'No, a lesser god – one hardly ever noticed.'

'Yes?' said Tutapu, impatiently.

Ragnu replied, 'The God of Hope.'

PART THREE

The Long Shark at Dawn

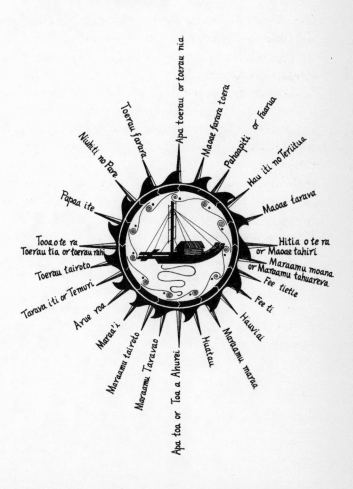

Toerau farara or toerau nia

Apa toerau or toerau nia

Maoae farara toera

Pahaapiti or Faarua

Hau iti no Teruitua

Maoae tarava

Hitia o te ra or Maoae tahiri

Maraamu moana or Maraamu tahuareva

Fee tietie

Fee ti

Hauviai

Maraamu maraa

Huatau

Apa toa or Toa a Ahurei

Maraamu Tavavao

Maraamu tairoto

Maraa'i

Arue roa

Tarava iti or Temuri

Toerau tairoto

Tooa o te ra
Toerau tia or toerau rahi

Papaa ite

Niuhiti no Pare

Toerau farara

1

Now that Tangiia had left the island, he too was a king, of the people he carried on his three pahi canoes. However, he was a king without an island and his mana was not yet strong enough to warrant a full taboo. Kikamana told him he would not move closer to the gods until he owned his own land, with its own particular set of gods, and until then he would not need to regard himself as truly sacred.

He was relieved to hear this, since it would have been difficult to live in the limited space on board canoe with almost a hundred people, and not touch and be touched by someone every so often, especially since he was the navigator and needed to be constantly moving around the craft, taking sightings, knotting his cord-device, memorising features. Priests could have screened him, but he had not enough of those to surround his royal person.

Had he great mana it would have been very dangerous for his people, whom he wanted to protect. To touch someone with great mana was like being hit by a bolt of lightning; such could result in the death of the commoner, whose body was not strong enough to resist the charge.

*

Tangiia's fleet was blown by the hurricane's edge off its intended course, which was due Apa toa on the wind flower, and instead he went in the same direction as Hitia ote ra. Fortunately the full force of the big wind passed them by, but they were caught on the periphery and pushed out into a region of the ocean which, after three days' sailing, became strangely still and calm. Kikamana told Tangiia this was because the hurricane Maomao had sent, to prevent Tutapu from following the fleet, was a gift that had to be balanced by a period of no wind.

'All gifts from the gods have their price,' she told him. 'We must wait until Maomao sees fit to send us the Goddess Hine-tu-whenua, to speed us on our way.'

They drifted along on a deep, wide current, having little choice in the matter since their paddles made little impression on the fast flow of warm water. Tangiia used the time to recheck their stores and make sure every man and woman knew their task on board the vessels.

It was Tangiia's intention to set Tangaroa up on the deck of *The Scudding Cloud*, behind his Tiki, so that the Great God of the Sea would have a view over the Tiki's shoulders at the ocean path ahead and help guide the ancestor to a new home.

'What's this?' cried Tangiia, on uncovering the totem taken from Most Sacred, Most Feared. 'This isn't Tangaroa.'

Kikamana was called.

'It's one of Tane's children,' she explained. 'It's the God of Hope.'

The young priest who had stolen the god was on board the third canoe and out of Tangiia's reach at the time, or he might have suffered a terrible punishment. Tangiia was at first incensed that his men had brought the wrong god, but then Kikamana told him to stop and think.

'What better god could we have with us than the God of Hope?' she said. 'Hope is the one thing we need to sustain us during our ordeals ahead. I see many trials in front of us, before we eventually reach a Faraway Heaven. We shall need to call on spiritual stamina to see us through, and this god can help us keep our hope alive, through these bad times.'

Tangiia was a young man and it was hard to quell his anger, but eventually he saw the wisdom in the Farseeing-virgin's words. He pardoned the young priest and his men, sending a white cowrie shell to the man to show him that he was forgiven. The fleet continued on its way in harmony once more.

The Scudding Cloud took the lead. Immediately behind the prince's canoe was *The Royal Palm* captained by Manopa, followed by *The Volcano Flower*, with Po in command. Po had risen in rank because of his famous voyage with Kupe and was now a highly respected ocean-going captain whose navigating skills were sought after by those who wished to cross leagues of water.

Kieto helped Tangiia with his daily duties during the lull, while Seumas, to take his mind off Dorcha, had agreed to have a new tattoo. This was an extremely dangerous and painful process which would allow little room in the mind of the victim for thoughts of unrequited love.

The tattoo was to be administered by Tangiia's second priest, Makka-te, since Kikamana would have nothing to do with touching the bodies of men.

Dirk took as much interest in seeing the tattoo kit laid out as did Seumas himself: the dog and boar teeth needles fixed to bamboo shafts, and the leaf-pouches full of the soot from burnt candle-nuts. Dirk sniffed at the soot and then sneezed, making Seumas laugh, even though he did not feel in the least bit merry.

'You crazy hound,' he said, ruffling the hair on the dog's neck. 'You might have guessed it would tickle your nostrils.'

Dirk had been the only pet dog in the kingdom of

Raiatea and Borabora and this was his status on board the three pahi. All other dogs were vegetarians and bred for the table; they were domestic livestock. Some Oceanians had been quite tickled when they saw how Seumas trained his hound, treated it as if it had some sort of intelligence. Many were scornful of this peculiar handling of an animal normally destined for a pot roast.

They were amused that Dirk slept at the foot of Seumas's bed, followed him everywhere, and protected the Pict against hostility from others.

One might as well, they told him, take a chicken for a wife.

Once, someone from another valley had caught Dirk in a net-trap in the rainforest. Thinking he was a stray, the man was about to slit his throat and barbecue him on an open fire, when Seumas appeared and struck the man.

When questioned about this extraordinary behaviour, not to say breaking of the law, Seumas told the chiefs who were judging him that a Pict would die for his dog, if necessary, for the hound would certainly give up his life for his master.

'But it's just a *dog*,' argued the judges, as if they were speaking about a lizard.

'This is not just a dog, it's *my* dog,' answered Seumas. 'I'm his owner and it's up to me to care for him. Besides,' he said, adopting a more practical approach, 'I feed him meat. He wouldn't taste good spitted and roasted.'

'You give the dog *meat*?' they said, looking at one another, giving up the argument. 'Valuable meat?'

'The dog brings *me* meat. He helps me hunt, fetches wild birds. He's my companion, and a damn good one.'

They fined him a pig and told him not to attack another man in favour of his hound, or he would be punished more severely the next time. They saw him pat the dog's head as he walked away from the temple courtyard, and the dog licked his hand, nuzzling the palm. Then at a snap of the

Pict's finger the hound fell into step at his heel. The judges shrugged at each other, as if to say who can fathom the mind of a mountain goblin who makes friends with creatures whose destiny it is to be eaten?

This was also the opinion of the priest Makke-te.

'The dog is stupid,' said Makka-te, a male virgin in his forties.

'Not *stupid*,' replied Seumas, 'just curious.'

He felt like arguing more hotly with the priest, whose attitude irritated him, but wisely refrained when he considered what the man was about to perform. Makka-te could make the operation as painful as he wished, without Seumas adding to any natural sadistic tendencies the priest might or might not have. Dirk might be stupid, but Seumas was not.

Seumas was no longer wild and hirsute, as he had been when first captured, but shaven and hairless almost to the crown of his head, where a long, thick plait sprouted out of a bed of red hair no bigger than the top of a sliced coconut shell.

The Pict sat cross-legged on the deck, his head tilted back slightly, while Makka-te began the pin-prick hammerings on his chest, making a tiny path of dark pigment. Seumas had asked for two hornbill beaks, one either side of his collar bones. Almost as soon as Makka-te started piercing him, he began wishing he had asked for much smaller songbird beaks instead. The pain drilled into his head making his brain reel.

The women, weaving baskets, gutting fish, and carrying out various other tasks around him, watched with interest the mountain goblin being tattooed. Children too, gathered in a circle around this event full of curiosity, there being little to keep their interest over the many slow hours on the water. Some were attached to safety lines, the little ones, while older brothers and sisters roamed free. They had seen men tattooed before, of course, but never the

goblin. Anything that happened to the goblin was of interest. Even the mariners who should have been paying
attention to their tasks, glanced occasionally towards the
tattooist and his victim.

Those on other canoes stared wistfully across the divide,
unable to get any closer to the proceedings. To swim, even
over a short distance, was dangerous, the currents being
swift and deliberate. A dugout canoe travelled between the
three pahi when necessary, but this boat only took one or
two men.

Seumas's pale skin and hard flat muscular body had been
an object of attention amongst the Raiateans and
Boraborans since he first arrived on the islands. They
would touch his shoulder or chest as he passed them, not
necessarily for sexual reasons, though this was not
unknown, but because of the fine texture and translucent
nature of his skin. Some found it a little repulsive, like a
lizard's belly, while others wanted to stroke him as if he
were made of soft fabric.

'See how stark it looks,' said one woman, as if Seumas
were not there. 'Like the markings on a white cone shell.'

'I think he's very brave,' said a young woman who was
known to be infatuated with Seumas. 'I think he's a great
warrior!'

Seumas turned to smile at this young maiden – whose
high cheek-bones and full lips had often tempted him – but
had his head sharply twisted back again by Makka-te, who
was like an impatient barber and not at all impressed by a
wandering target.

Thinking about the girl, with her supple waist and tightly
rounded bottom, Seumas remembered Princess Nau Ariki,
who was on board *The Volcano Flower*. Tangiia had not
yet dared face her, though her oaths and curses on waking,
and finding herself a captive of a man going nowhere, had
been sharp and loud enough to penetrate the roof of voyaging to its heart.

Kula had tried to throw herself to the sharks and Seumas was also reminded of Dorcha and her utter determination never to be touched by the Pict. Now Tangiia was having a taste of the bitter fruit swallowed by Seumas himself over the past decade.

There! And he had been determined himself, not to think of the Celt woman with her long legs and wild hair!

'Ow!' he grumbled, as a particularly white-hot pain went through his skull and pierced his brain. 'Watch it . . .'

But Makka-te was having none of this moaning.

'Are you a warrior or a pig?' he asked, pleasantly.

'A warrior,' growled Seumas.

'Then be silent like a warrior instead of squealing like a stuck sow.'

I'll give you stuck sow, my fine, pretty priest, thought Seumas, I'll puncture your arrogance the first chance I get, once this thing is done!

The tattooing process had begun in the late afternoon, which slipped swiftly into evening, there being no twilight in that part of the ocean. Kieto played the nose flute for him; beguiling tunes to take his mind off the pain. When the stars came out Seumas, lying on his back now, recognised the star group known to the Oceanians as White Squirrelfish, and another called Te rakau tapu, or The Sacred Timber. He liked the way Raiateans saw shapes in the star patterns, and gave them names.

Right across the heavens washed a swathe of milky white which was Mango-roa-i-ata, The Long Shark At Dawn, flung there by Maui who had caught it while fishing for islands in the creation. It was this rash of stars towards which the currents took them, into unknown waters, towards unknown islands.

Life on board a pahi was essentially ruled by the sea. The classic intervals of night and day were spliced together then cut into three equal slices, regardless of light and dark. If a storm ensued then everyone worked, never mind whose

shift it was when the storm arrived. The motion of the sea
dictated motion of the body.

Seumas had been born with the sea around him, on
Albainn, but he would never be as close to the ocean as
these people who had captured him. From the moment a
boy or girl was old enough to understand what was being
said to them, an Oceanian heard stories about the rigours
and exhilaration of life at sea. When a child first learned to
walk it would be wading in the waters of the lagoon, looking for shellfish, playing on the coral sands, the sea always
in its ears, always in its sight.

The rhythms of the tides were in an Oceanian's blood,
the coursing of the currents in an Oceanian's arteries. The
wide bowl of the roof of voyaging, with its horizons all
round, was almost always above his or her head, so little
time was spent inside a hut. On land the clean warm air of
the days and the balmy soft air of the nights were their
blankets, while at sea the wind and spray shaped them into
a hardy people, fit to travel over the great ocean which
was as much their home as the islands that dotted its surface in their thousands.

When a child was due to go on its first fishing trip it
would undergo a rite of passage, whereby it would be
wrapped in a bark-cloth skirt and painted with tumeric
dye. On return from the trip the youngster would be
washed with aromatic leaves and fed on taro pudding. At
not much older the child would be making model canoes,
of all types, in preparation for the time when it would
become a builder of full-sized vessels. And always the
sound of the ocean, always the sight of waves, filled their
waking days and sleeping nights. The importance of the sea
was impressed upon them from birth.

Seumas had seen them learn the wave patterns on the
open ocean, and gather knowledge of the star paths from
their seniors, and he knew he could never match these
people in their affinity with the great waters. They were

part of their world and he was an addition to it, surely grafted perhaps, but not an original branch. He could not match their ear for a change in the wind, nor the feel of their hand for a hidden ocean swell, nor their eye for an alteration in the wave patterns or a cloud on the horizon. He would always be an inferior on the pahi, though he knew he could match most men in single combat.

The pain from the tattooing process became excruciating and it was all Seumas could do to stop from crying out. Makka-te noticed this and asked for men to hold Seumas down, one to each limb. Seumas was about to protest, but the tattooist said, 'This is normal – there is no shame attached,' so he allowed himself to be pinioned. Makka-te began chanting now to the rhythm of his tattooing, using a variety of needles made from fish, human and bird bones. A comb was repeatedly hammered into the flesh using a heavy wooden stick.

As Makka-te's assistant was rubbing in some more soot from the burnt candle-nuts, Kieto came to Seumas.

'Shall I play some more tunes on my nose flute for you?' asked the youth.

It would help distract him from his agony. Seumas nodded and said, 'Yes – play me a song, Kieto.'

Mercifully, the process was finished by midnight and Seumas was left alone with his wounds and his pain.

The following morning his skin was inflamed and extremely sore to the touch. There was a red weal all around the wounded area, raised like an earth rampart. By noon the skin was swollen and puffy. He felt giddy and sick, and was going hot and cold in turns. Kieto made him lie down in the shade of one of the huts, where the youth began crushing some stems from a bunch of green bananas.

'What are you doing?' asked Seumas, faintly. 'Is that a poultice?'

'Yes,' replied Kieto. 'It'll help take down the swelling.

My grandmother did one for me, when I had my first tattoo.'

'This is not my first tattoo.'

'It's your first tattoo from a Raiatean priest – you should do as I say.'

The balm helped to relieve the soreness and swelling, and later Kieto administered some medicine from the nono tree, which was even more effective in healing the wound.

'Many people die from tattooing,' Kieto told Seumas, cheerfully. 'Beauty is not a thing the gods give easily to a man. You know how the first tattoo came to man?'

'No,' groaned Seumas, 'but I've got a feeling I'm going to be told, while I lie here helpless to defend my ears.'

'Well,' said Kieto, 'there was a prince named Tamanui who had a beautiful wife called Rukutia, but she ran away to another prince, whose name was Koropanga. She sent a message to Tamanui saying she had left him because she found him unattractive. You know what Tamanui did then?'

'I know what I would have done,' growled Seumas. 'Take my club and bash Koropanga's head in – then drag Rukutia back to my hut and –'

'No, nothing like that,' interrupted Kieto. 'He changed himself into a white egret with magic and flew up to his ancestors on the mountaintop to ask their advice. They told him they would paint his body, just as they painted themselves, and Tamanui let them. Unfortunately, once he was back in his own body and went swimming, the colours all washed off.'

'And I thought this was going to be a nice short story, so I could get some rest,' Seumas moaned. 'Get on with it.'

'Well, the prince went back again to his ancestors and asked them the *real* secret of their beauty. They told him that he had to have his body tattooed, but they warned him he might die of pain or sickness.'

'Thank you for reminding me again.'

'That's all right – anyway,' said the guileless youth, 'they cut long gashes in Tamanui's body and filled the wounds with a mysterious dye, which when his body healed would make him a beautiful man. Tamanui passed out once or twice, but he lived, and when he could walk again he went looking for his wife, who saw him from a long way off and asked out loud, "Who is that wonderful creature with the body of a god?" "It is I," said Tamanui, and Rukutia ran to him and loved him.'

'Did he beat her for being unfaithful?'

'Why, no, because it was *his* fault, for being so ugly before the tattoos.'

'I would have beaten her,' said Seumas, emphatically, taking great satisfaction in this thought, which helped relieve his pain. In his mind was a picture of a white-skinned, dark-eyed woman with long legs and wild hair submitting to his harsh treatment. 'I would have thrashed her soundly.'

'Then she would have slit your throat with a lei-o-mano while you slept,' replied Keito, with sound common sense.

'It might even be worth that,' sighed the love-sick Pict, 'to hear her begging for mercy – just once.'

'Who?' asked Keito, grinning.

'Why, Dorc—,' began Seumas, breaking off the word just in time and then saying quickly, 'this Rukuwhatsit woman . . . damn you boy, do you have to chatter all day? Get about your business, will you, and leave a man in peace?'

A long-voyaging sea bird landed near Seumas and was immediately chased away by an excited Dirk.

'Leave the bird alone,' moaned Seumas. 'Can't you see it's exhausted, dog? It needs to rest.'

Kieto said, 'That's a funny thing for you to say – when I first saw you, you were *strangling* birds.'

'I was doing it for a reason, not just for fun.'

'Tell me the reason,' asked Kieto.

'Then will you leave me in peace?'

'If you like,' smiled the boy.

Seumas explained, 'We caught the fulmars not for food, but for their oil. If I hadn't strangled the birds as I caught them, they would have been sick and the contents of their stomach would have been lost to me. It was necessary to wring their necks before they could disgorge the oil.'

'Ah, that explains it.'

'Now will you go?'

Kieto did as he was asked and left Seumas recovering from his ordeal, with Dirk lying beside him and licking his face occasionally, bewildered as to why his master was not up and walking around the deck.

On the evening of the third day Seumas was over the worst of his fever and was able to sit up. The ordinary fisherfolk had not been very successful in the waters through which the canoes drifted, and so Aputua, the chief of the shark-callers, studied the shape of the clouds in the other ocean above. Finally, he declared it a good and proper stretch of water for a shark hunt and ordered the shark-callers of all three vessels to listen to his commands.

'We must feed our people,' he told them. 'Go and find your threshing devices.'

Seumas was fascinated by this ceremony, which he had not witnessed before. He asked Kieto to explain things as they went along. Kieto began by telling him that because grey reef sharks had been plentiful around the islands, there had been no need for the shark-callers on Raiatea to work their magic.

'Watch this,' Seumas told Dirk. 'You might learn how to get your supper to jump out of the sea.'

Dirk was duly attentive, though it seemed he was not sure exactly what was expected of him.

Firstly, Aputua blew softly on a conch horn. The sound drifted out over the still evening waters. Others began blowing conches then, but with gentle notes. It was an enticing sound, alluring even to Seumas, whose ear was not musical.

Kieto whispered to Seumas, 'They are calling in the sharks to the area, but they must do it softly in case Magantu, the Great White Shark, hears the call and comes to swallow our canoes.'

Seumas watched the shark-callers line up, kneeling on the front of the deck. They then beat the water with their decorated paddles to attract sharks, which would be noosed with sennit cord, or speared with harpoons, and dragged on board. When the sharks failed to come, Kikamana threw magic stones into the water, which the sharks would swallow and then would be unable to prevent themselves from ignoring the shark-callers.

The shark-callers continued to thrash the water, while singing magic songs in the evening air.

Finally, there was suppressed excitement amongst them and Seumas looked over the edge of the vessel to see, in the light of the dropping sun, deep shadows and running streaks of darkness in the water below. Then the first great snout broke the surface, the jaws opened wide revealing a mass of teeth, and then slammed shut on painted paddle, taking a huge chunk out of the wood. A noose was dropped and then a harpoon struck and the snapping, writhing shark was dragged on to the deck.

Then another, and another.

The water frothed with grey shapes, red-and-white mouths, and dark, glinting eyes. It seemed the more sharks that were caught, the more eager were their comrades to join the landed harvest. Madness prevailed amongst the victims, who flung themselves at the threshing devices in a frenzy of excitement, as if to ignore the general lunacy would be to miss an invaluable experience, never mind that experience was death.

The shark callers were yelling instructions to each other, doing their best to keep out of the way of those who had caught a shark and were trying to subdue it with clubs, yet at the same time wishing to catch their own fish. It appeared to be pandemonium, though in fact there was an underlying sense of order to the proceedings.

Before Seumas could grab Dirk's ruff, the dog rushed forward barking and snapping himself, dangerously close to the first shark that had been hauled on to the deck. Dirk thought he could tackle the flip-flopping, jack-knifing creature, but in fact he was in danger of losing his head.

'Heel, Dirk!' yelled Seumas. 'NOW!'

The dog continued to bark, but glanced over his shoulder at his master, and on the second bidding returned to Seumas's side, growling softly in the back of his throat. Seumas clipped the dog's rump with the flat of his hand.

'Come on the first call,' said Seumas. 'Not the second, you ill-trained beast.'

'Who trained him" asked Kieto.

'Some fool soft on hounds,' answered Seumas.

When the shark-calling was over, the catch was skinned and cleaned. The raw flesh was cut and smoked over a small, stone-hearth fire on the deck of *The Scudding Cloud*. Fuel was precious, so the meat was cut into thin strips which would cook quickly and easily over the flames from the coconut fibres.

The meal was tough, but nutritious.

One hot night, while the crew were listless and inattentive, the pahi passed a small island. Kikamana had warned Tangiia that they were not to stop at this place. She told the king there were no provisions there and that it was a place like 'the island with the stink of ghosts' – an unhealthy piece of dirt.

Tangiia accepted what his high priestess had to say, without questioning her. She was the authority on mystical matters. He had limited knowledge of the supernatural landscapes and seascapes of Oceania, through which they had to slide from time to time, and he simply accepted her word. She had told him what the island was, and to whom it belonged, and he had nodded and shuddered, before going to his rest.

Seumas was not sleeping, but standing by the mast, staring at the forbidden island as they passed. There were dark shapes like large birds or fruit bats skimming the air above the island, their flight patterns tight and strangely limited. They swept and dived, swept and dived, as if trapped inside some invisible vessel that enclosed the whole landscape. They seemed to Seumas to be some kind of predatorial creatures, raptors perhaps, that sought small prey in the air.

The island itself looked quite scanty. He surmised that a man could walk around such an island in an hour. It was thickly wooded though, looking like a bristly hog's back on the darkness of the ocean. As Seumas watched he thought he saw a shape, running very fast along the sands of the beach – but then it was gone, into the thickets, if it was ever there at all.

Kikamana, the Far-seeing virgin, was standing near by, also unable to sleep for reasons of her own.

'Did you see that?' asked Seumas, pointing. 'Is there someone on that place.'

'Yes, there is,' she replied. 'That's why I want us to pass it quickly.'

She stared around her, at the night sky. There were swirling clouds running over the face of the moon; dark veils made of fine black hair. The surface of the sea was like liquid ebony, noiseless as flowing oil. These were strange hours on stretches of transcendental ocean where the delicate balance between the unnatural and natural world could be tipped either way by a word or a gesture, and a nightmare might begin.

At that moment a freak wave, perhaps Aremata-popoa, rose out of the soundless sea and swept towards the last pahi in the chain, *The Royal Palm*. A child of ten years or so had risen from her sleeping mat, to parch her thirst with coconut water, when the wave hit the canoe aft. The crew quickly clutched at fixings, holding on to the boat, but the young girl was carried off on the crest of the wave, towards the small island.

'That child!' cried Seumas.

'Oh no,' groaned Kikamana. 'Why can't he let just one fleet go by without claiming a victim?'

After this enigmatic remark Tangiia was woken immediately and told what had happened.

'I must go to the island,' said Kikamana, firmly. 'I must get the child before anything happens.'

'I will go with you,' said the king. 'We'll take Po and Manopa, and –'

'No, I must go alone,' replied Kikamana. 'He would slaughter you all. That's what he wants, to gather a crowd of people on his island, then to massacre them for his larder.'

Tangiia shook his head. 'You can't go alone – you must take some of your priestesses with you. They can help protect you.'

Kikamana shook her head, as sea anchors were dropped into the water and the dugout canoe was made ready for her.

'I shall take Seumas,' she said. 'His strangeness will confuse Matuku.'

By this time the two other pahi had come up alongside and had linked to *The Scudding Cloud*. Manopa and Po were informed that Kikamana and Seumas were going to the island. They nodded gravely and made a sacred sign in the air.

'Now just a moment –' began Seumas, who had not been consulted on his willingness to risk his life but before he properly knew what was happening, he was bundled into the dugout canoe and it was launched. He barely had time to snatch up a weapon, a patu club, in his right hand and a flaming brand in his left. Then he found himself being paddled over the oily waters towards the spit of land. It bristled in the moonlight, as if expecting its visitors.

'Who's on that island?' asked Seumas, fitting the brand to a socket and dropping the club. He took up a paddle to help with the rowing. 'Who's Matuku?'

Kikamana didn't answer. She simply picked up the weapon Seumas had brought and dropped it overboard.

'Wha—? What did you do that for?' cried Seumas. 'Now I'm defenceless. We're both without arms.'

'We cannot kill Matuku,' she stated simply.

'You'd be surprised who I can kill,' growled Seumas. 'There's not many men I can't fell in single combat.'

'I mean, we *mustn't* kill him, or we will put the whole fleet at risk – Matuku is a demi-god.'

At that point the canoe reached the beach and Seumas had no time to ask more questions.

At first it seemed to Seumas that the island was silent. Then he heard the crying of the child. It came from the middle of the clump of trees. Between the sobs of the child there was another less obvious noise, a kind of swishing in the air above the trees. He guessed this was the noise of the birds or bats he had seen from the craft.

'Come,' said Kikamana.

Seumas followed her in great trepidation. The stink of evil was on this place; he could smell it in the air. The grasses and weeds seemed to clutch at his ankles. The roots of the trees deliberately attempted to trip him.

He discovered to his horror that the earth beneath his soles was crawling with insects – he could not avoid treading on them, squashing them by the hundred. Ants, beetles, millipedes and other insects flowed over his feet, biting him, nipping his skin, stinging him. Spiders with bright eyes stared from the foliage; thousands of them on one bush alone. In the poor light from the torch he was not able to identify many creatures specifically, but he knew they

were unnaturally multitudinous and gathered in unusual
groupings. There were savage flesh-eating insects next to
mild plant-eating creatures.

The milling insects formed a band around the forest, like
a protective barrier.

As they went through the rainforest, the leaves brushed
their skin, and Seumas was aware of a new disquieting
presence.

'Beasties,' he muttered in disgust, shuddering in revulsion
as he noticed a clutch of long dark bulging shapes on the
arm carrying the torch.

When he shone the brand down by his torso and on his
legs, he could see dozens of them, scattered over his body.
There were many more on the priestess, even on her neck
and cheeks. Seumas felt his stomach turning liquidly over.

'Oh good grief,' he moaned. 'Kikamana, we're covered
in bloodsuckers.'

'Forget the leeches,' she said. 'Don't pick or knock them
off or they'll leave their heads under your skin. They will
rot and poison your blood. We'll get them off later.'

'Don't tell me how to deal with *bloodsuckers*,' he
growled, taking refuge from his repugnance in mild anger.
'I know how to deal with the beasties all right.'

Finally, they came to a clearing, in the middle of which a
white cage structure soared almost as high as the tallest
trees. So grand was it, in size and arrangement, that Seumas
might have called it a palace. It was complicated in design,
having several layers of meshed bars, which swept criss-
crossing upwards into hollow keeps and towers. The
surrounding trees had grown around and through the corners of the structure, so that it was firmly embedded in
their individual trunks, part of their galled growth, bolting
the massive cage securely to the earth. Hot winds blew
through the network, causing a low moaning noise, not
unlike the sound of pain.

Seumas could tell at once that it was fashioned of bones,

human bones by the look of them. He recognised thigh
bones and shin bones and skulls employed as locking
blocks and keystones. They were fused together in a tight
formation, so that a man could not pass his hand between
the bars. Inside the cage sat the child, sitting on the dirt. She
was crying softly.

'Great God of the Sky,' said Seumas, forgetting his
leeches instantly, 'what have we here?'

'Matuku's palace,' replied Kikamana. 'And there are his
toys, strung to the towers.'

Seumas stared up into the starry night and saw the birds
and bats again, but they were tied fast to the bone palace,
skimming around the heavens each on a long length of sennit string.

'Kites,' he said, recognising them at last and laughing
softly. 'They're bloody kites.'

He was able to reach up and pull one in. It was indeed a
kite, made of banana leaf stretched over a cross-frame. A
very simple design: the sort a Pict might make for his son
out of animal skin and sticks, the sort of kite that Seumas
had played with as a boy, on the cliffs of Albainn.

'You know these magical creatures?' asked the girl in
the cage, wiping away her tears.

'They're not *creatures*,' said Seumas. 'They're just bits of
leaf and string.'

'But Matuku has made them *live* – they fly through the
night and day – his sea-ancestors taught him how to
breathe movement into an ordinary leaf.'

'Rubbish,' snapped Seumas, shortly. 'I may be a savage
and a barbarian, but I know my kites.' He turned to
Kikamana. 'Look, we've got to get the girl out of there.'

With Kikamana's help Seumas managed to snap off a
large bough from a tree. The pair of them then tried to prise
open the human-bone bars of the cage with this lever. There
seemed to be no visible door to the palace. And the bones
were so welded together that it seemed impossible to enter,

unless they had some instrument to smash their way in. Seumas looked around the area for a large rock, but found nothing of any weight. It seemed the island was simply soil on a hidden mushroom of coral.

At that moment there was a crashing from the undergrowth and a figure appeared.

The figure stopped at the edge of the clearing. It was a naked man, but taller again by half than a normal man. There was long matted hair falling from his head, and thick hair on his chest and limbs. When he opened his mouth his teeth were sharply pointed. The man began to move forward.

Kikamana said softly, 'Speak to him – in your own tongue.'

Seumas cried, '*Ciod e a tha ort? Na biodh eagal ort.*'

The monstrous man stopped dead and his eyes grew round. He regarded Seumas with some awe. Seumas followed up his advantage and pointed to the bone palace, then waved the broken bough in the air before the creature's face.

'*Bi cho math agus an dorus fhosdgladh.*'

Matuku let out a cry of alarm and then fled back into the trees.

'You frightened him with your club,' said Kikamana. 'Now we'll lose him.'

'Not if I have anything to do with it,' Seumas said. 'This island's not big enough to hide on.'

He raced after Matuku with the branch still in his hand, chasing the great man through the forest tracks to the beach, over the river of insects, collecting more leeches on the way. There he saw Matuku run into the water until the creature was out of his depth and sank from sight. The giant man remained completely submerged, while Seumas waited on the beach. After a while it became apparent to Seumas that Matuku was not going to reappear. The big man with the pointed teeth had

drowned after all. Seumas looked backwards and forwards along the beach, thinking the creature might have
swum under water and emerged elsewhere, but there were
no footprints in the sand.

Returning to Kikamana, the Pict said, 'The man must be
dead – he went into the sea and didn't come out.'

Kikamana shook her head. 'Matuku can walk along the
bottom of the ocean bed – it's one of the tricks his sea-
ancestors taught him. I told you he is a demi-god – the son
of a mortal woman and Tawhaki, God of Thunder and
Lightning. He's a cannibal of ruthless character, eating raw
human flesh from his living victims. He likes children
because their meat is soft and sweet. What did you say to
him – in your own language?'

'I said, "What ails thee? Be not afraid."'

'And the second time?'

'I asked him to be so kind as to show me the door – to
the cage.'

Kikamana sighed.

Seumas asked, 'Will he be back?'

'I think he will – out of curiosity.'

The girl was still sniffling in the cage. She said, 'I want to
go to my mummy – I want my mummy.'

'And you shall soon, child,' said Kikamana. 'Be patient
now.'

Seumas waved the branch. 'Let's trap him in a net and I'll
threaten to brain him unless he opens the cage?'

'We cannot harm him, or even threaten him – Tawhaki
will destroy the fleet. To threaten to kill a son of one of the
gods, no matter how despicable he is, would be to ensure
our own doom. We must persuade him to open the hidden
door without intimidating him or hurting him in any way.'

'An eater of *babies*?'

Kikamana shrugged. 'Would you rather the fleet was
torn apart by lightning?'

Even as he spoke the words, Matuku came crashing

out of the undergrowth and pinioned Seumas's arms to his sides, forcing him to drop the branch. Matuku shrieked in delight at having caught the white demon so easily. He spat over Seumas's shoulder, into the face of Kikamana, who stood passively watching the Pict being slowly crushed to death. She stepped back, murmuring a karakia trying to protect Seumas with one of her magic chants. It worked for a few moments, then Matuku shook his head and squeezed hard. A rib cracked in Seumas's chest, then another. Kikamana, on hearing sounds, spoke at last, just as Seumas's head was reeling with red smoky pain.

Kikamana said quickly, 'If you kill the demon, he won't show you how to make a special kite.'

'Ahhh!' cried Matuku. 'Kite. Kite.'

The pressure was relieved for a moment.

Seumas groaned, 'What kite?'

'You must know another kind of kite,' muttered Kikamana. 'You said those are simple ones, he has there. Make him a more complicated one.'

'I – I don't know – I can't remember.'

'Kite!' shouted Matuku, letting Seumas fall to the ground. 'Make Matuku kite!'

'I – can't,' wheezed Seumas, finding it difficult to breathe through the pain of his broken ribs.

'Think!' flashed Kikamana.

She turned to Matuku. 'Let us have the child – we will make you a wonderful kite.'

Then to Seumas, 'Well?'

'Perhaps – I once met a wandering seller – we call them pedlars – he showed me a picture of a box-kite – a big square kite . . .'

'Make one, now.'

Matuku stood by, grinning wildly, his eyes shining with insane delight.

'Big kite! New Kite! Yes, yes.'

'I – I shall need some animal skin, some hide,' said Seumas, 'and some bamboo sticks – sennit string.'

Matuku rushed off, back into the rainforest.

While the creature was gone, Kikamana bound up Seumas's ribs with strips of tapa-bark cloth torn from her own gown.

'You'll be all right,' she murmured.

'I'm glad you think so,' replied Seumas, patting his padded chest. 'It still bloody hurts.'

'It's better than a crushed heart.'

Seumas smiled, grimly, 'That was crushed long ago – by someone with hardly any strength at all.'

Kikamana was aware of the sadness in his voice and touched his cheek with her fingertips.

'Even that might mend, one day.'

Matuku returned with all the kite parts, including some large pieces of thinly stretched hide and a sharp-edged razor shell. There were markings on the hide, drawings of a kind, which showed up under the flickering lights, but Seumas was too intent on considering his mental plans for the kite to bother too much with these. Seumas made a few more fire brands and arranged them in a circle around a mossy bank. Then he set about cutting the skins, at the same time instructing Kikamana on how to tie together the struts which would form the cage for the kite. He drew designs for her in the dust, showing her what the finished kite should look like.

'We're going to have to help each other here,' said Seumas, 'because I've never actually seen one made. I've just heard about it from the lips of another – seen a picture.'

Kikamana's intelligence was not lacking in any respect and she soon had a box-kite cage in progress. She prayed that Tangiia would not launch any kind of attack on the island, now that the pair of them had been gone for quite a long time. While the torches flickered away, under the eyes of both Matuku and his young prisoner, the kite took shape. Seumas asked for tree sap to seal the skin along the edges of the box, which Matuku seemed to find with remarkable alacrity, even in the darkness of the forest. It occurred to Seumas that the monster knew every corner, every tiny fraction, on this small island where he had been imprisoned by his father.

'There!' cried Seumas, as the dawn was reaching with grey-blue fingers over the sky. 'The box-kite!'

He handed the toy to Matuku, who took it with surprising gentleness into his hands and stroked it lovingly. Then Matuku produced a ball of sennit wound around a short stick from a hidey-hole in a tree. He tied one end of the string to the kite and then ran off along a rainforest path, to the beach. The other two followed him quickly, Kikamana praying out loud that the kite would actually work, that the wind would carry it.

'Maomao,' she said, 'Great God of the Winds – *make* this toy fly, if only for a short while . . .'

'Oh ye of little faith,' Seumas remarked, looking down into the beautiful priestess's eyes. 'It'll fly.'

And he was right. The kite lifted into the air with ease.

Matuku ran along the beach, his tall supple frame rippling with excitement, his laugh sounding over the waters, reaching the ears of those on the pahi canoes. They would be able to see, in the morn's light, that Seumas and Kikamana were alive and well. They might well be wondering what Seumas and Kikamana were doing, flying kites on the beach, when they were supposed to be freeing a little girl from captivity, but Kikamana hoped Tangiia would exercise patience, and trust her.

Matuku let out the string until the kite was a small oblong shape high above the island.

'Cloud!' he cried, delightedly. 'Up there, up there!'

He anchored it to a piece of coral jutting from the sands.

Kikamana said, 'And now, Matuku, your side of the bargain – you must release the child.'

Matuku suddenly looked sullen.

'Here we go,' muttered Seumas. 'The revoking.'

The Pict was convinced that the flesh-eating demi-god was now going to go back on his word.

From the sky, however, came a rumble like the growling in the back of a dog's throat. Matuku looked up, alarm in his eyes. There were no dark clouds in the heavens, from which the thunder might have come.

'Your father,' stated Kikamana. 'He does not think well of those who break their promises.'

Matuku stared at her, then after a few moments began walking the path to the palace of bones. Kikamana and Seumas followed him, once again passing over the insect barrier. By this time Seumas had been bitten and stung so many times he was almost immune to the pain.

While they watched, Matuku fiddled in a particular spot on the cage, pushing and pulling tiny needles of bone – a toe-bone here, a finger-bone there – slipping one backwards, another forwards, in an intricate series of movements. The locking device was like some strange puzzlebox of interlocking strips of wood, the kind that pedlars might sell to impressed peasants in the villages of Albainn. Finally the cage door swung open and its captive was released into the arms of Kikamana.

'I swear that door was invisible,' said Seumas, rubbing his sore ribs. 'Could *you* see it?'

'No,' admitted the priestess. 'Now let's get this girl back to her mother.'

'Yes, I want my mummy,' sniffed the child.

Seumas turned to look at Matuku, who nodded, his eyes still shining.

'Good kite,' said the demi-god. 'Fly good.'

In the dugout on the way back to the pahi, Seumas let

Kikamana and the girl do the paddling. He concentrated on burning off his leeches with a glowing twig, then doing the same for Kikamana. At a touch from the red-hot end, the leeches curled up, rearing their heads and tails and releasing their victim. The bites and stings from the insects would be treated with medicinal herbs, later in the day.

'Will these ribs mend soon?' he asked.

'They'll be fine in a few weeks,' said the kahuna. 'Just rest for a while.'

'Not much chance to do else,' grumbled the Pict. 'One thing though – it's a good job that hide Matuku brought us was cured to such a thinness. Anything thicker and the kite might have been too heavy to lift off the sand.'

Kikamana stared into his eyes. 'It hadn't been cured to a thinness – it was like that already.'

Seumas looked puzzled. 'I think you're wrong,' he said. 'What kind of animal would produce a pelt that thin?'

'That wasn't what you'd call a *pelt*,' replied Kikamana, calmly. 'It was human skin. Matuku always skins his victims before he eats the flesh from their bones. He keeps the cured skins flapping from a hidden tree.'

Seumas winced and stared at the box-kite, flying high above the beach, tugged at by the monster's hand.

'*Human* skin,' he said. 'That's disgusting.'

He looked at his own hands, remembering how easy it had been to slice the hide and cut it into shape, remembering the markings he had seen which of course he now realised were tattoos. Some dead person, some unfortunate shipwrecked mariner, was now flying over the island, looking down on his own interlocking bones, hovering over the creature who had skinned him alive, who yet held him captive on the end of a piece of string, tugging him into jerky motion.

That was something to think about, while the ribs mended in Seumas's chest.

As they passed the other two pahi, Seumas saw the

wistful face of Boy-girl, peering from behind the mast. Boy-girl gave him a plaintive wave. Safe on a separate vessel, Seumas waved back. Seumas had insisted that he be put on a different pahi to the desperate Boy-girl, otherwise his life would have been made a misery, unable to get away from Boy-girl's pestering.

'Come and see me?' cried Boy-girl, as the dugout passed.

'Soon,' Seumas lied. 'In a while.'

2

Twenty days after they had visited Matuku's island, during which one woman gave birth, one man died of natural causes, and a child fell overboard and was attacked by a shark, they were still drifting. They managed to save the child's life, but the whole left side of her body was paralysed.

The shark was duly caught and a ritual punishment took place whereby the shark had a line tied to its tail and was dragged backwards through the water until it was almost dead. Then a stinging jellyfish was caught and rammed down the shark's throat, which eventually swelled. The shark was then cut into small pieces and the less edible parts fed to boobies. Poetic justice for a predator who sometimes carried out sneak attacks and devoured exhausted booby birds resting on the water.

Several days after this event Tangiia sighted a circular cloud on the horizon and knew it to be one of those sky formations which clung to the peaks of mountains. He marked the cloud on his cord-device, which was growing quite lengthy and was strung with knots of many shapes and sizes.

'Keep a sharp eye out for signs of land,' he told his lesser navigators.

Then some white birds were seen, beautiful creatures
with long red tail-feathers, that seemed to paint the sky
with their bodies. Sometimes they even flew backwards in
their elegant dance. The Raiateans had seen nothing like
them before. They were clearly birds which remained in the
area of land.

Tangiia kept watch, noticing some rips in the sea to the
sun side of the canoe, and having his rowers move clear of
them. Some seaweed was found and given to the blind
Kaho, who felt its texture.

'I have heard of some islands which, on Raiatea, were
supposed in the direction of Ra. Dancing white birds and
coarse weed is to be found there. What is the colour of the
water, my son?' asked Kaho of Po'oi.

The child replied, 'The colour of an unripe coconut.'

'Ahh.' The old man smiled sightlessly. 'This is indeed
the place of which I have heard. We must be careful in
these waters. There are hostile peoples here.'

Tangiia thanked the old man.

The very next day they heard the sound of reefs on the
wind and finally, at noon, approached an island with a
lush green mountain rising from its centre. It was a sultry,
morbid-looking place where thick vegetation came right
down over the beach to touch the sea. The Raiateans could
see mangrove swamps in some of the coves, the trees standing on tall exposed roots, as if ready to run with spidery
legs away from the tide. Finally, the vessels came across a
stretch of sand which reached like a spit out into the sea.
Here they moored the canoes.

'We must take on some fresh water,' said Tangiia, with a
sense of foreboding warning him not to linger. 'It's not an
island I would wish us to populate.'

A six-man exploratory party was organised to seek for
fresh water, while others gathered drinking coconuts, and
anything else they could find, from the shoreline.

Manopa led the six-man expedition. Included within its

numbers were the young priest who had stolen the God of
Hope, Po and Seumas. Seumas's cracked ribs had almost
healed now and he was back to his normal state of fitness.

King Tangiia remained with the pahi canoes, though he
expressed a desire to go with the exploratory party.
Kikamana told him his place was with his people and that
now he was king he had a duty to protect his person from
harm.

'If anything happens to the party, we must cast off and
sail away – and you must be with us. Despite your youth,
you are our king and you must suppress your adventurous
nature at times like this. Without our king, we should be
lost in an unknown ocean without reason for being there.'

Boy-girl, who had been travelling on *The Volcano
Flower*, agreed with the priestess.

'You should stay here with us, to protect the women
and children with the rest of your warriors.'

Sighing heavily, Tangiia agreed, knowing that while the
canoes were moored together he would have to face the
onslaught of Princess Kula's wrath, from which the open
waters had protected him until this moment. Indeed, he
could see her smouldering form stepping on to the sand spit
at the very moment he was speaking with Kikamana. The
princess began striding purposefully towards the new king,
who uttered faltering apologies to his high priestess, before
walking quickly along the spit and down to the shoreline,
where he hoped to escape for a while in the near environs
of dense jungle.

At that moment, unnoticed by others, a bird was
released from a cage on one of the pahi. It was mobbed by
local frigate birds as it climbed into the sky and on hearing
the commotion Tangiia glanced up. He saw the frigates
attacking a stranger in their midst, but then shrugged and
took his attention from the scene, as the bird climbed
higher and out of danger.

Frigates were always attacking some poor feathered

creature, robbing it of food, or simply harassing it because
it was in their territory. The incident was instantly forgotten. There were important issues at stake and it was as
well not to be diverted by the vagaries of the natural world.

If King Tangiia had kept watching, he would have
noticed that the bird flew away over the ocean in the very
direction from which the fleet had come, and thus he might
possibly have saved himself future grief.

Manopa led his small party, each carrying a number of
empty gourds, into the interior. They were only lightly
armed and hoped to rely on flight if attacked by any war-
like peoples. No sight nor smell of smoke was detected,
however, and Manopa had hopes this piece of land was
uninhabited.

It was hot and humid under the canopy of leaves, and
insects stuck irritatingly to sweaty bodies as the party cut
their way through the vegetation with bone knives. The
air was heavy and difficult to breathe. Sometimes the stink
was unbelievably powerful when it rose from a mangrove
swamp where gas bubbles burst, releasing an ancient
organic stench into the enclosed atmosphere. Fiddler crabs
scuttled amongst the tidal reaches of the swamps and rep-
tiles hung from thick, dark-green leaves over the swilling,
brackish waters. It was a place where Moko, the Lizard-
God, might scatter his green, living jewels.

Apart from the obvious physical unattractiveness of their
surroundings the young priest told them he could sense
spirits in the foliage all around them.

'Dwarves too,' he murmured, with a shiver. 'I can feel the
Lipsipsip around us . . .'

Po groaned and Seumas asked him what was the matter.

'Lipsipsip,' said Po, glancing behind him. 'They are small
demons who live in rotting trees and black stones. Spirit
people, who devour you if you offend them.'

'How does one offend these creatures?' asked Seumas,

whose own country of Albainn was overrun with dwarves and giants, living as they did in deep caves and high on the hillside crags.

'Just by being here, if one is a stranger.'

'Quiet,' said the more pragmatic Manopa. 'Do you want to tell the whole island where we are?'

Manopa led his party towards the most likely area where a stream would fall from the mountain and cut its way through the undergrowth to the sea. They worked hard with their long bone knives, chopping away at tangles of vines and thick-stemmed, succulent plants that spread under the canopy. Finally, they were rewarded with the sound of cascading water.

'This way,' grunted Manopa, leading them into a clearing.

A thin waterfall dropped from a cliff as a silver flail and lost itself in a natural, mossy drain hole to an underground stream. Seumas stared around the glade, which was clearly man-made, in apprehension. He saw, on an otherwise smooth stump, the carved face of a god eating a lizard. The head and front legs of the lizard were poking between the god's lips like a swollen tongue. The carving's eyes were round and large, its nose long, and broad at the tip, its lips thick and brutish.

It was the head of the lizard that made Seumas shudder; it had the face of a terrified man.

'Who's that?' whispered Seumas to Po.

Po stared and shook his head, indicating that he didn't know, and did not *want* to know.

Behind the carving were painted totems, each about the size of a man's arm, projecting at all angles from the turf. There were animals and birds, as well as faces and skulls, carved on the totems. Dirty, bark-cloth rags hung from the mouths of some of the chiselled features, like frozen vomit. Spikes pierced the eyes of the carvings. In some cases the lips had been drawn back to reveal long, squared teeth.

The tongue of one wooden human face was as long as a man's intestines, and ran over the scrubby ground and down the throat of a totem, like a ribbon snake crawling into a hole.

Manopa's group were now quite terrified. They had clearly stumbled on to a sacred waterfall. It was a dreadful place, where the horror of awful deeds was almost tangible and could be tasted in the foul air. Each man expected that any moment a loathsome, drooling monster would spring from behind a stone. At that moment Po let out a yell.

'Arrrhhh!'

He dropped the gourds he was carrying and lifted his club to defend himself as a dense fern parted to reveal a man.

The stranger also jumped back and levelled his spear. He stuck out his tongue and went into a crouched stance. The yell of a war cry left his throat.

Manopa took hold of him from behind and motioned for him to lower his weapon. Po did as he was bid.

The wary stranger came forward, still crouched, followed by a number of other men in single file. If Manopa's group were going to attack, now was the time to do it, but they had been shocked by the encounter, and had lost the initiative. Manopa did not know how many of the local warriors there were in the vicinity and whether or not they were surrounded. The only method to employ here was hit and run, but their path back to the sea might have been closed behind them.

Manopa studied the natives with a practised eye.

They were tattooed, but with symbols not used by the intruders. Unlike the Raiateans, who regarded facial tattoos as distasteful, these warriors had bars tattooed across their noses and cheeks. In their features they were much like the Raiateans, though their heads were shaved except for two twisted horns of hair which projected from their scalps. Their stature was in fact somewhat stockier and shorter than that of the intruders.

Gradually more and more men came into the clearing and surrounded Manopa's party. They were all heavily armed and seemed by their demeanour and their bodily decorations to be outfitted for war. It would have been suicide to attempt to fight this many warriors in the tightness of the glade. Manopa waited for an opening speech from the natives, before committing his men to any course of action. He was not afraid to fight, but he wanted to give his men the best chance.

'Why have you come here?' asked one of the natives, who from his headdress appeared to be a chief of some kind. 'What are you doing?'

He spoke with a peculiar accent in a dialect used by all voyaging Oceanians; almost a separate language in itself. It was the tongue employed by mariners to communicate with each other when they met on the high seas, or in situations such as this, where strangers arrive on an island. It was a limited language, but adequate for its purpose.

'We touch nothing here,' said Manopa. 'We have not touched the water.'

'Water taboo,' snapped the chief.

Manopa said quickly, 'Yes, we understand.'

All the while they were carrying out this brief exchange, Manopa was aware that the natives were creeping around behind his group, in order to stare at something, and that those at the front were craning their necks to look over the shoulders of his own party. It took him a few moments to realise that the object of their interest was Seumas, who stood between the young priest and another man. Manopa and his men were so used to the strangeness of Seumas's skin, hair and eyes, that they quite forgot how odd it might seem to an outsider.

'Not albino,' said the chief, staring hard at Seumas. 'What is it?'

Manopa was quick to seize the moment.

'A demon we caught in a trap. We trained him to fight

for us. His eyes are made of blue shells. On the parts of his body where no sun has shone his skin is pure white.'

Seumas caught the drift of what was occurring here.

'*Tha e cho geal ris an t-sneachd*,' he said, telling them in the language of demons that it was as white as snow.

The chief's eyelids narrowed, he stepped back quickly, and the circle around the hapless group suddenly widened.

'He is a *demon*?'

'*Our* demon,' said Manopa.

The chief, who now felt it was required of him as the bravest member of his war party, went forward cautiously and touched Seumas on the chest with tentative fingers, which he quickly withdrew. Seumas stood quite still, allowing himself to be appraised and studied, from head to foot. His gingery-red plait he knew was a shocking colour to the Oceanians, and he had frightened many with his light-blue penetrating eyes. The chief seemed mesmerised by him.

Finally, the chief said, 'You eat with us,' and took the path by which he had entered the glade.

It seemed that Manopa and his band were expected to follow. Native warriors blocked the way back to the sea, so Manopa motioned for his small band to do as they had been told.

They were led into the interior and up the side of a mountain, to a flat shelf which was almost a plateau, except for the fact that it was overshadowed by a great curving hooked rock which rose behind the shelf and swept over it. Seumas noted that there was only one path up the steep ascent, which followed a narrow ridge over which they had to cross single file. On either side of the ridge, the width of a man's shoulders, the world dropped away to deep valleys below.

The village on the plateau was a fortress: almost impossible to attack. Seumas surreptitiously searched the landscape for ways of escape and it seemed that if the ridge was well guarded that action would be virtually impossible too.

The group were the object of much interest as they entered a large village of stone huts roofed with palm leaves. Sullen-faced women and children came out to stare at them as they passed, but there were no sounds of greeting or welcome; simply a ponderous silence. Seumas came under special scrutiny; some of the children hid behind their mothers as the party approached with him. Dogs came running from the village edge, barking and snapping at the strangers. One of them worried Manopa's heels until he kicked it and sent it yipping into a pack which was less bold and had kept its distance.

They were taken to a large, rectangular ceremonial area with a stone floor inside which were several platforms of stone at different levels and around which were houses of differing size and height. They were asked to sit in the middle of this rectangle, a temple which Seumas gathered was called a *tohua* in the local dialect. Drink was brought to them.

Gradually the temple began to fill with warriors, sitting around Manopa's group, until there were at least two to three hundred in and around the stone structure. Seumas had judged from the size of the village that there were more men somewhere else. There were houses to support at least two thousand people on the plateau and clearly not all of the warriors were present; the bulk of the fighting men were somewhere else. Perhaps out in their war canoes, fighting another local island, but more likely down on the shoreline, attacking the Raiateans.

'What is the name of this island?' asked Manopa of the chief, who could not take his eyes from Seumas.

'Nuku Hiva,' replied the chief, refusing to avert his gaze. 'You sell your demon to me? I give you many women, many shells, many red feathers.'

Seumas glanced at Manopa, who stared back stony-eyed.

'Yes,' he said at last, 'I'll think of a good price.'

'Good,' smiled the chief, showing an even row of teeth.

'Come the night – we eat. Tomorrow you tell me price. Now you want a woman for each man?'

Manopa's face set into a grim smile. 'Yes – good.'

Seumas knew the tactics, had used them himself in the clan wars. They were to be wined and dined and sapped of strength by lovemaking before being slaughtered. Feed your enemy, get him drunk, drain him physically, put him off his guard, then when he falls into an exhausted sleep, cut his throat.

Seumas wondered about the trading business, and decided the chief possibly had a perverted sense of honour which required that he offer to *buy* a demon rather than take it immediately by force. No doubt he felt it might be unlucky to simply massacre a group of men and then take their demon as spoils of war. A demon was something unusual and with unusual creatures you trod warily, careful not to upset any obscure gods, or break any cryptic taboos. At least the offer had been made and if the seller was not alive to take advantage of the deal then that was hardly the fault of the buyer.

'Good,' repeated the chief. He called something in his own dialect. Some wooden platters and giant clamshells of nuts and fruit were brought, and laid before him. The chief and his basket-sharers took their pick of the edibles, then offered some to Manopa's men, who also partook of the food.

After they had eaten, naked maidens were ushered from one of the stone houses. From their looks and demeanour they were of a different tribe, possibly from another island. Seumas guessed they were captives taken in a raid on some neighbours. They looked frightened and bewildered.

Each of Manopa's group was assigned a woman, until only Seumas was left alone. A nude mature female of thirty or so was pushed forward, in front of him. She was slightly overweight, but with pleasant features.

The local chief said something which Seumas did not catch and he turned to look at Po.

Po grunted, 'An enemy chief's wife – you're being honoured. Her husband is required for another ceremony.'

Seumas nodded, not knowing what Po meant about the
husband. The captured wife or daughter of an enemy chief
was a prize not lightly given.

The woman looked terrified and Seumas could well
understand why. Apart from being used as an object to
help subdue some strangers from across the ocean, she was
about to be handed over to a tattooed, white demon from
hell. Perhaps his cock would be made of fire? Or his loins
covered in fish hooks which would hold her to him forever?
Or his breath perfumed with the fragrance of deadly poisonous flowers?

Seumas turned away from her.

Po grabbed his arm and hissed in Raiatean dialect, 'You
have to do it – they will kill us where we stand if we don't
accept their gifts.'

'I'll take a few of them with me,' snarled Seumas, looking directly at the chief.

Po said, 'Yes, they don't want that – they want to soften
us up first – but give us a chance. Do what they want until
we get the opportunity to escape.'

Seumas turned back to the chief's wife. Already the other
Raiateans were lying with the young women on woven
mats, observed silently by two hundred or so native warriors. Seumas dropped his loin cloth to show the frightened
female he was not made of fire underneath, and that there
were no hidden traps beneath the bark-cloth. She stared at
his loins, then after a few moments, lay down for him on
the mats covering the stone floor.

When he took her in his arms she was trembling violently with fear. He stroked her hair for a few moments
under the direct scrutiny of the local chief, whose face wore
a puzzled frown. Seumas knew he was supposed to take the
woman dispassionately, without any show of affection, but
he could not do it. He had to at least show he was going to

be gentle to calm her terror if he could. He could feel her heart pounding against his ribs and when it quietened a little, he lay on his back and allowed her to penetrate herself, so that she could control the act.

She was still shaking when he entered her and her musty breath told him she was close to tears. Seumas soothed her with little sounds as she moved above him. He had not intended to reach orgasm, hoping for her sake to fake it, but in the end could not help himself and clung to her for a moment, holding her close to his chest. Then it was over.

She took herself away, obviously relieved that the ordeal had not been as terrible as she had imagined, and he watched her walk with a dignified posture towards the stone house whence she and her fellow captives had come.

The chief laughed delightedly and turned and threw a ripe fruit at the woman, striking her on the buttocks, splattering the tops of her legs, and up her back, with yellow juices and flesh. She paused in her stride to wipe her legs, then without turning around continued on her journey. The warriors around her jeered and poked her with sticks, until she finally left the courtyard.

In that moment Seumas hated the chief. It took all his reserves of spiritual strength to stop himself leaping on the grinning man and throttling him with bare hands.

The darkness came a little while after that and fires were lit around the temple. Seumas could sense a certain excitement in the air. Shortly after this he could smell the delicious aroma of roasting pork and realised that a feast was about to take place. Looking out towards the fires, he could see that there were carcasses being turned on spits over glowing charcoal. Kava was brought to them in coconut shells. Seumas noticed that Manopa and his men drank slowly and he did likewise, hoping the food would come soon or he would be drunk very quickly.

The evening air was redolent in and around the temple

and it was difficult not to feel comfortable. The cicadas stopped buzzing and the crickets came out, the night choir replacing the day with hardly a pause between. Torches were lit and placed all around the tohua, bringing shadows to life. Warriors moved from place to place, carrying wooden platters and bowls.

Finally the meat was brought. It smelled delicious and despite his situation, Seumas began to salivate. He had not eaten since mid-morning and his gastric juices were swirling in his stomach, trying to deal with the raw alcohol.

'Good,' he said, as a long haunch was placed before him. 'Food at last.'

Po gave him a sidelong glance, but said nothing.

There were no drums, or nose flutes, nor any kind of accompanying music, which Seumas felt was eerie. He guessed it was probably because the missing warriors from this community were down on the shoreline getting ready to attack the fleet from the cover of the forest. They would not want their enemies warned that the island was heavily inhabited.

Seumas could see Tangiia in his mind's eye, staring at the jungle's edge from the deck of *The Scudding Cloud*, wondering what had happened to his exploratory party, trying to decide whether he was going to cast off once the morning came around, or send in a search party.

'Eat!' cried the chief.

His warriors needed no second bidding and they immediately sank their teeth into the roasted flesh.

Just as Seumas was about to bite his haunch a woman brought him a leaf-plate with two round objects on it. Seumas knew immediately they were the testicles of the slaughtered beast. He had eaten all parts of sheep, goats and pigs before and was not squeamish about any part of an animal, be it brains, eyes or even intenstines. So long as it was well cooked, he would eat it, and thank the gods with a satisfied belch.

'You are being honoured again,' said Po. 'You must salute our host.'

Seumas looked towards the chief, braced himself, then smiled and rubbed his stomach. The chief grinned back through a mouthful of food. Seumas ate the two oval pieces of meat, finding them a little crunchy. He guessed they had come from a suckling pig, since they were quite small. The chief let out a delighted yell and picked up what looked like a plate of two eyeballs and a heart. These he proceeded to eat himself.

'The final insult,' said Po, under his breath.

'What?' asked Seumas, starting on his haunch.

'To eat the eyes and heart of a rival chief. Now the dead man can't join his ancestors.'

Seumas looked doubtfully at the long haunch of crispy, reddish-brown meat in his hand.

'This?' he said.

'His forearm.' Po nudged Seumas and pointed towards the cooking fires.

There, spitted and turning over the fierce heat from the charcoal, were three bodies. Seumas stared hard at the one closest to him, lit only by the glow from the fire, and realised it was not a pig as he had thought at first glance. A pig does not have a tongue that can be extended to curl around the spit like a snake around a stick.

It was – he could see it now – an eyeless and literally gutless man. A man whose hands were trussed around the back of his neck, and the elbows tied at the front, so that his arms resembled chicken wings. His legs were straight however and tied at the ankles. The cavity where his stomach, intestines, liver and lungs had been, was stuffed to overflowing with wild herbs. In place of his eyes were sweet potatoes. The hair on his head and body had been singed to tight, crisp curls.

Seumas could see that the hardwood spit went through the middle of the ankle bonds, entered the anus and disappeared into the torso, and reappeared out of the mouth. A man never had so straight a back as that man who turned on the spit over the charcoal fire.

'In the name of the gods,' he whispered. 'Did he feel anything or was he dead before . . .?'

'Before they cooked him? Probably he was dead – killed in battle. In any case they would have sucked his brains through a straw stuck into the eye socket. It's traditional.'

'Traditional?' breathed Seumas, wonderingly, as if this was a custom preserved for its quaintness. 'Tradition is it?'

The meat on the spit was a roasted-red colour, brittle crackling on the outside, and revealing soft blisters where the skin had split and the flesh was bursting through. Under the fire, which rested on raised volcanic rocks, was a long wooden tray like a short dugout canoe. The natural fats dripped continually from the roasting man, down sizzling into the fire, some of it flowing between the rocks and reaching the tray. A large pool of liquid human lard swam in the bottom of the tray into which women regularly dipped ladles to baste the meat in its own juices.

Seumas stopped chewing. The meat which had begun to warm him from within and had started to make him feel more at ease, now turned to cold clay in his stomach. He could feel the fatty fluids trickling through him, leaking into his veins, into every corner of his body, seducing him. This was the arm of a *man* like himself. Human flesh from a human bone. Meat destined for a burial mound, stolen from the mouths of worms.

Another thought struck him. 'What about – just now?'

Po shook his head.

'You took his wife and then you ate his balls – if you ever meet him in the Otherworld I should run away, very fast.'

Seumas felt like vomiting. This was the husband of the woman he had made love to, just a short while ago, this meal. He had just eaten the bollocks of a great chief. Perhaps not so great, if he was beaten in battle? Whatever, he wished he could spit them into the face of that other chief, sitting there with a grin on his greasy chops and his mouth full of another man's eyes. It was not only an insult to the dead man, it was also an insult to a Pict, to trick him into eating human flesh.

'On the other hand,' said Po with a tasteless touch of humour, 'a castrated ghost might not be much of a warrior.'

'I feel sick,' said Seumas.

'Eat,' muttered Po. 'You have to keep up your strength.'

Implicit in that remark was the warning not to *over*eat, for they would have to make their bid for freedom that night, and overindulgence meant lethargy. Seumas did not need to be warned about eating too much human flesh. Every swallow of meat made his stomach heave. It went down like grave earth.

'You are guests of Nuku Hiva people this night,' announced the local chief, smiling. 'You stay here, yes.'

It was not a question.

Dakuwanga the shark-god swam through the ether in the spirit world around the feasting mortals. Passing through rocks and trees, under the earth, in the waters of the streams, through mountains, along valleys, Dakuwanga searched for morsels and tidbits, fragments of a human soul. His wide crescent mouth below the blunt nose was ever open, while his tiny, empty-looking eyes searched amongst the shadows for souls on their way to Milu's Cave in the Land of the Dead. Ten thousand souls had passed through Dakuwanga's gullet.

While the mortals were feeding on the cooked human flesh of their enemies, the shark-god was busy hunting down and devouring their spirits, growing strong on their sau. Dakuwanga's energy came from the spiritual potency of the sacrificed victims of cannibals. A chief's soul was better than a warrior's, but the spirit of a kahuna was the choicest dish of all. Dakuwanga, however, was the scavanger of the spirit world and would eat any wisp of a human soul lost in shadowland.

Tangaroa watched the activities of Dakuwanga with some contempt. The Great Sea-God had little time for minor gods, even with eternity on his hands. His interest was purely as an observer. Unlike Maomao, the Great Wind-God, and Hau Maringi, the God of Mist and Fog, Tangaroa had not yet chosen sides between King Tutapu and King Tangiia. However, it had to be said that he was inclined to favour Tutapu, since Tangiia had blundered in his efforts to take an idol of Tangaroa with him on his long voyage. The Great Sea-God had not made up his mind whether or not he had been insulted.

For the present, he preferred to wait and see what mettle was in the blood of these two brothers; once he had made up his mind to support one or the other, or neither, then perhaps he would intervene and sweep aside minor gods such as Dakuwanga – or perhaps not.

Tangaroa, by his very nature, was a fickle god.

3

'The gods have deserted us,' moaned Po, as the group sat on the edge of the plateau on the side furthest from the ridge by which they entered the village.

Even as he spoke though, Hine the Moon-Goddess, came sailing out from behind a cloud and began to cross the roof of voyaging. Tonight she was Hine-keha, her bright form, as opposed to Hine-uri, her dark, invisible state. She illuminated the plateau with her radiance, revealing to the captives how hopeless was their position on the mountain.

There was a sheer drop of a thousand feet before them, and behind them two hundred warriors lay sprawled over the village grounds. Sometime in the night, when it was certain all the visitors were asleep, a death squad would rise up from amongst those warriors and quickly dispatch the visitors, sending them on their way to a grateful Milu.

Seumas stared out into the blackness.

'What are we going to do, Manopa?' he asked the gloomy leader of the expedition.

The big man put his head in his hands. Manopa was a good warrior, an exceptional fighter, and he was an intelligent man – but he was no lateral thinker. His plans and schemes were always straightforward, based on experience and knowledge of other well-tried plans and schemes. He had no answer for a highly unusual situation, except to attack his captors head on and try to reach the ridge without being cut down, a task he knew to be impossible, given the number of enemies out there.

'I don't know,' he admitted. Then he asked hopefully, 'Has anyone else got any ideas?'

No one answered. Po looked around him in panic.

'Someone must have a plan,' he said. 'Someone's got to have a plan.'

Silence. And more silence. Then Seumas stirred.

'I have,' he said, 'but it won't save you lot.'

Manopa said, 'You don't need to save yourself – they're going to let you live anyway, *demon*.'

'What sort of life would it be and for how long?' snorted Seumas. 'They'll put me in a cage until they need me, and when they realise I can't do magic, they'll spit me and roast me, like that poor bastard we ate tonight.'

Po frowned. 'How would you save yourself then?'

Seumas pointed to the edge of the plateau. 'I could climb down there and probably collect birds' eggs on the way.'

Manopa snorted. 'You couldn't climb down a face that sheer – you'd drop off before you got twenty feet.'

The Raiateans could shin up palm trees, scramble up steep tracks, balance on aerial walkways, but they were not good at straight rock-climbing on sheer faces, having little need for such skills on their home island.

Po contradicted his leader. 'He's right, Manopa. He can do it. When we found him, in the Land-of-Mists, he was climbing a cliff face just as sharp as this one. He was collecting wild seabirds from their nests, and the birds were attacking him too.'

'He fell off, didn't he?' snapped Manopa.

'No,' Po corrected Manopa, 'the woman Dorcha fell and *he* tried to catch her as she passed him. She broke his hold with her weight. I think he *could* climb down there.'

'Easily,' Seumas said.

'Well, then, save yourself,' muttered Manopa. The other men agreed, telling him to go quickly, while there was time. Seumas shook his head.

'I have a better idea – one which might save us all – if you have the courage for it.'

Po said, 'Tell us, quickly.'

'Well, it means you following me, putting your hands where my hands have been, copying my body movements, putting your feet in the cracks where my feet have been. If you follow me exactly, you should be able to make the climb.'

Po nodded, enthusiastically. 'I'm willing to chance it. If I fall it can't be any worse than having my skull crushed like a coconut and then being toasted.'

Manopa sighed and shook his head. 'There's a problem you haven't foreseen, goblin. You have to go down the cliff face first, with us following. How can we watch for your hand and foot holds, without falling off? It's impossible.'

'That's why we go *up*, instead of down.'

Manopa, Po and the other men looked up, to see the great hook of rock curving above the plateau, casting its black, wicked-looking shadow over the village. It was like some great fishing lure of the gods, Maui's perhaps, when he angled in the great empty ocean at the beginning of time, using his own blood for bait, and pulled up Oceania's islands, one by one.

'Up?' repeated Manopa, puzzled.

'Yes, up. If we throw a loin cloth over the edge here, so that it catches on a shrub down below, they'll think we climbed down. They'll go charging off over the ridge to reach the bottom of the cliff before we do. Then we'll come down and fight our way through whoever's been left here.'

One of the other men nodded. 'He's right, if we go up we can watch where he puts his hands and feet.'

'But we've got to come down again,' grumbled Manopa, short-sightedly. 'How do we get down? Fall?'

'We use some of those vines up on the crest, to lower ourselves,' Seumas said. 'We can't lower ourselves down a thousand-foot cliff, but we can from a hundred or so feet. Are you for it, or not?'

Manopa took one last look at the climb and said, 'Let's go.'

They waited until Hine-keha went behind another cloud and the captives could not easily be seen from the village. Then Manopa took off his loin cloth and threw it over the edge of the cliff. It floated out and disappeared into the blackness. 'Acchhh,' he said, disgustedly. He then snatched another man's garment and knotted a stone in its corner, before dropping it very carefully on to a shrub some ten feet below the lip. 'That should do it,' he said. 'Now climb, goblin.'

Seumas began scaling the curve of the hook. He put to good use the shrubs and other vegetation, including vines that ran down the steep face. He was wary of relying *too* much on the roots and stems of bushes, for though they clung tenaciously to the surface of the cliff, there was often not a great deal of surface soil and their grip did not allow for the weight of a man. At first he went too quickly for Po, directly behind him, even though he felt he was climbing at an extremely slow pace. His head was a little groggy still, from the effects of the kava juice, but he was not drunk. The knowledge that death was only a small misjudgment away was a sobering influence on him, as it must have been on all the climbers there.

Each man followed the movements of the man before him and in this way the group ascended the massive crag. The path of the climb took Seumas not only upwards, but to the side of the great hook as well, until the party were actually over a drop which fell into the fathomless valley below. He had no choice, for the lay of the climb was in that direction.

As the fickle gods would have it, the wind for which

they had been waiting many days now, sprang to life while they were desperately clinging to a piece of rock.

The man behind Po was the young priest who had stolen the God of Hope. He was no climber at all and made the mistake of looking down, when he should have been concentrating on watching where Po put his hand. In consequence, he chose the wrong hold, which crumbled under his grip. He fell out and backwards, into the void, clipping the naked Manopa behind the ear with his heel as he passed.

Manopa managed to hold on, but the falling man dropped away out of sight, only the faintest sound coming back to the group when his body hit the bottom. To his eternal credit the ill-fated Raiatean priest did not cry out on his descent to his death, knowing that to do so might mean the discovery of the climbers.

Po, trembling with fright, had to touch Seumas on the ankle to signal a stop. Po needed to recover his composure. For a few moments the shaken fisherman flattened himself against the rock, feeling giddy and shivering from head to toe, wishing he were on flat ground. The others below him did the same, glad for a respite, horrified when they thought of their position as insects halfway up one of the walls of the world.

Po then felt a tap on his head and knew he had to go on. He gritted his teeth and, looking up, continued the climb. Eventually, after what seemed more than a lifetime, the group reached a narrow ledge. There they huddled, waiting for events to unfold below them.

Seumas went on, further up, to collect a vine growing from the summit of the hook. He would have to dig it out by the roots with his bare hands, having no knife with him. He found a flat stone to use as a shovel and hacked away as quietly as he could at the base of the vine, finally loosening it enough to be able to wrench it free from its moorings.

*

There was a shout from below, which woke Seumas with a start. He had been dozing, his head against another man's shoulder. Their absence had been detected by the warriors sent to kill them. Men were running around with flaming torches now, looking in all the crevices, inside hollows, behind boulders. Then the loin cloth was found and the discovery was greeted with great excitement. Several lighted brands were thrown over the cliff, in order to look down below. One of the warriors stated that he thought he could see a body down in the valley.

There was a general call to arms then, with warriors rousing each other from their beds. Looking over the edge of the hook, Seumas could see the chief directing operations, sending his troops out to search for the missing guests. When the area of the plateau revealed nothing, the warriors began flowing along the ridge, their torches streaming like living fire balls.

The chief remained in the village, with a dozen or so of his men, while the rest of them crossed the ridge.

Seumas wrapped the end of the vine around a rock and held it there with his own hands.

'Down,' he murmured to Manopa.

The first man shinned down the vine until he was level with the plateau but still over the big drop, then he kicked out sideways, swinging himself like a pendulum, until he was over the lip of the plateau, when he let go and rolled. One by one the Raiateans went safely down the long vine, until there was only Manopa to go.

'I'm very heavy,' he warned.

'The rock's taking the strain,' said Seumas.

Manopa began climbing down the vine when Seumas suddenly noticed that the constant swinging had frayed the vine. It was too late to stop Manopa, who was almost at the bottom.

'God of Vines, whoever the hell you are,' growled Seumas, 'don't let this one break . . .'

He held his breath as the bulky Manopa began kicking awkwardly at a projection, trying to get himself within reach of the plateau. The other men were holding hands, so that one of them was reaching out over the lip, trying to catch Manopa as he struggled to get to them. Manopa spun precariously on the end of the vine, his face white with fear and exertion. He managed to stop the spin, but was still dangling helplessly.

Seumas took the vine in both hands, below the frayed part, and began swinging the man below. It took every ounce of strength in his body, but gradually the swings became longer and longer, until finally Po managed to grab Manopa's hand in a double-wrist grip. Manopa instantly and rather stupidly let go of the vine and almost dragged Po to his death. The chain of men held, however, and at last Manopa crawled over the lip of the plateau and lay panting in the dust.

The whole drama had been enacted in complete silence.

After a short rest, to allow the strength back into his arms, Seumas scuttled down to join the group.

'I prayed to the God of Vines for him,' he whispered to Po.

'What God of Vines?' asked Po. 'There isn't one.'

'Well, there should be – you've got a god for everything else – even breadfruit.'

The group, now depleted by one, crept off the rock shelf and back into the village. They armed themselves with whatever they could find: rocks, hunks of firewood, a fishing net, an adze left outside a hut. The remainder of the local warriors were gathered in the tohua, sitting on the temple floor, no doubt awaiting news from the world below the plateau. Manopa and his men attacked quickly and silently, throwing the net over the greater part of the assembly and proceeding to club them senseless while they fought with the folds.

A warrior not caught by the net came at Seumas

shouting oaths and wielding a wahaika club. Seumas flung a stone, catching the man in the throat, then followed up with a kick to the groin. The warrior was very strong and stayed on his feet, while Seumas grappled with him for possession of the club. Had he been fighting a normal man, the warrior might have won the struggle, but he paused to stare into Seumas's face, and realised his eyes were locked with those of a demon. The thought froze his muscles for a few moments, long enough for Seumas to wrest the club from his hand and strike him down.

With the wahaika club in his fist, Seumas began laying about him in a frenzy of blood lust. The madness of hand-to-hand combat was again upon him. There was only one way to survive in the midst of a battle, hacking it out amongst desperate bodies, and that was to fight in a demented and frenetic manner, to throw all sanity to the winds, to go berserk and put the fear of death in those enemies around you. To strike a man with madness in your eyes, and strike him again and again and again, until his legs went from under him and he disappeared from sight, down amongst the legs of hale warriors, to the ground below.

It had been a long while since Seumas had been in a battle, even a skirmish, and it recalled those times in his youth when clan met clan on Albainn's highlands, leaving the burns plugged with bloody corpses and the air reeking with the sweet smell of putrid flesh. Then there had been men with him, wearing the same cloth, bearing the same tattoos, yelling the same war cries. Then there had been the aroma of peat hags in his nostrils, a cold wind riffling his wolfskin cloak. Then there had been the prospect of a roast goat and hot mead to follow, sitting around the fire with men of his own stamp, his own culture, petting the dogs and scraping the gore from deerskin boots.

Now, at his side was another warrior, Manopa, who might have been his highland brother, blood of his blood, helping him to protect their family and glen from invading hordes of wild coastal tribes. Manopa was, Seumas quickly learned, a brilliant hand-to-hand fighter. The pair of them felled five warriors between them, while Po and the others dispatched and wounded the remainder, all except for one, the enemy chief.

The chief was a savage and skilful warrior, who though he had not claimed any lives from the group, had seriously wounded one man, and had damaged Po's left shoulder with a blow of his nokonoko kotiate club. The club was big and heavy, difficult to wield in a tight space, and the chief was now retreating into a corner of the courtyard.

Women now emerged from the houses near by and began wailing when they saw the dead bodies on the stone flags of the temple. Some of them rushed towards the group, stooping to pick up stones to throw. The chief, who was now in danger of being felled, took this opportunity to turn and run towards the ridge.

'Leave him to me,' said Manopa, picking up a javelin.

'No,' growled Seumas, snatching the weapon, 'that bastard humiliated me. He's mine.'

Seumas took three long strides and launched the javelin through the moonlit air. It flew silently towards the running man, falling short by several lengths. Manopa grunted.

'Now it's my turn,' he said, finding a feather-fletched spear amongst the array of weapons on the ground.

Manopa took a much longer run and the spear left his hand and hissed through the night. It arced beautifully, gracefully sweeping down towards its running target. The barbed point struck the fleeing chief just below the left shoulder blade and penetrated right through his body.

The chief turned with a surprised look on his face. His nokonoko-wood club, with its ugly, bas-relief carving of Oro on its head, dropped from his fingers. He glanced down, at the foot or so of spearpoint protruding from his chest, as if wondering what it was doing there. Then he

looked up with an annoyed expression at Manopa, as if
about to chastise a child for doing something naughty.
Finally his muscles sagged and he slipped sideways and fell
down the mountain slope, the spear catching on a rock
halfway to the bottom and snapping in two pieces.

'Good throw,' said Seumas, grudgingly. 'I missed my
footing, otherwise . . .'

Manopa said, disparagingly, 'Yes, otherwise you would
have got him – we all know that.'

The stones from the angry women were raining down on
them now, some of them as large as eggs, and there was a
serious danger of injury.

'Let's get out of here,' said Po, who was supporting the
wounded man. 'Now.'

Manopa took the limp man from Po and slung him over
his broad right shoulder. Then he ran towards the ridge, as
if carrying a sack of feathers. Seumas followed, wondering
again at the strength of Tangiia's second-in-command,
admiring it, envying it. Manopa was a good man to have if
you were outnumbered in battle.

As Seumas joined the other men on the ridge, and began
running across it, again he was mindful of the battles in the
highlands of Albainn: the hasty retreats, the running
advances, the speedy movements from glen to mountain to
glen. Even now, crossing this ridge, he recalled the scents of
the heather and pine, though the night air was actually carrying much more cloying perfumes of frangipani and
flowering ginger.

In the light from Hine-kena's brilliant sails, the group
found their way down the mountain tracks to the waterfall.
There they rested and drank, unconcerned for the moment
by the sacred nature of the pool, or the consequences of
annoying a local Tiki. The gourds they had dropped that
afternoon were still lying on the grasses around the glade
and they gathered these up and filled them under the falls.

Then they collected their weapons, slung the full, roped-

together gourds around their necks, and set off down the
last track to the shoreline below. They moved warily now,
knowing there were many enemy warriors in the forest.

They reached the beach without meeting any local warriors, where Manopa divested himself of his load. To their
dismay the pahi canoes were moored beyond the reef now,
probably using sea anchors. Tangiia had either already had
a tussle with the islanders, or he was being extra cautious.

'The able men have to swim out there and tell them we
have a wounded man back here on the beach,' said
Manopa. 'I'll stay with him.'

Seumas said, 'No, I should be the one to stay with him –
you're all better swimmers than I am.'

Manopa stared Seumas in the eyes, then nodded and
said, 'You're right.'

Without another word Manopa slipped into the water,
Po and the last fit man following, and they quietly swam
out into the lagoon. When they were halfway to the pahi
there was a shout from the rainforest. They could be seen in
the moonlight. Seumas hunched down in the foliage with
the wounded man, who was still unconscious, and made
ready to put a hand over the man's mouth in case he came
round and made a noise doing so.

A war canoe was launched from farther around the bay.
Seumas could see the island's warriors in their war finery:
the feathered helmets, the cloaks, the effigies of Oro held
up high by yelling priests, the decorated war clubs.

Manopa and the others were striking out for the pahi
now, and it looked as if they would reach it before the war
canoe caught up with them. More war canoes were launched
and the drums started pounding. By the time Manopa was
pulling himself up on to the deck of *The Scudding Cloud*,
there were thirty war canoes heading towards the Raiatean
fleet and more being launched all the time. The Raiateans
would be overwhelmed if they did not put to sea, which
Seumas was both glad and unhappy to see them do.

The crab-claw sails were raised in the wind, men got behind their paddles, and the large ocean-going canoes pulled away from the islands, heading out into the deep ocean. The war canoes were much smaller vessels and they had little hope of catching the Raiateans. Soon the large crab-claws dipped down over the moonlit horizon. The war canoes drifted to a standstill, turned slowly, and came back to the island, the drums still beating and the warriors still primed for a battle which was now out of reach.

When the war canoes reached the shore, the excited warriors leapt from them and into the rainforest, running off the pent-up energy which they had been storing for the fight. They were high on adrenaline and this vigour had to be expended in some way, now there was to be no killing.

There would be both relief and frustration in each of them. One half of their emotions would be telling them it was a good thing, they did not have to die for their king; the other half would be disappointed that they had not been given the chance to prove their worth to these intruders who had dared to step foot on their sacred isle without so much as a gift for their king.

Seumas remained hidden under the foliage that overlapped the shoreline like a fringe. There was a green tunnel there, between bank and water's edge, and it was this that hid the two men from sight. Seumas hugged the wounded man, praying he would not start raving in his illness.

Soon, however, it did not matter how much noise they made because on the plateau above a frenzy of hedonistic dancing began, with the drums thundering under the roof of voyaging, and whistles and flutes screaming into the night. There would be triumphant feasting in the villages, a loud mourning for the dead, an overindulgence in just about all bodily pleasures. The warriors had driven off an invasion force and they would be full of self-congratulations and arrogance.

The wounded man, whose name was Wakana, came to

consciousness at last in Seumas's arms.

'Where are the others?' he asked, looking up into Seumas's face. 'Where are *we*?'

'We're on the beach,' Seumas replied. 'Manopa and the others had to swim for the canoes – the whole fleet was chased over the horizon. I'm afraid we've been abandoned.'

Wakana was a young virgin whom Seumas had seen treading the fermented bread-fruit in the pulping enclosures on Raiatea. Apart from this rather unexceptional skill performed only by those young men whose purity was unquestioned, Seumas knew nothing about the youth. He did not even know if the boy could swim; there were one or two Oceanians who could not.

'We've got to get out of here,' Seumas told him. 'How about stealing one of those war canoes moored out in the lagoon? Can you swim that far?'

Wakana looked at him in disgust. 'Of course I can swim!' he began to get to his feet, then reeled over, clearly still giddy from his head wound.

'You can swim,' muttered Seumas, 'but can you *walk*?'

The boy passed out again for a few minutes and Seumas laid him down on the sand and crept along the green tunnel, wondering if he could steal a canoe by himself. He couldn't see any guards from where he was crawling, but that didn't mean there weren't any. They might be posted further up the hill. However, their attention would not be fully on their job, he knew, because of the noise coming from the villages.

Then, when he was a short way from where he had left Wakana, he heard the soft plashing of a paddle. At first he thought he might be hearing waves on the shore, or some animal or fish in the shallows, but when he concentrated he could fit a definite rhythm to sounds. They were indeed paddle strokes.

Seumas was certain there was a war canoe sneaking along the shore.

He lay flat on his stomach and regulated his breathing. Hermit crabs scuttled over his body. The ripples from the lagoon reached out, stroking his prone form. The *thump, thump, thump,* of the drums up in the village vibrated through him. He turned very slowly and began crawling back, returning head first along the tunnel of vegetation, to where he had left Wakana. When he reached the spot where he had left the youth, he found it empty. Wakana's body was gone.

Had the boy woken and, finding himself alone, crawled off somewhere else?

Or, the more likely thing was, given that Seumas had heard a canoe, he had been discovered and hauled away.

The sound of the paddles again, dipping softly into the warm shallows of the lagoon.

Seumas found his club in the sand and made ready to use it. If he was going to die he was not going to die *easily.* He shuddered as he thought that in perhaps a few hours time he might be a meal for laughing warriors, who would pick through the flesh between his toes with their teeth, swallow his eyes whole with relish, and suck the cooked brains from his upturned skull through straws. It was an ugly thought that made his heart race with revulsion, as he wondered whether his degraded spirit would be aware of what was happening to his body, and if he would have to be a silent witness to his own defilement.

'Goblin?'

A quiet voice drifted to him from the water.

'Goblin? Are you there?'

Seumas parted the leaves of the tunnel to see Manopa sitting in a small dugout canoe. Hunched near him, was Wakana. Relief swept through the Pict. Manopa had returned for him.

'Here!' he hissed, then slipped into the water and waded out to the canoe.

'Quickly,' Manopa said.

Seumas climbed into the dugout and soon they were shooting towards the open sea.

Manopa kept his eyes on a kaveinga, a star path, which Seumas knew would lead them to where the fleet was moored with sea anchors. Wakana was still in no condition to paddle, but Seumas did his bit, driving the dugout through the water, letting Manopa fathom the way. Finally they came to a place where there was a sweet fragrance in the air; a wide pool of silvery-grey ambergris lay on the ocean, glinting in the moonlight. In the middle of this waxy substance lay the three pahi canoes.

King Tangiia was there on the deck of *The Scudding Cloud* and he helped to drag the groggy Wakana on to the deck. The boy was then taken off by Princess Kula, presumably to be administered medicine of some kind. Manopa and Seumas climbed out of the dugout unassisted, then the small canoe was taken on board the large one. Dirk was there to greet Seumas. The dog accepted a heavy pat as an acknowledgement and whined with pleasure.

Tangiia came forward and slapped Manopa on the shoulders.

'Good – no wounds?'

'None,' grunted Manopa. 'Now I must take command of my vessel.'

'You're exhausted,' said Seumas, who was just about all in himself. 'Rest first, then drink with me. You saved my life – I have to give you my bond.'

'Give it to someone else, goblin,' growled Manopa. 'I went back for the boy, not for you.'

Seumas stared at the big warrior and then said, 'It doesn't matter – you came back. I need to thank you. You have to give me that chance to pledge my life to you.'

'Go pledge it to the fish,' said Manopa.

Tangiia's captain then walked over the deck, to the far hull where *The Royal Palm* was lashed alongside. Soon Manopa had ordered his pahi untied from Tangiia's and the two vessels drifted apart. Seumas looked bleakly at Tangiia.

'He doesn't mean it,' said the navigator king.

'Yes he does.'

Tangiia shrugged. 'All right, he does – but he would have still come back for you, if Wakana had been with you or not. He would have gone back for a pet bird.'

'That's a comforting thought,' said Seumas, drily. He promised himself that he would pay Manopa back in full, at the earliest opportunity, so that he would not feel beholden to the chief for longer than necessary. It was humiliating to be saved and then rejected by the saviour. Manopa had risked his life for a goblin; well then the goblin would do the same, when the time came, and their lines could diverge again.

Seumas nodded to where Kula was ministering to Wakana.

'I see you have your friend on board,' he smiled.

Tangiia shot a look at the Pict, to ascertain whether or not he was being mocked, and when he was satisfied the remark was purely conversational, he said, 'That's another story, my friend, for a long, hot day. In the meantime, I understand you proved yourself out there. Manopa says you saved all their lives, with your climb up the rock. You owe him nothing.'

'It's true I saved them all,' said Seumas, considering this remark. 'Without my climbing skills every single man of us would have been murdered. I'm surprised Manopa gave me credit, and I thank him for it, but the other thing is a one-to-one. I helped the group I was part of to survive, while he alone came back to lift me from the beach. I do owe him.'

'If you do, you do – but don't lose any sleep over it. We all owe something to someone. By the way, Boy-girl's been weeping. She thought you were dead.'

Seumas groaned. 'Does she know I'm safe now?'

'I signalled *The Volcano Flower* to that effect.'

The conversation ended there, for Tangiia's navigational talents were needed by his helmsman. The king went aft to issue instructions, while Seumas sank into a deep sleep on the deck, his dreams uncomfortably damp, as Dirk lay beside him licking the salt sweat from his tattooed body and growling at anyone who came near his resting master.

PART FOUR

Isle of Rapacious Women

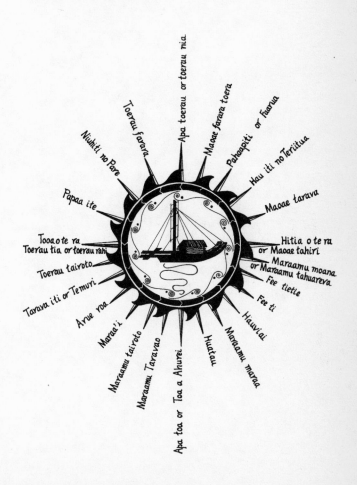

1

The Great Wind-God Maomao and the Great Sea-God Tangaroa had never been on good terms with one another. One of the reasons for this was because, by his very nature, Maomao found it necessary to stride about on his brother's back, and even flay him on occasion. These were circumstances under which Tangaroa felt humiliated and which infuriated him. There was no means by which Tangaroa could get his own back; the sea cannot punish the wind in any way. So any small opportunity for crossing his brother was swiftly seized by the Great Sea-God.

Maui, that puffed-up ancient hero of the Oceanian race, had been chattering in the Land of the Dead, about King Tangiia.

'He reminds me of myself,' said hero Maui. 'I was once a great voyager of the oceans, unafraid of men or gods, sailing into the unknown in my canoe. I prevailed because I was cunning and courageous, unconcerned by what the gods might fling at me, taking all in my stride on my passage through life . . .'

Tangaroa, who had little time for Maui whose trick of fishing-up islands had robbed the Great Sea-God of some of his territory, listened to this prattle with growing interest. Tangaroa was aware that King Tangiia was receiving support from the Great Wind-God and he saw a way of getting some of his own back, by appearing to support Maomao, but subtly putting obstacles in the course of the Raiatean fleet. After all, Tangiia had made no sacrifices to Tangaroa, even preferring to take a minor god, the God of Hope, as the fleet's guardian, rather than Tangaroa himself.

As for the atua Maui, Tangaroa had never forgiven the ancient hero for catching the sun, Ra, in a net of ropes and beating him with a stick. Maui had been displeased by the shortness of the hours of light and at first had tried to net Ra in some dry ropes, which the fiery body easily burned through. The next time Maui used a trick of wetting the ropes with seawater and this time Ra had been entangled and was soundly thrashed by Maui. 'Why do you flog Tama Nui-te-ra?' cried the sun, using the full name given to him by Rangi. 'What have I done to you?'

Maui said, 'Nothing, but you must promise to go more slowly over the sky to lengthen our days.' Ra agreed, but forever bore a grudge against Tangaroa for allowing Maui to use his water to wet the net of ropes, a thing Tangaroa had been unable to prevent, not having much control over the precocious Maui.

So, all things taken into consideration, Tangaroa was not inclined to help Tangiia, and in fact was on the side of Tutapu and Hau Maringi, Lord of the Mist and Fog. While Maomao was sending Tangiia's fleet a brisk wind to blow him to the island of Tahiti, Tangaroa sent an adaro to the fleet, to draw it off its present true course.

King Tangiia was on deck one morning when the waves were rolling hills that swept under the pahi. He could see the sails of the other two canoes rising and falling behind his own vessel, disappearing on occasion into a wide trough, then rising up again to tower above him on the crest of a tall wave. The people on their decks were like busy ants, continually adjusting and readjusting the sheets.

Tangiia was running before the wind Maraamu-tairoto on the wind flower, trusting to Maomao to fill the crab-claw sails and push the fleet in the direction of its true destiny. He had been noting the star paths and had fixed the present position of the craft under a fanakenga star. Then the dawn had come up and washed Rangi's face clean of kaveinga and fanakenga.

Around the king the crew and passengers were busy at their early morning tasks: the ever-present, always-busy bailers were rhythmically shovelling water from the hulls; the women were baking yams, cutting breadfruit, grating coconut, preparing the breakfast; the children were waking from a good sleep, salt-encrusted, bleary-eyed; the fisher-folk were preparing hooks with bait to trail alongside the craft; the navigators were noting the currents, the temper-ature of the water with their hands, the direction of the wind, the shape of the waves, the flight paths of different birds of the air.

Tangiia's mind was not on his people however, nor on navigation, but on the fact that Kula refused to speak to him, now that she had chastised him bitterly for abducting her and robbing his brother of his bride-to-be.

He stared down at himself, wondering why Kula did not love him. His body, he saw, was beautiful. The muscles were not too pronounced as to be knotted, but were like flat stones under his soft, brown skin. His hair he knew to be smooth and touchable, hanging like a black curtain around his broad shoulders. His feet and hands were well proportioned, both in themselves and relative to his torso and limbs. His face was pleasant to view, having no ugly blemishes or prominent features, such as a large nose. His eyes, he had been told, were like liquefied mud of the deepest brown.

And as well as all these handsome characteristics, he was a king!

Why, any other woman would have sold her father to

cannibals if it meant marrying such a youth.

'Perhaps it's my own self she does not like?' he sighed. 'My disposition and qualities of spirit?'

'What's that?' asked Kikamana, standing near to him.

Tangiia suddenly turned and looked at the Farseeing-virgin, an idea coming into his young head.

'Kikamana,' he said, 'has there been any instance where a woman has not loved a man, or indeed the other way around, yet the unloved has managed to turn the love of the unlover?'

'There is a story of a boy who invented a love potion,' confirmed Kikamana. 'He made the concoction from aromatic leaves and it boiled over and some fell into the mouth of his sleeping cousin. When she woke she went rushing down to the surf in which he was swimming and insisted he make love to her. They were both found dead in the cave of Bokairawata with the herb of mint growing all around them.'

'Is mint one of the ingredients of the love potion – do you know the other ingredients?' asked Tangiia, eagerly.

'Yes,' replied his high priestess, 'but we don't have them on board.'

'The very next island we see, I shall stop and pick the necessary aromatic leaves for you. But this must be our secret, Kikamana, as I'm sure you know who I shall want to drink the potion.'

Kikamana said she did, but warned Tangiia that meddling with such things as love potions and love spells nearly always ended in a disaster of some kind. Tangiia was desperate though. He had to have the princess. His heart ached for her, his loins ached for her, his head ached for her. If she continued to reject him, he told Kikamana, he might even have to end his own life, for he was so sunk in spirits as to contemplate suicide.

Not long after this Tangiia was staring moodily at the kava-dark sea, tired from lack of sleep and dispirited by his lack of progress with Princess Kula. It was early morning, the watch were tired and inattentive. Because they were running before the wind there was little to do except gaze at the sea and sky. Tangiia had his eyes fixed on a patch of ocean just in front of the craft. A ripple appeared, like a sea rip, and then something dark mingled with churning foam. There was a shape of a being the colour of seaweed, moving in an arc.

Tangiia watched as a creature broke the surface, rolling like a whale, though this was a much smaller beast. His eyes opened wide, for though the wavetops were misty with flying spray and occasionally frothed white, thus impairing his vision, it seemed to him that the creature was a man. A man, but not like any other the king had seen. The swimmer seemed less fish than human, but it owned definite features which suited aquatic conditions more than life on land.

Tangiia walked to the bows of the canoe to take a keener look.

The man-shaped creature had tailfins on his feet, quite visible to Tangiia when they broke the surface, and there were slits like gills on the back of his head, behind his ears. There was a shark's fin on his back, cutting the water whenever he slid across the surface, and on his head was a projection like the spike of a swordfish or narwhal. The man-fish turned on his back, pointed in a direction at a sharp angle to the course taken by the pahi, and seemed to beckon Tangiia to follow him.

The king found his voice at last.

'Look at that!' he cried. 'Can you see?'

His shout seemed to frighten the creature, which dived deeper immediately.

The helmsman turned the vessel, crying, 'Is it a log? Are we about to strike something?'

'No, no,' cried Tangiia, excitedly, pointing at the empty ocean, which flicked and danced before his eyes. 'There was a creature like a man! A man-fish!'

The mariner, who was an old seafarer, was familiar with Kuku Lau's tricks and thought the king was seeing things.

'Perhaps it was a dugong?' said the helmsman. 'They look very much like women, if you just catch a fleeting glance.'

The other members of the watch began to gather around the king now, as well as adults and children waking from their sleep. They all stared at the spot where Tangiia was pointing, seeing nothing but the waves. Then a fin broke the surface and some people shouted, 'There! There!'

'A porpoise,' said one of the mariners. 'Haven't you see a porpoise before?'

'That was not the beast I saw,' cried the king, angrily. 'I saw another creature, a man-fish I tell you.' He described what he had seen.

Makka-te came forward then. 'What you have described,' he told Tangiia, 'is an adaro – a creature of the gods.'

Tangiia was in a fever of excitement now. 'We must go after this marvellous beast. It asked me to follow it and went that way . . .'

Tangiia pointed a direction about three counts on the wind flower away from the present direction of the breeze.

Kikamana, who had now come forward, said, 'Is this wise, to change our course, King Tangiia? Maomao has sent us this wind. It has the blessing of Hine-tu-whenua. We should stay on our present course and not become diverted by strange sights that may prove to be nothing more than a fleck in your eye.'

'It was not a fleck in my eye, it was a wonderful creature. If you had seen it, you would agree with me. It is my decision that we follow this man-fish. I'm sure we're being shown the true path for our vessels. Signal to Manopa and Po that we're changing course . . . there! There it is again!'

As the king pointed to the adaro, which had again briefly broken the surface, all the attention had been on him.

When the heads turned, the man-fish was almost gone again, only the tip of his back-fin visible, and the flick of one fin from his feet.

'I saw *something*,' said Makka-te. 'Perhaps a shark?'

'It was the *adaro*,' cried Tangiia, frustrated almost beyond endurance. Then in a firm voice which brooked no opposition, he added, 'I want a watch kept in the bows with eyes for that creature alone. Every sighting must be reported to me in detail. I will prove to everyone here that I'm not mad – the man-fish is out there and we're going to follow it.'

Seumas was awake by this time and he watched in worried puzzlement as *The Scudding Cloud* altered course. He rose from his rest with Dirk at his heels, to speak with Kikamana, the Far-seeing virgin.

'It seems to me,' said Seumas, 'the king was out of his head for a while. Has he been drinking seawater?' They both stared at Tangiia, whose eyes were still fixed on the surface of the water ahead. 'I mean, he wasn't exactly raving, but he wasn't far off either. Does he know what he's doing?'

'He is the navigator,' Kikamana said. 'We must trust to his judgement for the time being, until he's proved to be wrong. At least this has taken his mind off his problem with Princess Kula.'

'Where is she?'

'Still tending the wounds of that young virgin who was wounded at Nuku Hiva Island.'

Seumas raised his eyebrows. 'She hasn't fallen for him – the youth I mean?'

Kikamana shook her head. 'No, I'm sure she hasn't. She still sees her place as being with Tutapu. I think she believes King Tutapu will follow us and take her home to Raiatea. Until that happens, or something convinces her that Tutapu is not coming for her, she'll remain a virgin herself.'

*

The night was sultry. The crab-claw sail puffed and died, puffed and died, as if it were gently breathing. The wind had dropped to a series of delicate cross-breezes. Tangiia caught a scent of something in the air, very faint, and needed confirmation. He called for Kaho, the Blind Navigator, and asked him if he could smell land.

Kaho sniffed the air and said that he could. 'Though in what direction it lies, I can't tell. The wind is dancing this way and that, tonight.'

'Fetch me a young pig,' Tangiia said to Po'oi, as always standing by ready to assist his sightless father. 'But keep things quiet. I don't want the whole vessel roused.'

Seumas, on hearing this, rose from his bed and went to stand with Tangiia. The king was much calmer now than he had been two mornings ago when he claimed to have spotted the adaro. Since then Tangiia kept telling others he was constantly sighting the wonderful man-fish, but no one else on board caught any more than a glimpse of fin breaking the surface of the sea, or a tip of a sawfish or swordfish horn.

However, Tangiia was no longer feverish, but very composed and deliberate in his efforts to stalk the creature he claimed was an adaro.

'Something new happening?' asked Seumas, quietly.

'There's an island out there somewhere,' Tangiia replied. 'I'm just about to find out in which direction it lies.'

Tangiia then ordered the sails to be lowered and the duty watch to take to the paddles. One of the crew signalled with a flaming torch to the following pahi that they were changing course. He received an acknowledgement.

At that moment Po'oi arrived with the pig, which Tangiia immediately picked up and tossed into the water. The animal made a splash, bobbed to the surface, and began swimming away from the vessel.

'Follow the pig,' Tangiia murmured to his helmsman. He then explained to Seumas, 'A pig's sense of smell is superior to ours – it will always swim towards the nearest land.'

'A costly navigational aid,' said Seumas.

'Not at all. When we land on the island the pig will be there and it'll only be a matter of retrieving it. You still have a lot to learn, Seumas, about us Oceanians.'

'I can believe that.'

A while after following the swimming pig, whose snout remained like a short breathing-tube above the surface, Seumas could hear breakers on a reef or beach. Tangiia ordered soundings to be taken, until the shallowness of the water was such that they could go no further. He then commanded that the sea anchors be dropped. Then he lowered a dugout into the water and indicated that Kikamana should join him in it. She obeyed without question, and Seumas had the feeling that she knew what all this was about.

'Don't you want to take some warriors?' asked Seumas, as the dugout began to push off. 'There may be hostile people on that island. Remember Nuku Hiva?'

'This island is too small to support people,' said Tangiia. 'We're going for some . . . fruit.'

'How do you know it's too small? You haven't seen it.'

Tangiia shook his head. 'I told you, you have a lot to learn. I have someone else's memory of this place,' he gestured at the ocean. 'Kupe has been here. He once told me about this part of the ocean – I can recognise features in the waves, the swell, and the sound of that reef. Do you hear it? All reefs sound different, Seumas. Islands have their own particular aroma too. I heard the sound of a bird – a particular bird. This is an island Kupe told me about, when I was twelve years of age. Anyway, there are no fires.'

'We didn't see fires on Nuku Hiva.'

'That was different.' With this unsatisfactory explanation left hanging in the air, the young king pushed off from the side of *The Scudding Cloud* with his paddle and soon all Seumas could see was the dark water all around.

The darkness swiftly gave way to the morning light and soon a flat island, not much more than a vegetated sandbar, appeared out of the grey dawn. The three pahi were anchored in pale-green water not far from the slow spread of the beach. By the time the whole fleet was awake, Tangiia and Kikamana were back, the dugout laden with coconuts and fruits, the pig sitting snugly in the bows and not at all put out by his trip.

After Tangiia had taken the opportunity to speak with his other two captains the dugout was taken on board again. They set sail before the sun became too hot. The wind was still not as strong as it had been until Tangiia had seen the adaro, but it was enough to sideswipe the vessels and keep them moving over the water, *The Scudding Cloud* still obsessively following in the wake of the marvellous man-fish which Tangiia said he saw from time to time.

Kieto had told Seumas that an adaro, apart from swimming in *water*, could also travel through the sky by crossing over rainbows.

'If they become angry with you,' he told the sceptical Pict, 'they shoot poisonous flying fish at you.'

'I'll remember not to anger one,' replied Seumas.

Later the Albannach went to King Tangiia and said, 'You didn't go to that island just for fruit – you could have sent some men and women for that – why did you go?'

Tangiia, who was squatting on the front of the deck, transfixed as usual, indicated that Seumas should sit beside him. The Pict, covered from ankles to shoulders in bark-cloth to protect his skin from the sun, his face shining with vegetable oil, squatted down easily next to the royal Raiatean. There was, as always a fine spray lifting from the water and drenching the deck of *The Scudding Cloud*, wetting everything at leg-level.

Tangiia whispered, 'I tell you this on pain of death if you betray me . . .'

Seumas nodded, wondering if he was about to be privy to some terrible state secret and whether he actually wanted to know.

'Seumas, my friend,' hissed Tangiia, not taking his eyes from the sea, 'Kikamana and I have gathered magic herbs from that island.' He turned and gave Seumas a strange smile. 'Soon the Princess Kula will be begging me to make love to her – *begging* – once she has drunk the love potion Kikamana is mixing. See – see the man-fish break the surface . . .' he ended, crying softly in preoccupied wonder.

'A giant turtle,' Seumas said. 'I saw a turtle. Listen, do you think it will work, this potion? Will she come to her senses and realise she is really in love with you after all? Is it fool-proof?'

Seumas had immediately thought of Dorcha and was kicking himself for not speaking with the Far-seeing virgin about such things. Perhaps she could have helped him win Dorcha, while they were still on Raiatea? Perhaps there was love for him in the Celt's breast which only needed awakening?

'Of course it will work. It *must* work. I must have that woman.'

Seumas sighed, heavily. 'I know how you feel.'

'Of course,' mused Tangiia, 'I shan't keep her in that condition – it would be wrong – so we collected the aromatic leaves to make a medicine which will counteract the effects of the love potion, once the Princess has given herself to me.'

'You intend to bring her out of her love trance?'

'Yes, once it is too late for her to go back on her commitment to me.'

Seumas raised his sandy-coloured eyebrows in surprise. All at once he felt distaste for the king's methods. To help someone fall in love with you was one thing. That was like wearing a sweet-smelling oil on your hair, washing your body in perfumed water and putting on fine clothes, in order to influence their judgement, make them reconsider your attractiveness. But then if that love could be taken away, just as easily, it was not the awakening of something dormant, already there, but the injection of a false emotion in the subject's breast. Seumas was not sure that he approved of this at all. His views on women and love had changed radically since he had arrived on the heavenly island of Raiatea. He had grown more tender in his thoughts, less savage in his ways.

'That's all very tricky. It sounds a little like getting someone drunk on kava and raping them to me . . .'

The young king looked at him angrily. 'You think I'm immoral, doing this? What choice do I have? She hates me. I can't stand it.'

'I know, I know,' said Seumas, softly. 'Believe me, I understand. For years now I have been going through the same thing. But this is very drastic.'

'If you tell a soul, I shall have you beheaded,' snapped Tangiia, his eyes hot with temper.

Seumas rose from his sitting position and stood over the young king.

'I shall tell no one. I simply ask you to consider what you're doing. I wouldn't do it.'

'You are not me – wait – there – there – did you see? You must have seen? Out there, in the crook of the wave. He beckoned. We must go on – go on . . .'

Seumas, thinking that they were now being guided by a madman, left the king staring ahead of the craft. Their navigator king's brains had been addled by some malevolent god, intent on leading the fleet to the edge of the world and watching them drop over into nothingness. The Pict thought there might be a mutiny on board soon, if the king did not come to his senses. There were already whisperings amongst the crew. He would have to keep an ear open himself, for he was considered close to the king, and when royal power was brought down, those standing next to it were often felled alongside.

It was difficult for Kikamana, on the great platform between the two hulls, to exercise the rights of a high priestess which made her profession worthwhile. Kikamana did not like people – or rather, did not like *crowds* – and on her home island she would be mostly alone in her temple. Her natural inclination was towards solitude and prayers, meditation and musings, during which time she considered deeply the workings of the universe, its symbols and its signs.

In her younger years Kikamana had learned, from older priests and priestesses, the fangu chants and songs which were important memory aids, carrying knowledge and power in their lines. She knew the weather and its patterns as well as any senior mariner, was aware of the shapes of the clouds and the temperatures of the wind which created squalls, or full-blooded storms, or dead calm. The landscapes and seascapes of her world were imprinted upon her mind like maps. Even among people renowned for the strength of their memory, she had phenomenal powers of recall. Inside her head were myriads of pictures with infinite detail, individual scenes she might only have seen but once in her life.

She was born the daughter of a weaver whose first three husbands died before she was twenty-four. One went to a shark, another fell from a coconut tree and broke his neck, the third died of a mysterious illness which made him first balloon like a puffer fish, then peel like an overripe fruit. Kikamana's mother took these deaths philosophically, but the priests at the time pronounced her taboo, thinking the gods did not intend for her to have a husband. Henceforth no man would go with her for fear of meeting a premature death. This aspect of affairs too formed part of her philosophy and her daughter was ambitiously raised in the belief that a man was not necessary to a woman's happiness and in fact might be more of a hindrance to a definite career. Since Kikamana later felt a natural inclination towards abstinence, this suited both mother and child.

Kikamana's mother was a religious woman who spent a great deal of time with her daughter, giving her the benefit of those stories which filled her head.

'Woman was the *first*,' she told Kikamana, 'for without a woman a man could not be formed. The god Rongo went abroad and fetched some pieces of clay and rock and these he gave to the god Tu, who made them into the shape of a woman using his spittle as mortar to keep the pieces together. The finished object was then handed to Tane who breathed warm air on the image, investing it with *spirit* and *breath-of-life*. The figure imbibed that life, a faint exhalation was heard, then a shudder went through the earth-formed female as the mortal spirit settled its home in her. Then at last the maid-of-clay opened her eyes, stood up, and was proclaimed – woman!'

Kikamana grew up in the belief that she was special and that her destiny was to be great and wise. She took this idea seriously, never doubting her mother for a moment. When she was fifteen and a man asked her to be his wife, she told him, 'I am saving myself for Maui.' This was very close to blasphemy, since Maui was almost a god.

'But Maui is in the land of the dead,' said the unhappy suitor.

'Precisely,' replied Kikamana.

At sixteen Kikamana went off to live in the mountains for ten years, where she found a cave and fasted. There her visions and dreams became real scenes and places. There were times when her visions manifested themselves and stayed with her for days, talking with her, passing knowledge to her. And other times when her dreams opened up and allowed her to walk inside them, gathering spiritual strength from their mana.

When the ten years were over Kikamana went down the mountain and rejoined the Raiatean community, where her powers soon became apparent and she was given one of the royal babies to watch over like a nurse. The child, Prince Tangiia, grew to manhood under her guidance. When he was fourteen Tangiia asked Kikamana to marry him, as many men had done before because she was so beautiful in spirit as well as body. She had told him to wait four years and ask her again. He promised her fiercely he would not forget to do it, that he would count the days, the moments, until he reached the age of eighteen years.

On his eighteenth birthday, just a short time ago, he had come to her in tears. He told her his honour was in shreds, his heart was broken and his spirit was torn.

'I cannot ask you to marry me, Kikamana, for I have seen a girl I love with all my soul.'

'And she is not me?' the mature Kikamana had said, smiling and stroking his head, teasing him.

'Why, no – she is a young maiden, a princess.'

'Then I release you from your promise.'

Tangiia had kissed her feet and left the temple with the tears still shining in his eyes and a smile on his lips.

He loved her, he told her later, as a brother, which he was, she being his half-sister.

He never again mentioned sexual love to her, until he asked her to make him a potion for Kula.

While Kikamana was at her prayers in the corner of one of the two huts, Seumas came to her and indicated that he would like to speak. Kikamana had not had a great deal to do with the Pict, since he never visited the temple on the island, as most Raiateans did, and seemed to avoid her at ceremonial feasts and other occasions. She had the feeling he was a little afraid of her, much like many other men, except he had an excuse. He was a newcomer and therefore wary of all priests of what was to him an alien religion full of strange gods whose names he had not learned as a toddler and whose ways were foreign.

Seumas sat opposite her in the darkness of the hut.

'There is a problem,' he whispered to her, for there were others in the vicinity. 'It's to do with the king.'

She appraised the pale, rugged man whose tattoos of beasts she had never seen in Oceania were symbols of his wildness. A long, thin rat, which was not a rat, chased an animal with tall ears and powerful back legs across his abdomen. There was a sharp-faced dog-creature on one shoulder and a larger, more hairy dog-creature on the other. Then there were the many symbols, curious curls, oddly shaped keys, that formed patterns over the flat muscles of his chest, around his decorated nipples.

His hair was like dry grass reddened under the sun. His muscular frame was lean, tall and compact. An angular face, becoming creased by the weathering of sun and salt water, held two sharp blue eyes that interested her more than any of his other features. She read a certain honesty in them. It was not the honesty of her own society, was not shaped by the same mind or culture. But nevertheless it was a trait to be respected as something he believed in and strove to keep pure; it was that aspect of him which was to be admired. He could also be, she thought, a loyal man if he found the right leader, the right ruler to follow.

Finally, his hands were touching hands, full of meaning, full of gravity. There was not a great deal of grace about him, when compared to an Oceanian, but his hands were graceful – gentle, tender, yet firm and strong.

'Are you asking me to commit treason?' she asked.

The eyes became worried, as if a misunderstanding had occurred.

'No, nothing of that kind. Simply to find the king again – the *real* king – before he becomes too lost to reach.'

'And where is he now?'

Seumas said, 'Deep down, inside himself.'

She liked this kind of talk. He sparred well. He had a certain intelligence. It was more interesting than talk of fishing, or weather, or discussing blocked bowels with overweight men, and sickly babies with fussy mothers. She had underestimated this man in the past.

'What are these,' she asked, pointing to his tattoos, one at a time. 'Tell me their names.'

He looked down at himself in surprise. 'No one has asked me that before – I think they believed it to be unlucky. You're not worried that I might really be a demon? Maybe when I tell you what they are, you'll be under my spell?'

'I'm the sorcerer,' she said, wryly, 'not you.'

He laughed. 'Getting above myself, eh?' He pointed to each shoulder in turn.

'This is called *fox* and this one here is a *wolf* – they're dog-like creatures. The fox is small but cunning, the wolf is strong and savage. I like to think I have something of both of them in me, like any respectable Pict.'

'You are a Pict?'

'That's my race.'

She nodded thoughtfully. 'And the scene on your belly?'

'Well, this long, lean chap is a *stoat* – he changes the colour of his coat in winter and becomes the *ermine*. Here, he's chasing a creature called a *hare*. He'll never catch him, because hares can run too fast, but he never stops trying. It's the dogged hunter after the uncatchable prey. A man running after a deer will never catch his quarry on foot – even if he is the fastest runner of his tribe – but there are secrets of the mind that will help the hunter bring down the deer.'

Finally, amongst the swirls and whorls which formed the designs on his chest, she pointed to one.

'And this?'

He looked down and then up again, smiling, and she knew she had been astute.

'That's one of the secrets of the mind.'

'What do you call it?'

'Them – they're really two separate parts of the same weapon, though the way they're drawn here it seems like they're one single thing – they're called a bow and an arrow.'

'And how do they work?'

He smiled again. 'That's another secret.'

'There's one creature you still haven't told me about – perhaps it's because you can't see it yourself. It's on your back. A wonderful-looking beast –'

'A *horse*,' he said, simply.

'It has a powerful, muscular body.'

'The ownership of one of these creatures will make a man a king, whether he's born of royal blood or not.'

'One can *own* a horse – like a dog?'

The Pict stood up and held his hand level with his own shoulder.

'The height of a horse would reach at least to here,' he said.

Despite herself, Kikamana was surprised. The dimensions of the beast on Seumas's back were impressive. If one could own such a creature, perhaps it was useful in war, to bite and tear at one's foes, or kick with its hard-looking feet? Or flay the skin off a man's back with that tail? Perhaps it could be trained to stamp enemies into the dirt. It certainly had terrible eyes in that long head, cavernous nostrils for snorting fire, and whips along its neck.

'I suppose,' she said, 'this *horse* is another secret.'

'Of course,' he said, smiling and sitting down again.

'Like this *iron* you once spoke of?'

'Like *iron*.'

She said, 'You seem to have so many secrets your head must be ready to burst.'

He laughed. 'Me? I'm a poor, simple man, an ignorant peasant of a man. Someone else discovered the secret of the bow, of iron, of the horse, not me. I merely make use of the thoughts in another man's head, when the opportunity arises.'

'It seems to me that you can't have the horse or iron in our world, but you could make a bow and arrow.'

'Does it seem like that to you?' mused Seumas. 'Well then, that's how it is, isn't it? But I'm not going to show one of you how to make them. I still have old loyalties to consider. One day you people will return to Albainn, or the Land-of-Mists as your Kupe called it, and you'll want to conquer my people. If I tell you my secrets, then you'll know as much as your enemies, who are my cousins and brothers, my aunts and uncles, and sisters. Why, that would be *treachery*, Kikamana. Treason of the worst kind.'

She nodded and laughed. He really was an interesting man. Not a demon, but a man. One day she might have to use her powers to find keys to those secrets of his. But for now, it hardly mattered. They were not necessary to her.

'You came to see me,' she reminded him, 'about the king.'

His face took on a worried frown. 'I understand from him that there's a plot to make Kula fall in love with him – using some potion made from herbs.'

'He told you this?'

'Yes,' said Seumas, 'in an unguarded moment.'

'And?'

'I want to know if you approve of this plot, or whether you're simply carrying out the king's orders.'

Kikamana sighed and pulled her bark-cloth wrap more closely around her.

'My honest opinion is that it'll lead to more sorrow for King Tangiia in the end.'

Seumas nodded, as if this was the answer he had expected.

'I also understand,' he said, 'that you have another potion, which has the opposite effect?'

'The corrective. Yes, I can brew that too.'

Seumas leaned forward, close to her ear. Kikamana felt a certain distaste at having a man's lips so close to her face, but she realised he was merely trying to impart something. She listened intently.

'Why don't you,' whispered Seumas, 'just give this – corrective – to the king? Pretend to give Kula the love-juice, but instead give her something harmless. Tell the king he needs to take the potion too, but give him the corrective.'

'And the purpose of this?'

'To make the king fall out of love with Kula. Once he doesn't love her, it won't matter that we've tricked him, will it. She'll mean nothing more to him than a pig's orphan.'

Kikamana raised her eyebrows. 'You have a strange way of describing emotions.'

The Far-seeing virgin sat for a while and thought over this scheme from the Pict and it seemed to her to be the answer to several problems. Her integrity as a high priestess would have been stretched to the limits, if she had been party to the enslavement of a lovely young woman. As it was, Seumas's plan offered the king escape from his misery, and Kikamana herself an ethical way out of her dilemma. The king would no longer be entranced by Kula, captive to her charms, but free to concentrate upon the main task of navigating. He had for too long been brooding, his heart full of longing, his head spinning with the very real torture of unrequited love. Once freed from his obsession, the whole community would benefit.

'Excellent,' she told Seumas. 'An excellent plan.'

'Good,' breathed Seumas. 'I hoped it was.'

Kikamana said, 'Leave everything to me, but let me ask you, have you been this close to a king before?'

'Never – I told you, I'm a peasant – a bird-collector, a lowly warrior.'

'Well, you seem to have taken to court intrigue as if you were born for it.'

Seumas smiled, saying, 'You must think there's no limit to my talents. By the way, you can give some of that potion to me – the stuff that makes you fall out of love.'

Kikamana frowned a little, then said, 'Ahh, the dark-eyed Celt. Are you still pining?'

'I shall always pine,' replied Seumas, grimly. 'Though *pining* is not the word I would use. I still have hopes that one day she will come chasing after me.' He grinned, sheepishly.

'There's always hope,' replied Kikamana. 'After all, we carry the God of Hope with us, here on this very pahi.'

'By accident.'

'Accident or design, it matters not – he is with us and will watch over us, for we revere his image.'

He stood up then, and left the hut, walking out into the bright sunshine. Kikamana could see him afterwards, standing on the bows of the canoe, his legs entangled in the rainbows produced by the fine spray, his head somewhere in the clouds. Their conversation had given her a great deal of respect for the Pict. She hoped there would be more talks.

King Tangiia was by the mast, surveying the roof of voyaging with a critical eye. It seemed that a squall was about to descend upon the fleet. The wind was strong, the waves increasing in size and strength. Maomao was about to give Tangaroa another whipping. Tangiia had been following a te lapa streak at the same time as urging his rowers to catch up with the marvellous man-fish who was still drawing the fleet off its chosen course. The king had made some nets in which he hoped to catch the weird creature and study it at close hand.

Behind *The Scudding Cloud*, the other two pahi were visible, keeping in sight-contact with one another. All six crab-claw sails were straining at the seams in the rising wind. Children were huddled in the huts, protected from the flying spume by the bodies of their mothers. All able-bodied men stood by, ready to handle the sheets, if the sails had to be rolled up suddenly to reduce the area exposed to the wind.

During Tangiia's visit to the other canoes, while they were moored by the sandspit island, both captains had argued strongly with Tangiia on the folly of pursuing the adaro, but Tangiia would listen to neither of them. It seemed he was bewitched by the creature and would lead the fleet to its doom rather than give up the chase.

Near to the mast, just inside the doorway of one of the huts, sat Princess Kula. When Tangiia cast a casual glance her way, she glared at him, wasting no opportunity to let him know she hated him. She was shocked and surprised when his returning look was one of indifference. Normally his expression would either be one of piteous unhappiness, or one of defiant determination to win her in the end. In either one she read of his forlorn hope of love from her.

The look that he had just given her, however, appeared to indicate that he couldn't care less whether she loved or hated him. It was as if she were *nothing* to him.

Kula was puzzled. She knew that all she should feel was relief, that the young man was over her at last. She tried to tell herself how glad she was that he would not bother her any longer with those wistful stares, or with his whispered entreaties. No more would she need to scorn him, turn her shoulder to his advances, curl her lip in contempt whenever he tried to accost her. It was a *good* thing, wasn't it?

Yet she felt puzzled. What had happened to change him so abruptly? Young men, and indeed young women, could not switch from love to indifference in a moment. Was he faking his feelings, trying to make her think he had gone cold on her? Yes, that must be it. She would test this theory.

Kula stood up and adjusted her skirt. Her clothing was damp and clung to her trim figure, emphasising the firm-ness of her breasts and the gentle curve of her hips. She stepped out on to the deck and looked up, pretending to examine the weather. Then she turned to Tangiia and said in an offhand tone, 'I suppose you will manage to beat the squall to calmer water?'

He hardly looked at her, replying, 'It would be best if you returned to the hut.'

'Why – are you afraid for my safety?' she asked, haughtily.

He turned and looked at her with empty, cold eyes. 'Your personal safety is your own concern, not mine. I have the fleet to consider. I can't be bothered with individuals.'

Again she was shocked by the complete lack of regard in his expression. This was not acting! He really was more concerned with his duty than he was with her well-being. In the past he had whispered that he would die for her, kill for her, destroy the fleet and all its passengers and crew if she willed it. Now it seemed he could not care less whether she was swept overboard by a freak wave and sank to oblivion!

'Thank you for your advice,' she snapped. 'I'm well able to take care of myself.'

'Stop bothering me with your chatter, woman. Get in the hut with the others. I'm trying to outrun a storm here.'

He turned away from her and began issuing orders to his crew. Despite her indignation at his summary dismissal, she was impressed as always by his seamanship. He seemed to have the situation completely under control. There was a strong air of authority about him that went beyond his age and his rank of navigator king and was inherent in him as a man. She returned to her place in the hut, while the mariners dashed around the deck, loosening sennit sheets, tightening stays, rolling up the crab-claw sail. While they worked, the seafarers chanted a song to the great god Maomao:

'O wind from the top of the world!
Sprung from the chasm

Carrying the scudding clouds over untravelled
   horizons.
Great wind of Maomao,
Made manifest in the waves of the ocean,
fleeing before the fury of your roar
whose tempestuous blast
swells the rushing tumult of the sea . . .'

The women too had their duties, in trying to keep the pandanus flour dry, the pigs from stealing the almonds and
chestnuts, the breadfruit and coconuts from rolling away,
the sugar-cane from being stolen by the children, the gourds
from breaking, vegetarian dogs from making too much
noise, and the mountain apples from shrinking in the salt-
water spray.

Of the nearly one hundred people on board *The
Scudding Cloud* there were few who had nothing to do
once a storm threatened.

2

How the Great Wind-God loved playing with his whips! He lashed the back of Tangaroa with his flails until the Great Sea-God's skin rose in giant blisters, to burst and flow in all directions, the white momentary scars running with the rush of fluid. And Tangaroa's tears of anger and pain were evident in the clouds of spray and spume, only to be whisked away by the mighty blast created by Maomao's flogging.

Maomao's great winds opened the heavens for two other terrible storm-gods to enter: Apu Matangi, feared by all mariners, God of the Howling Rain, and his equally vicious brother Apu Hau, God of the Fierce Squall.

The Raiatean fleet were caught on the edge of this storm, which Maomao intended as a warning. The Great Wind-God was annoyed with King Tangiia for allowing himself to become entranced by the adaro. Maomao knew that men were fickle, inquisitive creatures, weak of flesh and spirit, and the gods could play with them as a child played with toys. It grieved Maomao that he had to remind his fledglings that their task was not to become sidetracked by wondrous sights, but to seek a new Faraway Heaven, somewhere on the wide world of the ocean.

*

To those on board the three pahi canoes, the wind and the sea had become one entity, inseparable. The air was white with spray which lashed at the mat sails, shaking them as if they were the branches of a tree. The masts creaked and threatened to snap and go flying out into the darkness. It was day, but it was night, and the canoes were flung between the wavetops like coconuts tossed from hand to hand at harvest time.

The Raiateans wailed and cried to their gods, begging for mercy, thinking they were all about to drown, while the crews fought with lines and paddles, trying to keep the canoes heading into waves that changed direction with almost every sweep of water. There were mountains where there had been plains, immense troughs that fell to the centre of the earth.

At times the vessels were almost vertical, falling down a sheer wall of water. It seemed at those times that they must plunge bows-first into the heart of the ocean and continue down to be buried under the massive deluge which had overwhelmed them.

At other times they clawed their way up precipitous slopes like a man tries to climb a cliff of loose scree. It seemed on occasion that the wave up which they were ascending would curl over and enfold them in its bosom, loving them to their deaths. Then miraculously the wave would flatten, the hump of water would run under their hulls, lifting the pahi high above the world, and then another mighty trough would appear before them, and they would stare down into its maw and once again feel that they were about to disappear into the salivating mouth of the Great Sea-God Tangaroa, who was displeased with them.

How flimsy their majestic pahi canoes seemed to them now, the pegs loosening in the hulls and flying free, the lashings on the logs squealing and shrieking like live creatures, the timbers grinding and grating and trying to change places. Those fixtures which had taken ten men to tighten, using capstans of rope, rock and pole, were now easily unfastened with the twists and turns of the crazy flood.

Here and there the currents met with such fierce opposition to one another that vortexes appeared, swirling in dizzying rings which turned to hollow cones. The crews fought as if they were mad, to keep clear of the sudden maelstroms that came and went like the furious ghosts of ancestors. Sometimes the vessels were caught and carried, racing, around the lip of one of these giant whirlpools, until terrified men and women dug in their paddles and fought against the suction with wide, wild eyes and frantic arms until they managed to pull themselves free.

For a day and a half they were battered and beaten, exhausted beyond sleep, until they finally emerged from the side of the storm into a place of calm.

It was in this tranquil state that Kikamana consulted with Rangi, through the medium of her ancestors and confirmed what she and Boy-girl had suspected for a long time, even before landing on Nuku Hiva. Rangi the Great Sky-God sees all things under his roof of voyaging, for nothing is lost from his gaze except those trapped inside Hau Maringi's fogs and mists.

Kikamana learned that the fleet was being stalked; someone was in pursuit. Her atua would give her no names, for the ancestors and gods will not provide such details, but a great flotilla of canoes decked out for war followed in their wake, an angry and violent admiral at their head.

When she spoke with Makka-te about this, he pronounced her knowledge unsafe.

'One cannot trust one's atua's *completely*,' he said. 'Ancestor spirits are inclined to exaggerate. Perhaps there are but one or two vessels following us? I shouldn't alarm the king unduly. It will only make him anxious.'

At first Kikamana saw the sense in this advice. If the king was worried about a pursuer it might impair his ability to navigate. It was enough to find his way across the vast ocean and to contend with the elements and gods, let alone concern himself with a hunter. Yet, in the end, her conscience would not let her withhold the information. Knowledge passed to her from their ancestors was not meant to be kept secret, otherwise it would never have been given in the first place.

Kikamana held a meeting with King Tangiia and Makka-te.

'Someone is after us – they hunt us over the seas. I had a dream before we came to Nuku Hiva that there was a dark cloud tracking our wake across the ocean. I spoke with Makka-te about this, but he said we should not alarm you until we were sure.'

Makke-te nodded thoughtfully. A naturally reserved and private person, he was a priest whose feelings were never wholly evident. He was, however, respected for his gravity and impartiality.

'Well,' continued Kikamana, 'now I am sure.'

'Who is it?' asked Tangiia.

Kikamana shook her head, but Makka-te said, 'We can guess who it is – the man so blinded with hatred for you, he cannot see straight . . .'

Tangiia said, 'My brother?'

'Who else?' muttered Makka-te, grimly.

It was a green ocean into which the adaro had led their navigator king, with a curious green light to the sky. Rangi and Tangaroa were wearing similar verdant cloaks. It was a still place, with barely a breath of wind blowing. The fish there were lazy and seemed not to care if they were caught or went free. Their torpid forms floated to the surface, dull in their lethargy. Their eyes did not shine, but were filmy and grey. Their scales were lacklustre too, barely reflecting the greenness of the sea and sky around them.

Weed floated in great clumps, going nowhere, becoming

entangled with the paddles, slowing the fleet to a standstill at times. There was ribbon seaweed, and the blistered variety, but worst of all was the blanket weed, thin strands that had multiplied to become an impenetrable mass of green slime. It almost seemed to crawl up the gunwales, like an animate creature, in an attempt to overwhelm the canoes.

In the patches where there was no weed, flotillas of listless jellyfish hung in the water, trailing their frills and streamers in a desultory fashion. They pulsated sluggishly in the hot day as if gathering their strength for some long journey, and when a hapless fish glided into their path only then did their tentacles drift out and sting the creature to death, afterwards to hold the corpse in a loose embrace, waiting for it to rot.

'I don't like this place,' said Kula to Kikamana. 'It has an air of decay about it.'

'It is a place we should leave as soon as possible!' agreed the priestess.

They meandered languidly in this green, slumberous world, until they came upon an exposed reef without an island, part of an underwater ridge that ran like a whale's dorsal fin along a stretch of ocean. On this lonely place the waves beat slowly and with deep, resonant tones, as if drumming against a vane of coral-tipped rock that went down a thousand fathoms.

Here the women and men seafarers disembarked to collect their preferred diet of shellfish which had been denied them on the voyage, since it was necessary to eat such fare on the day of the gathering.

Using bone hooks to feel under the ledges, for fear of being bitten by fish or stung by the waving fronds of pretty anemones, they collected the bounteous harvest of the reef: the gastropods – strawberry tops, green helmets, harps, conches, mermaids' combs, violet snails, textile cones, murexes, shiny olives, white cowries, spires and variegated screws; the bi-valves – frog shells, clams, scallops, thorny oysters; and finally, the stickers – the abalones, limpets, barnacles.

The treasures of the reef, which the Raiateans had done without on their voyage so far, were eagerly garnered like glittering jewels, their colours, shapes and patterns unmatched by any other set of animate creatures over the whole and copious earth. The shells themselves would become ornaments, or containers, after the molluscs had gone for sustenance. The harvesting in itself was a time full of excitement and chatter, even in such a place of strange light and sonorous sound.

After the feasting was over they set off again and in the evening of that same day came upon an island.

There was no reef encircling the island, which had the same torpid atmosphere about it as the sea in which it rested. In the centre of the island was an arrogant volcano with an open mouth, breathing sulphur gases into the atmosphere. The smell of these gases mingled with the heavy, cloying perfume of orchids and wafted across the bay inducing a heavy-lidded sleepiness on the Raiateans. Thick-winged birds circled on high thermals, like the dark souls of forgotten precursors.

The Raiateans felt drugged and insensible, unable to think straight.

King Tangiia said, 'This time *I* shall take some men ashore and gather provisions.'

'Is that wise?' asked Kikamana. 'We know nothing about this place. Why not let Manopa go, or Po? They did well enough on Nuku Hiva.'

'Yes, that's why it's my turn,' said the young man. Then in an extraordinary outburst, cried, 'Why does that woman keep looking at me like that? Get her out of my sight.'

He was referring to Princess Kula, who turned and went away of her own accord, her face a scene of misery.

At noon the men were collected, the dugouts lowered

into the water, and their king joined them. They paddled towards the shore and landed on the beach without mishap. Immediately, they began gathering coconuts from the palms along the beach. Then the search began of the hinterland for yam, taro, sweet potato, breadfruit, plantain and banana. This was unusually easy. All were found in abundance, much to the surprise of Tangiia.

The dugouts, with two-man crews, ferried the goods back to the pahi canoes standing offshore. When it appeared that enough had been gathered, Tangiia then took his men further inland, to the base of the volcano, where the rich soil made the vegetation thick and lush. It was coming on evening and the greenness had changed to a rosy glow, partly due to the sunset, and partly due to the red hotness of the volcano's mouth.

Here an unbearable weariness came upon the party and they sank to the mossy floor of the rainforest and fell into a slumber. All except Tangiia, who, though fatigued, forced himself to stay awake in case they were attacked by hostile natives.

When the women came, Tangiia was not sure if he had fallen into a dream. They were the most beautiful creatures he had ever laid eyes on. Had he been of a sound spirit he would have been instantly aroused as the naked women silently lay down beside his men, one or two to each.

'Men,' whispered Tangiia, hoarsely, 'keep your senses – don't be bewitched . . .'

One of these wondrous females came to him, smiling, her breath smelling of sugar, her hair of sweet-scented oils. Her eyes were unfathomable, as deep and rich as the roof of voyaging at night. Her skin was dusty-dark, soft as frangipani petals. Her parted lips were wet with tonguing, desire evident in their trembling. There were shadows on her lovely face, where the high cheekbones met her eyes.

She bent down to him and pressed her bosom against his

chest, wrapping her thighs around his right leg. He could feel the hard nipples rasping against his skin. The mound between her legs was as soft and as yielding as a ripe fruit.

On the mossy bank below him, Tangiia witnessed his men, now awake, making love to the women in their arms. There was a raw, revived energy in them as they struggled with the effort of carnal enjoyment. However, each man soon came to the point of ecstasy, but once his orgasm was over, another woman came to him and aroused him again, beginning the passion all over again, from start to finish. The men seemed unable to resist the onslaught of these gentle but persistent maidens, who were insatiable in their sexual appetites.

Again and again the men performed, becoming more and more exhausted with each encounter. Yet still the women continued with their whispered supplications for love, love and yet more love. The men groaned and begged to be left alone, but each new orgasm brought a fresh companion, and the cycle seemed endless.

As Tangiia stared down upon this unreal scene he felt powerless to stop it. It was true that he himself was able to resist the charms of these lovely females, but he felt so drugged by the languid atmosphere he could make no move to assist his men. One by one the women came to him too, to stroke his body, whisper unintelligible words into his ear, and attempt to mount him even though he had no erection.

Finally, he managed to scream at the top of his voice and with his lei-o-mano he slashed at the woman crawling over his body, desperately trying to arouse him.

The blade seemed to pass through her form, though she leapt to her feet and ran into the rainforest. Her fleeing gave Tangiia the strength he needed to get up. Once standing he charged down the incline to the glade where his men were in the last throes of love. The women scattered before his attack, disappearing like wraiths into the undergrowth.

Tangiia quickly gathered his men together, to lead them back to the shore.

Two men were already dead, their bodies drained of their lifeforce, while the others could barely stagger back to the shoreline. There they quickly boarded the dugouts and paddled back to the pahi canoes.

'Make sail immediately!' Tangiia cried, then went to see the priestess Kikamana.

He explained to Kikamana what had happened and asked if she had an explanation.

'There is an island,' she told him, 'called Kaitalugi, where shipwrecked seafarers are washed up on to the beach. There they are seized and raped by a crowd of naked women. Once a woman has had one man, the next one will take him, until the men finally die of exhaustion.'

'This must be that island,' said Tangiia, fiercely. 'The man-fish led us here.'

'You were bewitched by the adaro,' agreed Kikamana.

'Now these monstrous females have killed two of my men!'

Kikamana's eyes turned hard and she shook her head. 'If they are monstrous, it's because men have made them so. These women were banished from their home islands, set adrift in open boats and left to die. The Great Sea-God led them to this island, just as he has led us, to give them a home.

'Now the injured sau of those women seek justice and revenge for their maltreatment. They have the power of enchantment, the power to bewitch men. They wait for shipwrecked seafarers, who are unable to resist them, manifest themselves in human form, and rape the men to exhaustion and death. I myself do not blame them – their grievances were many . . .'

Tangiia asked, 'What did they do to deserve banishment?'

'Refused a man intercourse, cried "rape" when they were

being taken against their will, ran away from violent husbands.'

'But these are not crimes.'

'They were on some islands, in some places, at one time or another. Perhaps there are still islands where the woman has no rights and is treated worse than a dog? Considering all things,' Kikamana added, 'the men die a painless death – you could say they kill themselves. Poetically.'

Tangiia hung his head for a moment, then said, 'I've come to my senses at last. We must sail with the wind, let Maomao take us to our destiny . . .' He paused to incline his head towards the entrance to the deck hut, which had darkened with a form. Seumas had entered, his dog at his heel. After a moment of silence Tangiia continued, '. . . what I don't understand, is how I was able to resist those women, while my men succumbed?'

'I gave you a drug, just before the storm – don't you remember?'

'I remember you gave me a *drink*,' said Tangiia. 'You gave one to Princess Kula, at the same time.'

'Hers was a harmless concoction.'

'And mine?'

'A potion to enable you to resist love, in all its forms.'

Tangiia frowned again. 'Why would you give me a potion like that, without my permission?'

'You were besotted – with – with the *adaro*. I believed the concoction would cure you of your obsession.'

Tangiia nodded, thoughtfully, 'I see – yes, that makes sense – but now I want you to give me something to counter the drug. It bothers me, this tampering with my emotions, my feelings. Next time, you should persuade me, not give it to me without my consent. You could have poisoned me.'

'I shall remember that, King Tangiia.'

After the king had left the hut, Seumas came forward and placed a hand on Kikamana's shoulder, staring into her eyes.

'I could have sworn you told a lie there, high priestess, but of course for a person with your views on morality, that's impossible. I must have been mistaken.'

Kikamana gave him back the stare with full measure.

'Be reassured, you *are* mistaken.'

'Yes, yes, I thought I was. Come on, Dirk, let's get out on deck, I think the captain's come to his senses at last. We're heading back on our true course again. Come on, boy, don't dawdle in the presence of a great lady.'

Dirk barked, loudly, looking from the lady to the man and back again, aware that something was amusing his master, but being a dog, was never going to know what it was.

Boy-girl's obsession with Seumas had begun the day she saw him stagger from Po's canoe after the great Kupe's magnificent voyage of discovery. A man with a pure white skin! He was ugly to her, yet he was beautiful. She was both repulsed and attracted to him, and this is where fascination begins. There was a desire to touch, but a fear of touch.

Boy-girl had been fourteen at the time, running around decorated with shells and flowers, but naked. Already tall and willowly, though thin rather than slender at this age, her movements were not as artistically feminine as they were to become. She was still, at fourteen, quite gauche.

'Horrid,' she said, as he passed her, his wobbly legs still unused to the firmness of the ground. 'Horrid demon.'

The demon turned, his salt-white, salt-encrusted skin blinding her with its brilliance in the bright tropical sun. His red hair fell around his shoulders like the long feathers of a precious bird. Hawk-faced, hard-mouthed, he turned his terrible eyes upon her.

When she stared into those eyes, she saw they were an eerie, washed blue and deeply penetrating. Those eyes saw deep into Boy-girl's soul, searched every corner of her being, and she was chilled by a strange fear.

Boy-girl let out a gasp and stepped backwards.

A savage sound came from the demon's mouth as he snarled at her, making her back away even further.

Then Boy-girl realised there were two of them – two white demons – and she stared in wonder. But Seumas was the one who had caught her eye first and he became the object of her obsession. From that point on she wanted to be near him, around him, as often as she could get away with it. Other Raiateans scorned her for it, laughed at her, because they saw only in Seumas a strong man weakened by his obvious displays of masculinity, a man desperate to be seen as a man. Someone who had continually to prove himself tough and uncompromising must, they said, be at heart a very poor specimen of a human being.

But Boy-girl looked deeper than her fellow islanders, having a sharper intellect than most and a wisdom born of the ruthless, detached study of people, and saw the real compassionate strength beneath the weak show of hardness.

When she was older, and her sexual appetites were much stronger, she wanted Seumas with every fibre of her being. Her fantasies were always of him and though she eventually learned to control her obsession there were times when she thought she would go mad with desire.

For his part, Seumas felt his contempt for these islanders was fully justified since he had met this creature – clearly a male – covered in feminine trinkets and wiggling its bottom as it walked. His disgust for what he considered unwholesome girlishness had been effectively deepened by this meeting. On the other hand, he had developed a lasting respect for Kupe and Po, but as navigators and seamen, not as men. He still felt he could beat any one of them in single combat.

Seumas was given an abandoned hut which he was told was his own, unless he wanted to build another. Since he had no idea how to go about building a dwelling out of local materials he repaired the one he had been given and hoped it would not fall down before he had learned the native crafts. He was told he had the same rights as any other islander, though he was never to go off in an ocean voyager without a Raiatean on board.

Dorcha was given a hut close by, but she soon moved when she learned that she and Seumas were to be near neighbours. Dorcha built a teak and coconut hut with a pandanus leaf roof. She seemed to pick up in a week what it took Seumas to learn in several months.

At first the islanders stayed away from both of them – all except Kieto and Boy-girl – but gradually they grew less fearful and then they came to satisfy their curiosity. Seumas barked at them, but they got used to this, and soon one of the young women was sleeping with him.

Boy-girl ambushed this woman, savagely pulling her hair, and tried to claw out her eyes.

Boy-girl was brought before the council and told to stop this kind of thing or she would be banished to an uninhabited island. Boy-girl complied with the ruling, but wept bitter tears into her rolled-mat pillow that night.

Seumas said to Kieto one day, 'I think I am stronger than any of your men – they look too smooth and fat to be good warriors. I think I could beat any man here.'

Kieto, unused to bragging, replied, 'If you think that, you must be right. No one has seen you fight, Seumas, so I must take you at your word.'

After this Seumas began strutting around the island, making people step aside for him on narrow mountain paths, growling at anyone who stared too long.

'I could tear your face from your skull,' he would cry. 'I could blind you with one blow with my fist.'

Not because they were afraid of him, but because they were not familiar with this kind of boast, they looked at him nervously and then hurried on. He began to think of himself as invincible. Men who believe themselves invulnerable actually become overawed by their own power and very often take to bullying. Seumas became a bully.

One day he met a man named Manopa on a jungle path and expected the other to step aside.

'Out of the way, moron,' snarled Seumas.

When Manopa did not relinquish the path, Seumas tried to shoulder past the broad man.

Manopa, short but solid, remained firm.

Enraged, Seumas swung a fist at Manopa's head.

Manopa gave him the hiding of his life.

Seumas crawled back to his hut where Kieto was waiting for him.

'What happened to you?' asked the boy. 'Did you meet a terrible demon?'

'I met a man called Manopa,' mumbled Seumas through thick lips and bloodied gums. 'He must be the best fighter on the whole damned island.'

Kieto said, 'He's a *good* warrior, but there are others who are better. Kupe, who is close to the gods, can beat him of course, and Tutapu, and possibly even . . .' and Kieto continued with a list of names that made Seumas wince.

'You mean to say,' said the Pict, 'that he's not that unusual?'

'He's a chief and a very good warrior, but there are many of those on the islands.'

'Just that?'

'Yes.'

From that point on, Seumas began gradually to revise his assessment of the natives. He realised they did not have to prove themselves men every hour of the day, because they were secure in the knowledge that they *were* men.

The night he was beaten, Kieto tended his bruises with local medicine, but Seumas was in a poor condition. One blue-black bruise extended over the whole of his left side and was agony to the touch. In the middle of the night, he felt Kieto rubbing balm into this wound, and was relieved to find that the fire went out of it almost immediately and he was able to sleep.

When Seumas woke the next morning, he found Boy-girl curled up alongside him.

He rolled away, alarmed. 'Wha— What are you doing here, creature?'

Boy-girl opened her eyes sleepily and smiled at him.

'I came to help you – I have mended your hurt side.'

'You slept with me!' cried Seumas, appalled.

'Yes, but you didn't do anything,' said Boy-girl, in a voice that revealed a mixture of annoyance and wistfulness. She was now seventeen and sexually active. 'You were hurt too much to do anything.'

'I don't like boys,' cried Seumas. 'I wouldn't have done anything if I was hale.'

Boy-girl smiled and rattled her shells. 'You never know,' she sighed, 'you might change your mind . . .'

As soon as he was well enough, Seumas built a door to his hut, with a bar on the inside, so that he could lock it.

In those early days Kieto used to take him hunting for birds with a slingshot. One day Boy-girl asked to come too.

'We're going hunting, not dancing,' said Seumas, disparagingly. 'Those shells would frighten away an army of birds.'

'I always leave my jewels at home,' said Boy-girl.

Despite Seumas's protests, Boy-girl did come with them that day. The three of them went up into the rainforests to explore the deep valleys between volcanic hills. There it was lush and green and full of life. It seemed the world of the hinterland was thick-stemmed juicy plants, diaphanous mists drifting on the moist air, sudden waterfalls, and lightning streams that cracked down through rock and leaf-mould earth.

Under the canopy, inside the green world, Seumas

remarked, 'This is indeed a wonderful land – it's not *my* land, but it's like a good woman – moist and warm and beautiful.'

Boy-girl grunted.

Kieto said, 'This *is* your land now, Seumas. You will become part of it, just as we are.'

Seumas looked at the boy, now in his tenth year. Already Kieto was showing signs of leadership. The other boys of his age, even some of the older ones, looked up to him. He was asked to take them on fishing expeditions or hunting birds. He would organise these trips with care and attention to detail, making sure every member of the party had a part to play, ensuring the best possibility for a good catch or a fine hunt. Seumas had heard what Kupe had once said, that one day Kieto would lead the invasion force on Albainn.

'You will want my help, when you attack the Land-of-Mists, young man – you shall not have it, no matter how hard you try to make me one of your own.'

Boy-girl smiled sweetly. 'Oh, you will be one of us, Seumas, there's no fighting *that*.'

Seumas began to get angry. 'I say I will not! I have my own mind, I own my own soul. I say I shall never be traitor to my kind. Nothing will turn me into a betrayer.'

Kieto said, 'You will never be traitor to your own kind because *we* will be your people. It is us you will not betray – those others, on your old island – they are not your people any more.'

He said it with such conviction that Seumas almost went into a fury and struck the boy. However, he kept his temper and stared at these two young people, both utterly confident that he would not remain an Albannach at heart, but would become an Oceanian, a nomad of the wind, before the time came to attack the land of his forefathers.

'We shall see,' he growled at last. 'You'll see that I'm right. You are children. You have no concept of what's in a

grown man's heart. When you're as old as I am, then you
will know how impossible it is that I could betray my
people. But one thing you will never completely know
or understand – the fierce pride of the Pict, the pride that
he has of his homeland, of his clan, of his birthplace. It
is steadfast.'

Boy-girl said seriously, 'That may be so, Seumas, but
you might not be able to help yourself changing. You're like
a taro root taken from one island and planted on another.
At first you refuse to flourish, because the new soil is not
like your old earth, even though it might be richer – yet,
you *will* grow, because the need to survive, the need to live,
is strong.'

'I shall *grow*, but not as an islander.'

'Your soul will mellow in our heaven, Seumas, and you
will be grafted to us.'

This disconcerted Seumas so much, he decided to change
the subject.

'I want no more arguments – let's get on with the hunt.
Boy-girl, what are you doing here anyway? You should be
back on the beach collecting pretty shells . . .'

At that moment a large bird flew overhead. With astonishing speed Boy-girl whirled her slingshot and let fly,
striking the bird on the breast. It fell from the sky, almost at
their feet. Seumas was amazed by her skill. He stared up at
the heavens, then down at the dead wildfowl.

'I made a mistake,' Seumas said, 'unless that was a lucky
shot?'

'It wasn't a lucky shot,' Kieto answered him. 'Boy-girl is
one of the best slingshots on the island.'

Boy-girl smiled warmly at Seumas.

'You are mistaken about a lot of things, my lovely
demon, but don't worry, all will be revealed in time.'

'Don't you try any magic on me,' warned Seumas, panicking a little. 'Don't you do that, or I swear I'll treat you
like I used to treat fulmars. I'll wring your skinny neck.'

Boy-girl gave him another sweet smile.

'I mean it!' said Seumas.

Boy-girl pouted. 'Oh, you silly creature, of course I won't make you do anything you don't want to – where would be the fun in that? Anyway, I didn't mean *that*. The trouble with you, Seumas, is you're obsessed with sex . . .'

Seumas learned a lot that afternoon, hunting with the two people who loved him most on this strange island in this strange ocean. He learned that there was more to Boy-girl than just a pretty face. She was not empty-headed, but intelligent, incisive and an excellent hunter. He was beginning to respect and fear her. Kieto, too, he had discovered was astonishingly single-minded. The youth was not as sharp and deep as Boy-girl, but he was constant to his path. Yes, Seumas believed that one day Kieto would invade Albainn – whether he would conquer it was another matter, but Seumas was determined that nothing, nothing he as a Pict had to offer would be given willingly.

On the way back to their village, bloody birds strung about their necks like pendants, Seumas was taken by his hands, one on either side – Kieto held his right hand, Boy-girl his left. He did not pull away, recognising the simple friendship and honour that was being bestowed upon him as an outsider. It felt uncomfortable, the silky palm of Boy-girl especially, but he bore it, knowing to remove his hand now would be a horrible insult and would do irreparable damage to their relationships.

'One thing is certain,' he said, 'you pair, young as you are, have given me friendship, even though others have laughed at you for it. A Pict never forgets something as valuable as that – I am in your debt. From now on, your enemies are my enemies. I would die, or kill, for you both.'

He said it half in jest, but they all knew that underneath, Seumas was serious.

PART FIVE

The Relentless Pursuer

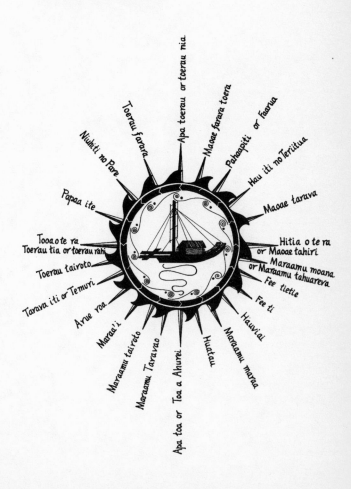

1

It was night.

Out on the ocean, approaching the island of Fatu Hiva, were three thousand lights from flaming torches. They illuminated the darkness like giant candles as they floated slowly towards the Bay of Virgins. The natives of Fatu Hiva were gathered on the beaches, watching the massed flames draw ever closer, knowing that each one of the brands was held by the hand of a warrior. A foreign fleet had arrived at their island and seeing the number of lights on the vessels which approached, they knew they could not match the invasion. Their chief waited in trepidation for the storming of his island, knowing resistance was useless against such a powerful force.

One of the island's fishermen had been out on open waters during the day and had seen a fleet of tipairua canoes, some thirty in number, all with black sails, heading towards his home island. The canoes had a war-like appearance with their fast v-shaped hulls and had alarmed him. He had fled back to the island as fast as he could, arriving just as dusk was settling. He informed his chief of what he had seen and the whole tribe went down to the beach in despair, to await the arrival of this awesome flotilla.

The lights off-shore were as numerous as fireflies and the local chief knew they had been lit for a purpose and were meant to intimidate him. Indeed, as he waited in agitation, he *felt* very intimidated. A smaller fleet of five hundred, or perhaps even a thousand warriors, would have had him armed to the teeth and waiting with fury in his breast. But the scale and size of this attack was unprecedented and he felt powerless to offer an opposition. His courage had turned to pork jelly.

So, he waited, with gifts of food, carvings, precious shells, red feathers, turtle shells, etched gourds and other treasures at his feet, ready to buy the lives of himself and his islanders.

The chief had removed a necklace of human teeth, taken from enemies, which he usually wore around his throat. The stick crowned with a human skull, normally shaken in defiance at strangers to the island, was hidden under a mat. His war helmet, of feathers on a frame of human skin, was still on its pole just inside the door of his house.

He made himself look as small as possible, stooping and hunching his shoulders, appearing thoroughly pathetic. He had smeared fire-soot on his tattoos, to hide those which proclaimed him a great warrior, afraid of no man. He had brought his three fat wives and their younger children, to show that he was a family man, and not inclined towards war.

Two of the prettiest girls in the tribe flanked him; they were his oldest daughters. He would hand them over without a murmur if necessary. Dishonour before death, in such circumstances.

The fleet moored outside the reef and a small outrigger canoe was launched to come gliding over the reef in a movement timed with the rhythm of the waves. Crossing a reef either way, and landing or launching in beach surf, was the most dangerous part of boatmen's manoeuvres, especially when the reef and beach were unknown to the mariners. Islanders ran into the surf, eager to help beach the outrigger and its crew, anxious to accommodate the foreign admiral.

Men and women on the beach began a song of welcome to the strangers, and a dance which proclaimed that the island was peaceful towards the newcomers. Garlands were brought forward and placed around the necks of the suspicious outlanders.

The crew of the outrigger were armed for war, but when they encountered no resistance and made certain no treachery was intended they signalled the tipairua that all was well. A second outrigger was launched and the fleet's admiral soon stepped out of the surf and on to the beach to confront the local chief, who could see at once by the feathered helmet of the arrogant-looking newcomer that he was in the presence of a great king. He made gestures of obeisance, waved his hand over the array of gifts, nodded smilingly towards his daughters.

'I am King Tutapu of Raiatea and Borabora,' said the stranger in haughty tones. He used the language of seafarers. 'I have some questions to ask of you.'

'Please,' said the chief, 'you are welcome at my fire. Come and rest. There is food and drink . . .'

Canoes of warriors from the fleet were being ferried down to the beach now and the gifts were being loaded into the outriggers and shipped out to the tipairua canoes. King Tutapu, surrounded as always by his attendant priests who were also his bodyguards, followed the local chief up to the village, where there was a huge fire with several suckling pigs roasting on spits and many bowls of fruit and vegetables surrounding it.

The king was seated comfortably on a wooden stool and offered a drink of kava juice. One of his priests had first to perform a short ceremony over the kava, to make it worthy of a king and his mana. This ritual seemed to irritate the king a little, since it delayed the quenching of his thirst.

His retinue of priests noticed this and got to work on the rest of the food within a reach of the king. A roasted, impaled wild bird, stuffed with herbs, honey and ants' eggs, was purified for his consumption and placed at his right elbow. A dish of dried beetles, quails' eggs, sea worms and boiled crabs was placed at his left elbow. In front of him were laid platters of cooked turtle's flesh garnished with berries and beans.

The chief sat at the stranger's right hand, while his two lovely daughters, still unsure of their fate and looking frightened and glum, sat on the left side. One played fretfully with a necklace of shells around her slim throat, while the other was anxiously biting her bottom lip. Dancers began swaying around the fire, singing songs of peace and goodwill towards all men.

The king's lesser retainers were arriving now and seating themselves around the fire, waited on by local people. The chief was alarmed to see that one of these newcomers was a woman with a white skin and wild black hair. She looked to the chief very much like a vis – a creature which scratched out the eyes of victims with its long nails and then lapped the blood which flowed from the sockets. In fact the chief looked upwards quickly, at the night sky, to see if the vis was accompanied by its constant companion, a flying corpse still wrapped in its mat and known throughout oceania as a balepa. Certainly this creature *shined* in the firelight, which was one of the things which gave the vis away to human onlookers.

'What are you staring at?' asked Tutapu. 'My goblin?'

'Ah,' replied the chief, much relieved, 'a tapua? I thought she was something else.'

Once Tutapu had eaten and drunk sufficiently the chief asked him tentatively, 'Er, to what do we owe the honour of this visit from the King of Raiatea and Borabora?'

Tutapu turned a dour face on the chief. 'I'm looking for my brother,' he said.

'Your brother?' laughed the chief nervously. 'What makes you think he might be here?'

'My brother is Prince Tangiia, who left our islands with three pahi canoes and a god belonging to me. The theft of that god has caused me much anguish and loss of prosperity. He stole from Raiatea's Most Sacred, Most Feared, the God of Hope. An island cannot live without hope – it moves into decline, decays and falls apart. Its people have no heart, no spirit, to face the future. It rots from within.

'My brother also stole my future bride. I mean to kill my brother and retrieve my possessions.

'On board my brother's fleet is one of my own men – a spy –who has been releasing homing birds at regular intervals. I have been following the flight path of these birds, sailing my fleet in the direction whence they came. That path leads me to your island.'

'Not to *here*, King Tutapu, surely?' said the chief, falteringly. 'I –I well – we have seen no other fleet.'

Tutapu stared at the chief disconcertingly. The chief became agitated by this look, knowing by it that his life was in the balance. It behove him to do something. The only thing he could think of was to stand up and make an announcement.

'People of my island,' he cried. 'Listen to me. This great king . . .' he smiled obsequiously at his guest, 'Tutapu by name, has come in search of a robber, his own brother, a man of foul ways. Is there anyone here who can help the king? The brother, curse his repulsive name, is voyaging in three great pahi canoes and is believed to be in this part of the ocean.'

The chief anxiously searched the faces of his people in the firelight to see if anything had registered.

No one spoke.

The chief had visions of his village being razed to the ground, the men all clubbed to death, and himself (along with the tender babies) spitted and roasted alive, while all the females and young boys were raped. He could offer his services to the invader king of course, in return for his own life, but there was no room on the canoes for the whole village. He kept this idea in abeyance, until he was sure that none of his people had seen or heard of anything to do with the matter.

'Anyone at all?' he cried, desperately.

Of course, he might be able to kill the king in single combat, but how would that help him? And somehow, looking at the tall, disdainful warrior-king, the chief had an idea that it would not be an easy thing to subdue this man.

'Anything?' he cried, plaintively.

His men all looked down at the earth. His women shuffled on the soles of their feet. Not a sound came from them.

Why doesn't one of you stand up and tell a lie? thought the chief, angrily, wishing he had done so the moment King Tutapu had put the question to him. *Pretend, make up a story about three pahi canoes with savage crews who sank a cousin's fishing boat. Fabricate a tale. Are you all so stupid?*

No one spoke.

'I think . . .' began the chief, wondering whether a quick smash at the stranger's skull with his patu club, then a glorious last battle, which would almost certainly lead to his defeat and death, might not be the best option after all.

However, the decision was taken away from him by a cry in the night.

'I have seen these three pahi canoes!'

The chief whirled. 'Who spoke?'

'Me! Polahiki, here – in the captive's hut!'

At the back of the village was a small, strong hut built of hardwood. It had no windows. There was a heavy log roof and a thick trapdoor without a handle. It was only three feet high, so that any man of normal height kept inside the hut would have to be on his knees the whole while, yet it seemed too short for a human inhabitant to lie full length within its walls. The whole structure was smeared on the outside with dogshit. Dead, rotting rats hung from the eaves. There was a slit through which a slim container of water or food could be passed. Through the slit, crawling with cockroaches and ants where slops had been spilt and had dried, poked some fingers with dirty broken nails. Blowflies crept over the fingers and in and out of the crack.

The smell of the hut and its unwashed inhabitant was nauseating.

'The prisoner,' said the chief, relieved. 'We took him on the last raid.'

'You raided another island?' questioned Tutapu. 'Which island was that?'

'No, no – they raided *us*, great king. They attacked a village on the far side of Fatu Hiva, taking the inhabitants away, carrying them back to Nuku Hiva. That's where those men come from. The Nuku Hivans are a war-crazy people, O king, unlike us who strive for peace and harmony.' He smiled silkily at the unmoved Tutapu. 'We arrived at the raided village just before dawn to find these two fiends, these dregs of a since-departed war fleet, still remaining, looting and pillaging graves. We took them prisoner, to hold them as hostages. One of them has since died, of, er, *neglect* and zealous overseeing, if you understand me.'

'Bring the speaker here,' ordered Tutapu.

The man from Nuku Hiva was brought before Tutapu and forced to his knees. He would have actually gone down on his knees quite willingly, if they had let him. He smiled through the pigshit that had dried on his face, flung there by angry villagers when he had run the gauntlet. A huge hut spider was caught in the tangle of his hair and struggled there, trying to free its hairy legs. He seemed not only unconcerned but actually oblivious of this arachnid.

There were bruises and lacerations all over the fisherman's body and his left arm hung limp, as if broken below the elbow. He knew he was in the presence of a great war-lord and the right answers to the questions might bring him his freedom.

'You have seen these three pahi canoes?' he was asked.

'Not personally, O great one, but when I arrived back at Nuku Hiva after a few days' fishing out on the open sea, one of our chiefs lay dead and several of his bodyguard were also dead – killed by seafarers who had called at Nuku Hiva the day before I arrived home.'

'Were there any names? Can you tell me a name? You go free if I hear a certain name.'

The man picked at the hardened pig dung on his cheek.

'No, O great king, but I have something just as good as a name, something just as sure. Can I bargain with you, O Royal One? What is on offer here, may I ask?'

Polahiki was procrastinating, playing accepted local games, but he had misjudged his audience.

An angry Tutapu leapt to his feet and raised his kotiate club.

'Tell me guickly, before I smash your skull!'

'A demon, great king,' gabbled the terrified fisherman, hand up to protect his head. 'A demon as white as that one over there by the fire,' he pointed. 'Only it was a male tapua – a white demon who spoke strange harsh words – words from the Otherworld. This tapua killed one of our chiefs. He fought like a demon would fight – with high screeching yells and strange movements – not like a warrior from Oceania at all, but like a madman from the Underworld. Does this answer your question? Do not kill me, O king. I'm not worth the effort of washing the blood and hair from your club.'

Tutapu slowly lowered his weapon, staring at the man in front of him as if ascertaining whether or not he was telling the truth. Finally, he nodded, briskly.

'Clean this creature and put him on my tipairua,' ordered the king. 'Men, eat and drink your fill, then load the canoes with provisions. Dorcha, come here. Talk to me while we walk back to the shore. I want your opinion.'

The grateful Nuku Hivan fisherman was led away, knowing he would live, even if he had to sail with a foreign fleet.

The local chief heaved a sigh of relief, glad to be out of the spotlight at last. His daughters were whisked away into the rainforest, ordered not to return until the great fleet had left the shores. The chief then set about trying to preserve as much of his produce and goods as possible, by whispering to his villagers as he passed them, telling them to hide some of their breadfruit, taro, pandanus flour and other provisions in covered pits in the rainforest, so that they would have something to eat once the invading forces had gone from the island.

The Great Sea-God showed his favour towards the flotilla of tipairua canoes by giving them a favourable current to follow in the direction of the fleet of three pahi canoes. Tangaroa was not especially fond of Hau Maringi, the God of Mists and Fog, whose prejudiced efforts on behalf of King Tutapu were forever being thwarted by the Great Wind-God. On the other hand, Kuku Lau's mirages, in favour of Tangiia, were becoming less effective because of Tutapu's knowledge of her partisanship.

On the whole the gods did not like to be witnessed interfering in human affairs, but tended to do things on the sly. Io, the Father of the Gods, could be unusually harsh towards a god, great or not, who showed partiality and prejudice towards individual mortals. Meddling in earthly matters was considered to be rather beneath a god's or goddess's full attention. A casual adjustment here and there during an idle moment was acceptable, but a full-blooded interest might lead to more serious consequences.

There had been wars amongst the gods before. Their jealousy of each other's powers was legendary. Their imperious tempers were always close to the surface. Human conflicts might easily overspill into a divine war, if the gods took the affairs of humankind too seriously. So they pretended superficial interest and worked their ways through cunning.

After Tangiia had left the shores of Raiatea for ever, Tutapu had been willing to let him go, even after the discovery that a god had been stolen. It was true that Tangiia was a thief and a kidnapper, having abducted Princess Kula, but Tutapu was ready to swallow these insults if it meant that he did not have to kill his brother and slaughter a large proportion of his subjects in order to become king of the two islands.

However, following Tangiia's departure something seemed to go wrong with life on Borabora and Raiatea. It was not that disasters arrived to destroy the islands in the shape of winds or waves, or disease or famine, or stronger invading forces, but somehow the *life* seemed to go out of the islands.

There was the dull pall of depression hanging over the community which never seemed to dissipate. Everyone was listless, apathetic, and little work was done. Crops were planted in a desultory fashion, simply stuck in the ground without the usual rotting fish often buried with the shoot or root to fertilise it and help it to flourish. Little hunting was done, hardly any fishing, no gathering. People sat about their huts and moped, remarking that life was one long boring day after another and that death was beginning to look attractive.

'What's happened here?' asked the frustrated Tutapu of his high priest Ragnu. 'Why all this lethargy, this indolence?'

Ragnu had the answer ready. 'Your brother took the God of Hope with him, my king. Without hope we cannot survive. Without hope we shall languish and die. No one can live without hope – not for ever.'

Tutapu had brooded on this and came to see the truth in Ragnu's words. The God of Hope might be a minor god but he was absolutely essential to the well-being of the islands' peoples. No one could survive long without hope; eventually despair would engulf them and wither them away.

'Can we not carve a God of Hope?' he asked Ragnu.

The high priest's answer was plain. 'We already have one – the fact that it is out on the ocean is an unhappy circumstance for the people of these islands. There are not *two* Gods of Hope, only one.'

So Tutapu ordered the building of a mighty flotilla of ocean-going canoes, but with a war aspect to their design. These were the thirty tipairua canoes, each of which would carry a hundred people. In order to build them Tutapu had to deforest the island of Borabora and this caused him great anguish. He blamed his brother for the devastation of his favourite island and swore that instead of placing a rotting fish at the roots of each new sapling, as it was planted, he would put the decomposing corpse of a man, one for every new tree.

The king sent for Dorcha, who was ushered into his presence.

'I am going to pursue my brother across the great ocean,' said Tutapu. 'We have to recapture the God of Hope. I shall destroy my brother and then return here, to these islands. I intend to kill every one who went with him on that voyage and you have often expressed the desire to extract some sort of revenge on Seumas, who I understand was instrumental in your first husband's death? You may come with me on my expedition and fulfil that desire.'

Dorcha hesitated for a few moments, then replied, 'Good – I shall make ready.'

'Will you take your two husbands with you?'

Of late the twins had been quarrelsome and bad-tempered. Dorcha had been considering leaving the hut and finding herself a new home. The twins did little but squabble with each other over petty issues like who left an item where, and whose turn it was to do a chore, and Dorcha was thoroughly fed up with them. In fact she was sick to death of living with men and had decided to do without them. Until now she had deliberately avoided becoming pregnant, making her husbands wear a root skin over their penises when they made love to her.

Now she was regretting that, for a child would be a good companion for a woman alone.

The reason Dorcha had agreed to go with the expedition was not because she still desired Seumas's death, but because life had lost its meaning after he had left the islands. It had been a mistake to let him go alone, for when he was around she had some target at which to direct the anger that simmered in her breast. Tormenting Seumas had become one of her reasons for living, so she now believed, and since he was no longer there an emptiness had begun to grow within her. She could account for the feeling inside her no other way. Why else would she feel bereft? Why else was she experiencing a feeling of loss, if not for the joy of inflicting suffering on the hated Pict?

'I would prefer it if my two husbands didn't come,' Dorcha told King Tutapu. 'They bicker too much.'

The king agreed with this decision. In his opinion twins brought bad luck upon a voyage. This had been contended by his grandfather and he had no reason to disbelieve it. The twins would stay behind on the islands, when the flotilla sailed.

Once the tipairua canoes were built, and equipped with mat crab-claw sails stained black to symbolise the gravity of the expedition, Tutapu appointed his cousin Haari as regent and set sail. In his heart he carried no hatred, but a determination to destroy his wayward brother. He intended to hunt Tangiia down and slay him, thus to recover the God of Hope and end all contention to Tutapu's kingly authority.

Tutapu felt he had justice on his side, only occasionally recalling that it had been his own threats which had chased Tangiia from the islands in the first place.

Tutapu's course was apa toa on the wind flower.

The king was, like his brother, a good navigator, having been taught by the same tutor, their father. Tutapu was especially good at short-haul navigation and always knew when the flotilla was close to islands. His keen eyes were able to detect *reflected waves*, which were of a barely discernible different shape to ordinary waves on the open waters.

Reflected waves are those waves caused by rebounding off an island or reef, rather than simply the product of wind and currents. By calculating their direction it was possible for a navigator to determine the location of an island or atoll.

Also, Tutapu was a great bird watcher. He knew those species of bird which slept ashore at night and fed on fish out in the open ocean during the day. In the early morning the birds flew out to the fishing shoals and when night came they returned to their island nests. Thus they were land-finding for a keen-eyed navigator, who could follow their direction.

Dorcha asked him one day to teach her the names of the birds which helped him find land.

'The makitopaa, mauakena, katoko, ngao and rakiia,' replied Tutapu without hesitation. 'But you would have difficulty in recognising which was which, when they are high in the air and have the sun behind them. They are all booby and noddy birds. We do not use for example the frigate bird, ropaa uvea, or the nanae, the sooty tern. These are unreliable.'

'What about that one up there,' Dorcha pointed to a white bird with a long, slim, red tail, which seemed to dance backwards in the sky. 'It's very beautiful.'

The bird was as elegant and lovely as an heavenly spirit. Its white trailing feathers wafted the air with such grace that Dorcha believed it was nothing less than the soul of a goddess, made manifest in the warm currents of the air and the torn lacy spindrift of high lazy waves. It was delicately fashioned from sea spume, light and airy as a cloud, and it danced in the blue sky with entrancing movements, bewitching the watcher. Dorcha felt her own soul dancing with the bird, using a light zephyr as a trapeze, floating between earth and ocean on angel's wings.

'I don't know the name of this bird – it must be local to these islands,' replied Tutapu.

A partially washed Polahiki, with badly cropped hair and crooked teeth, was sitting not far away on the deck, waiting to be called officially into the presence of the king. His scrawny body had been oiled, to protect the king's nose from its usual offensive odour, and the fisherman had been given a new, long, bark-cloth skirt which gave him a strangely stiff carriage when he walked, as if he was unused to clothes. The only tattoos he bore were around the lips of his mouth, making it look larger and grimmer than a normal mouth. His broken arm, which had set badly at an angle, had been rebroken by a kahuna and placed in wooden splints.

Polahiki said, 'I know this bird. It is called toake, the tropic bird, and we hold it sacred.'

Dorcha was fascinated by the man's mouth, which resembled the orifice of a large fish, opening and closing in the manner of such fish when they lay gasping on the deck.

'Do you use it to find land?' asked Tutapu.

'Some of us do, others say it is not reliable,' replied the fisherman grinning. 'Last night by the fire you saw the maidens dance the courtship dance of the toake bird.'

'I wasn't watching,' replied Tutapu. 'I was more interested in obtaining information.'

At that moment the helmsman called for the king's

assistance in determining the angle of the vessel's wake to the canoe's path through the ocean, a necessary exercise in order to find the extent of the craft's leeway drift. The task called for a well-trained eye and a delicate, correcting touch on the steering oar.

Dorcha was about to enter one of the deck huts, when Polahiki spoke to her again.

'What are you?'

Dorcha was stepping carefully amongst men and women who were seated on the deck weaving fishing nets. She turned and stared at the gnarled fisherman, then returned to his side. Having lived amongst the Raiateans and Boraborans for so long now, their interest dulled by familiarity, she was surprised by someone who found her an object of curiosity.

'What do you mean, what am I? I'm a woman.'

Polahiki reached out and touched her leg, which she withdrew sharply.

He said, 'I've never seen a creature like you before. You must be made by magic. Who made you?'

His gaunt face was looking up at her expectantly, as if he thought he was about to hear some secret of the universe.

'Who made me?' she laughed. 'My mother made me.'

'And your father?'

'Well, he had a little to do with it, but not much. I'm told my mother met him on the road to the southern lowlands and they spent the night in the heather. Apart from a brief coupling, it was my mother who did all the making.'

'Ahh, and was she of the same paleness of skin?'

'Just the same,' smiled Dorcha. 'Except that she was more beautiful than me.'

'I'm very glad for her sake,' said Polahiki, 'because you are quite ugly.'

Stung by this, Dorcha said, 'I know I'm not young any more – I shall be thirty in a few years – still I have a good face and a good body. I'm not yet a crone.'

'I know nothing of your age, but you have an ugly skin – and those marks around your cheeks and nose – what are they?'

Dorcha touched her face. 'Freckles? Some men like them.'

'Not me,' shuddered the scrawny fisherman. 'I think they're hideous. You look like a lizard that's losing its scales. Is the white demon who killed one of our chiefs – is he your brother? Were you spawned by the same lizard-woman?'

'No – that is, I wasn't spawned by a lizard. I'm a person just like you.'

Polahiki shook his head violently. 'Oh, no, you're not like me – I'm a real mortal. I may rob graves and corpses, but at least I'm true flesh and bone.'

Dorcha said, 'I find *you* quite repulsive too. You look like a man of sticks. You have no meat on you.'

'Me?' cried the fisherman. 'How can you insult me, you pasty sow? The reason I'm thin is so that my fingers can get into small places, reach into graves without digging too much. Anyway, it helps when you get captured by foes.'

Dorcha had decided it was best to ignore the man's insults, since they seemed to get worse when she chastised him.

'How does it help?'

'Why,' he grinned, his teeth long pegs in his narrow jaw, 'who would want to roast and eat me? A chicken would make a better meal. A rat would be tastier.'

She nodded. 'I see what you mean.'

'I shall make myself useful to this king of yours. It seems he is about to have a battle with his brother? There'll be a few corpses around afterwards, I expect. Eh?'

'It's not a prospect for joy,' she chided him.

'Oh yes it is – plenty of bodies to rob of their necklaces and bracelets. Many weapons to gather. Plenty of stones and precious shells. An abundance of red feathers to pluck from the helmets of the fallen warriors. There'll be a singing in *my* heart after the fight. And the beauty of it is, you see,' he said in a confidential manner, as if imparting trade secrets, 'it doesn't matter who wins and who loses. Just so long as the fight is bloody and leaves plenty of carcasses.'

'You're disgusting,' said Dorcha.

'Yes and I want to be rich as well.'

She left the gloating fisherman and stepped again through the squatting people on the deck, trying to keep her feet clear of the nets which were growing in size and number. Inside the deck hut Dorcha sat next to a young girl of fourteen who had become her constant companion on the voyage. The girl's name was Elo and her mother had died shortly after the fleet had set out from Raiatea. Her father was a bailer and had little time for her, so Dorcha had partly adopted the young person.

'Have you cut the yams like I asked?' said Dorcha, sitting next to the girl.

'Yes,' said Elo, turning a smiling face on to Dorcha, melting the Celt's heart. 'Just as you asked.'

'Good,' smiled Dorcha, hugging Elo. 'The wind is picking up and these waves are making me a little woozy. Do you have a story to tell me, to take my mind off the sea?' Dorcha was actually feeling fine, but she knew that Elo liked to be of use. She lay with her back against a stack of pandanus flour leaf-packs.

'Last time I told you a story about Hine-keha, the Moon-Goddess,' replied the girl, 'but this time I have a tale of Maui.'

'Oh, Maui,' groaned Dorcha. 'Is there no end to stories of Maui?'

Elo laughed. 'No, there are many – listen, this is the story of when Maui was named Maui-of-the-many-devices . . .'

In the days when 'fire' was the sole property of Mahuika, a witch and one of the mothers of the ancient clans, Maui used to eat his fish raw. One day he decided he was tired of this tasteless food and made up his mind to get fire for his people, so they could roast their fish and make it more appetising. Mahuika was a terrible ogress, however, and ate men whole. It was said of her, 'She devours human beings as swiftly as her fire devours kindling.' A celestial chicken guarded her hearth and warned her of any attempt to steal her fire from its grate.

Maui however was not called Maui-of-the-many-devices for nothing! Even though Hua-hega refused to tell Maui where Mahuika lived he managed to find her house. Mahuika was truly horrible in appearance, but the courageous, small-statured Maui showed little fear. She ran at him with her mouth open, ready to eat him, but Maui cried, 'Look who I am! Your grandson Maui. I have come to pay you a visit.'

Mahuika stopped short and began to ask him questions about his background and where he came from. Finally, he asked her to give him some fire. Since her fingernails were made of fire, she pulled one out of her hand and gave it to him. He ran back to his canoe, but the fire burned his palms and he let it fall into his wooden canoe. It burned through the bottom and dropped into the sea, which of course put it out.

Maui had to return to Mahuika and ask her for another nail. This happened many times until the old woman lost patience with him and screamed, 'Have my hearth!'

Maui was immediately ringed by walls of flame from which it was impossible to pass through without being burned. In order to escape, Maui changed himself into a hawk, but even then the flames singed his feathers as he tried to pass over them.

This is why the hawk has reddish-brown feathers today.

Maui then changed into a fish and dropped into the ocean, but the fire was making the water boil and he had to leap out on to an island.

The island, called Whakaari, began to burn and is still burning to this very day.

Maui then called on the Gods of Rain, Sleet and Hail – Ua, Nganga and Whatu – to extinguish the fire. Only these three gods working together managed to put out the flames.

Mahuika was almost drowned in the flood they produced between them, but managed to throw her fire into the branches of a kaikomako tree, where it remained burning.

The kaikomako tree's wood is still used to make people's fires: the long-headed flames of Mahuika's hearth fire are trapped inside and released when the wood is rubbed vigorously against another wood.

No one knows what happened to the celestial chicken, but many believe Maui cut kindling from the kaikomako tree that very day and ate the bird for his supper. It was his first cooked meal. It was so tasty that thereafter he preferred roasted fish and meat to raw food and passed this on to his people.

Now that his brother's fleet had deviated from a straight course, the homing birds released by the traitor would not be seen by King Tutapu. It behove the king to listen to his high priest, Ragnu, and follow that man's inclinations. Ragnu informed his king that the Great Sea-God was showing them their path, with his ocean currents, and Tutapu had no choice but to follow where he was being led, trusting in Ragnu's judgement.

After many days sailing they entered a part of the ocean where the skies were stretched tightly like a light-blue skin over the roof of voyaging. The wind was slight but gusty and there was a chop on the surface of the sea. The current was strong enough to travel without sail, but the mats remained on the mast, swinging this way and that in changeable breezes. Tutapu wanted to waste no power in reaching his goal.

One evening the vessels, strung out like a snake with a line between each one in this relative calm, passed slowly by a distant island. The island consisted almost entirely of a single mountain with a flat top whose silhouette showed stark against the red sky. Men and women gathered in silence to stare at the island, while Ragnu performed a sacred dance and sprinkled the evening air with chanting and songs. One of his young priests played a nose flute, but no drums were sounded.

Dorcha asked Elo, 'What is that island? Why are people staring at it with such awe?'

'It's the drum of Lingadua.'

'Who is Lingadua?'

Elo said, 'Why, he's the God of Drums, of course – he only has one arm, but when he beats his drum the world shakes. His drumskin is made from the Great Earth-Goddess Papa's hymen, stolen from her while she was in her first ecstatic embrace with the Great Sky-God Rangi. We must not sound our own drums here, or the one-armed Lingadua will steal their voices . . .'

Darkness came swiftly as Ra fell into the sea, but before they were out of sight of Drum Island, Whatu the God of Hail sent down a shower out of Rangi's domain. Hailstones the size of pebbles came raining out of the sky, hammering against the tipairua canoes, driving through the roofs of the huts. Inside the huts were Tutapu's war drums and the hailstones pounded on the stretched hides of the drums, and on the hollow log-drums, and the sound reverberated over the ocean.

People themselves were struck down by the hailstones and hunched there becoming bruised and battered. Out on the ocean the water was hissing and pockmarked. The world was a white blur for some time as the hard sky shattered and fell on the unsuspecting Oceanians. Then finally the shower stopped just as abruptly as it had begun.

On all the decks of the canoes people began to rise,

helping each other to their feet. Gourds had been shattered by the force of the hail and their liquid contents were flowing over the canoes. The leaf-roofed huts had been almost stripped of their covering. Hailstones still lay in layers on flat surfaces and heaped in natural pockets.

Ragnu was grim. 'Our drums have sounded within the province of Lingadua. If he heard them, he'll be angry. He'll steal the voices from our war drums and we'll be at a disadvantage when we next go to fight.'

'It wasn't our fault. We didn't beat the drums ourselves,' said King Tutapu.

'How is Lingadua to know that? He's an irritable god and doesn't stop to think before he acts. I'm sure we'll have trouble from him in the future.

'In any case, we know which side Whatu, the God of Hail, has taken in this conflict. He must favour your half-brother, Tangiia.'

King Tutapu rapped his knuckles on the nearest drum and it resounded through the hut.

'It seems he's left them with their voices,' he said.

Ragnu was doubtful. 'We'll see,' he said.

There were holes in the mat sails which had to be repaired and the decks were swept clear of the melting hailstones. Gradually life settled back into its normal routine. A new shift came on. Bailers toiled at their never-ending task, the steersman handled his steering oar, the look-out woman's keen eyes scoured the ocean ahead for any floating objects.

King Tutapu followed a star path which led to a constellation called Small Face with Small Eyes, and on through the Running Beast, the largest magellanic cloud of the roof of voyaging. He took these sightings not to find the way to where they were going, but to remember where they had been.

It was the natural duty of every Oceanian navigator, king or commoner, mentally to chart the great ocean on which they voyaged. Only in this way were memory maps assembled, to be passed on to descendants, so that journeys could be retaken and perhaps extended, to stretch the limits of known seascapes and oceanic knowledge available to seafarers.

One day perhaps the great-great-grandchild of King Tutapu would return again to Lingadua's drum.

The king went to his rest after midnight, that time of the dead pulse, when all things stand still for a moment.

He was woken from a bad dream by three beats on a drum.

Pulling a cloak of feathers around himself for warmth, he hurried out on deck, to find all was peaceful and still.

'Did you hear anything?' he asked of the deck watch.

'Some distant thunder,' said one man. 'Too far away to concern us.'

Tutapu stared out, into the darkness.

'Three claps of thunder?'

'It may have been three,' answered the man, casually. 'I didn't keep a tally.'

'Next time be more attentive,' snapped Tutapu, 'or you may be counting severed fingers.'

The man swallowed hard and stared with white, frightened eyes.

'Get back to your duties,' Tutapu growled. 'Keep a sharp watch – that means ears as well as eyes.'

He went back to his own hut and spent a restless night. The next morning he was woken to be told three fit men had died in the small hours. The cause seemed to be heart failure.

'Each one has a bruise on his chest, above his heart,' Ragnu told Tutapu, 'as if he has been struck by a heavy club.'

'Or a drum stick wielded by a one-armed god,' muttered Tutapu. 'Is this punishment, or is it merely a warning? The deaths of seamen is no penalty for a king. I have the feeling

I'm going to be disciplined further, when the time comes.'

Ragnu could not disagree with his king and suggested a human sacrifice to try to appease Lingadua.

'That would probably be the best thing,' said Tutapu, 'though I have a feeling we might be too late.'

A young male virgin was chosen and brought to the front of the king's canoe. He was bound with sennit cord, hand and foot, and placed on an improvised ritual platform made of wood. A garland of leaves was placed around his head.

The youth's eyes were wide with fear, until Ragnu sat and talked to him, telling the young man he would become a great spirit in the sky, an atua, and that one day men would worship him and treat him with more respect than a mere king. Ragnu then gave the youth of bowl of porridge, in which there were secret spices known only to the priests, and the youth became docile and willing.

'The gods and our ancestors are hungry for sau,' cried Ragnu, in the ceremony that took place under the roof of voyaging. 'Here is food for the Lord of the Drum, Lingadua, whom we have displeased!'

So saying Ragnu slit the youth's throat with an obsidian dagger. The body fell forward and the scarlet blood splashed forth, staining the deck. It flowed over the stern of the craft, into the water, leaving a widening red wake. Foam became red froth until the surf spread and died.

The dying boy lay there, oiled, muscled, beautiful, his tattoos still fresh, his eyelids fluttering like butterflies. The gods had given him a superb body and they had taken it back before age had withered the flesh and time had corrupted the spirit. Indeed, the young man had been chosen for his almost perfect form.

There was chanting then, as the body drained of fluid. The youth's mother was distressed. She had already lost one son to the sea, the boy having fallen from the masthead and broken his neck at the beginning of the voyage. Friends comforted her, telling her that she had yet a third son who needed her love.

Nevertheless, she slipped quietly overboard later that night, surrendering herself to the embrace of Tangaroa.

Dorcha had witnessed the whole affair, indeed had seen many like it since coming to Oceania. In her homeland of Albainn the men were savage and would fight at a moment's notice, tear out an eye, or sever a limb. There was a kind of terrible fury bubbling inside an Albannach's brain, which overflowed when some delicate trigger was touched. They were like wolves, those men of her homeland, instinctively attacking in the subconscious knowledge that he who does not strike first might not live long enough to strike at all. It was defensive.

This calm deliberate taking of life, however, was not within her experience. She had heard horrible stories of sacrifices down where the Angles and Jutes lived. There, it was said, human victims were burned alive in wicker effigies. Giant basket-men were stuffed with dry hay and straw, then screaming people were crammed inside the cages and set alight. Holy men called Druids were said to be responsible for this heinous rite; priests carrying out a spring time festival, a sacrifice to the fertility gods of flower buds and bird eggs.

But she herself had not witnessed such ghastly sights and the sacrifice of young men and women affected her deeply.

'You do not approve?' King Tutapu said to her, as she stared at the young man's body in the moonlight. 'Others forget him quickly, but you remain here.'

'It is not up to me to approve or disapprove of a king's command – I simply do not see it as necessary.'

'The individual is not important,' explained Tutapu. 'The community as a whole, everyone, must be protected against the impulsive wrath of fickle gods. This man has given his life for the many. It is a brave and wonderful thing to be able to sacrifice oneself for the benefit of the population. I hope I may be given the opportunity one day.'

She stared into his eyes and saw that he meant every word he said.

Dorcha had come on this expedition, not because she still harboured a grudge against Seumas, though her quarrel with him was still as hot and troublesome to her. She had come because she had been dissatisfied with her life back on Raiatea. Some inner voice had been urging her to strike camp, move on, seek a new home. This was in itself rather fickle, since she had told Seumas – and meant it at the time – that she wanted to settle down and live a comfortable life on the two islands.

Yet people do not stay the same, she told herself. They change constantly. It reminded her that one should not use the word 'always' or the word 'never', since they formed promises which must eventually be broken, unless the person who made them was fashioned of stone or wood – or straw.

2

Tutapu woke that night from a deep sleep. The air was hot and humid. Not a fly was stirring, the livestock was still, no man was abroad. He rose from his mat and went out on to deck to find all his crew asleep, even the helmsmen and bailers. The duty watch was nowhere to be seen. Bodies lay everywhere in a seemingly fathomless torpor. They were draped over rigging, sail mats, gourds and fishing nets. A woman lay on her side using her fat little boy, who was also in a drugged sleep, as her pillow. A man hung over a steering oar, as if he were a piece of washing drying in the moonlight.

It was as if a goddess had passed her hand over the boat, her hands dispensing sleep dust.

'Is anyone awake?' called the king, his voice deadened by the stillness of the night. 'Who watches over my canoe?'

No one answered.

He failed to rouse them with his call and was loath to touch them because he was taboo.

Strangely enough, the only movement came from the corpse of the sacrificed youth, still half hanging over the end of the canoe, his limp arms trailing in the water, his cut throat gaping like the open mouth of a giant frog. The ripples of the boat's wake made the youth's body roll gently from side to side, as if he were about to stand up and announce his return.

King Tutapu stared out over the kava-coloured sea. There was a sluggish calm that weighed oppressively on the night. The boat floated on this languid water as if carrying a cargo of opiate dreams. It slid slowly and silently, a vessel in slumber. Above him the stars were like glistening heavy stones imbedded in a dull sky. Between the boat and the stars the clammy air seemed to hold as much moisture as the sea itself.

The other twenty-nine tipairua drifted on behind. He could see them in the moonlight, like hard shadows on the ocean. They seemed to have no life in them, as if they were simply bark following bark naturally along a captivating current. No sailors steered them, nor even stirred on their boards. They were just driftwood which happened to resemble canoes, running in the track of the king's own vessel, caught by the same rivers of warm surface water, sliding over the heavy ocean.

Then, when he looked out over the bows, he saw a path of deep purple appear on the surface of the sea. The path led to a cave which had opened itself in the waters, a cave which led downwards into a nether land.

Tutapu now guessed what was happening. He had been murdered in his sleep by one of his subjects. Or his heart had stopped in the night, without warning.

But then he heard a voice, coming from the cave.

'*Tutapu, come to me.*'

The voice was like the sound of the wind blowing through the husk of a coconut. Or the rustling of dry grasses on a hill. Or the whisper that lives in an empty seashell.

Yet he knew at once it was the voice of his father, calling to him from the Land of the Dead. '*Come to me,*' repeated his father. '*Son, I must speak with you. Do not be afraid. Come. Bring no weapons. Eat nothing. Bring one of your babies.*'

But Tutapu *was* afraid. A man might be fearless in battle and the most dangerous exploit hold no terrors for him, yet when he is faced by the gaping maw that is a tunnel to the Land of the Dead, he feels such fear it almost strangles him.

Yet, he knew that he had to go – he was *compelled* to go. He would have rather not gone, for there were horrors there which he knew would leave a canker on his soul. He was going to see the dead, the empty ones, in their own foul habitat. They were not coming to his house, a terrible enough event; he was going down into theirs. He was taking the path walked just a short time ago by the sau of the sacrificed youth. Would he now have to meet this boy, perhaps pass him on the way to the underworld, the living being quicker of foot? Would the boy be angry with him? Perhaps even attempt revenge for an early death?

'I must get it over with,' he murmured to himself. 'If I must go, I shall go now.'

Tutapu picked up a club, but then remembered the last three commands of his father. It was hard not to take a weapon with him. He felt secure with the club in his hand. Yet he had been told to take nothing except a baby.

A child was sleeping nearby, close to his mother, one of the king's cousins and his concubine. Tutapu dropped the club and reached for the boy. When he held him in his arms, he stirred. Tutapu took little interest in the children born to his concubines, since they were not recognised as his sons. The boy would, if he lived to grow to adulthood, become a vestal priest and serve one of his half-brothers, a *true* son of king and queen. Just as Ragnu was an unrecognised half-brother to both himself and Tangiia, and Kikamana was their half-sister. The priests of the people needed to have some royal blood in their veins, in order to be immune from the taboo king's mana.

Tutapu studied the infant's smooth complexion, his half-open mouth, his chubby limbs and round little belly. Tutapu was not an ogre and he knew the mother would be heartbroken to find her child gone in the morning. Sentiment welled in his breast as he stared down at the beautiful child. In the end he knew he could not take the boy with him. Instead he took from the boy's arms a bark-cloth rag doll. The child stirred in his sleep, but did not wake. Tutapu put the infant back by his mother's side and stepped over the edge of the canoe on to the water.

Once on the purple path he walked down into the open mouth of the cave.

Milu stood there, at the opening to Te Reinga, but he spoke not a word to Tutapu, since the king was a living spirit.

The old king's voice came to Tutapu, in his head.

'*Speak not to the God of the Dead. Look not into his eyes.*'

Tutapu did as he was told, passing the beautiful pale form of Milu wrapped in his cloak of white and lilac flower petals without glancing up, though he was sorely tempted to do so.

The sea was spongy under the king's feet, yet firm enough to hold his weight. Once below the surface of the water the walls of the cave turned to crystal, with veins of coloured stone running through it. He could hear the sound of his own footsteps on the floor of the cave, as if he were walking on the hard hollow crust of a baked mudflat.

He did indeed pass the youth, who neither turned his head to look, nor spoke a word. The boy did not appear as happy as Tutapu might have expected. He had, after all, been chosen for the beauty of his body and his spirit, and it had been expected that he would remain in that perfect form for all eternity. Instead, the young man looked as if he were made of dingy sand, blown gently down a hillside; a swirling cloud of mournful dust, broadcasting such sadness it enveloped Tutapu as he passed and greyed his heart. Tutapu might have choked on the youth's misery, had he not hurried on down the tunnel, out of reach.

When he reached the end of the tunnel, the Land of the Dead lay before him, vast and unearthly. It was a place of blacks and greys, a land of moving shadows and shades. The ground was covered in sharp stones and jutting rocks, and nowhere was there any colour. It looked impossible to cross.

A man stood at the end of a valley, decorated for war.

The figure's tattoos stood out in relief – strong and heroic in nature. There was a magnificent helmet on his head, of many feathers, though none of any bright hue. In his right hand he held a patu club and in his left a shield. Though the man's frame was thin and wasted, there was about him an enormous aura of strength.

Tutapu recognised the figure as being that of his father.

Stepping out of the end of the tunnel, Tutapu was startled to see a giant naked goddess blocking his way. She was in fact at the exit to many tunnels, from many areas in the living world, squatting there, her vagina like a massive cave itself, surrounded by bramble bushes with wicked thorns. Into this living cave she fed the shattered bodies of men.

Newly dead people were coming out of the many tunnels. Some were immediately snatched up by the monstrous goddess, as tall as ten palm trees, and covered with nails and teeth. She dashed those she picked up against rocks, smashing their skulls and breaking every bone in them. Their broken bodies were pushed, limp and shattered, up inside her womb.

When her eyes rested on him, Tutapu reached automatically for his club as he prepared to defend himself. His hand found nothing and the goddess merely gave him a gruesome sharp-toothed smile. He knew then that if he had produced a weapon, she would have crushed him instantly.

'You are not one of the dead,' she said. 'You have no business here.'

'Who are you?' he asked her boldly. 'What *is* your grisly business?'

'I am Nangananga,' she cried, her long black hair flowing down her body and stretching like a bridal train.
'Goddess of Punishment. My business is with men who
lived their whole lives without taking a wife. Bachelors are
the curse of mankind.'

'It seems a harsh punishment for choosing to remain
single,' said Tutapu. 'Why, even now a youth is on his way
to this land whom I sacrificed to the gods. Is this to be his
reward?'

'I am only interested in men past marriageable age, not
in young virgins such as your victim. My task is to punish
those who might have added to the strength of the people,
by bringing forth progeny. Return to your canoe, King
Tutapu, I have my work to attend to. You keep me from it
with your chatter . . .'

'I come to speak with my father.'

'Give me one of your children,' she demanded. 'I must
eat one of your babies, or you cannot pass by me.'

It seemed to him that he would not hear his father's
words, that he must return to the canoe. It was hard, considering his father was within sight. To be so close to his
father, yet not be able to hear his words . . .

He remembered the infant's rag doll.

'Here,' he cried, whipping it out of his waistband. 'Take
my child.'

Nangananga snatched at the doll and without inspecting
it she swallowed it whole.

'Pass, then,' she said. 'Quickly.'

With that the giant goddess, whose pendulous breasts
swung this way and that with such force when she moved,
they shattered obsidian rocks to slivers, turned away from
him. Her hands, with their long talons, reached out and
snatched an elderly man as he left the exit of a tunnel. She
dashed his skull against a stone, smashed his bones to
splinters.

To his horror Tutapu saw that the victim was not

senseless, but was still aware, his eyes rolling in his pulped head, groans issuing from his gaping mouth.

'I must take me a wife as soon as possible,' muttered Tutapu, moving on. 'I must catch up with my brother and marry Kula before I come to this place.'

Tutapu was met by his mother, who said nothing to him, but crooked a finger and walked ahead, leading him through the maze of whetted and barbed rocks. He followed her, silently, wondering at her form. Instinctively he knew that even if he questioned her, she would not answer him.

Crossing Te Reinga, the Land of the Dead, Tutapu was aware of a great thirst, accompanied by ravenous hunger. There were inviting fresh-water streams running between the rocks and the food of the dead, ngaro, was distributed like guano over the rocks. He might have drunk from one of the streams, or eaten some of the ngaro, had not his father's voice rung in his head.

'*Eat nothing, drink nothing, for if you do you will have to remain in the place where you now walk.*'

Tutapu's father waited at the edge of a seething ocean, between sheer rocks, standing on the last Stepping Stone, a jetty. Not far from him stood his first wife, who had waited for him and led him through the bleak boulder-strewn landscape to the jetty for the canoe to carry all dead souls. His third wife, the mother of Tangiia, was there also. And now his second wife, Tutapu's mother, joined them.

There was indeed a boat there waiting, ready to take the old king across the sea to the silent village of Nabangatai, the place of invisible souls. Since he had been a warrior in life, he would have to fight with Samulayo, God of Death in Battle. Win or lose, Tutapu's father would then go before the Serpent-God, Dengei, who would interrogate and judge him according to his deeds. Tutapu knew all this, from the stories told by priests.

'Son,' said the old king, splendid in his battle attire and wearing his war face, 'I have not much time, so I must tell you now what you must do. You must turn your flotilla round and return to your home islands. Forget your brother, who has fled your wrath. Let him make his own kingdom, away from yours, in a new Faraway Heaven.'

Tutapu felt a flare of fury in his breast, despite the awe in which he held his warrior father's spirit.

'You could have told me this without me having to travel to the Land of the Dead. It has not been a journey without perils. You sent me commands, why not tell me about my brother?'

'Because you would not have taken my words seriously. I wanted you to know how grave is your situation. To do that, I needed you here, where I can look into your eyes.'

Tutapu tried not to look into his father's face.

'But Tangiia has done me a great wrong. He has stolen one of my gods and has abducted my bride-to-be. How can I let him get away with these crimes?'

'He is your brother.'

'*Half*-brother,' corrected Tutapu.

'Yet you are both my true sons. If you persist in your venture, one of you must join me here. When I was alive that did not seem a terrible thing, but now I'm dead I am aware of the waste of such a young life. You are two kings, you can both be great in your own spheres, but you must remain apart.'

'I'm sorry, Father, but I must destroy my brother, before he destroys me. I must recapture the God of Hope, marry the woman who was intended to be my wife, and right those wrongs perpetrated by Tangiia.'

The old king sighed. 'On your own head be it, then – but remember, it might be you who falls in battle.'

Tutapu said, 'I think not, Father – and in any case, I am willing to risk it.'

'Have pity on a dead king's son.'

'No,' said Tutapu, determinedly. 'It is impossible for me to feel pity for Tangiia.'

'I meant you,' said the old king.

'I need no pity, I need *revenge*.'

His words echoed around the Land of the Dead and the old king saw that he meant them, and that he was wasting his time.

'Then go,' said the old man, turning away to step into the sombre, stately canoe, whose decorating long black feathers made it appear like some giant scavenging bird, resting on the murky waters. 'Go now.'

The canoe pulled away, its invisible crew hauling on the sheets, raising the feathery crab-claw sail. The great bark was covered in dark effigies of gods unknown to living men. There were black banners that might have been the souls of the damned flapping from the mast and stays. In the place above the Land of the Dead, which would have been the sky in the real world, the clouds gathered like vultures. Tutapu watched his father go with great sadness in his breast. He had been a good father, a good king, and now he was nothing but a shadow.

Tutapu turned and retraced his steps through the boulder-strewn land to the mouth of the cave, where Nangananga worked tirelessly at weeding out the bachelors from the married souls and burying the former for ever in her womb.

When Tutapu stepped out of the cave, on to the sea of the real world, the purple path was gone. The sea became real water and he shouted in alarm as he began to sink. A shout went up from the canoe, which he recognised as Ragnu's voice.

'The king has been sleepwalking! He drowns!'

An ordinary man, one of the fisherfolk, reached out with an arm and clutched the king's hand, hauling him aboard.

Tutapu lay there, exhausted and dripping, while Ragnu came to him and stood over him.

'I saw you sleepwalking, my lord. You stepped out into the night as if you were going on a stroll. I was too late to prevent you from going over the side.'

Tutapu sighed. 'I have been on a journey.'

'In your dreams?'

'A momentous journey.'

He looked around him, for the mother and child, then remembered he had forbidden children under the useful age of twelve to be present on this voyage.

'My own dreams disobey my commands,' he murmured to himself, 'then cause me to forget I ever made them.'

The king went into the hut to dry himself, since there was a chill wind that night. He thought about his father's words and though he wanted to find room for them in his heart, he could not do it. His kingly breast was too full of other things to allow such feelings inside. It was in his destiny that he should find his brother and take his revenge.

'Perhaps the old man was trying to protect his younger son?' said Tutapu to himself. 'Perhaps I was not his concern at all, but Tangiia, my faithless brother, was his real interest?'

With this jealous thought in mind he fell into an uneasy sleep for the second time that night.

The fisherman who had saved the king, instinctively reaching out a hand to a drowning man, realised afterwards he had touched a taboo person. The man fell ill a little time later, wasted away, and died. King Tutapu was told of the man's death and asked, 'Was he married?'

'Yes, my lord,' said his priest.

'Good, then we need mourn his loss of life, but not his death, for he is safe.'

With this enigmatic statement puzzling his brain, the priest went to the man's relatives to try to comfort them.

PART SIX

The Time of the Green Lizard

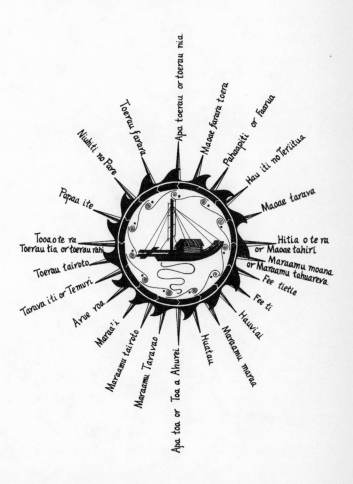

1

After they had left that heavy, dream-like part of the world to which Tangaroa's adaro had led them, King Tangiia's fleet set sail in a stiff, clean wind. They traversed the ocean, following Tooa-o-te-ra on the wind flower, almost retracing their voyage to Nuku Hiva in the opposite direction. Kikamana told Tangiia they would come perilously close to Raiatea if they continued their present course, so the king ordered a slight change of direction, and headed for Tahiti.

The king himself had never been to this island, not more than a few days sailing from Raiatea, but several of his men had touched its shores. These men spoke of a people friendly to the Raiateans living on an island rich in resources. They were not certain of their reception, given that this was a fleet of three large canoes and not a fishing vessel of a few men, but they felt reasonably confident they would not be attacked without preliminary negotiations taking place.

At the end of twelve days' sailing, Tangiia could see a lagoon reflecting on the cloud base. This stretch of the voyage had seen the birth of three babies, the death of one old woman and the disappearance during the night of a young, healthy, male bailer.

The vanishing of the young man was put down to Amai-te-rangi, the god who fished for people from his home in the sky. Someone said they even saw the line being whisked back up to the clouds, with something wriggling on the end of it.

While Tangiia was adding knots to the mnemonic cord-device, Kaho the blind navigator, the Feeler-of-the-sea, put his hand in the water. After a short while Kaho announced that there were many islands in the vicinity.

'The water is warmer here – this is a calm place – we are approaching Tahiti.'

A particular swell, unfelt by others, which Kaho had discerned by the motion of the boat to be dead astern until now, had changed its course. This swell had its origins thousands of miles away in the upper trade winds, beyond the equator. It had gone down like a sea serpent diving to a depth to where its coldness was no longer distinguished by the blind old man, and warmer, surface currents had taken its place.

That evening there was a minor tragedy. No one lost their life but when the shark-callers were beating the water, a great white shark hid amongst smaller cousins milling around the canoes. It rose suddenly, catching the shark-callers unawares, and took a man's leg with its crescent mouth. The leg was severed at the knee and the man pumped blood into the water, sending the other sharks crazy with excitement.

The wound was cauterised quickly and medicine used to sedate the victim. There were many injuries amongst the shark-callers, and some amongst other professions too. A body lost various parts during its journey through life – an eye taken out, a hand or an arm severed, a foot or a leg lost – the Oceanians did not consider this to be a major tragedy. If the victim lived, the body adjusted, and if the old job called for four limbs, two good eyes and perfect hearing, why, then the injured person took up another line of work, which did not require them.

Since it was too dangerous that evening to carry on fishing for sharks, the creatures being maddened by the blood in the water, and snapping at every shadow, the people used another method of fishing. They smeared some paste made from hotu nuts on a coral club which they then dangled in the water. The fish who came to investigate this substance were stunned by it, then when they floated to the surface were lifted from the water.

The following morning an island came into view. Its mountains were a fantastic labyrinth of pinnacles and gorges, with eerie windows in the myriad peaks of rock. It seemed a place where spirits dwelt high up in these mysterious, jagged forests forming a fairy kingdom at the top of the island. Strange wisps of cloud encircled irregular igneous vanes of stone and every peak was like a claw, and every uncanny claw covered in tiny beaks of rock. A land which had swallowed birds. This was the taboo island Moorea, an island close to Tahiti.

'This is a sacred place,' Tangiia said, emphatically. 'We will not land here.'

They sailed on to the greater island, Tahiti. This place too was volcanic, but the mountains were less ghostly and covered in green rainforest. There were beaches beyond the reef, where people could be seen washing clothes, gathering shellfish, chattering and laughing together. On seeing the fleet these people pointed and gestured, some of them running up the beach to inform others that there were visitors to the island.

Tangiia moored the pahi canoes just inside the reef and waited for a reception committee to come out to meet them.

Seumas stood on the bows, not at all convinced that the Tahitians were friendly, and when a war canoe was launched a little while later, this confirmed his fears.

'Here they come!' he called to Tangiia. 'Are we going to have to fight?'

Tangiia came forward and stared at the oncoming war canoe. It was a massive craft, longer than the pahi canoes by at least another third. There were no sails, but Seumas counted 144 paddlers, 8 steering oarsmen, and many warriors on the large elevated combat platform in the bows, surrounding a nobleman in war feathers. There were at least 300 people on board the canoe. Even the paddlers sitting on the gunwales were armed and ready to leap into action. There was packed muscle-power on that craft, strong fit warriors who had not been wearied by months at sea and a restricted diet.

The prow of the magnificent craft swept upwards in two great v-shaped curves. There were totems rising from the hulls, covered in elaborate carvings, some of which had coloured banners flowing from their heads. The royal personage, encircled by his priest-bodyguards, had a tall helmet whose edging feathers spread like a large fan above his head. Around his neck was a decorated u-shaped collar, also fringed with precious feathers, though smaller than those which bordered the helmet.

Standing beside the nobleman was an important kahuna wearing a helmet shaped like a fish head, the mouth open and revealing rows of sharp teeth. A frill hung from the back of this strange headgear, protecting the priest's neck from the sun. In his hand the kahuna held an engraved hardwood staff.

'Do we fight?' asked Seumas, agitated. 'Are we just going to stand here?'

Kikamana said, 'Don't be so impatient for bloodshed, Seumas. If they were serious about fighting they would have sent a dozen war canoes, not one. This is more in the nature of a royal barge . . .'

The canoe finally came up alongside and warriors leapt from the combat platform on to the deck of the king's pahi.

There was a lot of yelling and thigh-slapping, rolling of eyes and tongue-showing, until finally the man wearing the royal helmet stepped on board the pahi and introduced himself to King Tangiia as the son of the King of Tahiti. He invited Tangiia to return with him to the island in the war canoe.

Despite Seumas's misgivings, Tangiia accepted.

Once the king had stepped on board the war canoe, outriggers with excited young women and men came shooting over the breakers to the reef. Barely touching the surf their light canoes seemed to fly like birds. They came with garlands and sweetmeats, fruit and juices to drink. They sang to the seafarers who had come to their island, helping to steer the three great pahi canoes over the safest part of the reef, throwing the hibiscus blooms on to the decks.

By the time Tangiia reached the beach he could see why these people had no need to put on a greater show of strength than just one war canoe. There were a great many of them; too many to concern themselves with subduing a small fleet carrying well under three hundred souls. King Tangiia took an escort of men and women, the most attractive of his people, to meet the king of this wealthy and well-populated island. Crowds had amassed now, along the sands, of men, women, children and dogs.

'I am King Tangiia,' said the navigator proudly to his host, 'and these are my people. We have fled the islands of Raiatea and Borabora, where my father ruled but is now dead. My brother has proclaimed himself king of those islands, but is fearful of my presence. Therefore I am bound for unknown parts of our ocean, to find a Faraway Heaven for my people.'

The King of Tahiti, surrounded by his retainers, nodded gravely.

'I am King Kopu, the Morning Star. Welcome to my island. I knew your father, young man. He was a wise and good ruler. Your brother Tutapu is also known to me and I respect his strength of purpose. You are young. You have the mark of the adventurer on your face. You have done the right thing, by removing this threat to your brother's authority, whether the danger of usurpation is real or not.

'Now,' he proclaimed, 'there will be a feast. You must tell me of your adventures on the great ocean.'

King Morning Star, a fat man twice as large as Tangiia, was then carried at shoulder level on a decorated platform by twelve youths, three on each corner pole. They led the procession, with Tangiia walking beside his host, back to a village at the foot of a great mountain. There the fat king clapped his hands and ordered meats, fruits, vegetables, fish and shellfish to be brought to the cooking fires. Dancing began again with the most beautiful maidens Tangiia had ever seen, swaying and singing, while the drums beat and the flutes trilled.

The heady fragrance of blossoms mingled with the smell of rained-upon earth and drifted down from high mossy valleys, where clouds of waterfall spray drifted as ghosts, keeping the rock towers green with furze and fern. Birdsong was in every narrow cleft, every hollow, echoing around rock walls which soared to the clouds, gathering light on their ascent. Petals floated down from tall spires of stone, to the rainforest far below, delicate fingernails of alpine flowers.

'Feasting, love, laughter!' the cry went up.

Mats were brought covered in designs which Tangiia was told were made by cutting stencils from broad leaves, the artisans amongst the Raiateans noting this new technique for decorating their wares for future use. Palms leaves were placed over the heads of the visitors, protecting them from the sun. Fresh clear water was brought from sparkling waterfalls which fell from the mountains of this beautiful island. It was obvious to the Raiateans that the land was bountiful and this was a rich and prosperous place which had known little strife and much harmony.

Sacred kava drink was brought and shared only between the two royal personages present.

King Morning Star noticed the one white body amongst the many brown and asked King Tangiia for an explanation.

'This is a captive of Kupe the Navigator, from a faroff place known as the Land-of-Mists. He is a free man and now sails as one of us. Do you wish to speak with him?'

'He is not a supernatural creature?'

'No,' said Tangiia.

'How disappointing, but indeed, he seems quite exotic none the less,' King Morning Star said, staring at Seumas as the Pict walked amongst the bowls of fruit, his dog at his heels. 'I shall talk with him later. Does he speak the tongue of seafarers?'

'Now he does, but he also has a darker tongue, of which we have not entirely been able to cure him.'

'I should tear it out at the roots with tongs!'

Tangiia smiled. 'Unfortunately that would rob him of his new tongue too and I must say I like talking with him. He has interesting ideas and can throw a different light on problems that need to be solved. His method of thinking is unusual.'

'Quite. I'm not surprised,' said Morning Star, 'and he seems to have a peculiarly strong attachment to his livestock. Does he think it will be stolen?'

The Tahitian king meant Dirk, and again Tangiia explained that in the Land-of-Mists men used dogs for hunting and treated them like human beings, a fact which astonished Morning Star so much that he wobbled on his stool, his fat body shaking.

'You mean they don't *eat* their puppies?'

'They feed their dogs meat, which makes the flesh of the animals unpalatable.'

'Incredible,' said the Tahitian king, shaking his head in wonderment. 'How fortunate for us that we live in a civilised part of the great ocean, and not in this strange land where skins are pale as fish bellies and dogs are raised as children.'

Tangiia made a mental note to pass that one on to Seumas later, when the Pict was getting above himself.

Ra finished his slow journey over the face of his father, Rangi, and Hine-nui-te-po urged Hine-keha to come out of hiding and show her bright visage to Papa.

During one unguarded moment Tangiia caught sight of Kula, sitting on the far side of the fire talking to a neighbour. He could see her face through the high flames, appearing and disappearing as the fire waxed and waned. Fiery sparks flew between them as the bark of the firewood peeled and rose on the hot air. Kula's head then turned and her eyes met his through the wavering long-headed flames. He read something in her sad-eyed stare which caused his heart to beat with excitement.

Turning to King Morning Star, Tangiia said, 'I must speak with that woman over there – she is Princess Nau Ariki.'

The king looked surprised but nodded.

Tangiia stood up and walked to the shadows of some huts. He stood there and waited. After a short while Kula rose and joined him. She came to him and stood before him.

There were flowers behind her ears and garlands decorating her throat. Her hair had a silver sheen to it which took his breath away; its blackness was deeper than the darkest night out on the great ocean, yet bearing the flush of shining white stars that made the Long Shark at Dawn. Her small pointed breasts with their dark nipples, below the streamers which flowed like waterfalls from her collar bones, rose and fell slowly, as she regarded him in silence. She was as beautiful as any goddess, or fairy, or mermaid. She might have been born amongst the lovely shells of the ocean, a princess of the coral kingdoms below the waterline.

Tangiia wished to crush her in an embrace; he longed to enjoy her softness, her sweet-smelling skin. He wanted to lick the sea-salt from her eyelids. He needed to kiss her eyebrows, her high-boned cheeks. He wanted their sensitive noses to caress one another. He desired her long legs to be entwined about his waist, his spear buried deep in her secret mossy target, her tongue searching his ear like a warm, wet snake, her two pointed breasts attacking his own with their sharp tips. He wanted to *possess* her body, utterly, completely, with profound tenderness and with an unruly passion.

'I love you,' she said, breaking the silence.

He could not believe what he had heard. He croaked hoarsely, 'You – you love me?' His mouth felt as dry and hot as a bone left lying in the sun. His stomach was an empty glade where leaves fluttered in strong breezes. His heart was fired clay on which the feet of running men pounded.

'Yes,' she said, fiercely. 'I had a duty, but that duty can never be fulfilled now. It's time to forget our old life, isn't it? Time to begin a new one.'

She seemed like a predator circling a prey, closing in gradually, coming near for the pounce – yet she had not moved in person, only in mind and spirit.

'Kula,' said Tangiia, caught unawares by the burning intensity of her words, 'are you sure? I thought you hated me – I thought . . .'

'Of course I hate you. I hate you as much as I love you. Sometimes I could drive a dagger through your heart,' she said, ferociously. 'Yet,' her eyes turned liquid, 'there are times when I just want to lie with you in the dust and let our bodies pound together, rhythmically, making the sound that women make early in the morning pummelling the grain with their poles in the hollow stones, creating clouds of fine powder . . .'

'Will you be my wife?'

'I shall be your princess, your slave, your mistress and your queen. I shall be all women to you, and you shall want no other. I *demand* you take no other. I can endure no companions on my husband's love mat. No other woman shall sport the patterns of its weave on her buttocks. I alone must carry the badge of my husband's lovemaking.

'If all this is understood, then I am yours.'

Tangiia's soul soared to the roof of voyaging, where Oro's Body, the brightest star in the sky, shone hard and bright.

The king took her hand and led her back to the firelight. There the dancing and feasting had continued, but on seeing Tangiia and Kula hand-in-hand, word passed quickly and the people of Raiatea rose almost as a single unit and turned towards them.

King Morning Star, who was not fully aware of what was happening, feared that a sudden subversive attack was about to take place, that the Raiateans had risen at a previously given signal and were about to fall upon their hosts.

'Ware the intruders!' he cried.

Tahitian warriors leapt to their feet, snatching up their weapons, ready to do battle. The whole atmosphere was tense with speculation and suspicion, until Kikamana, the Far-seeing virgin, stretched her arms and said, 'Tahitians – you have nothing to fear! Our king has found himself a bride.'

At that moment Tangiia lifted the hand he was holding and presented Kula to his people.

'Behold,' he cried, 'my queen!'

A mighty cheer went up from Tangiia's people.

The King of Tahiti stared solemnly for a moment at this extraordinary sight, then he began laughing, his whole body shaking with the effort, the fat on his belly and breasts wobbling, his jowls rippling, his bottom jiggling. On seeing him laugh, his people laughed too, and waved their weapons in the air not in anger but in delight. Then the Raiateans were moved to laughter, until the whole place echoed with the sound of mirth and merriment – and none were as happy as Tangiia and Kula.

'There's going to be a wedding!' cried Morning Star, laughing. 'We're going to have a marriage.'

It was the Time of the Green Lizard, a time of calm and peace. In periods when the weather was fine, the sea was tranquil, the colour of the light was misty-blue and soft as a moth's wing, then the Great Sea-God Tangaroa would change himself into a green lizard and bask on a rock in the sun.

Tangiia consulted with Makka-te and Kikamana, the Far-seeing virgin, and both agreed it was safe to rest a while in Tahiti, since the portents showed their pursuer to be several months behind them, lost somewhere on the great ocean. Since Kula was about to become his bride and queen, Tangiia felt it was right to consult her also, on their future. She too believed that a period of relaxation would do the Raiateans no harm.

Kula said, 'We must refresh the energy of our people, or their spirits will shrivel inside them, and they will not be able to go on. Our wedding will also be good for them. It will add cohesion to your rule – much strength and vigour results from the merging of a royal couple. It can only be good for us.'

King Morning Star insisted that the bride should have a new house for her wedding night and men were sent into the rainforest to cut hardwood posts for the uprights, bamboo poles to line the walls horizontally, and reed thatch for the roof. The splicers set to work on the binding ropes; the carvers prepared the upright posts, turning history and legend into tangible form; the wood masons cut the joining pegs, the rafters and beams, the blocks and pins, the frames.

While the craftsmen joiners worked their art, kahunas appealed to the spirits of ancestors, asking them to favour the young couple with their good will, not to demand human sacrifice on such a happy occasion, and to bless the house with their presence whenever it pleased them.

'You're a lucky man,' sighed Seumas, speaking to Tangiia. 'The woman of your dreams – it doesn't happen to many of us'

Seumas was sitting on a log, at the edge of the rainforest, Dirk lying at his feet. The dog had one lazy eye open, but was clearly enjoying a noon-day doze. Tangiia had paused to talk with Seumas as he passed by.

'Yes,' replied the young king, but he answered with uncertainty in his voice.

It was clear to Seumas that now the deed was about to take place, Tangiia was going through that time most young men experience just before their wedding, when they begin to wonder if they've done the right thing. Marriage brings responsibilities on top of those already in hand, and what was more it meant that another person had to be consulted over most decisions. 'I'll go fishing today and just idle away a watery noon,' became, 'Is it all right to go fishing?' Freedom, in the sense that one could do exactly as one liked with one's time, was gone for both parties. There was a call on that time, for family duties, and later, 'Is it all right to go fishing?' would become, 'Shall I take the children off your hands for a while?' Even kings of Oceania had family responsibilities.

All this, Seumas knew, was going through Tangiia's mind. It wasn't that the youth did not love his betrothed – he loved her to distraction – but he was panicking a little about what he was taking on. Life would never be the same again. It would not be as lonely and miserably insecure, but it would not be as free and easy either. And what was more, it was supposed to be *for ever*. Any mistake was an eternal one. It was no wonder he felt like bolting into the rainforest and hiding there until it had all blown over.

'You don't look like a man who has just won the prize of a lifetime,' said Seumas.

Tangiia shrugged. 'I'm – scared.'

'Of what?'

'That things won't go right – afterwards.'

'You have to *make* them go right, work at it – that's what it's all about.'

Tangiia snorted, 'How would you know – you're not married.'

'No, but I have been. And I've thought about marrying Dorcha a million times and I know that marriage to her would be hell in some ways. She's a very fiery woman. She can be an unmanageable one. I would be exchanging the hell of loneliness for the hell of the battleground – but, by the power of the Oceanian gods, I'd do it tomorrow if I could.'

'You wouldn't feel like running away,' said Tangiia, sourly, 'no, not you.'

'Maybe,' Seumas said, 'but look, you think you're scared. What about Kula? She's feeling all those things you're feeling – and on top of that she's probably worried about the first night of the marriage bed. Don't forget she's a virgin. How would you like a stranger to ram a stiff fleshy part of their body into a place you've never had any-thing put before?'

'I'm not a stranger.'

'You are to her body. How does she know you won't become one of those violent husbands who beat their wives in secret? She's got to take that chance, too. No, my friend, it's *she* who should be afraid, not you. Hers is the bigger risk.'

Tangiia nodded gravely and sighed. 'I suppose you're right, but like Dorcha she's a very spirited woman too. Do you really think it will be a battleground? Will we have to fight with one another for supremacy in the family house?'

'Not if you listen to her with as much attention as you would listen to another man, respect her intelligence and judgement, don't take her for granted, be sensitive to her needs, trust her, and remember to be tender.

'And just think, a spirited, intelligent woman is the ulti-
mate prize – would you want to be bored out of your
brains for the rest of your life with drivel and small talk?
What kind of a man would want that? Only one who
wishes to dominate his partner because he's dominated by
his fellow men.'

Tangiia grinned. 'You would make a fine husband,
Seumas.'

Seumas grinned back. 'No, I'm just good at passing on
advice to others. In fact I'm just a barbarian. I used to treat
women like dogs. That advice was given to me by one of
your own people – Kupe – when we first met. Kupe is a
very wise man – it's good advice, when you think about
it. If you respect the woman you love, then you respect
yourself, because *you* chose her, no one else, and your
judgement's at fault if afterwards all you want to do is
stay out of her sight.'

'Seumas,' said Tangiia, solemnly, 'you must share my
basket with me and others, before my wedding.'

This was a great honour for the man they called 'the
mountain goblin' and Seumas was struck mute for a
moment. Finally he managed to speak.

'Accept the thanks of a Pict,' he said. 'I've done nothing
to deserve it, but I'm grateful you should consider me
worthy.'

King Tangiia shook his head and smiled. 'And bring that
hound with you, if you have to.' He nodded towards the
dozing Dirk, who had not moved a muscle in the last hour.

Dirk immediately lifted his head, cocked an ear, and then
looked from one man to the other.

'I swear,' said Tangiia, amazed, 'that dog knows every
word we speak.'

'Every word,' smiled Seumas, patting Dirk's head.

Kula was indeed feeling as if she wanted to run into the
rainforest and keep on running until she met the sea again,

but not necessarily for the reasons Seumas had put to Tangiia. Kula was convinced that she was doing the wrong thing, according to her duty to her father and the gods, and that she was being selfish in giving in to her own passion. She wanted Tangiia, but felt she was wrong to want him and to submit to that desire.

It was late evening, the surf was booming along the reef creating a distant backdrop of sound, and the crickets were vying with the tree frogs in choral competition. Fruit bats rustled their drumskin wings at the top of palms. There was the occasional thud of a coconut falling from a tree top to earth, a constant danger to strollers when the fruit was ripe.

Kula was sitting on the shore just above where the waves were rippling amongst the coconut husks and dead, brown palm leaves that littered the beach. Hermit crabs scuttled under the arch created by her legs, wearing the various shells taken from dead molluscs. She stared at the place where redness had given way to darkness lit with bright islands of light.

'I'm not strong,' she said when praying to her favourite goddess Hine-keha. 'My will is weak.'

Hine-keha, the Bright Lady, had loved many, including a mortal who found her amongst some kelp in her dead phase, as Hine-uri, the Indigo Lady, after she had been floating in the sea. The handsome young man was a prince named Rupe. She took on human shape as he parted the seaweed which had entangled her form. Thinking she was a maiden who had fallen into the sea and almost drowned he lifted her from amongst the flotsam and jetsam and pressed her to his bosom to give her some warmth. They fell in love and she bore him a child, Tuhuruhuru.

'You know about love,' Kula said softly. 'Your duty is to love your husband Marama, but yet you have turned from that duty to love other gods and even mortals, so please do not judge me harshly for turning from my duty . . .'

Kula was feeling vulnerable. She was racked with home-sickness, wondering who was feeding her grandfather, and what the rest of her family were doing right at that moment. All her old basket-sharers, the girls who used to accompany her to the pool under the waterfall, were back on the islands. She had made new friends of course, new maidens who shared her food with her, and one in particular – a girl named Lolina. Still, she missed her old basket-sharers, and her parents and grandfather, and her sisters.

'Are you finished yet?' called Lolina.

'Yes, I'm coming,' replied Kula, enjoying the warm breezes which blew from the direction in which lay her old home. At that moment a silvery fish-shape leapt from the waters of the lagoon, into the moonlight, and entered the waters again with barely a light splash. It seemed to Kula that this was a sign which told her she was doing the right thing, at least by Hine.

'Hine-te-ngaru-moana!' breathed Kula. 'Lady of the Ocean Waves, I'm sure it was you!'

'What?' called Lolina.

'Nothing, nothing . . .'

Kula went to join her friend and together they ran bare-foot over the grass to where others were waiting to greet them. Baskets of fruit and roasted fish, with breadfruit and plantains, were brought to the group. Then the maidens began to eat and chatter at the same time. One of them told Kula she was so lucky '. . . he's such a handsome man, the king.'

'Not so much a man,' replied Kula, 'more of a youth.'

'But he's the *king*. His manhood is conferred by his rank. A youth can't be king.'

'So you say,' Kula answered, taking some breadfruit, 'but I say differently. What's more he's a youth who has injured me, my family and former intended husband.'

Lolina looked puzzled by this remark.

'Aren't you in love with him then?'

Kula looked her friend directly in the eyes. 'Of course I am, but he must be punished all the same, for abducting me – if not by the gods, then I must be the instrument. The honour of my family is at stake, which means my *own* honour, since I'm part of that family. I will not let anyone, even someone I love, stamp my honour into the dust. Not without punishment.'

The other maidens were aghast at this speech.

One cried, 'You will be his wife. You must go to him in humility and love, not with vengeance in your heart.'

'I go with love and a desire for justice,' said Kula, simply.

'What will you do?' asked Lolina, fearfully, thinking her friend the princess quite capable of taking up a patu club and braining her new husband during their first coupling, while he was helplessly in the throes of ecstasy.

'I shall withhold my virginity until we find a Faraway Heaven.'

The anxiety of the maidens turned to horror at these words. They felt sure the king would kill his new wife, if she refused to give him her body. Either that or he would abandon her and find a lover, which would be so humiliating she would have to kill herself.

'But what – what if he insists?' asked the terrified Lolina.

'You mean if he rapes me? I hope he does,' Kula said, calmly. 'Then his suffering will be more intense and will only need to be over a short time period. We won't have to wait then, until we reach a new island. He's not the kind of man who could rape a woman, especially the woman he loves, and not feel terrible guilt. I'll goad that guilt with sharp words, until he can't stand it any longer. Once he's paid for abducting me, then we'll be free to live a long and happy life together, unmarred by his bad deeds of the past.'

'If you live that long,' groaned Lolina.

"True,' smiled Kula, 'if he doesn't kill me in a fit of rage.' She became thoughtful for a moment, before adding, 'I hope he doesn't for his sake – he'd never forgive himself.'

At the time Kula was sharing her basket with her maidens, Tangiia was doing the same, with his companions. The special guests at this basket-sharing were Boy-girl whose new lover, Ranata, was a friend of the king, and Seumas. Also present was Makke-te, Aputua the leader of the shark-callers, Kaho the Feeler-of-the-sea, Po, Manopa and one or two others of lesser rank.

Boy-girl had the peculiar and distinct status of being eligible to share baskets with both men and women. She was clearly enjoying herself at this gathering, until the king asked her a question.

'Kikamana says a dark force is coming this way. Can you confirm this?'

Boy-girl nodded. 'There is something beyond the horizon, racing across the waves towards us.'

Tangiia asked the question Boy-girl was dreading.

'What is it?'

'I don't know,' admitted Boy-girl. 'I can't even tell if it's human, demon or god-like. Its identity is being protected by magic. All I can see is a dark cloud hiding a nefarious presence – and the cloud is rushing this way. Perhaps it's a monster sent by your enemies?'

Since Tangiia only had one enemy that he knew of this information was a little redundant.

Tangiia grumbled, 'What's the use of having Farseeing priests, if they can't tell you anything.'

Boy-girl said, 'I'm not a priest . . .'

'Don't split hairs with me,' Tangiia growled.

Manopa said, 'Come – this is a social gathering, my king – let's not quarrel here.'

Manopa was able to use such strong words with Tangiia because of his high rank and age. He was the rock on which Tangiia stood. Manopa was steadfast, loyal and true, and his physical strength and mental control made him a formidable foe and a stalwart friend.

Manopa was not an intellectual, like Boy-girl, but he thought things through with great thoroughness and made decisions based on evidence and hard facts.

Where there were none of these, he used his experience and reasoning powers, and the mariners under his command respected him immensely, knowing that in the event of something terrible happening – like a great storm – Manopa would remain calm and in possession of his faculties. He would see them through the greatest adversities with a calm, authoritative voice and not the slightest show of unease or lack of confidence.

Manopa's figure standing firmly on the deck of his pahi, almost as if he were carved from the woodwork, issuing commands while the waves loured above the vessel and crashed around its hulls, inspired great efforts from his sailors. It instilled complete confidence in him.

Not a man easily swayed by emotions, Manopa was one of three husbands married to the same woman. He found his duties not irksome but demanding, and he only had a certain amount of time to give to a wife. A wife with one husband was always waiting for her man to return to the fireplace, to the bed, or to the meal table. Manopa gave of his all to his work, before even considering returning to his home and his bed. His present wife enjoyed the status of being connected with Manopa, but did not fret and whine if her husband, being only one of three, was only around a short part of the time.

'Pass me a mango,' said Po to Manopa.

Po was quite unlike Manopa, which was strange considering they were of the same rank and did the same job, that of captaining a pahi. Po had four wives, was as thin as a shadow, and his sense of humour was what kept his men at their posts during a crisis. During the recent storm, he had bellowed at the wind and the waves, 'Is that you,

Tangaroa? All right, do your worst – punish us puny sea-farers for some imagined insult – see if we care. Is *that* the worst you can do? That wave was hardly even worthy to be called mountainous. Surely you can produce a bigger one than that? Oh, wait – yes – I take it back. I see one coming on the horizon – my god, it's monstrous – it'll swamp us for sure . . .'

The sailors would all raise their heads in anxiety, to witness a piddling little wave coming towards them, and realise their captain was being sarcastic. They would chuckle at Po's ranting and raving, which would spread to the women and children, and no matter how much the storm tossed their frail craft, they would be jollying each other along and giggling at Po's antics.

Po threw a piece of mango to Dirk, sitting beside his master.

Dirk looked at the chunk of fruit as if he had been offered a bat's turd.

'What's the matter with your dog, Seumas? That's good food I've given him. The other dogs would be fighting over that by now, if I'd thrown it to them.'

'You know he doesn't eat fruit,' snapped Seumas. 'If you want to feed him, give him a scrap of meat.'

Po reached into the basket and pulled out a chunk of meat which he then tossed to Dirk. Tangiia looked at Po disapprovingly, but Po just winked at his king. As a reliable captain and second navigator he could get away with almost as much as Manopa. The dog leapt on the cooked flesh and began to devour it with gusto. Po sniggered.

'What's so funny?' asked Seumas.

Po said with a snicker, 'That's his mother.'

Seumas shot a look at the piece of meat and then realised he was being teased. Dirk's mother must have been killed and eaten long ago.

'Are you calling my dog a cannibal?' he asked Po, in a soft threatening voice. 'Nobody insults my dog.'

Even Po was surprised by the quiet menace in Seumas's voice.

'What's wrong with being a cannibal?' he asked, pleasantly. 'Every man here has eaten human flesh at some time, even you.'

'I'm talking about you insulting my dog.'

The whole party had suddenly gone still. No one chewed or swallowed their food. All eyes were on Po and Seumas. Everyone knew Seumas was a awesome fighter in single combat. Po had seen him in action several times and had no wish to meet him hand-to-hand over the sensibilities of an animal which should have formed part of the pot roast.

Po said nervously, 'Oh, come on, Seumas, it's not one of your children – it's just a dog.'

Tangiia made things worse for Po. 'Dirk is like a child to Seumas – like one of his own sons.'

Seumas stared hard at Po, while the captain fidgeted with his food for a moment.

Finally Po burst out with, 'Oh, all right – I apologise, Seumas. I'm not going to fall out with you over livestock.'

'Not to me,' said Seumas, evenly. 'To Dirk.'

'To the dog? Oh, listen – look Seumas, the dog – after all – well then, dog, I'm sorry. There.'

'Say, "I'm sorry, *Dirk*." That's his name. He doesn't like being called "dog".'

'But he is a *dog*,' expostulated Po. 'He might not be a walking pork chop, but he is a blasted dog after all . . .'

'Right, that's it – sic 'im, Dirk.'

Dirk instantly left the meat and stood up, his nape hairs bristling, his teeth frighteningly bared. There was a growl beginning in the back of his throat, which curled there, rolling slowly out of his mouth. His eyes showed their whites.

Po said quietly in a high voice, 'Seumas . . .'

'All right, boy, sit,' said Seumas casually, going back to his eating.

Dirk settled again with his meat, while the other men returned to their food, chattering amongst themselves. Po sat there sweating for a moment, breathing quickly, his eyes upon his shaking hands. When he looked up again, everyone was staring at him and grinning broadly. Even Seumas.

He suddenly realised what was going on.

'It was a joke,' he said. 'A rotten joke. That wasn't funny, you know. I thought for a moment – Seumas, that wasn't funny. I almost crapped myself . . .' Then he saw the funny side of it himself and began laughing, along with the others. So many times he had been the teaser, the one who mocked and heckled, and now he had been on the other end. It was quite funny. He showed them he could take a joke, by laughing with them, but he swore to himself he would get even with his friend Seumas. If it took him the rest of his life he would get even.

The tall, willowly Boy-girl, with her hair dangling with ribbons and shells said, 'Tell your dog to attack me, Seumas.'

Seumas said, 'No, I don't want him to hurt you.'

Boy-girl smiled. 'He won't hurt me – just tell him . . .'

Seumas shrugged, then turned to Dirk and said, 'Kill,' pointing at Boy-girl.

The dog left the ground with hunched shoulders as if it had been kicked into the air, its eyes flashing, its mouth salivating and the jaws clashing together. The men around Boy-girl, including her new lover, vacated the area instantly. Boy-girl simply sat there, waiting, until the dog was an arm's length away, then she turned and stared into his eyes.

Dirk immediately came to a halt. He then went down on his haunches, still staring at Boy-girl, his tongue lolling out of the side of his mouth. Then, at a whisper from Boy-girl, he lay his head on his front paws, and regarded her with limp eyes.

'What a nice dog,' she said, reaching out to stroke the animal. 'What makes you so afraid of it, Po?'

'I'm not a bloody magician, that's what,' answered Po with his usual bluntness. 'He would have eaten me.'

Seumas was astonished at the speed with which Boy-girl was able to subdue Dirk. When he called the dog, it remained where it was, annoying him. He whistled and called again. Still no response. Boy-girl said something and finally Dirk stood up and went back to Seumas, its face registering the fact that it knew it had displeased its master.

'It took me a year to train this dog as a killer,' said Seumas, peevishly, 'and you turn him back into a puppy within a minute.'

Boy-girl smiled sweetly. 'He knows you love me, that's why he's nice to me,' she said.

Boy-girl's new lover shot Seumas a look of jealous hatred.

I don't need this, thought Seumas. It's bad enough having Boy-girl pressing herself against me at any opportunity, without having to look over my shoulder for jealous lovers coming out of the dark with a knife in their hand.

'Boy-girl, you know that's not true. I only like *real* women. Tell your new friend that we're just good chums.'

'We're just good chums,' said Boy-girl to her lover, but in a tone which implied that there was more to it than that. 'Seumas only likes *real* women.'

Seumas shook his head, ruefully, wondering whether he would ever manage to shake the tenacious Boy-girl from his life.

2

On the night of the wedding the airy spirits who inhabited the sky were in a happy mood. As always, they were playing ball games with superb dexterity amongst the clouds. The spirits of the sky were fair of skin, which made them an ancient race of beings, related to the ancestors of the Oceanians.

There were other spirits, less cheerful, in lost villages in the earth, in the water, in all the elements, spirits known to men as the 'gloomy ghosts' because they have no knowledge of fire and they eat their food raw. Once two fishermen stumbled on such a village and were told that they could eat with the spirits but if they laughed they would be killed. They were forced to swallow raw whale meat, even though they had found driftwood on the beach and had carried it under their arms to dry it. After the men left, they never laughed again.

And in the forest the bird-spirits recalled the time they had built the first canoe for the hero Rata, while the woods echoed with their songs.

A royal wedding was a cause for celebration amongst the spirit world, as well as amongst mortals.

King Morning Star was nothing if not generous and the food for the wedding feast was supplied in plenty.

There were sixty different kinds of yam, baked and roasted sweet potatoes, suckling pigs smeared with honey and roasted over slow fires, pit stews of dog and wild bird meat, fermented breadfruit, chickens stuffed with coconut and banana, Tahitian chestnuts, wild birds' eggs, crispy ants and beetles.

Then there were the seafare dishes, which outweighed the meat by far, consisting of sharks' roe, barracuda, squid, cuttlefish, an abundance of shellfish, reef fish, eels in thick sauces, turtle-meat kebabs, turtle eggs, sea weeds of various kinds, crabs and lobsters, anemones and skipjack.

The fires were lit, the dancing began. The bride and groom sat one on either side of the Tahitian priest who was to perform the marriage ceremony. Flowers, bamboo and streamers, and decorated mats were everywhere, on the ground, adorning the houses and huts. Wooden personal gods marched out of the houses and stood in yards. Totems were dusted and set in the ground. Ahu had been raised for the sacrifices, though Tangiia had stipulated there were to be no human sacrifices at his wedding, only those of animals.

There were blooms in people's hair – Seumas and his dog were both decked in frangipani blossoms.

'You look very pretty,' Kikamana said to Seumas.

Po added, 'You'd better stay out of Boy-girl's way, or you'll wake up from the kava drink tomorrow to find yourself married to her.'

Boy-girl herself looked stunningly beautiful in a tapa cloth dyed red. She was so tall and elegant she towered over most of the Tahitians, yet her carriage was perfect. She refused to stoop to listen or speak to those below her height and her deportment was to be envied.

The bride and groom were quiet and serious, not looking at each other, possibly feeling quite shy.

King Morning Star was his usual jolly self, ordering food to be put in his mouth, calling for a particular dance, drinking enough kava juice to kill an ordinary man.

Seumas ignored Po's advice and drank kava juice until it ran down his chin and chest. Halfway through the evening he jumped up and began dancing, much to the consternation of Dirk, who kept running through people's legs in an effort to keep pace with his master. The dog could not understand what was happening.

Sometime in the late evening the marriage ceremony took place, but by that hour Seumas was so drunk things began to get a little fuzzy and unco-ordinated. The dancing picked up in pace and Seumas especially felt his feet hopping in a furious manner, determined as he was to keep up with those lithe figures around him, to whom dancing was a natural expression of joy.

The drums were beaten with such skill and speed it made Seumas giddy to look upon the musicians. The trilling of flutes filled the air, patterned the night. Seumas's soul had trouble keeping up with his body, as he jumped and leapt and swayed and kicked.

Towards the end of the night, he found himself dancing opposite a bright-eyed girl whose features were so shiny and delicate they might have been fashioned from fragile seashells. She smiled at Seumas, as she swayed before him, her slender arms waving like fronds, her slim, beautiful legs peeking through the grass skirt, tantalising him. She was beauty in absolute and Seumas danced with his mouth agape, wondering how he could have missed seeing such a wonderful maiden before now.

However, when he happened to glance around him, it seemed that there were many more like her – dainty, ethereal creatures with small, heart-shaped faces. Their hair was like black rain falling over their sweet, pale features. It seemed to Seumas that if he touched one of them with a fingertip, they would bruise like ripe fruit. The maiden dancing with him kept smiling gently, a smile he was sure was an invitation.

'Do you want to go somewhere?' he asked, huskily, his

feet still jigging with the dance.

She nodded, slightly, still wearing her serene smile.

'Just a bit more of the dancing first, eh?' he cried, quickening his pace, feeling quite elated at this conquest. 'Just to wear off the drink a little.'

The girl took his hand in her own and he marvelled at how tiny it was. She tugged at him, trying to draw him in amongst the rocks at the edge of the rainforest, but he still had not danced his full measure, and laughingly pulled her back again, into the cavorting throng. Her bright eyes looked at him questioningly, and he said, 'Just a few more steps.'

Finally, he had exhausted his energy and she was able to lead him to a soft, mossy bank between two great boulders. There she lay on her side, inviting him down with her. He was only slightly astonished to see she was completely naked, realising he was so drunk his powers of observance were practically nil. Her small, pale body hardly made an impression in the spongy moss, so slight and weightless she seemed.

He lay down with her, puzzled at the haze that surrounded her in the way that a bright mist often encircles the moon. Her breath was like that of perfume breathed from flowers. Eyes he had seen only in distant dreams shone from the petal-soft complexion, the need in them strong and evident.

Dirk crept around the boulders and lay not far away, sensing he was not welcome at this meeting of two humans.

Seumas took her head in his hands, cupping it like a sweet apple to be savoured, and bent to kiss her.

Her lips had the tang of wild fruit and her tongue tasted of honey. He kissed down her face to the bare shoulders, as intricately formed as that of a bird. When he reached her breasts, quivering with passion, he stopped – then opened his lips as if to drink, before taking one of them inside his mouth whole, so small and sweet were they. Her legs parted and the perfumed breath came faster and faster.

'Oh, my darlin' lovely girl,' he moaned. 'Thank you for choosing a rough man like me.'

The first rays of the dawn parted the air above the two great boulders, as Ra's shafts began to penetrate the day. Rangi's domain was swiftly overtaken, the light chasing away the darkness into unknown regions. Seumas tore away his loin cloth and drove upwards with his hardened penis –

– only to find himself stabbing at empty air.

'Wha—?' He looked down to see a shape dissolving into the moss. Where the maiden had been was nothing but mist. She had disappeared with the dawn and he was making love to twigs and leaves – to Papa, the Great Earth-Goddess.

The shock, on top of the massive amount of kava juice he had drunk, caused him to pass out.

Seumas spent the best part of the morning lying naked on the lichen-covered rocks. When he woke the sun was beating down on his head, punishing him for his overindulgence. Dirk was lying beside him, one eye open.

Seumas rose and staggered off to find the water hole, drinking down great draughts of the cool liquid when he found it and cursing himself for being so weak willed. Then, as he was splashing his head, he remembered the maiden he had almost made love to at dawn. Had it been a dream? Perhaps kava juice, taken in vast quantities, produced false images in his brain, made him see things that were not there.

Po arrived at the pool then, and he too splashed his face with cold water.

Po said, 'Did you see the tipairu?'

Seumas, lying full-length at the edge of the pool with his face half in the water, looked up dripping.

'Who?'

'The fairies,' said Po, excitedly. 'The Unequalled Ones, they came down to the dancing last night – very late –

when they knew no one would pay much attention to them.'

'Were they . . .?' and Seumas described his maiden.

'That's them,' said Po. 'Beautiful creatures. They live in the high pools and hanging gardens up in the mountains – I was told by the villagers last night. It seems they don't always come down, but they did for us.'

Seumas said, more to himself in wonder than to Po, 'I almost made love to a fairy.'

'You what?' laughed Po.

'She vanished into mist, when the dawn came.'

'Sure,' said Po, mockingly. 'A fairy fell in love with a grisly old mountain goblin, yet not a single beautiful young warrior could get an Unequalled One into the forest on her own? Please, don't insult my common sense, Seumas. Go and joke with someone else.'

'I tell you I did,' said Seumas angrily. Then he became quietly anguished, his voice full of regret. 'I tell you she took me to a mossy bank and – I kissed her breasts, her small, sweet breasts – they tasted of – of rose petals – and she almost gave herself to me – she almost . . . it was a matter of a few moments. If the sun had been a second later, I would have had her. Maybe it was my fair skin? They had pale fair skins too. If I'd just had a little more time – the sun – and I'm *not* old – I'm not even thirty yet.'

'That's *old* when there are handsome youths of eighteen and nineteen around, with not a blemish between them. Look, I'm not saying you didn't have a woman. You probably picked up one of the Tahitian wives – they're a pretty free lot on this island – but I shouldn't tell her husband if I were you. It always helps to keep it quiet afterwards. Don't brag about your secret liaisons, Seumas – it isn't manly.'

'*It was a damn fairy,*' shouted Seumas, thereby making a sharp pain go through his head, as if a wooden stake had been hammered between his eyes. '*I could have had her, if Ra hadn't come between us.*'

'Have it your own way,' sighed Po. 'Never mind you were too drunk to see straight. Just keep away from the kava juice in future, or you'll have fairy children to look after, as well as a stupid dog.

'And if you did abduct a fairy from the fire dancing,' said Po, admonishing him sternly, 'then I would have expected the gods to stop you raping her. She would have destroyed you with her mana. No wonder Ra rose early this morning. It was to prevent you from violating one of his fairies and to save your worthless goblin hide. If he hadn't, you would have been a smoking piece of meat now, struck down by lightning of your own seeking.

'The lust of some men,' added Po with a fatherly shake of his head, 'often astounds me.'

'That's rich, coming from you,' Seamus snarled.

'I never meddle with the fairies,' replied Po, haughtily. 'I've got more sense than *that*.'

With that the captain got up and walked away from the pool, leaving Seumas wondering whether the kava juice really had been responsible for his night apparitions.

Tangiia emerged from his house the morning after the wedding with an angry look on his face. Manopa, on seeing the king, knew immediately that all had not gone well in the marriage bed and put it down to a sexual failure. After all, both parties in the marriage were virgins. Perhaps Tangiia had been over-excited and had brought forth his seed too early? Perhaps he had been too anxious and had not been able to achieve an erection? Maybe the bride was too terrified to let him enter her? These were not uncommon problems on the first night.

'Well, what are you standing around for?' growled Tangiia, storming past his second-in-command. 'Haven't you got any work to do? It's this place! It encourages idleness.'

The king went off into the rainforest, presumably to find the pool where he could wash.

'Definitely,' Manopa muttered to himself. 'No doubt about it – a personal failure.'

Around the village men and women were emerging from their huts and houses, bleary-eyed and hung over after the feasting and drinking at the wedding. Children, always the first to be up, were running around playing games. The older ones were already doing their chores, lighting fires, pounding seeds, fetching fresh water. The women came out next, rubbing their faces, calling to the children to come and eat, or to do this or that, taking swipes at cockroaches with a handy log. Finally the men staggered out, bad-tempered, scratching their heads or their genitals, or both, many of them with full bladders or bowels, or both, heading towards the nearest clump of bushes.

Manopa noticed Po, down by the shore, talking to some returning night fishermen who had gone out after the wedding. There were always some who took advantage of the fact that others were over-indulging, using the opportunity to fish in grounds not strictly their own. He called to Po.

'Come here, will you?'

Po glanced across, frowned, and said a few more words to a fisherman, before walking slowly across the warming sands, over the under-tree grasses, to where Manopa stood.

'What is it?' asked Po. 'What's the crisis now?'

Manopa told him about the king.

'Well, what do you want *me* to do about it?' asked Po. 'Service the queen?'

Manopa glowered. He didn't like foul-mouthed talk, like Po and his fishermen friends. Besides, talk like that, about the queen, was not only tasteless, it was treason. If Tangiia had heard Po he would have been felled by a club in an instant. Po knew it too. His expression told Manopa that Tangiia's number three knew he had gone too far with that remark.

'I'll pretend I didn't hear that,' Manopa said, pompously. 'What I want you to do is have a little discussion with our king. You know the kind of thing I mean? Tell him it can happen to anyone, whatever it is that's bothering him. Tell him it's quite normal for a young man, a virgin, for things to – things not to work as one expects them to, especially after a wedding where the drink flowed so freely. Give him a fatherly talk about first nights . . .'

'Me? Why don't you do it?'

'You're older than I am – more of a father figure – and you're better at these things than me. I'm a bit too blunt – I don't have your – your social skills.'

Po flicked his head irritably as if to say, oh sure, me again.

After a while he said, 'Oh, all right – but you'd better be within call. If he goes to bash my head in, I want you close by to stop him. An ordinary man doesn't take kindly to advice about his sex life, let alone a king.'

'It depends how it's done,' said Manopa. 'I'm sure you can find the right way and the right words. If I may make a suggestion, get him on his own by the bathing pool and start talking about yourself, when you were first – well, when you married your first wife, as a young man . . .'

Po stiffened. 'Nothing went wrong on *my* wedding night, I'll have you know. I was as hard as a totem and I gave her what for at least six times. She was begging . . .'

'Yes, yes,' snapped Manopa, losing his patience, 'no one's interested in your sexual prowess. *Pretend* can't you? Make it all up.'

'I'm not telling *anyone* that I had trouble on my first wedding night. I'd be the brunt of all the mariners' jokes. My status as a captain would be worth nothing.'

Manopa regarded the tall, skinny captain with exasperation.

'Why can't you do something to help your king?' he said. 'Why do you have to turn a simple chore into a massive problem?'

'If it's so simple,' snapped Po, 'why don't you do it?'

'Because – because I can't be as *subtle* as you.'

Po nodded. 'That's true.'

At that moment a dripping King Tangiia passed by them, flinging words over his shoulder.

'Still standing around, Manopa? I see you've passed this bad habit on to Po. Idleness is not a good friend.'

Po glanced at the king and then looked back at Manopa.

'Remember,' hissed Manopa, 'subtlety.'

Po nodded, then yelled after Tangiia, 'Couldn't you get it up then?'

Tangiia stopped in his tracks, his back still facing the two men. Manopa felt like sinking into the sand. His heart had shrivelled in his chest to the size of a dried nut kernel. He stared at Po in horror, knowing that Po was going to tell Tangiia that he, Manopa, had told him the king had failed to make love to his bride on the night of the wedding. He was going to die.

'Why are you doing this to me?' he squeaked at Po. 'Do you hate me so much?'

Po waved some fingers in Manopa's face, as if to say, don't worry, I have the situation well in hand.

Tangiia came back, his face stricken with misery.

'What did you say?' he asked Po, in a quiet voice.

'I was just telling Manopa here that you were a real man after all. He's not so far away from us, after all, I said, even though he's a king.'

'What are you talking about?' asked Tangiia.

'You know, not being able to do it, on your first night. It happens to everyone, even Manopa here – strapping fellow that he is. Why,' he smiled, 'it's almost a tradition amongst us virulent types. It's because we're so eager, so rampant.' He made a gesture with his fist and forearm.

'You mean virile,' muttered Manopa.

'Yes, that's what I mean.'

Tangiia looked from one captain to the other, slowly, then said in a very tight voice, 'I understand you're trying to allay any concerns you believe I might have, but my marriage bed is my own business. But I'll tell you this – there's nothing wrong with my potency. It has nothing to do with me, you understand? Now I don't want to have to talk about this again – ever.'

He turned away and marched back to his house.

Manopa looked disgustedly at Po. 'Virulent?' he said, shaking his head.

Po shrugged. 'You're better with words than me.'

Tahiti was a land of pleasure at that time, with King Morning Star at its head. Corpulent, amiable and fun-loving, the king was as close to a hedonist as a man could get. He had seventeen wives, all of them pretty, some of them fat. There were feast days by the score, throughout the year. The king had revived as many old customs as there were gods to support them; so long as those customs involved either food, drink or sex, with dancing and music in between, he would make it a law.

Morning Star's favourite god was Rongo-ma-tane, the God of the Sweet Potato, a food he devoured in vast quantities. He would have made the sweet potato taboo to everyone but kings, if such an action would not have resulted in famine. As it was, most men and women were careful not to be seen by their king to be eating the vegetable, let alone wasting it.

Rongo-mai was another god to whom the king paid special deference, since he was God of Comets. Because the king was one of the stars in the heavens, he paid particular attention to this region of the world, and he loved falling stars and comets. His special treat was to lie on his back outside his house, looking up to the roof of voyaging, and watching the stars, counting meteors until he fell asleep. Then his priests would carefully lift him on the specially strengthened mats and carry him indoors.

Much as this idle pleasure suited Manopa, he saw his

own king being sucked into a life of indolence. The Raiateans were beginning to make themselves too much at home. Some were building their own fishing canoes instead of borrowing a Tahitian outrigger. Others married local men and women, thus giving themselves a stake in the kingdom. Some took on posts which were unpopular amongst the Tahitians, like being responsible for the clearance of the beaches near the village.

Manopa went to see Tangiia in his house. The king had been brooding ever since his wedding night. Kula was there, making supper for the two of them. It seemed like a nice domestic scene. Kula was welcoming, showing Manopa to his mat, offering him a drink. There was a lightness to her voice which was absent from that of the king's. Tangiia watched after his wife, as she moved about the room, his eyes on her every moment. His expression was not angry, nor even sullen, but a little vacant, as if he were somewhere else.

Manopa got to work.

'I've sent for Kikamana. We must have a discussion, the three of us.'

'What about?' asked Tangiia, picking at the weave in the mat on which he was sitting.

'We must leave this place, we've been here almost six months,' said Manopa.

'What's wrong with it?' asked Tangiia, desultorily.

'What's wrong with it? There's nothing wrong with it, except that it's only a spit away from your brother's kingdom. Sooner or later there'll be mariners from Raiatea or Borabora visiting these islands and they'll carry word back to your brother. It's not safe here. We have to move on.'

'In a little while.'

'But our pahi are gathering barnacles and weed on their hulls out there. The sails are rotting with lack of use.'

'Get some men to drag them out of the water – scrape their bottoms. Make some new pandanus sails.'

Manopa said, 'That's not the point –'

At this moment Kikamana arrived.

Manopa said to Kikamana, 'Tell the king what you told me earlier – about the dark force.'

Kikamana nodded. 'King Tangiia,' she said, 'we must leave these shores. I believe your brother is very close now, leading a flotilla of tipairua canoes. My dreams are full of black sails and blood-red seas. We must go on. Our destiny is not here, but on some island we have not yet known.'

Tangiia paid attention now.

'If Tutapu is out on the high seas, who's guarding the islands of Raiatea and Borabora?'

'We can't go back there,' Manopa said. 'Eventually Tutapu will head towards home and he'll find you there and slaughter us all. If we leave now we have a chance of getting far away – of losing ourselves amongst the islands and reefs at the bottom of the world.'

Kikamana said, 'Manopa is right. Your place is on a new island with a new nation.'

'We're getting fat and lazy here,' complained Manopa. 'Look at our people. They were hardy mariners a few months ago, now all they do is look forward to the next festival day. The time of the green lizard is on us. We know Tangaroa favours your brother – the Great Sea-God is making life so easy for us with these fine days, this good weather, on this beautiful island – and it *is* a beautiful island – we don't want to leave.

'The problem is, it's not *our* island. When Tutapu gets here, how do you know Morning Star won't side with *him*? He's the older brother, the one entitled to the kingdom.'

'What does my new wife say?' asked Tangiia, testily.

Kula glanced over at the intent group and shrugged her shoulders.

'It's not my decision,' she said.

'You're the queen, aren't you?' Tangiia answered back.

'I – I haven't yet got used to that fact. It will take me

some time before I feel able to offer you helpful advice. Until then, you rule by yourself, you must do it on your own.'

'Like a lot of other things around here,' muttered Tangiia, and Manopa gave his king a startled look.

'Well,' continued Tangiia, 'domestic quarrels apart, I suppose you're right. We should continue our voyage. Tangaroa deliberately allowed us to reach Tahiti because it's so tantalisingly near our old home. He's made it a haven of rest and beauty for us. Well, he'll beguile us no longer with his tricks. I'll bet he'll have the waves crashing on the shoreline within an hour, trying to stop us from getting away.'

Manopa stood up, relieved that the king had come to his senses at last.

'I'll start to make preparations at once.'

Kikamana also got to her feet, her long-flowing tapa robes rustling against the mats.

'It's the right decision,' she said.

She too left the house.

Tangiia turned to his wife. 'So that's why you've been holding out. You knew Tutapu was on his way and you've been saving yourself for him.'

She lifted her eyes and stared at him defiantly.

'If that's what you want to think.'

'What else should I think?' he said, heatedly.

'You should think that your wife has her reasons for restraint at this time, that she would never have married you unless she loved you, that she had no way of knowing that your brother was pursuing you, and that you should be thinking about becoming a man in your own right.'

She left him, standing there, and went out with a gourd to fetch some water from the stream.

After a moment he called softly after her, 'How can I become a man, if you keep rejecting me?'

*

The fleet left Tahiti on a fine morning bearing delicate wisps of cloud like streamers in Rangi's sky. There were dancers on the beaches to say farewell to Tangiia, Kula and the rest of the courageous seafarers, once more embarking on a voyage into the unknown. On the beaches too were the Raiateans remaining behind, most of them with mixed feelings. They had found a new home, it was true, but their comrades were going on to more adventures. Adventure too has its appeal and many would regret they stayed behind to wonder at the fate of their former king and the bold families who accompanied him.

All along the shoreline were huge rocks, half buried in the sand. There were unnoticed symbols on the rocks which dotted the shoreline. Such scratches could have been made accidentally, by the spears of fishermen, or sea creatures, but in fact had been left by the traitor amongst Tangiia's people. They were secret marks left for a pursuer. Marks which would be recognised by that pursuer or his kahuna.

PART SEVEN

Cave of the Poukai

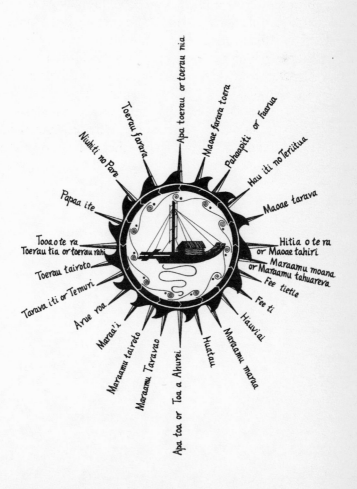

1

'Even when the stars are not visible, the shape of the waves will tell you which of the three seas you are in, be it the darkest of nights,' said Kaho, the blind navigator. 'One need never be so lost that one doesn't know in which part of the great ocean one is sailing.'

Seumas shook his head. 'They all seem the same to me – at least, big ones and little ones, but the shape? They don't have any shape, do they? Not a regular shape.'

They were standing on the deck of *The Scudding Cloud*. Kaho, his head tilted a little, was obviously enjoying the feel of the sea wind on his face. He sniffed deeply, inhaling the ozone, filling his lungs with pure air. Seumas knew what the Feeler-of-the-sea was experiencing. Tahiti had been a beautiful island, but the smells of people living together, of cooking, sewage, animal dung, and rotting waste, pervaded every corner of the village. Out here on the ocean, the atmosphere was untainted by any odour from humankind.

'Oh, when you've lived as close to the ocean as we have, using it as a second home, treating it as an extension of the land, then you can recognise shapes in the unshapely.'

Seumas said, 'But even if you know which corner of the world you're in – those *corners* are pretty big stretches of water.'

'Most of the ocean's currents follow the prevailing winds,' explained the expert Kaho. 'It doesn't take long to know and understand the mean set of the seas, and information can be passed on through generations. But it would take more than a lifetime for an outsider to learn these things, so give up any ambition you may have to be a navigator.'

'There's no such ambition in my breast,' said Seumas, emphatically. 'I just like to talk with you.'

He stared out over the sea, a deep green colour under the lowering clouds. There was a brisk blow lifting the wavetops, feathering their tips. Sheets and lines were flapping on the craft, slapping against wood.

'In my old country,' Seumas added, remembering, 'the ships always hug the coastline. We don't make long voyages like you people – the open sea is too full of dangers.'

'You should learn to trust to wave, wind and star, like the Oceanians,' said Kaho, before going off to rest.

'I trust the elements,' said Seumas to Dirk, 'as far as I could throw a pahi. And as for these gods of yours . . .'

They were now sailing in the direction of Papaa-ite on the wind flower, following one of the trades. They had left Tahiti six days previously. Some of the people had elected to stay behind and live on Tahiti, about thirty in number. These were mostly men and women who had married Tahitians.

Assisted by Kieto, Tangiia was standing by one of the masts, knotting his cord-device, charting their progress. Tangiia was now wisely running before the wind, trusting to Maomao. He had promised himself and others that he would not be diverted by any tricks used by Tangaroa.

Kikamana, who had dream-knowledge of the gods through the sau of atua and Tiki, told Tangiia that Tangaroa was peeved rather than angry with the navigator king, for bringing the wrong god on the voyage. It was not so much the refugee Raiateans whom Tangaroa was trying to spite, it was Maomao the Great Sea-God. This was actually a quarrel between the gods, a jealous tiff between the supernatural beings who shared the world with humans.

Tangaroa could of course, if he wished, crush the expedition with one mighty tidal wave, and be done with it. Instead, he wanted to use the refugees to tease the Great Wind-God, to annoy Maomao by thwarting their plans. At the same time, Kikamana was told by her atua and informants, Tangaroa and Maomao were on the surface pleasant to one another. Io, the Supreme Being, would have it no other way. Io always expected harmony between the gods and goddesses and rather than upset the Old One, the most ancient of the gods, the supernatural inhabitants of earth, sky and sea maintained outwardly congenial relationships.

Tangaroa, who had indeed appeared as the Green Lizard to the island of Tahiti, thus bringing about the good weather and encouraging laziness and procrastination amongst the Raiateans, now brought a reef of spirits up from the depths of the ocean, to cause Tangiia's fleet of pahi to be diverted. This eater-of-canoes was brought just to the surface of the water, where it could be seen by the navigator king as rips in the ocean. Maomao, rushing by, would not notice the new reef, right out in the middle of the ocean, so far from land.

Tangaroa was hoping to alter Tangiia's course by the merest fraction. What began as a fraction often developed into a major change of direction the farther one sailed. In this way Tangaroa planned on leading the fleet to another of those parts of the ocean where the line between the real and the unreal was to be crossed, where the languid noons lulled wayward seafarers into a dreamy-weary state of mind.

Here the mariners' brains would fill with smoke under a hot sun and calm sea. Their judgement would be blunted

by their inability to tell the substantial from the illusory,
and they would be lost in their own imaginary world where
anything could happen.

The navigator king saw the rips on the surface of the
ocean and immediately changed tack to avoid them.
However, the coral reef was a good deal longer than
Tangiia had at first guessed and he had to circumnavigate
the whole ridge, thus altering his so-far steady course
across a broad sea.

At midday, three days later, the weather turned humid
and hot. The sails were still full, the wind still blew, but the
ocean remained as flat as a mountain pool. People sought
the shade, finding the sweltering sky too much to bear.

There was a sound like the buzzing of insects in the air,
though no such creatures could be seen. Fresh vegetables
and fruit tasted dry and fibrous on the tongue. Bark became
crisp and curled away from bare wood. Drinking water
became warm in the gourds and failed to quench the thirst.

In the ocean itself, there were knots of sea-snakes floating on the dull, oily surface, as if they had become
accidentally entangled and were doomed to die struggling
with one another until the last gasp.

This energy-draining weather lasted many, many days,
until finally land came into sight, like a dark mouth on the
horizon. In the hard-edged light of the afternoon, it
gleamed dully, its heat-waves rising like fronds from its
dense stone. It was a long low island with a squat central
ridge. The ridge was bare rock at the top, melting into
jungle beneath.

There was the cloying perfume of blooms in the air, making it difficult to breathe.

In the natural harbour there was no reef and the remains
of palms, without their tops, projected from the sea off-
shore. It seemed the ocean had reclaimed some of the land.
The trees were black and rotten for the most part, but

Tangiia found a stump strong enough to which he could moor his drifting pahi.

He then called to *The Volcano Flower* and *The Royal Palm* to moor up alongside *The Scudding Cloud*. The sound of his voice was leaden in the dull, heavy atmosphere. His call was returned stolidly by the other two captains.

Manopa came on board, followed by Po. Kikamana and Boy-girl attended the conference of the captains, joined by Kula, who exercised one of her privileges as queen. Opinion was divided fairly evenly. Manopa, Kikamana and Kula were for leaving the area immediately. The Farseeing-virgin said the portents were bad. On the other hand, although Boy-girl agreed with Kikamana about the portents, she felt that the crews, including the captains, could do with a few days' rest before setting sail again.

'Everyone is weary,' said Boy-girl. 'If none of us goes ashore, I feel we can risk sheltering in this harbour for a short while.'

Kikamana nodded. 'Boy-girl's right. If we do stay, the island should be forbidden territory, to all crew and passengers on the pahi. Not even the captains should put a foot on those sands. Not even a kahuna like myself must touch solid earth.'

'I shall feel uneasy even out here,' said Kula, shuddering when she looked at the island. 'There's something very sinister about this place.'

So it was settled that no one should go ashore and that the crews would rest for two days before the fleet continued on its journey.

'Seumas, Seumas, the boy's gone.'

'Wha— what's the matter?' asked Seumas waking from a deep, uncomfortable sleep.

His mouth was dry, he badly wanted a piss, and his brain felt sluggish and ponderous.

He looked up to see Po standing over him.

'Kieto, the boy. That fool dog of yours suddenly took it into its head to flop in the water and swim to the island. The boy saw it go – he took a dugout and went after it.'

'Dirk? Kieto?' He rubbed his drooping head. 'What did the hound do that for? He's never left my side without an order before. You know that.' Seumas looked over the inert water at the island. Nothing seemed to be moving there, not even the wind.

'We'll have to go after him.'

Po said, 'Tangiia gave an order than no one was to set foot on the island.'

'Where is Tangiia?'

'Asleep. They're all asleep, except for one or two fishermen. I can't wake the king or Manopa.'

Seumas said, 'It's this place. How come you didn't fall asleep like the rest of us?'

Po lifted his head and showed Seumas his nostrils.

'I stuffed some herbs up my nose, because I didn't like those tree blossom smells, wafting over from the island – I prefer the stink of fish to the tricky smell of perfume. Whenever I catch a whiff of flower fragrance, I end up getting married again. That's how I got my three wives, letting myself be charmed by an overpowering scent.

'And in my opinion that perfume in the air is what's sending people to sleep. So I'm breathing the tang of cooking herbs, not the fumes from that island. I thought some of us should stay awake. You should try it too. Kula has.'

He gave Seumas a handful of damp herb leaves. Seumas duly blocked his nostrils with some of them.

'Kula's awake?'

'She did the same as me, when she saw what I was doing.'

'Well,' said Seumas, rising to his feet, 'it's up to us then. Are you with me?'

Po nodded. 'I'll round up all those people I can wake.

Some are more soundly asleep than others. Then we'll go and look for the boy.'

'And my dog.'

Po rolled his eyes to heaven.

Kula helped the captain of *The Volcano Flower* to stuff herbs in the nostrils of other men and women and eventually there were enough awake to form a search party.

'I don't want anyone asleep over *there*,' warned Po, pointing to the island. 'We don't want to be looking for you too.'

'They'll be all right,' said Kula. 'I hope there's some fresh cool water on that island. All the water here on deck is warm, from lying in the sun.'

They took two dugouts, one with Po, two fishermen and two other women – the other carrying Seumas, two mariners and Kula. When they got to the beach they pulled the canoes up above the high-tide mark and decided to split the search party into two separate groups, one going left, the other going right.

'You walk along the beach that way, and we'll go the other,' said Po. 'When we meet up, on the other shore, we'll take a path each inland. I just hope that jungle was too dense for that stupid dog of yours and they've stuck to the shore.'

Seumas didn't argue with the captain. He and Kula and the two mariners began to walk along the beach, calling for both Kieto and Dirk.

The foliage was a tangled mass at the top of the beach, rolling like a dark green wave. All along the shore were dead shells, bleached coral and white driftwood. Sometimes this litter was so deep it was difficult to walk. They trudged on, seeing no living creatures on that usually busy margin where land met sea – no crabs, no mudskippers, no myriad of insects.

'Kieto? Kieto?' Kula called in a clear, lyrical tone that she hoped would carry.

'Dirk?' cried Seumas, in a sharp voice. 'Here, boy – here. Come, Dirk. Dirk? Dirk?'

Occasionally Seumas would stop to whistle, while the two mariners put their hands over their ears, hating the shrillness of the sound. The whistle seemed to hit the heavy, humid air like a fast bird hitting a wall. It carried no further than did their shouts, which also fell to earth like dead birds and were lost in the crammed flora of the island.

At one point they found human bones, picked clean by some unseen creature. The backbone was scattered over a wide area, little sockets that had come unhinged. The leg-bones and armbones were missing, but the ribcage was still there, with the skull inexplicably imprisoned within it, staring out through the bars. It was as if the head had locked itself inside the cage, to escape from something ghastly on the outside.

'Wait,' said Kula. 'I hear something!'

They listened hard and indeed there were some shrill cries, coming from the hinterland.

Seumas said, 'Come on.' He gripped his obsidian-edged club in his right hand and began hacking a path through the jungle. Kula and the two mariners did the same. To their surprise, the deeper they went, the less dense became the growth, until finally they found a stream beside which were some prints, both boy's and dog's.

'Good,' said Seumas, 'we're on the right track.'

They followed the stream until they came to a clearing where a rock face, half hidden by vines and foliage, appeared as a backdrop. Out in the clearing was a huge totem, a living tree carved in antiquity, which soared upwards in a multitude of faces and forms to a small crop of green at its head. The figures on its trunk and along its branches had been so cleverly wrought, there was always bark flowing between them to allow the sap a continuous path, thus ensuring the life of the tree.

Growth had distorted the images on the massive totem,

still resplendent with buttress roots, the middle of each vane standing as tall as Seumas. Organs – lips, eyes, noses, genitals – bulged from the carved faces and loins of the ugly figures. Staring at the twisted, warped features made Seumas feel giddy and ill, so horrifying were they. It was as if the tree-totem had deliberately grown galls and knots in places to emphasise gross parts of the now unrecognisable faces.

A hole in the trunk had become a hideous mouth with curled lips around it. A fat gall was now a bulbous nose, with cavernous nostrils beneath. Knots formed crazed eyes, veined and staring fixedly. A thick, stunted branch had grown to an ugly phallus, thrusting wildly at the sky.

And there were thousands of such faces, such torsos, from the roots to the topmost branch of the tree.

Around the base of the tree, all the undergrowth was dead, covered by a blinding-white crust of bird lime. And all down one side of the tree too, this bird lime ran like a frozen river, down from the phallus-branch which had obviously been used as a perch by a multitude of birds. Pure white faces on one side, brown on the other, all forming part of the same tree-totem. A totem whose eyes could see in every conceivable direction at once. A totem from the top of which the world could be viewed.

'Horrible,' said Kula, shuddering.

Spirits fluttered amongst its leaves, registering disapproval at her words.

'Yes, but look between the roots,' said Seumas.

Kula did so and saw that there were two living figures curled up asleep between the vanes of two buttress roots.

The party went to the foot of the giant tree and tried to wake both Kieto and Dirk.

'If they're so sound asleep,' said Kula, 'who was it that called?'

Seumas had no answer to this question.

Neither boy nor dog could be stirred, so one of the

mariners lifted Kieto on to his back, using the youth's arms to hold him there. Seumas heaved his dog up on to his tattooed shoulders, draping him around them like a scarf, gripping the hound's paws to keep him secure.

'Let's get out of here,' said Kula, 'before we find out who carved this monstrosity.'

'They must be dead, those people,' said one of the mariners, a man called Pungarehu. 'The faces look so old.'

'Not up there,' Kula said, pointing. 'Look, the higher the figure, the cleaner the wood. Up near the top they are quite fresh . . .'

Seumas added, 'They must be some climbers, to get up there and manage to carve faces so high off the ground.'

At that moment the sky darkened as it seemed that a cloud came sweeping low over the top of the cliff. The whole glade went cold as the area around the massive totem was thrown into the shade. It was more than the cold produced by a drop in temperature; it struck a deep, nefarious chill at the core of every soul present. Something wicked was casting that shadow, a fiend with a heart of pure obsidian.

Seumas looked up and his curiosity turned to a feeling of terror as he witnessed the arrival of a giant raptor, with claws and hooked beak large enough to grip a man. Just one of its great wings was enough to blacken the sun. The terrible bird of prey began circling the glade at an incredible speed, in small tight sweeps. Its piercing eyes were on the group below, as if preparing to stoop for a meal. Seumas had no doubt this was the creature which used the phallus branch as its perch.

Suddenly a shriek loud and shrill enough to skewer the brain began to fill the glade as the monster gave throat to its fury. The sound rose still higher, and yet even higher. Seumas's eyes watered as the scream penetrated his skull, threatening to shatter the fragile vessel which held his brain into a thousand small pieces. The giant bird of prey continued to wheel over the glade at a tremendous speed.

'The poukai!' cried Kula, her hands over her ears.

The group were strung out across the glade. Seumas and Kula were leading. Kula grabbed Seumas's arm and pulled him towards the trees at the edge of the clearing. Seumas, the dog a dead weight on his shoulders, followed willingly. Pungarehu, carrying Kieto, also turned towards the tree line. The last man however was closer to the totem and in a panic he dashed for the shelter of the buttress roots, waving his arms about his head as if to ward off the dreadful talons of the monster bird.

This waving action of the mariner's must have attracted the bird's attention, because he was chosen as its victim. It dropped from the sky like a rock, falling on the hapless mariner and snatching him from the ground before he reached the totem-tree. Seumas, now in the trees, witnessed the sickening sight of the mariner being carried wriggling and screaming, to the top of the cliff. There the bird took him in its enormous bill and shook him silly before smashing his head against the rocks. The waving arms and legs went limp and floppy.

'Oh no,' whispered Kula.

The poukai first picked out the eyes with the point of its beak, stuck its bill into the mariner's mouth and pulled out his tongue like a long, red worm, jerking it three times to tear it from its roots. Then the hideous freak pecked open the stomach of the lolling corpse and pulled out intestines like grey string, stabbing at the liver and other lights, eating the man from the inside out.

Blood and brains dribbled down the face of the cliff into some swamp water at the foot, as the body of the mariner was jerked this way and that in the bird's efforts to pick its bones clean. Every so often the bird's great head would look up from its task and stare around, as if watching for enemies.

When it had partially eaten its victim, the poukai flew to

the totem-tree. There it found a suitable perch at the top of the tree and began to chisel at the trunk like a woodpecker, as if drilling for grubs beneath the bark. After a while it became apparent that it was hewing a face in the wood.

The face was recognisable.

'It's *him* – my sailing companion,' cried Pungarehu, as the features of the dead mariner began to take shape on the bole of the tree. 'It's carving my friend's face.'

The bird looked down at the source of this sound and let out a loud, echoing *cark* – a mocking tone.

'We must leave,' said Seumas.

The group took the path through the jungle, back to the pahi, before the death mask was finished. Kula helped Pungarehu carry Kieto, so that they could jog a little. They reached the two dugouts and cast off almost on the run. Po's dugout remained on the shore, testifying that he and his party were still walking somewhere on the island. Hopefully they had stuck to the beach as planned and could be picked up easily.

Seumas paddled as if he had mechanical arms, desperate to reach the pahi before the bird should decide to follow them. Even before they were two boat lengths from the ocean-going canoes, he was shouting, 'Everybody up! Everybody awake? We must leave here now. Tangiia, Manopa – everyone on your feet. Get the sails up. Call the paddlers . . .'

People moaned in their slumber, one or two stirred and went up on to their elbows, weary and overblown with too much sleep and too little rest. Tangiia began to wake now, as Seumas leapt aboard. The king sat up, his face creased, sleep dust in the corners of his eyes. 'What's happening?' he mumbled.

'A giant bird!' cried Seumas helping the others carry the two bodies on board. 'The poukai, Kula calls it.'

'The poukai?' the king reached for a gourd and splashed water on his face. 'Oh, I remember the tales –'

'Here,' said Kula, going to him. 'Stuff this in your nose – everyone, fill your nostrils with damp herbs.'

'We have to get away from here,' Seumas babbled to Tangiia, his voice just a shade away from hysterical. 'You haven't seen this creature – it's a monster. Come on, get up, you lazy tics, on your feet.' He slapped a few backs. 'Get up and raise the sails, get to the paddles . . .'

He began kicking at the sailors in earnest. Most of them were still snoring deeply, lying on the bare deck, oblivious of the danger they were in. They rolled over, some staying asleep, others complaining in thick voices about being woken. One man lying in a hut took a swing with his fist at Seumas's ankle, angry at being disturbed, thinking Seumas wanted to steal his comfortable nest of sennit ropes and pandanus leaves.

'Are they dead?' asked Tangiia, unable to help himself yawning. 'The boy and the dog?'

'No, they're alive,' replied Kula. 'They're just asleep.'

Suddenly, Tangiia frowned. 'The poukai,' he murmured. Then more angrily to Seumas, he said, 'You risked my wife's life, taking her over there. It was forbidden.'

'The boy Kieto went after the dog without telling anyone. He was probably afraid we wouldn't go and fetch the hound. We had to go and get him back,' said Kula. 'There were only a few of us awake. Po is still over there, with four others. This is no time to be blaming people for doing what they had to do. Best get the sails up and go round the island to pick up the lost party before they're attacked.'

'Seumas and Po should have known better than to take you,' the king said loudly and persistently.

'They didn't take me – I went of my own free will. I'm not a pretty bird to be kept in a cage. I go as I please.'

Tangiia took this without a change of expression, then he rubbed his face again in irritation.

'What's making me so *weary*?' he grumbled. 'I can't think straight like this. I just feel so drowsy.'

'It's the perfume from the blossoms on the island's trees – push some more herbs up your nose. We have to get on, quickly, or that monster will pick us off the decks like insects.'

'Yes,' cried Seumas. 'We have to find Po and then get out into the deep ocean as quickly as we can.'

At that moment one man, an ordinary sailor, stepped forward and stood in front of Seumas.

'No,' he said. 'That bird is a menace to mariners and seafarers – we must rid the island of the creature.'

Seumas saw he was faced by the sailor named Pungarehu who had carried Kieto back from the island.

'What? Are you mad?' yelled Seumas. 'Nothing would make me go back there. Nothing.' He shuddered, violently.

Seumas had been truly shaken by his encounter with the monster. Never before had he witnessed such a scene as the attack on the dead mariner and he knew he would see that hideous head with its long curving beak, its glittering eyes, in his nightmares. Even now he could see the stubby red tongue of the bird deep in its throat, as the huge bill yawked wide in that ugly scream of triumph and fury.

Pit Seumas against a mortal foe, be he dwarf or giant or ordinary man, and Seumas would stand and fight. But against this brute bird he felt nothing but terrified revulsion. All those years on the cliffs, stealing fulmars from their nests, had come back to haunt him. This was retribution, this great feathered fiend, this bird-god come to claw out his guts, pick out his eyes, hook out his heart, for the theft of helpless birds on the cliffs of Albainn.

'We must go,' he muttered, shaking badly.

Pungarehu said softly, 'We must kill the bird. It is our duty as mariners. This poukai preys on our kind.'

Seumas turned half-crazed eyes on the sailor.

'And how do you propose to do that?' he cried.

King Tangiia was fully awake now and came and stood beside Seumas.

'Yes,' asked the king, but calmly. 'How?'

'I shall brain the creature with a stone axe,' replied Pungarehu. 'One of the large axes stored in the first deck hut. Seumas still has a squealing pig he made many years ago – he can make it screech to attract the poukai. We need to get the bird in a place with trees, so that it cannot easily take to the air.'

Tangiia frowned. 'The screaming pig Seumas made was burned – I saw it go on the fire myself.'

'Then he has made another one,' said the dogged Pungarehu. 'There are several mariners who know he has one – we've seen it in the second hut, wrapped in tapa-bark cloth. He brought it on board one night before we sailed from Raiatea. We were curious and had a look. It's there all right – the shape of an octopus with stiff legs and a body made from pigskin.'

Tangiia turned to Seumas. 'Is this true – you brought another of your living-dead pigs with us?'

'It's not *alive* in any way,' snorted Seumas. 'It's a musical instrument like a flute . . .'

'It makes a noise like a pig in pain, not like a flute,' argued the king. 'It makes a noise like a boar being castrated with a blunt stone knife.'

'It's *not* alive,' insisted Seumas. 'I never brought anything back to life. I'm not a sorcerer. The noise it makes is beautiful to the ear of a Pict or Scot – you just don't appreciate the sound. I like to play.'

'Then you must play for Pungarehu,' said the king, firmly. 'You must make your pig squeal for him. See if the poukai monster appreciates your music. See if you can beguile it with your mountain goblin's flute.'

'No – no – I can't. Not that. It's like a terrible dream. I can't do it. I can't.'

Tangiia whispered in his ear, 'Are you a *warrior*? I was beginning to think you were like us. But you seem to have grown cowardly. Are all Albannachs cowards like you?'

'But this is different,' hissed Seumas. 'This bird has come for *me*. I know it.'

'All the more reason to kill it then.'

'Yes, but – someone else. I can't play. Look, my hands are trembling.' He held out his quaking hands for inspection. 'My fingers won't find the right holes on the chanter.'

'Will it matter?' asked Tangiia with a touch of sarcastic humour. 'Who can tell the difference?'

'I can,' hissed Seumas, his fierce pride in his clan's marshal tune making him rise to the challenge.

'Then make your fingers obey you.'

Only a little more persuasion was needed, for Seumas was growing in confidence all the while. He had been badly frightened on the island, but he told himself now that he could only die once, and he had thwarted death several times in his younger years. He should have died when he fell off the cliff into the sea, but Kupe plucked him from his grave. He should have died on Nuku Hiva, but somehow he had survived. There were many other, earlier times. If anyone should have died before now, it was him.

'I hope I don't run,' he said to Pungarehu, 'when I see that bird again.'

'You better hope *I* don't run,' said Pungarehu. '*You're* the bait.'

They both touched the God of Hope for luck before leaving the ship and paddling over to the island. Seumas had his bagpipes with him. Pungarehu had his great stone axe, a monstrous weapon that was used to fell hardwood trees. It had a haft as thick as a man's wrist and an obsidian head, chipped to a sharp edge, bound to the haft with sennit cord.

They beached the canoe and retraced their steps to the jungle clearing. Seumas was almost hoping that the great bird had gone and flown away somewhere, but it was still at the top of the cliff, picking at the carcass of the mariner. The plan was to stay within the trees, which were sparse but would hamper the bird's flight. Seumas made ready with his bagpipes, while Pungarehu positioned himself in the lower branches of a tree.

Seumas blew up the pigskin bag, and then began playing, his fingers dancing nimbly along the chanter.

It was a pibroch he played, a marshal dirge, and even before the first few notes wailed over the glade, the bird left its perch and began to wheel.

Once again the fear knotted itself in Seumas's windpipe. It was all he could do to find air to fill the bag. If Pungarehu had not been with him he would have surely run away.

As he played, Seumas stared unbelievingly as the wind rushed through the bird's feathers creating a sound almost equalling that of the bagpipes in volume. The tail of the bird was shaped like an arrowhead, with long side stream-ers. These whipped the treetops as the poukai swooped and dived, trying to find a way in to the creature who was making all the noise. Shadows flickered over the two men as the bird cut through the shafts of sunlight above the forest. Seumas felt like a highland hare, about to be taken by a golden eagle; to be ripped open while he was still alive and feeling pain, and his eyes and tongue pecked out.

Come on! his mind yelled. *Get it over with.*

The poukai then let out one of its ugly screams, com-pletely drowning the pibroch. It landed swiftly on the turf of the clearing and came running into the rainforest, half as tall as the trees. Its pace was phenomenal and at last the Pict's nerve broke. Seumas spat out the mouthpiece and turned to run for cover, as the monster weaved amongst the trunks, heading straight for him as fleet as any highland stag.

Seumas turned once, to look over his shoulder, and saw a large bright pair of eyes bearing down on him from the darkness in the canopy of the rainforest. The small knot of fear in his throat became a large twisted clout. He was going to die, he was sure of it. That hooked beak was about stab him in the back and pierce his lungs on the way through.

'Ahhhghh! Pungarehu?' he cried. 'Where are you?'

Had the Oceanian already taken to his heels? Seumas wouldn't have blamed him. He would hate him with his dying breath, and curse his progeny, but he wouldn't blame him.

The ground was a snake pit of tree roots. Seumas's foot caught in one of these and he fell headlong forwards. He hit the earth with a thump, winding him. He rolled on to his back and held the bagpipes up in front of his face in a vain attempt to protect his eyes.

'NO!' he yelled.

The poukai's beak jabbed and pierced the pigskin bag, forcing air through the pipes.

'Whhhheeeeeeeyyyy,' went the pipes, nasally.

A moment later Pungarehu dropped from his hiding place in the tree, on to the bird's back. The mariner swung his axe and shouted, 'Here, monster, up here!' for all the world as if he were calling a dog to his side.

The shocked poukai half opened its wings, forgetting that flight in the rainforest, however few trees, was impossible. The poukai began to run, with Pungarehu standing between its wings, a foot on each joint. It seemed as if the poukai was preparing to take off as it weaved amongst the trees, its wing tips brushing the scattered trunks.

Now, Seumas inwardly cried, *hit the bastard now*!

As if he could read the Pict's thoughts, the mariner swung the great axe at the bird. The monster sensed a blow coming and averted its head, but the wily Oceanian was not aiming at the poukai's skull – he was striking at the left wing.

The stone axe struck the creature squarely on the leading edge of its wing, shattering the bone.

The poukai screamed. It began to drag its dead wing,

unable to close it now. Its run turned into a circular movement as it realised it was trapped in a ring of trees. The
vicious head came up and over its shoulder, as the poukai
attempted to peck Pungarehu from its back. Its great beak
clacked as it tried to bite Pungarehu, but it had not the
room to twist itself half-circle and snatch him with its bill.

Using the follow-through motion of the axe to form an
impetus for the next blow, Pungarehu now swung right
and broke the other wing, leaving the giant bird screeching
in rage and pain, trailing both its wings.

It tried to escape Pungarehu's murderous stone axe, by
running back to the glade, but it had lost its equilibrium
and its broken right wing caught a tree, sending the monster crashing to the ground. The brave Pungarehu then
stepped forward on to the neck and battered the poukai to
death, splitting its skull with the edge of the axe and letting
the brains bubble forth.

The poukai gave one last pathetic *cark* and died. Its
great, soft body, still full of warmth, lay jammed between
the trees, the branches brushing its back in the wind.
Pungarehu jumped down from the bird and plucked as a
trophy a giant primary feather from the trailing edge of the
wing. The feather was as tall as a pahi mast and would
make a sail in itself.

Seumas came forward and slapped the mariner on the
back.

'You did it! That was a great feat. They'll make up songs
about this, Pungarehu – and I hope you get all the credit. I
panicked there, at the end.'

'I was scared too,' admitted the seaman, smiling. 'My
blood was racing like a young river.'

'You kept a cool head and got the job done.'

'To tell the truth,' said the abashed mariner, 'I lost my
nose plug and went into a drowsy sleep up there in the
branches. It was the wail of your dead pig which woke me.
If I had not heard it cry, you would now be carrion.'

Seumas stared at his companion and felt a cold sweat trickling down the hollow of his back.

'You fell asleep?' he said, quietly.

'Yes.'

'Then the God of Pigs must indeed have been watching over us,' breathed Seumas.

Pungarehu grinned broadly at the humour and rested his tired arms on the handle of his axe.

'You are indeed an Oceanian, Seumas,' smiled Pungarehu. 'Only we can joke about such serious matters.'

'Oh, no,' argued Seumas, 'Albannachs are good at that too.'

One who was not too happy with Pungarehu was the Great Wind-God Maomao, until now a friend of the fleet. The birds of the air were Maomao's children; they played in his warm currents and caressed his brow with fine, soft feathers. They filled the atmosphere with their nursery cries and made patterns of their flight to amuse the Great Wind-God.

'This nobody Pungarehu must one day pay for killing the king of the birds,' said Maomao to Papa the Great Earth-Goddess. 'He has slaughtered one of my children, not for meat or feathers, but simply because it was there.'

'It killed and ate his friend,' Papa reminded the fickle god. 'Men are emotional creatures – passionate about friends and family.'

Maomao was only slightly mollified by Papa's speech defending the actions of Pungarehu and never quite forgot the wrong the mariner had inflicted on the wind-god.

After the death of the poukai, Po and his band met them in the forest, having circumnavigated the island. Together the whole band of men and women climbed the cliff behind the totem, at the top of which they discovered a cave. In the entrance and deep inside the cave were piles of human bones and skulls. Sorting through the skeletons they found many necklaces, bracelets and amulets, belonging to the victims of the poukai.

They returned with these to the glade and hung them on the great live totem as a symbol of respect and deference to the ghosts of the cave and clearing.

While they did this, Pungarehu carved one last death image on the trunk, that of the poukai itself.

The party returned in triumph to the bay of the dead palm trees, where the pahi were moored. There they were greeted by King Tangiia, to whom Pungarehu gave the feather as a tribute, and wild celebrations followed. That night they sailed away from the island and this time Tangaroa was better pleased, having struck at his old rival Maomao, by having his own favourite people kill his favourite bird. It satisfied the Great Sea-God's appetite for revenge for a while.

PART EIGHT

Out of Tawhaki's Armpits

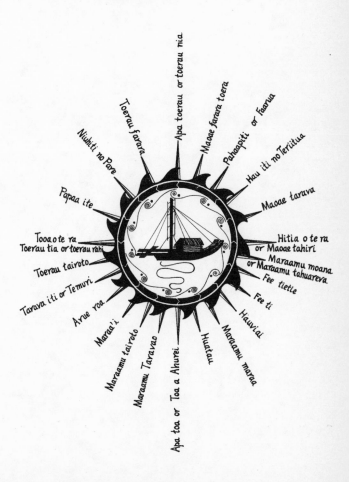

1

The name of lightning is Uira.

He is given life by the God of Thunder and Lightning, Tawhaki, not through a womb as with a mortal woman, but out of his armpits. Tawhaki *is* thunder, but to bring lightning Tawhaki spreads forth his arms and calls for the long jagged strips of blinding light, and flat pulses of brightness, that are Uira.

Uira fell in furious mood on the flotilla of tipairua canoes three days out of Fatu Hiva. It was not that Uira was angry with King Tutapu, or that he was taking sides in the fight. What brought Uira down from the skies were the sixty masts, bearing the sixty black sails, of the thirty tipairua.

Uira always sought out masts which stood high above Tangaroa's ocean, and sixty of them at once was just too easy not to miss. Uira the feller of trees brought down seven of the sixty masts, rigging and sails too, causing havoc on the decks of the tipairua.

Following this onslaught, Maomao sent Hau-iti-no-teriitua on the wind flower, to blow against the flotilla. An angry King Tutapu found he had to beat against the wind, all the way from Fatu Hiva, so then the king struck out towards Maraamu-tairoto on the wind flower and

reached the island of Rapa, almost at the bottom edge of
the ocean, only to be told by Ragnu that the Great God
Tangaroa had come to him as a sea snake at sunset and
informed him that King Tangiia was now in Tahiti.

'Tahiti?' snarled Tutapu. 'What's my half-brother doing?
Trying to get back to Raiatea and steal my islands?'

Tutapu set sail again towards Torau-farara on the wind
flower, only to find once again that he was beating against
the gale.

The king refused to stop at any island, so anxious was he
to catch his brother before he left Tahiti. The fisher folk
had to put trolling lines in the sea, to feed the hungry thousands on the move. There was famine on the tipairua, and
after a few months scurvy had begun to take a strong hold
amongst the seafarers. Polahiki, the fisherman picked up on
Fatu Hiva, complained bitterly to Dorcha that he was being
misused.

'I'm not one of you people,' he complained. 'Why should
I starve or catch some disease, just because your king wants
to kill his brother?'

Dorcha looked in distaste at the lice-infested fisherman.

'You probably brought more diseases on board with you
than anyone else here.'

The grimy, black-toothed Polahiki said he resented such
a remark, coming from a mountain goblin's mouth.

One day, when the wind was in the wrong direction,
Tutapu caught the drift of one of Polahiki's complaints.
The king was pacing the deck at the time, trying to concentrate on his navigating, wanting to curse Maomao for
obstructing him, but fearful of arousing more anger from
the Great Wind-God. The whining he heard from Polahiki
irritated him.

'Hurl that man overboard,' he ordered two of his sailors.

Polahiki heard the command and threw himself on the
deck, clinging with his gnarled fingers on to Dorcha's
ankles.

'No! No!' he shrieked. 'I'm sorry, my lord. Please, for the love of the gods – don't drown me. I'm not worthy – I'm not worthy – I'm not worthy . . .'

They ripped his hands away from Dorcha's flesh, where the nails had penetrated, causing her great pain. There were deep scratches where the fisherman's fingers had been. Then they heaved the struggling, shrieking man above their heads.

Polahiki then gripped one of the masts as they passed it and refused to release. He screamed and cursed them when they hit his fingers with a log. He bit one of the mariners savagely on the wrist as the log struck his hand.

Polahiki then clutched at one man's hair, and when his fingers were prised open, at another man's hair, until finally one of them held him while the other broke the fingers of his right hand, four at once.

He screamed in pain.

They then broke his left wrist.

To give him his due, Polahiki was obdurate to the point of insanity. He wrapped his legs around the neck of one of the mariners, locking his ankles. It took two more mariners to prise those legs open, with a thick bamboo pole, and by that time the man in the neck-lock was almost dead.

Tutapu watched all this in irritated amazement.

Finally, four men had one limb each and they tossed the wriggling, shrieking Polahiki into the air. He landed in the sea with a splash and disappeared from view.

A little later the fisher folk on the stern announced that Polahiki had caught hold of one of the trolling lines and was being dragged along by the canoe.

'Cut it loose,' snapped the king. 'He's slowing me up. Get rid of him *now*. If I hear that man's name again, I'll burn out the eyes of the person that's used it.'

The fisher folk did as they were told, but Polahiki kept grabbing other trolling lines, careless of the hooks that must have been penetrating his flesh. Finally, they managed to lose him and he was left thrashing in the sea – only to be picked up by another tipairua in the wake of the king's canoe, who probably believed that Polahiki had simply fallen overboard.

Dorcha washed her wounds in sea water, hoping they would not become infected. She thought it was entirely possible due to the filthy state of Polahiki's nails, that she would get some demon in her blood. She could see the culprit far behind, picking fish hooks from his arms with his teeth.

'I hope they tear you!' she yelled.

Then she felt bad about it. The poor man had broken bones, torn flesh, and lungs full of water. It was a miracle he was still alive. Dorcha was to find however that Polahiki was a born survivor. Even while on board the king's canoe, fit and healthy men had been dropping to the deck of fever and illness, while Polahiki's scrawny, sickly-looking frame seemed to resist every demon malady or injury known to humankind.

It was night and the stars had crystallised in the sky.

'I've heard enough stories about Maui,' said Dorcha, 'tell me a story about a woman.'

'I can tell you another story about how the first woman came to the world,' said Elo sweetly.

Dorcha sighed. 'That will do for a start.'

'In this story the first woman was made by the Goddess of Mirages . . .'

'A goddess making a woman – we do things for ourselves that's a *good* start.'

Little Elo frowned and said sternly, 'Please don't interrupt, Dorcha, while I'm telling the story.'

'I'm sorry, I'm sorry – go on,' replied Dorcha, suitably chastised.

'The Goddess of Mirages shaped the first woman from the heat waves of the midday sun, that time of day when mirages usually appear. This first woman was given a name. She was called Marikoriko and she married Tiki the first man –'

'Didn't have a lot of choice, did she?' interrupted Dorcha, tartly.

Elo put her head to one side and tightened her lips.

'Sorry, sorry – go on.'

'Well, Marikoriko and Tiki had the first child ever born on earth, who was a girl baby –'

'Another girl! Excellent! – sorry, sorry. I'm just wondering what we needed men for after this. Go on.'

'This first child was called "Lady of the Early Gentle Floating Shadows". Rainclouds appeared in the sky when she was born and these filled the rivers, but not so that they flooded, so that they flowed calm and serene, providing water for the people to drink . . .'

'When the people came along of course, because at first there was just Marikoriko, Tiki and their baby girl.'

'Yes, later the people came, but before that the First Child asked for light in the world and morning broke.'

Elo smiled sweetly and fell silent.

Dorcha looked at the girl and then said, 'Yes – what about the story?'

'That *is* the story,' said Elo.

'That's it?' cried Dorcha, incredulously. 'That's all of it? What about the story where a woman saves the world?'

Elo frowned again. 'I don't know of any story like that.'

Dorcha stared at the girl, then at the sky, then at the sea, and said finally, 'I do. Or at least, I know one who tried.'

'Tell it to me then.'

Dorcha said, 'There was once, in the far corner of my island, a Celtic princess, who was raped by invaders when her father died. The invaders from across the seas stole her kingdom and sacked the holy places, murdering the Celtic priests and warriors who tried to stop them. When the princess complained she and her sister were savagely whipped and raped.

'So the princess gathered together many of her own warriors and led them against the invaders. The invaders were very strong people and their warriors were many, but the princess was a great fighter and she and her people killed thousands of the invaders, driving them out of her kingdom.

'Two great battles she fought and won, then on the third she was defeated by sheer weight of numbers – she died defiantly spitting in the face of her enemies.'

Elo's eyes were wide with wonder at this tale.

'She sounds a truly remarkable lady, this princess of your race.'

Dorcha nodded. 'She was.'

'What was her name?' asked Elo.

'Her name was Boudicca.'

Elo repeated the name slowly, having trouble with the pronunciation.

King Tutapu, who had been standing by the mast knotting his cord-device, overheard this story, and said, 'I am interested in this Boudicca of yours – you say she defeated a superior force of warriors? To do this she must have had something which the invaders did not have – not because she was a woman, but because a small force always needs an edge, to conquer a large force. The gods were with her, I suppose?'

'And the goddesses.'

'And her people were very angry,' he added, 'while the invaders had only their greed to inspire them?'

'Just so,' answered Dorcha.

Tutapu said, 'You would like to be such a woman? To fight like a man?'

'Not like a man, like a warrior queen. I don't like the work men leave to women.'

Tutapu shrugged. 'What else can you do?'

Dorcha stared into the king's eyes. They were standing just a short distance from one another. She knew she could not touch him, for he was taboo and she had not been given protection by the kahuna, but just at that moment Tutapu was very attractive to her. He had a regal stance, he radiated power, and he was extremely handsome.

She said, 'I've been watching you, listening to you speak with your helmsmen. I've watched you with your knotted cord-device, noticed your sightings and heard your soundings. I would like to be a navigator too.'

Elo gave out a little gasp, but the king smiled.

'Have you discovered any of my secrets?' he asked.

'Yes. I can recognise many of the kaveinga stars, and the fanakenga stars.'

He nodded to the roof of voyaging. 'Find me the Taro.'

She looked up and then pointed out a group of stars. 'That's it there, with its stem and leaves.'

'Very good,' he said, raising his eyebrows. 'And the Adze?'

'There – handle and blade.'

'The Octopus Tentacle?'

"There.'

'I'm impressed,' he said, 'and I'm sure you know many more of my secrets, but those that are most important take a long time to learn, like the names and directions of the swells, the shape of waves, the long- and short-flighted birds, the te lapa . . .'

'I'm learning all the time.'

He questioned her for a long time as the tipairua glided through the night. She could tell he was fascinated by her correct answers to all he asked. When, on rare occasions, she did not know the answer, she told him so bluntly and he then relieved her of her ignorance. Finally he nodded thoughtfully and asked her one more question.

He held up his cord-device. 'And this – can you do this and map our way across the world?'

'That might take me years to learn, but I have this.'

She reached into her blanket smugly and produced a kind

of a rectangular frame as long as her arm and half as wide. There were strips of split bamboo criss-crossing it haphazardly. Some of the strips were bent into a curve, others were straight. There seemed to be no order or reason to the irregular network of strips but dotted about, again seemingly at random, were small cowrie shells stuck to the bamboo.

King Tutapu looked surprised. 'What is that?'

'It's a similar thing to your knotted cord-device. See, the whole thing is the great ocean and the slivers of bamboo criss-crossing it are journeys made by great navigators. The cowrie shells are stars. See, this one is Tiuriuri, the Evening Star, and this one Te Tino A Manu . . .'

King Tutapu did not take the device from her, because he was afraid his mana might harm her, but he went close and studied the bamboo chart, nodding thoughtfully.

'Yes, yes – I see how it might work. Who taught you this device?'

'Polahiki,' she smiled.

The king screwed up his face in distaste. 'That filthy creature?'

'He's a seafarer, for all his dirt – and he is from a different people, who have different ways.'

The king grunted, unconvinced it seemed.

He said no more for a while. Dorcha put her bamboo chart away and she and Elo chattered. Then Elo fell asleep on the deck. Dorcha too was tired and was about to lie down, when King Tutapu said, 'From tomorrow you will help me navigate. I want you to keep a record of our voyages, just as I do with my cord-device. Do not show it to me, unless I ask you to, otherwise we shall influence each other's recording. Ragnu will be told to raise your status to that of priestess. You are not a virgin, so you cannot hold high office, but there are priestesses with special duties who are not maidens.'

'But I am not your kin – the priestesses share your father with you . . .'

'You are sufficiently different from an ordinary person to warrant holding office.'

'If you say so.'

'I say so, goblin.'

She looked at him, startled. 'Shall I do it?'

'I command it,' replied Tutapu.

Dorcha was silent for a moment, realising she had won a great victory. She was to be a priestess – and no common man was allowed to assist the king in his navigating. It was an *awesome* victory. She would have a useful job that was nothing to do with cooking, cleaning or gathering. She was to be a hunter at last – a hunter of secret signs in the night, a hunter of shapes and colours in the day, a hunter of *passage*.

'Thank you,' she said humbly.

Tutapu waved the thanks away with his hand.

'It is deserved.'

Maomao, having heard about Tangaroa's tricks which had led King Tangiia's fleet first to the Isle of the Rapacious Women, then to the Island of the Poukai Bird, decided it was time to do the same to the flotilla of tipairua.

Maomao blew the thirty ships with their black sails in the direction of a certain island where dwelt a giant called Flaming Teeth, whose fangs were fiery logs which flared and spat sparks when he breathed in and out.

Flaming Teeth loved the taste of charred human flesh and spent his days looking out to sea, hoping for a ship-wreck on the shores of his island. When a log the size of a great tree trunk burned down to a stump in his mouth, Flaming Teeth would reach in with long thin fingers and pluck it out, pushing a new log into the empty socket.

Tutapu, impatient to find his brother, did not want to land on the island. He ordered his men to fight against the strong wind, to paddle as hard as they could. Finally, with his men exhausted, King Tutapu had to concede defeat.

The helmsmen could do nothing to prevent the ships from being driven towards the beach, so fierce and unrelenting was the wind.

However, the Great Wind-God's timing was wrong, because when the flotilla was blown hard up against the shore of the island it was night and the giant's teeth were plainly visible, as he slept on the side of a mountain. Sparks flew up in brilliant showers, above the rainforest. The sky was lit up by the tall flames, hiding the stars beneath their light.

Although the wind was pushing the flotilla up against the shore, on the island itself the air was strangely calm, as if the island were enclosed in a great bubble. The air was muggy and dense like the atmosphere of a sweltering swampland.

Tutapu gathered together eighty of his strongest men and went ashore quietly, hoping to surprise the giant, but the crickets saw the men – all armed with huge rocks wrapped in sennet netting so that they could swing them like clubs – and called to the giant to wake up and defend himself. The pitch of a cricket's song is high enough to penetrate any other sound, including the furnace roar of Flaming Teeth's mouth.

Flaming Teeth, whose arms were as long as his whole body, and whose hands rested next to his feet while he slept on his back, sat up. Only half awake he asked the crickets if they had called him. The flames roared out, scorching the treetops, as he called out his enquiry.

The crickets all answered at once, in a confusing chorus.

'Of course we called you,' they said. 'What's the matter with you? Do you want to be struck down in your sleep?'

One of the giant's long spidery arms bent, the elbow near his knee joint, as a hand came up to scratch his scalp with its straggly, lank hair.

'What?' he cried, flames roaring forth. 'What say?'

The crickets asked him again if he wanted to die, and

this time his other hand came up to scratch at his wispy pate.

'What say?' he flared. 'What say?'

At that moment Ragnu instructed his men to whistle and trill like birds, to scare the crickets into silence.

The crickets, surprised to hear birds singing at night, were struck dumb immediately. They did not want to give away their positions in the grasses to birds who might come, seek them out, and eat them. Eventually, when the crickets failed to answer him for a third time, the giant lay down to sleep again, thinking he had dreamt that the crickets had been calling him.

Ragnu said to King Tutapu, 'It seems we have a very stupid giant here, who scratches his head in frustration, every time he's asked a question. But it's not possible to confuse him in this way, because the heat from his mouth, and the roaring noise of the fire, doesn't allow men to get close enough for him to hear what is being said to him.'

Tutapu thought for a while and formed a plan, sending some of his men back to the tipairua. While they were gone he told other mariners to tie logs to the giant's hands with sennit cord, being careful not to wake him. Eventually the ones who had been back to the canoes returned bringing with them whole pig skins filled with sea water. These had been smeared on the outside with precious, sweet-smelling honey.

'Now,' whispered King Tutapu, 'we must get up level with his head.'

They passed the great giant on either side, carrying their large pigskin water containers on two-man poles. All around them, the forest was singed and charred where the giant had accidentally set fire to the undergrowth with his burning incisors and molars. The forests, hillsides and valleys were empty of human life and most large animals. Long ago the giant had eaten all the pigs and dogs of the island, and then started on the humans. The terrified people had run away to hide in the caves in the hillside, but Flaming Teeth easily winkled them out with the use of his long thin arms.

When Tutapu's seafarers reached a height level with the giant's head, but at a safe distance from the terrible flames, they made catapults out of springy saplings.

The giant's teeth flared and roared with each breath taken, the flames reaching higher than the treetops. It was impossible to get close to him, so intense was the heat from his fiery jaws. His mouth was a furnace which withered all the grasses around it and men were beaten back by the scorching flames to a place behind some rocks. Even there the giant's sweltering breath made it difficult for them not to swoon.

At a signal the mariners in the forest began to catapult the pig-sized water containers into the giant's mouth.

Flaming Teeth, thinking in his sleep that he was eating something tasty and sweet, chewed on the honey-covered pouches of water and punctured them. Salt water poured into his mouth, dousing the flames on his teeth with a hissing and fizzing. The giant then sat up, choking and spluttering, his mouth pouring steam and smoke in equal quantities. Without the fire the giant's island was plunged into pitch blackness. Never before had Flaming Teeth been subjected to the darkness.

'What's happened?' he cried. 'Why can't I see? Am I blind? Why is my mouth so wet? Why is it salty? Where are my precious flames? Who is on the island of Flaming Teeth, whose friend is Maomao the Great Wind-God?'

He ground his charcoal teeth together and huge damp splinters of charred wood sprayed forth.

'Who asks all these questions?' cried Tutapu. 'What is your name?'

Flaming Teeth immediately reached up to scratch his head at this question. He struck himself a brutal blow on his own skull with the log tied to his wrist. A yell of pain escaped his lips .

'Answer me quickly,' Tutapu cried, 'are you indeed blind?'

This time the other hand came up and struck the giant a blow on the other side of his head.

'Ahhhhggghhhh!' he screamed. 'Who strikes me?'

'Who strikes you indeed?' called Tutapu. 'Tell me his name and I'll kill him with my club.'

The giant's hand came up again, to scratch his skull, and he struck himself yet again, a terrible blow which made the forest ring with its echoes, wailing in anguish as he did so, crying to the gods to help him fight off his invisible opponent.

'Someone is attacking me in my blindness,' cried Flaming Teeth. 'A monster with thousands of shining eyes.'

He meant the stars, which he had never seen before, his fire having been so bright it overpowered their light.

Tutapu was relentless with his questions, asking one after the other, until finally the giant had beaten himself senseless. Tutapu's men then went forward. They built a platform on stilts, on which they raised a huge rock. This they let fall on the giant's skull, smashing it, and killing him stone dead.

They left the giant's body on the hillside, it being too heavy to move. Maomao blew through the giant's wispy hair and moaned across the great caves that were his nostrils. Maomao was not pleased that one of his adopted children had been slaughtered by King Tutapu, but Io spoke to him and told him he should recognise that it was he who had forced the king to land on the island and that it was partly his own fault.

Maomao had no option but to agree with the Father of Gods and gave Tutapu a fair wind to Tahiti.

Tutapu gathered stores and provisions and set sail once more for Tahiti, where he hoped to find his half-brother.

It was a clear, warm day with gentle breezes lifting the

palm leaves like unseen hands. Up on the slopes of the Tahitian mountains a lookout spotted a line of black dots on the horizon. He called down to a runner, who went straight to the king's basket-sharers and informed them of what had been seen. The basket-sharers spoke briefly to the king's high priest. The high priest went into the king's house with the news.

King Morning Star, indolent and lazy in times of peace, was no slouch when it came to protecting his precious homeland. He immediately ordered the launching of a hundred and fifty war canoes. By the time Tutapu's mighty flotilla approached the reef, Morning Star's force was lined up ready for battle, with Morning Star himself in the front line.

Tangiia's force of three pahi had been of little concern to Tahiti, but three thousand warriors in canoes decked for war and bearing sinister black sails was a definite threat.

Drums sounded in the bay as the two fleets approached each other. There was much noise as the warriors sang out their battle songs, asking Oro the Great War-God to grant them victory in the coming battle. A single flush of spears left the leading Tahitian canoe, killing one of Tutapu's men and wounding a woman, before the Raiatean and Boraboran king held up his arms.

'Peace!' called Ragnu, across the water, to the head Tahitian kahuna.

'Peace,' agreed the high priest, after conferring with King Morning Star.

Tutapu signalled that he wished to step on to the Tahitian king's canoe and speak with King Morning Star, as the two great armadas faced each other uneasily in the wide bay.

Safe passage was granted and Tutapu, resplendent in his war helmet and carrying his club and lei-o-mano, leapt from his canoe on to that of the Tahitian king. He greeted King Morning Star with respect and then asked him if

Tangiia was present. They spoke formally, with evident reserve and pride.

'Ah,' said Morning Star, 'the Relentless Pursuer. You are King Tutapu, who desires the death of your half-brother?'

'I am that man,' said Tutapu.

'And if I say Tangiia is with my warriors in the bay?'

'Then I shall do my utmost to destroy your fleet, though I die in the enterprise,' said Tutapu. 'I must have his life, for he stole one of my gods and will ever be a threat to me.'

King Morning Star nodded, his great cheeks quivering.

'You would wish me to give him up to you then?'

'Yes.'

'That I cannot do, because he is no longer with us – he left the island some days ago.'

The disappointment showed clearly on Tutapu's face, but he raised his head and said, 'Then I have no quarrel with you.'

King Morning Star nodded gravely and said, 'No, but you were prepared to attack my island, to take a guest from my hands by force, and therefore I refuse to allow you to land and gather provisions. You will sail away from my island now, or face my warriors in a sea battle which you will surely lose.'

Tutapu glared angrily at the Tahitian king, but he reminded himself that it was Tangiia he wanted, not a war with Tahiti. Such a war might be prolonged for generations and ruin both peoples with the waste that war brings. He looked around him, prior to returning to his tipairua.

'I see amongst your warriors and rowers, people from Raiatea,' he said. 'These are traitors to my lands.'

'They are Tahitians now,' Morning Star told him. 'They have married into my family.'

'Your family?'

'All my people are my family.'

Tutapu muttered, 'I see.'

Morning Star said on their parting, 'I have no quarrel

with you, King Tutapu. I recognise your right to kingship of your islands and I respect that right deeply. You
are the oldest son of my great friend, your father, and I
have no wish to interfere in your quarrel. If you had
come to me in vessels decked for peace, instead of war, I
should have welcomed you with all the ceremony due to
a king.

'But you came prepared for war, if not with your
brother, with anyone who stood in the way of your
brother. Your father would not have done this – he would
have changed his sails, the posture of his canoes, the attire
of his men, and he would have worn not his war helmet,
but flowers in his hair. You have much to learn, Tutapu,
about kingship.'

'Perhaps I have,' said Tutapu, wisely. 'Kingship is new to
me. Perhaps the passing years will give me more wisdom.
But my men are weary. Would it be too much to ask that
we remain anchored here for a few hours, while they rest?'

'This request is granted.'

Tutapu returned to his tipairua in thoughtfulness, rather
than in anger. He was still upset by his reception, but he
had to admit to himself that he had not chosen the wisest
method of approach. The Tahitian king was right about
that, he had much to learn, but the lessons were coming
thick and fast.

When he reached his vessel, he said to Ragnu, 'I would
like to slaughter every Raiatean on that island.'

Ragnu gripped his club and said, 'Let us do it.'

Tutapu shook his head. 'No, no. There's no sense in
depleting our warriors by fighting a war with the Tahitians
for a few grubby traitors. It's Tangiia I want. What we
must do is speak with one of those traitors and find out
which direction Tangiia took, so that we can follow him.'

'Our spy must surely have left signs for us?'

'True, but any such signs will be on the island – if we

cannot wander on Tahiti at our leisure, then we have little chance of coming across them.'

Ragnu said, 'There'll be Tahitian sentries on the beaches, watching us like hungry sharks. But one man might be able to slip through.'

'Who?' asked Tutapu.

'I'll go myself,' said Ragnu.

'If you are not back within a stipulated time,' warned Tutapu, 'I shall have to leave without you.'

'Understood,' replied the high priest.

When evening came Ra and Hine-keha passed each other in the sky without a sign.

As the daylight faded and the moonlight waxed Tutapu shouted orders to his crews, already briefed, to make ready to sail, commands that could be heard from the beaches of Tahiti. While the activity, designed to look speedy and efficient but actually just another delaying tactic, was in progress Ragnu slipped into the water and swam quietly parallel to the reef. When he reached a place where the sentries were thin on the ground, he swam ashore and crept up the beach into the rainforest.

From there he made his way back to the loose-knit cluster of several villages, where most people were still outside their houses and huts gawping at the foreign flotilla, watching as the sailors ran around the decks, hauling on ropes, tightening rigging, raising sails.

Ragnu moved around unobtrusively in the moonlight, searching features, until he found a familiar face.

He went back to the darkness on the edge of the rainforest and called the man's name.

'Over here,' he hissed.

The man looked back, frowning, clearly puzzled.

'What is it? Who's that?'

Ragnu didn't answer. He simply waited, hoping the man's curiosity would get the better of him. It was a successful ruse and eventually the Raiatean ambled over to him, saying, 'Who is it? What is it you want? I want to see Tutapu leave.'

When he was close enough, Ragnu grabbed the man by the throat and dragged him into the bushes. There he proceeded to strangle the man, having had the advantage of surprise, until the man's eyes bugged and he was clearly only seconds away from death. Only then did Ragnu release him.

'Uhhhhhh,' moaned the man, once he had recovered his breath.

'Wha— you – you tried to kill me . . .' He rubbed his throat which carried the marks of Ragnu's strong fingers.

Ragnu pulled a kotiate club from his loin cloth and threatened the man with it.

'One word from you, to warn your friends, and I'll smash your skull. Now, I want to know some things from you! If you fail to give them to me, I'll send a kabu to you in the night and you'll die of fear. Have you seen the faces of men who die of fear? The terror makes them open their mouths so wide their jaws become unhinged. Their eyes jump out of their sockets on to their cheeks. Their nostrils bleed . . .'

The man, whose face was hidden by shadow, said nothing. He was still clearly very weak from the ordeal of his strangling. He was kneeling on the ground. Ragnu was behind him gripping and stretching him by his long hair, bolt upright, while at the same time standing on his ankles. In his right hand Ragnu held the kotiate club, ready to strike if the man should utter a sound loud enough to alert the Tahitians.

It was a delicate balance. The kahuna did not want to alarm Morning Star's warriors and cause a major incident, perhaps leading to war. At the same time he had to get the information he wanted from this man.

'Tell me!' hissed Ragnu.

At that moment Ragnu felt the man tense and knew he was going to shout for help. A sound came out of the man's mouth which was abruptly cut short as Ragnu decapitated him with the edge of the kotiate club. Ragnu was disgusted in himself, for having chosen a man prepared to die rather than give him the intelligence he needed. He tossed the head into the forest where it landed with a thump similar to that of a coconut falling from a palm.

The noise the man had made had not been enough to alert the people watching the boats. One woman glanced behind, but when Ragnu made a thrashing sound in the bushes, similar to the sound made by a large lizard when it scrambled through dead leaves, she turned back and said something to her neighbour, who giggled.

Ragnu's problem was now time. Tutapu could not delay the departure for much longer and Ragnu realised he would have to get back to the tipairua right away. Cursing, he made his way to the beach, dreading his next meeting with King Tutapu. Once on the beach it occurred to him that perhaps one of the sentries might be a Raiatean and he could club the man senseless and take him back to the tipairua with him. Once he had someone on board the king's canoe they could set sail and torture the man at their leisure, being almost certain to obtain what they wanted.

Ragnu slipped behind a rock and peered over it at three sentries standing together, chattering and pointing occasionally at the foreign flotilla of canoes.

None of these three men looked familiar, but as Ragnu stared at them, he noticed something on the rock itself which showed faintly in the moonlight from Hine-keha's bright face.

It was a mark scratched into the stone surface by someone Ragnu knew well – King Tutapu's spy.

It was a cryptic symbol for papaa-iti on the wind flower.

'Got you!' murmured Ragnu, in triumph.

The high priest then crept away from the three sentries

and found a place on the beach where he could wriggle down to the water like a turtle without being seen. Once in the warm waters of the great lagoon he swam out towards the tipairua, only to see with consternation that they had already begun sailing away. When Ragnu reached the reef, the last tipairua was riding the surf over the dead, white top-coral.

Tangaroa had witnessed Ragnu's failure to get back to the flotilla in time and sent Aremata-rorua, the long-wave, to assist him. Aremata-rorua, normally feared by mariners, rose up in the lagoon and swept towards the reef. On his way the long-wave gathered Ragnu on its foaming crest and bore him over the dangerously sharp coral, into the ocean beyond.

Aremata-rorua continued his surge out into the deep ocean, until he reached the flotilla of canoes with their ominous black sails. There he petered out.

Ragnu was helped on board the last canoe, which then broke line and took the high priest to Tutapu's tipairua. One of the king's lovers, a young man of extraordinary beauty, was surprised to see Ragnu boarding the canoe and called to his lord that Ragnu was saved. Tutapu emerged from a deck hut. He had evidently been weeping and Ragnu was touched by the fact that he had been so missed by his king.

'Papaa-iti,' Ragnu said.

Tutapu's eyes opened a little wider, then he called to his helmsman.

'Papaa-iti on the wind flower!'

Once he had received an acknowledgement King Tutapu motioned for Ragnu to follow him into his hut. There was a girl in the hut, another of the king's paramours. The king continued to enjoy the bodies of both men and women, so long as they were young and sweet, or were special, like Boy-girl.

Tutapu's sexual appetites were not particularly strong or unusual, but they were definite. The king admired loveliness, in all its forms, for beauty – like sad music from flutes – made him cry. Beautiful youths and girls were invested with exceptional temporary powers by the head kahuna, to protect them against the king's mana. Thus, taboo to all other commoners, the king was able to satisfy his lust without harming his lovers.

The girl left the hut once she saw Ragnu entering.

Ragnu recounted his adventures on the island.

'They'll discover the beheaded corpse of course, if they haven't already done so – but who's to say it was not a local murder. No one saw me go ashore or return to this canoe. Even if the Tahitian king suspects something, there's little he can do to prove it, even to himself.'

King Tutapu said, 'You've done well. I shall reward you when we reach our home islands.'

'Your satisfaction is reward enough,' murmured Ragnu.

2

One day, five years after Seumas had arrived on Raiatea, Kieto had come running to him.

'Quickly, Seumas – it's Boy-girl. She's fallen over a cliff!'

To his eternal shame the first emotion that passed through Seumas's breast was a feeling of relief. At last he would cease to be pestered by the creature. Almost immediately however, he felt a sense of shame, and made brief enquiries.

'Is she dead?'

'No, she's caught on a ledge halfway down. There's a huge drop into a gulley below her. If someone doesn't climb down to her with a rope, she'll die.'

'Someone? Me, I suppose.'

Kieto looked at the Pict and shrugged. 'You're the best climber on the island.'

Seumas quickly gathered some sennit ropes from the corner of his hut and followed Kieto out into the sunshine, saying, 'I suppose I should feel flattered. What was she doing on the cliffs anyway?'

'Collecting birds' eggs.'

'Trying to steal their feathers, more like. All right, lead the way. I'm right behind you.'

Kieto took off at a run with Seumas on his heels, into the rainforest at the edge of the beach. They ran along jungle paths, up steep slopes, until they reached the tops of some cliffs on the east side of the island. Kieto went to the edge immediately and looked down. Seumas followed him.

There was Boy-girl, a good way below, with the sea birds swooping and diving around her. She looked like a wounded bird herself, with her ribbons flying. Clutching a pinnacle of rock that jutted from the cliff, she had since fallen a short way further down from the ledge which had first borne her weight. Far below was the greenery of the rainforest, with rocks piercing the canopy like white knives. A heavy mist clung to the tops of the trees and wound around the points of stone.

'Hold on, Boy-girl, I'm coming down,' yelled Seumas.

Boy-girl's frightened features looked up at him.

'Hurry,' she whispered into the wind. 'My arms are getting tired.'

Seumas tied a rope around the base of a tree and then began abseiling down the rockface, past shrubs laden with nests, until he reached Boy-girl. She stretched out an arm for him, but he held off for a moment. This was an opportunity not to be missed. Seumas would never have another like it.

'Boy-girl,' he said, 'I'm going to save you – but you must first promise me you won't bother me so much.'

'Wha— what do you mean?' shrieked the terrified Boy-girl. 'Get me up there.'

'Not until you promise,' said Seumas, firmly. 'I don't mind us talking once in a while, but I won't be pestered any more. I'd rather see you fall.'

Kieto, who could hear everything that was going on below him, called out, 'Seumas – *please.*'

'No, not until she promises.'

Tears began to stream down Boy-girl's face.

'I'd rather die,' she squealed. 'I'll let go *now*. Here, I'm letting go – and it'll be your fault.'

But she didn't let go, and Seumas waited patiently, inwardly ready to grab her if her arms gave way, but outwardly indifferent to her fate. Their eyes were locked and for all Boy-girl could see, Seumas was ready to let her die.

'All you have to do is promise,' he said. 'Then you can have the rope . . .'

Boy-girl sobbed for a minute, then nodded.

'All right,' she said. 'I won't pester you so much.'

'You won't pester me at all.'

'I'll try not to.'

Seumas realised this was as much as he was going to get out of her and finally reached across and put the rope in her hands.

'I can't climb up,' she whispered. 'I'm too tired.'

Bridging himself between two rocks, Seumas freed his own hands to tie her wrists together. Then he looped her arms around his neck and began climbing upwards. When he was part the way up he realised Boy-girl, pressing hard against his back, had an erection.

'Boy-girl, stop that!' he snarled.

'I can't help it,' she whined. Then she sniggered.

'By the gods, if you're doing all this on purpose, I'll kill you,' muttered Seumas.

He reached the top of the cliff and then dumped her unceremoniously on the ground. Kieto was still looking shocked.

'You were going to let her fall,' he said.

'I wouldn't have done that,' Seumas grunted. 'I was ready to catch her. But I got my promise.' He looked at Boy-girl, who was lying on her back, recovering from her ordeal. 'You did promise, you know. No more bothering me.'

Boy-girl looked away. 'I know.'

Kieto walked Seumas back to his hut.

On the way, Kieto said, 'Thank you for coming, Seumas.'

'Don't mention it. It was an opportunity I couldn't ignore. At last I'll get a little peace.'

'Is that all you can think of?'

'Yes, Kieto, it is. If you were me you'd know how it feels to be chased from morning until night. I feel trapped all the time, here on this island, with someone who won't leave me alone.'

'Oh.'

A little while later, just before they parted, Kieto said to Seumas, 'You know, Dorcha said exactly those same words – the words you just spoke to me – not a day ago.'

After he had gone Seumas sat down in the darkness of his hut and mused. So Dorcha thought him a pest, did she? He was doing to her, what Boy-girl was doing to him. Was she then as repulsed as he was, concerning physical contact? Did she want him to avoid her completely? If that was the way she felt about him, why, she would have her wish. He was not a man to force himself upon anyone. She could go to hell, for all he cared. He needed neither sight nor sound of her.

And so, for a while, he managed to keep out of Dorcha's way, and not see her. But his hunger for her eventually overcame his sense of pride and shame, and he found himself peeking through bushes, going to the stream for water at certain times of day, hoping for a glance of her, or hoping to hear the sound of her voice on the warm air. Once, she caught him hiding behind a tree, watching her go by, and she remonstrated with him angrily.

'Don't you think I need some privacy?'

'I thought I was giving you plenty,' he told her miserably. 'I've hardly followed you once this past twenty days.'

'I'm supposed to thank you for that?'

So things returned to normal after a while. And though Boy-girl kept to her promise, more or less, for longer than Seumas kept to his, she too began to run into him more frequently, bothering him. In the end Seumas gave up worrying, both about Boy-girl and whether Dorcha was angry with him. He followed Dorcha, Boy-girl followed him, and little changed over the years until the time came for the great expedition.

PART NINE

The Tree of Many Branches

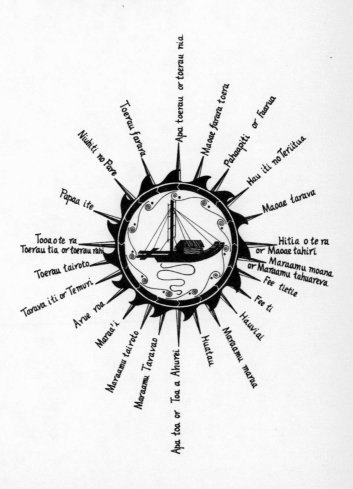

1

'This is a story about Maui,' said Kieto.

'Who else?' smiled Seumas, lying in the midday heat, stroking Dirk with one hand and shading his eyes with the other. 'Go on, what did he do now?'

'Well, when the world was fresh and new, all the winds were wild and blew in every direction, all at once, creating great turmoil and disasters. It was impossible to use a sail on a canoe. So one day Maui fought with the winds. He wrestled them until they submitted – and so he brought them under control.

'Tua-Uo-Loa promised to blow in one direction only – up from the bottom edge of Oceania. And Matuu from the top of Oceania, in the opposite direction. Furthermore, they agreed that only one of them should blow at any one time, unless the God Apu Hau released them from this rule for a short while.

'Mata Upolu, who blows from the left side of Oceania, and Tonga from the bottom left, were also subdued.

'Each of these winds has its own shape and strength, and its own particular ways, which I will describe to you if you wish.'

'I can do without it – go on with the story. Did any of the

winds survive this drubbing by Maui? Any of them tell him to go peddle his clay pots elsewhere?'

Kieto shook his head solemnly. 'No – but Maui took pity on the gentle breeze, Fisaga, which was allowed to roam free.'

'A generous fellow, Maui.'

At that moment there was a shout that land had been seen and everyone stood up and stared. On the starboard side of the canoes great fountains of water could be seen gushing up into the sky with regularity. They appeared to be geysers, with gaps between the spouts. It was a while before the word went round that this was the sea, rushing in beneath a shelf of rock with holes in it. The force of the wave sent tall columns of water hissing through the holes like a forest of waterspouts, only to change to spray and mist a few moments later, carried away by the wind.

'What a sight,' said Seumas.

These were rugged islands where the landscape rose steeply from the shoreline. This was a high kingdom, where the fringing reefs were built on volcanic rock. Here moved the god Ruau-moko, who was still inside his mother Papa's womb, struggling to be born. The one god who never would be given birth, but was destined for ever to kick and roll inside his mother, causing the houses of men to tumble on the earth, and the trees to fall, and the rocks to split and rattle down the mountains. Ruau-moko made massive cracks in the earth, trying to open his mother's womb and escape, but none of them were ever wide enough to let him out. They passed one island that Kieto recognised.

Kieto said, 'I think I know this land, from my voyage with Kupe – it's the island of Savaii.'

'Will we stop here?'

Kieto shook his head. 'I do not think so – there are many people who live here already. They have no use for more.'

Before they sailed away from the region, Tangiia ordered sacrifices to be made, and chants to be sung. This was the land of Kai-n-tiku-aba, the sacred tree, which at one time grew on the back of the Father of the Gods, but was broken off by a destructive man called Koura-abi. Until then the whole population of the earth had dwelt under the tree's shade, but once it had been broken they turned to violence and war, and through conflict were gradually scattered over the whole vastness of the world, and they learned the meaning of sorrow.

The three pahi then headed in the same direction as Hauviai on the wind flower. On the way they saw a fisherman, whom Tangiia took on board and questioned, asking him if he knew of any uninhabited islands in the region. The fisherman, who was from Savaii and clearly nervous, told Tangiia that he believed there were islands in line with Hauviai which had no people on them.

'Who told you this?' asked Tangiia.

'One of our great navigators, King Karika,' said the Savaiian fisherman. 'He has been wandering the ocean in search of a new land and the Great Sea-God Tangaroa has told him in a dream of a beautiful island in the direction you are voyaging.'

'I too have been voyaging a long time and my people are weary,' Tangiia said. 'It shall be a case of who gets to this island first – and I intend it to be *me*.'

With that King Tangiia ordered full sail. The fisherman was set adrift in his own canoe again and the fleet sped across the waves towards their destination. On the way they met a great storm, where Tangaroa and Maomao, each wanting their favourites to reach the uninhabited island first, had a furious struggle with each other.

Tangiia in his haste to reach the island before Karika refused to allow his men to take in sail and at the height of the storm, one of the pahi was swamped by a great tidal wave from Apu Matangi, God of Storms and the Howling Rain, aroused to action by the struggling of his fellow gods on this wild stretch of the great ocean.

The Volcano Flower, Po's pahi, was smashed and sank. Tangiia at last took in sail and turned about to save as many souls as he could, as did Manopa with *The Royal Palm*. They managed to rescue many of the people, though at least a third were drowned, but more importantly the great canoe was lost.

Po was among those rescued and he grieved for the loss of his vessel and his passengers and crew. He attached all blame for the loss to himself, though others told him he had done all he could to keep *The Volcano Flower* afloat. None could charge him with a mistake in judgement, though such an error would have been understandable during so fierce a storm.

Men, women and children were shared between the two surviving canoes, but space was cramped and food and water was scarce. Tangiia beat himself about the head and chest, until he was stopped by Makka-te and Kikamana. He wailed that he was responsible for the deaths of his people and no one contradicted him for kings too have to learn to take responsibility for their actions. That evening he finally made an appeasing sacrifice to the Great Sea-God, Tangaroa, who forgave him for his previous indiscretions and accepted him to his bosom.

'Milu,' cried Tangiia, into the dying breath of the storm, 'look after my people for me – treat them well – for it is I who should be walking the purple path to your kingdom, not they.'

The two pahi continued on their journey, following the navigational signs the Savaiian fisherman had given them. The weather became fair, with a fresh wind that blew them swiftly over a rippling sea, a sea on which that wind chased fleeting shadows and evanescent patches of light.

There was a feeling on board the two canoes that they were at last heading towards their destination. A quietness settled on the Raiateans. Makka-te did some tattooing, for young men who had passed the age; Seumas groomed his dog and made it a rattan collar, into which was woven coloured strands of bark-cloth; Tangiia stood by the mast most days, staring at the horizon, looking for that shade of light green on the bottom cloud which signalled an atoll or island; Po and Kula comforted grieving relatives of those drowned souls: Aputua the shark-caller busied himself making lures; Kikamana the Farseeing-virgin remained aloof, staying inside one of the deck huts; Kaho the blind Feeler-of-the-sea tested the waters continually for a change in temperature, while keeping his son Po'oi amused with tales of great voyages, his memory map perfect in every detail.

One night they passed a conical island which glowed red at its top, but Kikamana told Tangiia this was not the island they sought and to keep on course.

Kaho came to Tangiia one morning to inform him that the temperature of the water had changed dramatically.

'Could this be the volcano island we passed?' asked Tangiia.

'No,' said Kaho, 'the currents are coming from the wrong direction for that.'

Tangiia kept a close watch on the surface of the sea that day and noted seaweed and driftwood.

Towards evening a lookout sighted a large voyager craft sailing parallel to them.

Tangiia climbed the mast and studied the vessel, which was taking the same line as the two pahi. It was under full sail and seemed to be keeping pace with Tangiia's canoes. Tangiia slipped back down the mast.

'More sail,' he ordered his crew. 'Bailers, I want you to work much harder. Get rid of every drop of surplus water, it's only extra weight. Po, organise some people and throw overboard anything we don't need from now on. Kula, signal our intentions to Manopa – we must outrun that canoe over there. It has to be Karika. We must beat him to the island.'

The bailers worked frantically, shovelling the water from the two hulls with their half-coconuts, changing shifts more often so that rested men and women could take over from the weary workers. Po went through the craft, section by section, tossing overboard anything that was of sentimental value only, or obsolete so far as the voyage was concerned. Manopa, when he received Kula's signals, began doing the same.

Tangiia knelt down before Tiki, imploring his ancestor to help him in his endeavours. He asked Maomao for more wind, to give him more speed, though by now the other craft was close enough to receive the same wind. He begged Tangaroa to open a smooth channel for him, without him having to battle against strong eddies and currents, having the swell behind him. The God of Hope was brought out into the sunshine, to inspire the crew and passengers with confidence in their undertaking.

The gods seemed to be with Tangiia, for he was granted all he asked, but the strange canoe seemed also to receive such assistance, because it kept pace with *The Scudding Cloud*. Kikamana was asked to pray to Whatu, the God of Hail, to pelt the other craft with huge hailstones, and to Tawhaki, to strike down the captain of that vessel with Uira, but no answer was received from either god. Kikamana told Tangiia that the gods had decided it was to be a contest between the two men only – himself and Karika – and that the gods were betting on the outcome, urging on their favourite, but would not intervene.

'A race, is it?' said the Raiatean king. 'Then let it be so!'

Tangiia used every ounce of his seamanship to get speed out of his pahi. Trawl lines were taken in. The rigging was tightened until it hummed, the masts bent like bamboo stems in a high wind. The wind then sang through stays and sheets. The high, curved bowsprits were like hungry mouths eating waves, flecks of foam flying from their jaws.

The deck huts were taken down and stacked flat. The

cargo was distributed over the deck platform. All those not
working were told to lie prone, to lower their wind resistance.

Gradually the Raiatean craft began to outstrip the
Savaiian vessel, nosing ahead.

'Ha, ha!' cried Tangiia. 'Now we shall see who has the
best canoe, who is the best captain!'

Seumas cried, 'She's changing sails – for bigger ones by
the look.'

Indeed, the other vessel had raised a large red crab-claw
sail on the port side and was doing the same on the starboard side.

Despite the size of the vessels they were now skipping
over the wave tops. They hardly seemed to touch the surface of the water. Spume flew from the bows of the pahi. It
hissed along, with the wind pushing hard. *The Royal Palm*
was left behind, to follow as best as it could. The two
racing vessels danced ahead, first one easing in front, then
the other.

Tangiia had never before been at such a high speed. It
seemed to him that they were racing for the edge of the
world. It appeared to him that they were bound for disaster. If they should touch so much as a small floating log
with their bows, there would be a catastrophe. Any small
object like a coconut in the water would go through the
hull like a catapulted rock through a taut banana leaf.

'The island!' screamed Po, through the wind. 'Port side.'

There indeed was an island. It rose out of the sea like a
great green whale. Even from this distance Tangiia could
see that it was indeed a Faraway Heaven. Its lush jungled
interior had a mountain ridge dominating it. Around the
edge of the island, shaped like a jellyfish, was a coral reef.
The closer they came to this reef they could see it was tight
in places, up against the shore, and looser in others. But
nowhere did it reach right out into the ocean like some
island reefs. It had a beautiful turquoise lagoon studded

with smaller islands. Puffs of clouds decorated the high, dark-green peaks.

It was a perfect island, not too low like some atolls, vulnerable to tidal waves.

Not too high like others, and so drawing too much rain. Perfect.

'*My* island,' screamed Tangiia, waving his fist at the other canoe. 'Keep away from my island!'

A man standing by the mast on the other vessel waved a weapon in the air. Tangiia knew that this must be the famous Savaiian captain, Karika. His exploits were known throughout Oceania. He was a great navigator in his own right and it seemed he had chosen the same time to look for a new island as Tangiia, or had been spurred on to do so by the gods. If the gods were responsible, they were cruel in their sport, to match two such men against each other over so important a prize.

The reef drew nearer and still the two vessels were neck and neck. Neither waited for a good wave to cross the coral teeth that could have ripped their canoes to pieces, they simply hoped for a crest to coincide with their landing. As it was, both craft slid over the reef without damage, and raced for the shallows.

Once close to the beach the craft had to be slowed.

Tangiia ran the length of the deck and dived into the water. Cheered by his people, he swam, striking out for the beach. Karika did the same, his people also giving voice. If there had been nothing between the vessels, there was now nothing between the men, for they swam stroke for stroke, neither gaining on the other, neither falling back. Tangiia's lungs were bursting, his muscles screamed at him, but he dug deep into his reserves of stamina, knowing that all depended on him winning.

The two swimmers reached their depth at the same time, struggled through the water, up through the surf, and reached the warm sands of the island simultaneously.

It was a dead heat.

They both fell on their backs, gasping for breath, sucking down air.

Wild birds whirled above them, as if anticipating what was to come next.

When the strength returned to his body Tangiia leapt to his feet, whipping out the shark-toothed lei-o-mano from his waistband.

Karika, seeing he was in danger, did the same.

They circled one another, warily.

'My island!' growled Karika.

'Mine,' said Tangiia. 'I have sailed too long and far to give it up to you.'

'My people have voyaged for many, many months.'

'My people have battled with the elements, fought with monsters, defied the gods to be here.'

'Mine too,' shouted Karika. 'They have suffered too long to be turned back to the sea now.'

'Go away,' said Tangiia, slashing at his opponent, 'find another island.'

'This is my island,' cried Karika, dodging the blow and thrusting at his antagonist. 'You find another one.'

Out in the lagoon a skirmish was taking place between the two vessels. Spears were flying through the air. Warriors from *The Scudding Cloud* had taken to dugouts and were trying to board the other vessel. Some of Karika's warriors had done likewise and were trying to find a way to climb on the deck of *The Scudding Cloud*.

The two would-be kings of the as-yet-unnamed island jabbed and slashed, trying to find an opening through each other's guards, each hoping Oro,the God of War, was favouring him alone.

Suddenly, out of the mêlée in the lagoon came a terrible scream. Tangiia looked up quickly to see Po, standing on the deck of *The Scudding Cloud*, a spear through his chest. The point of the spear had entered through his breast bone and exited between his shoulder blades. Blood gushed along the shaft as the captain of the sunken *Volcano Flower* staggered forward, his eyes wide with pain and fear.

'Tangiia!' he called. 'I'm – I'm –'

Po tottered to the edge of the deck, then fell headlong into the water, the haft of the spear sticking into the sand at the bottom of the lagoon and holding up the body in a grotesque fashion, like a skewered sacrifice.

Po was dead.

Tangiia dropped his guard, so distracted was he by Po's cry.

At that moment Karika could have plunged his dagger into his adversary's soft stomach and ripped it open like the belly of a fish, but for some reason he held back, stayed his hand.

All fighting had ceased on the canoes with the horrible shout let out by the dying Po. Tangiia let his arm fall by his side. Karika did the same. The two men just stood there, staring out at the body which wafted back and forth in the ripples from the waves.

Blood stained the waters in an ever-increasing circle. If there were any sharks in the lagoon, they would soon be in the area. Feelings of alarm swept through Tangiia. It was one thing to lose warriors fighting an enemy, quite another to have them torn to shreds by ravenous sharks.

'Get out of the water,' yelled Tangiia, to some men and women who had either jumped or fallen overboard in the struggle. 'Get on the canoes!'

'Quickly!' cried Karika, in tune with his adversary's thoughts of danger.

Those in the water recognised the peril they were in and thrashed back to the canoes, to be helped aboard by those already on deck. Karika's people were assisting Tangiia's people on board their craft and the same was happening around *The Scudding Cloud*. Soon enough there were fins cutting the water, around the body of Po. Hammerheads!

The corpse too, was hauled on board. Dugouts were launched and the crews and passengers of both vessels began ferrying themselves to the beach.

Once on the beach the two sides separated again and faced each other on the sands. There were wounded amongst them, from the skirmish. One of Tangiia's men was bleeding from a shoulder wound. Another was pouring blood from behind his ear, where he had been struck by a club. A young woman had a broken wrist. There were similar injuries amongst Karika's people.

Tangiia and Karika were foremost, their weapons still drawn.

'What shall we do about this,' asked Tangiia. 'I want no more of my people to die.'

'Nor do I wish any more deaths on my people – they have suffered enough already. We lost a canoe out on the ocean – Magantu, the Great White Shark, bit through one of the hulls and swallowed three bailers whole.'

'We also lost a pahi!' exclaimed Tangiia. 'My people have died of fevers, of violent weather, of treatment from hostiles, of encounters with monsters and demons.'

'Mine too.'

Karika was silent for a moment, then said, 'Single combat then, between us. Whoever wins takes the island and the loser's people leave. Agreed?'

Kikamana now stepped forward, between the two men.

'This is unnecessary,' she said. 'The island is big enough for both peoples.'

Tangiia shook his head. 'This has to be.'

Seumas, his patu club in his right hand, called to the king of the Raiateans, 'Listen to your high priestess.'

'It is not your place, to speak at such a time,' interrupted Makka-te, angrily.

'No,' said Seumas, 'but I'm doing it anyway. I have been on the same voyage as you, I have some say in how it ends. This is a good island. All together, Raiateans, Savaiians, we are few. It can support us and many generations to come, without any hardship. I say listen to Kikamana.'

'Yes,' cried Kieto.

'Be quiet, boy,' snapped Makka-te. 'This is a decision for a king, not for goblins or boys.'

Kikamana said. 'Why not share the island? Why not rule this land together?'

Tangiia turned to Kaho, the blind, old Feeler-of-the-sea.

'What do you say, my old friend?'

'Kikamana is right,' said Kaho, lifting his blind face to the breeze, 'the land smells rich enough for us all.'

At that moment a conch horn sounded and drums began to beat a martial rhythm. *The Royal Palm* had now arrived in the lagoon with Manopa standing on the deck. His warriors were armed and ready for war. A statue of Oro, roughly hewn during the long voyages, was lashed to the mast. Manopa had on his war helmet and his war cloak of yellow and red feathers, which fluttered in the wind. He looked truly formidable. The Raiateans had the edge now, commanding positions both on the beach and out in the lagoon. It no longer needed to be single combat; Tangiia's forces were twice those of Karika's.

Tangiia turned to study his opponent, a young man like himself with a fine physique. He could see that adventure on the high seas had shaped Karika's character much in the same manner as it had shaped that of Tangiia himself. Karika seemed a modest sort of man, with a strong sense of honour. He could have slain Tangiia very easily just a few moments before, when Po had distracted his king, but he stayed his hand. Tangiia was sure there were many similarities between the two of them. They might even grow to like each other.

'I would agree to a trial on that basis,' said Tangiia. 'Six months to see if it works.'

Karika stared at his opponent and nodded slowly.

'It is better we both live a little longer, certainly, and

enjoy some time on this beautiful island. I would agree to a six-month trial, after which if it does not work out, we draw lots and the loser takes his people and leaves.'

Thus it was agreed between the Savaiians and the Raiateans that they share the island, perhaps for six months, perhaps for ever.

That evening Karika and Tangiia drank kava together on the sands of their new home. They talked for many hours. It was a good meeting, since they found they had much in common.

When Tangiia asked Kula what she thought about the arrangement, she said, 'When you can resolve differences as important as this one without resorting to violence, then I believe you have truly become a king.'

Po's sau walked the purple path to the place where Milu stood waiting for him. Po was a voyager, a man whose life had been entwined with that of an ocean which *was* the history of the Oceanian peoples. There were many deeds against his name, many journeys, many storms. He was a hero. Milu bowed his head slightly as Po approached him, acknowledging Po's status.

Po returned the gesture and then stared beyond the God of the Dead, into Death's kingdom. It was a solemn place, but not without its grandeur. There was a certain opulence in the use of mother-of-pearl for its pathways, in its dark, shiny obsidian walls and black waterfalls dropping down infinite chasms. It was not a comfortable place, but there was a kind of restfulness about the dimness of the light. It shone like those dark-blue, dully polished shells found in the deepest part of the ocean.

Moreover, Po had nothing to fear from Nangananga, having three wives to guarantee his safety. Since they were all three alive it would be his dead mother waiting for him, ready to guide him over the sharp rocks and through the maze of boulders. In the Land of the Dead it is the women who are supreme, with their strong wisdom, their deep intelligence, and their understanding of emotion. It is a place where infinity and eternity mingle and there is time to ponder the puzzles of the world. The men there are lost for a time, having to come to terms with their spiritual feelings, while the women have already spent a lifetime doing just that and are already prepared for death.

The boat of dead souls would be waiting for Po, its black feathers whispering sacred fangu.

Po moved forward as Milu stood aside to let him pass.

Po hesitated on the threshold and turning to Milu began, 'The sad thing is –'

'– you discovered the secret of life, just as the spear entered your chest and dispatched you here,' finished Milu.

'How did you know?'asked Po, surprised.

'It's always the way,' sighed Milu.

The island was indeed a place worth the voyage.

A strong person could walk around it in a day, but it had flat fertile land which flowed inwards for a good way, then climbed upwards into craggy but green heights.

Tiki was given thanks, as was Maomao and all the other gods who had assisted them on their great voyage, even Tangaroa who had at last been appeased by the Raiatean king.

The separate cargoes of tubers, roots, shoots and cuttings, from all three canoes, were ferried ashore and planted. These were their most precious possessions, for they would provide the new island people with their food over the coming decades.

There was fish in the lagoon, and shellfish in the coral beds, and pig and dog – even the ever-present rat was there to provide meat in times of famine – but fruit and vegetables had been developed over a long period of their history.

The cuttings and roots they had planted would keep them and their children healthy and fit for such trials as the

gods and an uncertain future might throw in their way.
Pens were built for the stock, land was marked and shared
out in equal lots for all families, single men and single
women. Huts were built for the commoners and houses
for the royal families. Posts were carved, ahu made for sacrifices to the gods, temples were constructed with marae,
gods were sculpted from local stone.

Po was buried with due ceremony on the slopes of the
island, in sight of the lagoon. There were sacrifices to him,
of chickens and pigs. Many mourned his passing, especially
Kieto, who regarded him almost as a second father.

Canoe building began in earnest then of váa and pu hoe
canoes, both outrigged vessels. These were craft with u-
shaped hulls having a capacity from two to six – one man
would have difficulty in managing the boat – used for fishing in a lagoon or close to a reef. The hull of one of these
craft was hollowed from a single tree, with straight sides
and a vertical stem. The slightly raised stern formed a platform behind, from which the fisherman threw his net or
line.

People also began work on váa motu, larger outrigged
canoes for crossing short stretches of open ocean. This craft
had a tall mast supported by bamboo poles and a stay
attached to the stern. A bouquet of feathers or leaves would
crown the mast before a sailing, a symbol of peace to other
mariners. On the end of the boom, fixed freely at the base
of the mast, was a plume of delicate trailing feathers to
assist the helmsman in finding the direction of the wind. A
huge paddle called the hoe fa'atere was used to steer the
craft.

On the seventh day Tangiia and Karika were inaugurated
as the first kings of the island. They were to govern together
for the first six months and if all was well, thereafter until
one of them died. It would be the dead man's eldest son
who would rule after both kings had gone, thus protecting
the kings from each other. They might kill themselves to

ensure their line, but they could not murder their co-ruler to make it so.

If the eldest son of the first-dead king was deemed unsuitable, because of mental illness or some other restricting factor of his birth, or if he had no wish to rule, a completely new king was to be chosen by the high priestess from the virgin males of the island. The selection was to be made at random from the fittest, most intelligent of the candidates; this to be determined by a series of tests run by the priests. This would help to protect the lives of newly born royal babies from ambitious members of either imperial family.

Tangiia's royal house was not yet constructed and he and Kula were spending the nights in a hut away from the huts of their people. Now that Tangiia had been invested as king of an island, he was taboo, and had to take the precautions necessary to prevent ordinary people from receiving a lethal charge of his mana.

On the evening of the eighth day he lay on his mat as usual, weary from the day's work, when Kula quietly lay down beside him.

He was surprised. Ever since the night of their wedding on Tahiti she had slept on her own mat, at a respectable distance from him.

'Do you wish me to sleep elsewhere?' he asked.

'No,' she whispered, shrugging her skirt from her, 'I want you to hold me.'

He took her in his arms and very soon they were making love for the first time. Tangiia felt he was in a dream as his beloved moved with him, murmuring her pleasure in his ear, giving him all he had ever desired from a woman. After they had both satisfied one another, they cried in each other's arms.

Early in the morning, before the parrots had woken and begun strutting their perches in the trees, Tangiia leaned over and said to her, 'Why now?'

'Because I promised my father I would not give myself to anyone but a king – you, my lord, were only a king in name, but now you are a king in land and people.'

'I see,' he said. 'And this is why you gave yourself to me at this time?'

'That, and because I have found during the voyages, and when you confronted Karika, that you are truly a man of great courage and honour, capable of compassion, tender and loving, and all the things I wanted in a man. You have many faults of course . . .'

'I do?' he queried, frowning.

'Yes,' she smiled, putting her fingers to his lips, 'but I forgive you for them.'

He was quiet for a moment and then laughed.

'Thank you, and I forgive *you*.'

'For what?' she asked, archly.

'For bewitching me with your beauty.'

They laughed together, just as the first parrot started shrieking at his neighbours, waking the rest of the world.

2

There were no very young children on Tutapu's expeditionary force, only males and females over the age of twelve. The king had warned his people that any babies born on the voyage would be thrown overboard. However, among such a large number of people there will always be men and women who fall in love and cannot wait to consummate that love. Consequently three couples, the women pregnant, had already taken dugouts in the middle of the night and set themselves adrift, willing to face death rather than watch their child thrown to the sharks.

Yet Tutapu was not regarded as a bad king, or even a particularly harsh ruler. Many kings would not have bothered to warn the people of the consequences of their actions and would have killed the babies anyway. Many kings would have taken time out to hunt down and punish the perpetrators for stealing a dugout. Tutapu was simply single-minded, obsessive, in his desire to find his half-brother and execute him. Any obstacle, however small, in the way of that goal was dealt with ruthlessly. Babies were a distraction – they required constant attention – and Tutapu wanted his people to be as single-minded as himself in the endeavour.

Unlike Tangiia and Karika, Tutapu had lost none of his vessels. At the time the other two new kings were at the initial stages of building their new kingdom, Tutapu was on course for the island of Savaii. A lookout called to say a dugout with two people had been sighted off the starboard bow. The couple were recognised as the last pair to steal away in the night, presumably because the woman was pregnant. It seemed that fast currents had carried the lighter vessel ahead of the flotilla, but now the trade winds had given the latter speed enough to catch up with the smaller craft.

As the tipairua drew closer to the dugout it was apparent that the couple were close to death. By the look of them they were dying of thirst, there being little enough room to carry drinking coconuts or gourds on a dugout.

'Shall we pick them up?' asked the helmsman.

'Sail past,' ordered Tutapu.

Dorcha, on hearing this, said, 'But they're almost gone – they won't make it to an island.'

'They should have thought of that when they stole one of my dugouts and crept away like thieves in the night.'

Dorcha watched as the thirty tipairua with their black sails ignored the dugout, which went drifting through the squadron of vessels. Those on board the tipairua knew better than to look at the dying couple. It was as if there was nothing there but a floating log, to be avoided in order to prevent collision, but not to be studied intently.

The dying woman, recognising a relative, feebly raised her hand above the gunwales of the dugout, but her cousin ignored the wave, knowing he was under the eyes of the king.

To Dorcha it was a harrowing sight and though she had seen some callous acts in her time, this one sickened her beyond endurance.

'We must stop,' she said. 'This is not a good thing to do – wayfarers in trouble in my homeland are always given assistance. Anyone who refuses to help a traveller dying of hunger or thirst is dealt with harshly, if not in this life, then in the next.'

King Tutapu raised his eyebrows and said, 'You mean, even a king stops to assist a beggar?'

'No, that's not what I mean – and of course there are brigands who would rob a corpse, let alone a dying man – but most people see the sense in aiding a person in trouble. It might be *you* next time.'

Tutapu shook his head, adamantly. 'These are not wayfarers we have come across by accident, these are people who disobeyed my commands. *I* am not likely to steal away from my own tipairua, so it could not possibly be me. Another king would have ploughed through the dugout, drowning the occupants.'

'Perhaps even that would have been kinder,' said Dorcha.

Tutapu folded his arms and looked at her for a moment, then he ordered his signaller to send the last tipairua in the flotilla back to the dugout.

'Tell the captain to sink the canoe.'

'You mean, take the couple on board first, don't you?' prompted Dorcha, anxiously.

'No,' Tutapu replied, turning cold eyes on Dorcha, 'I mean to drown them. You yourself has said this would be better than leaving them to die of thirst. So be it. This is your doing and you shall take the responsibility. They shall have a quick death and let no one say Tutapu is not a magnanimous ruler, capable of compassion.'

Dorcha was stunned by this act of cruelty, but she said no more, knowing that she could not move Tutapu. He was an obdurate man whose mission he saw as too important to be delayed even a moment by disobedient subjects. The couple had wronged him, had even now distracted him from his purpose, and so the Relentless Pursuer would have none of them. They had ordered their own execution the night they had made love without taking precautions and had conceived a child.

And so it was done. The dugout was sunk. The couple were drowned.

And it seemed to Dorcha that no one thought the worse of the king for his actions. Was it just that a king's deeds were above reproach because of his god-like status? Or did the people really approve of his actions? All that time she had spent with these Oceanians, and still she did not know them.

Nor did they know her, for shortly afterwards the king came to her and asked her about the course they were maintaining, and whether she believed it to be correct according to her bamboo-and-shell device. It was clear from his manner that he expected she would have forgotten all about the execution. It was obvious he thought she had engaged in a minor disagreement with him and had lost the argument, and there was an end to the trivial matter; that no bad feeling existed between them.

On the contrary, Dorcha was still appalled by what had occurred, and could not conceive of things ever being the same between her and the king again. She had seen human sacrifices performed by willing young men and women, she had seen harsh punishment meted out to malefactors for misdemeanours, she had witnessed judgements she considered poor, but had accepted all these as part of a culture she had no influence over.

It would have been so easy, however, for Tutapu to take the dying couple on board one of his craft. It would have been the act of a noble heart and mind. Had he done so, she would have respected him as a great man of honour.

Now, she despised him.

Yet she was alone in that feeling.

Even Elo would not speak against the king.

Tutapu's flotilla reached Savaii, where he learned that Tangiia had gone in search of an island which was also being sought by a Savaiian voyager, Karika. A fisherman had seen Tangiia's pahi and had taken the news back to Savaii that a battle was about to take place over the contested island. Both voyagers knew in which direction the island lay, it was just a matter of who reached it first, and if that king could hold on to it in the face of an invasion.

Tutapu cried to Tangaroa, 'Don't let him die by another hand – it must be my weapon that takes his life. Mine is just retribution for stealing the hope from my kingdom. If he should be killed, surely it would be best done by the brother who loved him once, who grew with him to manhood, who turned his hand against his flesh and blood only when a kingdom was threatened.

'You know that brothers must be sacrificed for kingdoms, that kin must be put aside for kingship, that thieves and robbers must be brought to book, though they be tied by family bonds to their prosecutors. Save his head for my club, his heart for my dagger, that he may die by one who has loved him, rather than by an enemy who despises him. Grant me this, O Great Sea-God!'

Dorcha's feelings for King Tutapu were confused and ambivalent. She both admired and detested him. He was a brilliant captain and navigator, and possibly even a great king, but his greatness was dominated by petty fears and jealousies, and his concerns motivated by selfish dreams. He wanted perfection for himself and his islands, and when he saw that such flawlessness was not there, he looked for someone to blame. His eyes had settled on his only brother.

He was also, she thought sadly, lacking in compassion. There was a coldness which filled him that left no room inside his heart for mercy. A momentary gain towards his goal was more important than the lives of a dozen commoners. His ambition was indeed blind to all but its own ends.

Yet he was not a man utterly convinced of the rightness of his actions; his feelings were in conflict with themselves.

Dorcha could see the torment Tutapu was going through, now that he was closing in on his brother. She recognised that the king of Raiatea and Borabora did indeed bear a fraternal love for Tangiia, but through circumstance felt compelled to hunt him down and kill him for the sake of peace of mind. While Tangiia lived Tutapu felt he could never be secure in his kingdom, that one day Tangiia might launch an expeditionary force against him and wrest the heaven of Raiatea from his grasp.

'He stole one of my gods,' Tutapu kept repeating, when he felt the need to justify the chase.

'And your future bride,' Dorcha reminded him, quietly.

'Yes,' he agreed, distantly, 'and Kula.'

The flotilla sped over the ocean, following Hauviai on the wind flower. Maomao stayed behind them, as if helping them towards their destination. There were no more forced diversions to strange islands. It was as if the gods too had become single-minded in their efforts to bring the two brothers together in mortal combat.

One morning Dorcha was awakened by the shout of a lookout, telling everyone within earshot that land had been sighted.

She stared in the direction at which the lookout was pointing and saw a dark hump-backed whale in the distance.

'The island,' said Dorcha, suddenly coming to terms with her own reasons for this voyage. 'Seumas is there.'

'Have you come to hurt him, Dorcha?' asked Elo. 'Have you come to remind him of what he did to you?'

'I keep changing my mind,' replied the confused Celt. 'My husband's ghost tells me one thing and my heart, another.'

'Then why did you come? Why did you join the king's expedition?'

Angrily, Dorcha snapped, 'I don't know.'

'I'm sorry, Dorcha. I won't ask again.'

Dorcha, remorseful, turned and hugged the head of the girl to her breast.

'I'm sorry too, Elo. Who knows why I came? Dark reasons, good reasons? A mixture of both? Perhaps I've come to make my peace with Seumas?'

Elo said wisely for her years, 'That would be the best thing.'

PART TEN

The New Heaven

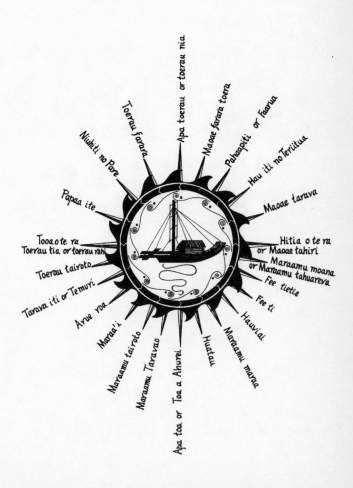

Toerau toerau or toerau nia

Apa toerau or toerau nia

Maoae farava toera

Pahaapiti or faarua

Hau iti no Teriitua

Maoae tarava

Hitia o te ra
or Maoae tahiri

Maraamu moana
or Maraamu tahuareva

Fee tietie

Fee ti

Hauviai

Maraamu maraa

Huctau

Apa toa or Toa a Ahurei

Maraamu Taravao

Maraamu tairoto

Maraa'i

Arue roa

Tarava iti or Temuri

Toerau tairoto

Tooao te ra
Toerau tia or toerau rahi

Papaa ite

Niuhiti no Pare

Toerau farava

1

Thirty tipairua bearing black sails were seen on the horizon by the lookouts on the mountain.

The news was quickly relayed to the two kings, sitting in the marae of a new temple, in the process of being built for Rangi, Hine and Papa. One such temple had already been constructed for Maomao and Tangaroa. There would be another to Tane and Rongo. The mountain itself, where stood a needle rock, was reserved wholly for Io, the 'Old One', the Father of the Gods. There would be smaller places sacred to Ra, Hau Naringi, Kuku Lau and Ua. Neither king had seen the need to raise a temple to Oro, not this early in their reign on their new heavenly island.

The kings, minor chiefs, priests and their retinues gathered at the marae outside Tangiia's house, within earshot of Kula, who had been preparing tapa-bark cloth for dyeing, but who had stopped work like everyone else to listen.

'An invasion force,' said Karika, 'but who?'

Kikamana provided the answer.

'It is Tangiia's brother. His feather-banner flutters from the masthead of the leading tipairua. He has followed us here from Raiatea. I warned of his coming. My dreams have been full of his warriors' shadows.'

Tangiia sighed. 'Is it really Tutapu?'

Kikamana said nothing more, knowing the question was rhetorical in nature.

'Thirty vessels,' said Karika. 'If they're full, it means we have to face three thousand warriors.'

'Not *we*,' said Tangiia, placing a hand on the other's arm, 'that's my brother out there. This is my war, not yours.'

Karika clasped his fellow king's hand.

'We rule this island together – any threat to its peace is a threat to us both – *I* am your brother now. We will fight side by side. My warriors are your warriors – they are all *our* people. I would have expected no less from you.'

Tangiia sighed. 'Tutapu's men will lay waste to the whole island. He has a reputation in war, of slaughtering a conquered enemy. I loved him once, but he has grown into strangeness. I believe too, that he is a better warrior than me.'

'If we die,' Karika insisted, 'we die together.'

Tangiia nodded. 'In that case, prepare our men for war – we shall meet Tutapu on the beaches. The advantage will be with us, since his warriors can be engaged as they try to leap from their canoes into the surf. Manopa, Seumas, you will lead half my warriors, Makka-te and Kikamana the other half.'

'Where shall you be?' asked Seumas.

'I shall be at your head of course, but I want to be free to concentrate on a personal battle with my brother. Once one of us dies, the battle will be over. Karika, I expect you to deploy your warriors in the way you know best.'

'They can go under the command of your officers. I shall fight by your side, to ensure you have a fair combat with your brother. He will be sure to have his own bodyguards.'

Tangiia nodded. 'Yes, no doubt he will. Now, where are those officers? Manopa? There, good – and Seumas too. Kikamana of course . . . where is Makka-te?'

At that moment Makka-te was dragged across the courtyard by two young priests. He was trussed hand and foot, and looked sullen and defiant.

'What's this?' cried the young king.

'Some sentries caught him signalling to the enemy fleet,' said one of the priests. 'Since the sentries were commoners and couldn't touch him, they sent for us.'

Tangiia stared unbelievingly at Makka-te. 'You – a traitor?' he said softly.

Makka-te looked into the face of his king and sneered. 'Traitor to whom? My loyalties have always been with your brother. I joined your expedition knowing in my heart that he would never let you alone. It was impossible for him. With you alive he would have never felt safe. Now, thanks to me, he has caught up with you.'

One of the priests cried, 'He's been releasing birds to show Tutapu the way. He left a symbol on a rock at Tahiti, to point the direction on the wind flower. Everywhere we have been he has left signs for Tutapu to follow.'

Tangiia paced up and down in front of Makka-te, stopping every so often to stare at him. In the end he said, 'Can you see into the future, priest?'

Makka-te smiled grimly and nodded. 'I see you roasting one who would have been your half-brother, had it not been that his mother was a king's concubine.'

'You think I should roast you?'

'I think you *will*.'

Tangiia shook his head. 'Take him down to the shore line,' he told Makka-te's captors, 'untie him and throw him into the water. He can swim out to my brother's canoes. I want no more of him.'

The other priests were aghast. 'Aren't you going to execute him?'

'No,' replied the king. 'This meeting between my brother and me was inevitable – it had to be. Makka-te has helped to bring that about sooner, rather than later. He has chosen his side in this battle, let him go to it.'

Makka-te looked puzzled, clearly expecting some sort of trick. Was Tangiia going to strike him down as they marched him away? Was there some hidden code in his words to his priests that meant they were to cut his throat on the way down to the beach? It didn't seem possible that Tangiia would let him go, a self-confessed traitor, a spy in his midst.

'Now,' cried Tangiia, striding out, 'we must arm for the fight. Sound the war conch!' he ordered a priest. 'I shall dress for the battle. Kikamana, prepare the marae for sacrifices to the gods. We can ill afford to slaughter livestock at the moment, just when we are beginning our life on this island and our breeding stock is low, but we must bring ourselves to their attention.'

At that moment a messenger came running, to fall at the feet of King Tangiia.

'King Tangiia,' cried the man, 'your wife –'

'What about my wife?' said Tangiia, whirling on the man.

'She – she has swum out with Makka-te to the tipairua in the bay. She has gone to your brother.'

Tangiia turned quickly to see that the spot where Kula had been sitting, mixing the dyes, was empty.

He let out a long cry of anguish.

Kula reached the tipairua before Makka-te, being a better swimmer than the middle-aged man. She climbed, dripping, on to the deck. Her wet hair was plastered against her scalp. There were droplets of water clinging to her breasts which glistened with colours in the bright sunlight. Her dusky skin was unblemished and smooth. She looked truly beautiful.

She faced a King Tutapu dressed and armed for war.

'You have no need to fight,' she said. 'I have come to you.'

King Tutapu stared hard and puzzled at the woman

before him, then his expression changed as recognition came to him.

'*Kula*,' he said. 'Forgive me – I have not seen you for so many years – not since my father brought you to show to me when you were fourteen.'

Makka-te was hauled on board. King Tutapu went to him immediately. 'You revealed yourself to him? I told you to remain amongst them.'

'They found me out,' said Makka-te, struggling for breath. 'I didn't reveal myself – I was discovered.'

'What are their numbers?'

'Male warriors? Fewer than three hundred, but many of the women are prepared to fight.'

'Three hundred?' queried Tutapu, frowning.

'Tangiia has made an ally. Karika, the Savaiian. They rule the island together.'

'And Karika is prepared to fight with him?'

Makka-te said, ironically, 'They are closer than brothers.'

Kula ran forward and clasped the tall, muscled king around the knees.

'You have no need to fight, I am here now. I shall be your wife –'

Makka-te sneered. 'She is already the wife of Tangiia. They married in Tahiti. She has been on his love-mat since that time and is no longer a maiden.'

Tutapu shrugged, pacing the deck. 'What do I care for maidens? Does experience make them worse lovers, or better? Virgins make terrible wives for men with strong, healthy appetites. If I want a virgin I can take one, any time I choose. I am the king. My father promised me Kula for my wife. My wife she shall be.'

Kula spat triumphantly at Makka-te's feet and then let out a cry of relief.

'Let's sail away now, then – away to Raiatea and Borabora? Leave Tangiia to his island,' she cried.

Tutapu turned and looked at her. Ragnu was staring at Kula with interest written on his features. Near by, Dorcha was also watching the scene with concern in her eyes. Everyone present, except Kula and perhaps Makka-te, knew in advance what the answer would be from the king.

The king said, 'He still has the god he stole from me.'

Kula blinked, then shook her head, saying, 'But it's only an idol – a minor god, hardly significant.'

'He has robbed me of Hope,' cried the king loudly. 'My brother has taken away my joy. How can I live without hope?'

'But surely,' said Kula, now on her feet, 'this is just a feeling, *inside* you? It's all in the mind. You can have another God of Hope carved. Tane is with us all, in his many forms – isn't that so, priest?' She appealed to Ragnu.

Tutapu did not even let his head kahuna reply.

'Tangiia must die,' said the king. 'I must wipe out the insult of his theft. How else can the sacred be cleansed, except with blood? It has to be.'

'Then what did I come to you for?' wailed the distraught queen of the island. 'He will be grieving my loss. He will be full of anguish at my going.'

Tutapu raised his eyebrows. 'Do you care?'

'I *love* him,' cried Kula. 'I should be by his side. I came to you because it was my duty to do so. I came to prevent any bloodshed.'

'Then you're a fool,' snapped Tutapu.

Kula turned and collapsed into Dorcha's arms. Dorcha held her, stroked her brow.

'Nothing can stop the fight,' said the Celt, softly and sympathetically. 'Tutapu is determined.'

Dorcha might have used the word 'obsessed' for it would have been a more accurate one.

The king then ignored Kula in order to lay out his battle plans. 'Ragnu, make ready for the attack! It seems my brother is preparing for an assault on dry land, since he hasn't launched his pahi. That does him credit. Three pahi against thirty tipairua are poor odds for a sea battle. He'll stand a better chance against us, when we're struggling on foot through the surf to get on to the beach.'

'In that case, shouldn't we wait?' asked Ragnu. 'He'll have to come out to us eventually, if he sees we're not going to storm the island? We can blockade the fishing. Without fish they'll eventually run out of food.'

'I can't wait that long. We'll lose more men, but still the odds are heavily in our favour. I will lead five tipairua into the shallows as a frontal spearhead. This should draw all Tangiia's forces to that point on the shoreline. Then you will lead the right wing and Hioiutu the left wing, each of ten tipairua. Five tipairua will remain by the reef, as a rear guard and to prevent any of the enemy from escaping in boats. You will await my drummer's signal to attack the flanks.'

'What will be the signal?' asked Ragnu.

'Seven rapid beats on the drum.'

Tangiia's men were arranged in a crescent all round the bay. Sacrifices had been made to the Great War-God, Oro, to ask him to fight on the side of the islanders. No one on the beach held out much hope that the war god would stand in their ranks however, for being the God of War, Oro was usually a friend of the strong and an enemy of the weak. Tutapu would be making the same sacrifices and asking for the same support. It seemed likely that Oro, given his lust for death and destruction, would favour the side most likely to win.

Nevertheless there were totems to Oro planted all along the sands, and priests carried Oro sticks carved into visages and bore Oro images made of feathers above their heads. They chanted their battle hymn to the stamp of feet on hard earth. The voices were full of hope, but there was dread among them, facing such fearful odds.

Oro, Great War-God, give us your strength!
Let the enemy be consumed in the huge fire,
Where you, Great War-God, throw the evil demons
You have vanquished, to smoke and burn.

Oro, Great War-God, let your three daughters,
Axe-eye, Head-eater and Escape-from-a-hundred-
   stones,
Be with us in the coming fight.
Let them slay our enemies by the thousand.

Oro, Great War-God, send your son,
Faithful Friend, to keep our courage high.
Oro, Great War-God, come yourself
And kill as many of our foes as please you!

The chant rang out over the sands.

On the tipairua, similar chants were in progress.

Tangiia was full of sorrow. His wife had deserted him and had gone over to the enemy. She had lied to him when she told him she loved him. If he survived the battle he promised himself he would cut her throat the moment he saw her, to stop her lying tongue from beguiling him again. She deserved no mercy. She was worse than the traitor in his camp.

Karika stood on his right side, a stranger not so long ago, now a friend willing to die for him. Karika carried a patu club and a canoe-breaker – a lump of volcanic rock lashed with sennit, with which to smash the hulls of canoes. The canoe-breaker could also be a fearsome weapon in hand-to-hand fighting. It was heavy and required time to swing, but it mashed to pulp any enemy head it met in the way of its arc.

On Tangiia's left was Seumas, a strange weapon in his hand – a wooden shaft bent into a curve and tied in place by a piece of taut sennit cord. Into the cord Seumas had fitted a tiny spear of thin bamboo, just as long as his arm. It was fletched with feathers at the notched end, while a sharp obsidian point weighted the other end. Seumas had shown he could fire the spear, which he called an 'arrow', a great distance when he drew back on the weapon he called a 'bow'. He told Tangiia he had not wanted to show the Oceanians this weapon, but since the odds against Tangiia's force were so great, he had to use it.

On Seumas's back was his set of bagpipes.

Dirk was at his side.

Midway down the bay on Seumas's wing was Manopa, a steady, solid, formidable figure amongst the ranks of warriors.

Kikamana in her long flowing cloak of feathers and leaves was on the other wing, with her force of thirty virgins, strong maidens with supple limbs. Kikamana was plying her magic, laying about her protective spells, and sending invisible darts of sickness and disease towards her foes. Kikamana called on demons and fairies alike, to join the fray.

Even the tall, willowy Boy-girl was there, shells in her locks, her tattered ribbons flying in the breeze. In her right hand was her deadly slingshot. In her left, a lucky charm, a puppy's foot fitted to a short stick. She wore poisonous flowers in her garments today, for their potency, and for their dark beauty, to put fear into the enemies she faced. She knew if she could look into a foe's eyes, that foe could be turned to an unwitting friend for the duration of the battle.

Tangiia stared along the line of warriors, either side of him. They looked colourful and fierce, their tattooed muscles rippling in the sunlight, their faces twisted and ugly with savage intent. They danced their war dances, their thigh slaps and projected tongues defying the enemy. The chiefs' war helmets fluttered in the wind. They all appeared to be full of heart for the coming fight, unafraid, indomitable.

Yet he knew they were really hollow, his men, and the belief amongst them was that they were all going to die.

'Come!' he called them. 'Be brave! You are fine warriors, fine fighting men and women. You must have the faith in yourselves, that I have in you. I know you will conquer today and the mighty foe will fall like severed flowers.'

A ragged cheer answered these words, vacuous and uninspired.

Just then, a lookout called from the top of a palm

'Someone comes in a váa motu canoe – two people! They ride the reef. I think it is Kupe. Kupe comes to us!'

Tangiia stared at the place where the lookout was pointing and, sure enough, there was Kupe, standing at the mast while another, smaller man managed the rudder paddle. Kupe waved. He swept down in his little canoe, past Tutapu's tipairua squadron, and across the lagoon. When the váa motu approached the beach, the other man was hidden by the boom and the sail, and when Kupe dropped the sail, this man was nowhere to be seen. All that could be said of him was that he had been short of stature and his loin cloth had hung low.

Kupe leapt from the canoe, on to the strand.

A vigorous cheer went up from the warriors all along the shoreline. Kupe had come! Kupe, the great voyager and warrior, slayer of the giant octopus, had come to join the new islanders in their fight against an oppressor.

Tangiia ran forward and rubbed noses with Kupe.

'My friend,' said the king. 'How did you know where to come?'

Kupe smiled. 'Why, you saw my companion?'

'Yes, but I didn't know him – who was he?'

Kupe grinned more broadly and shouted for all to hear. 'That was the mighty Maui, come from the bosom of Hine-nui-te-po, Great Goddess of the Night and Death, to fill your warriors with bravery and heart. Maui is with you in the coming fight! Maui guided my canoe to these shores, to give you support against your brother. Tutapu should never have come here.'

The word was quickly passed along the line of warriors – Maui was with them. They might not have Oro in their ranks, but Maui the Trickster, Maui of a Thousand Devices, Maui who outwitted Te Tuna and his friends was with them today, Maui the Sun-beater, Maui of the Friendly Fire, Maui who Fished Islands. Their hearts swelled with courage, their hands grew stronger and they squared their shoulders and stood tall.

'Maui is with us!' the cry rang out. 'The day is ours!'

Kupe, older but still strong, hefted up a spear and took his place between Seumas and Tangiia.

'Where is my friend, Po?' he asked, looking down the line of warriors. 'I hoped to see him before the battle.'

'Gone,' replied Seumas. 'Killed in skirmish.'

'By whom?'

'By those who are now our friends.'

Kupe nodded, wisely. 'Then Po will be mourned by me, but not avenged.'

The squadron of five tipairua swept forward, detaching itself from the flotilla, just as dark clouds rolled over the sky like carrion crows. The prows were carved idols of Oro, their mouths sneering, revealing pointed teeth, the eyes hidden beneath heavy brows. Banners fluttered from the totems on the decks, warriors chanted songs of death, King Tutapu called for victory.

Tangiia, thinking that his brother had decided to establish a beach-head, called his warriors to his side. Using the waves, the squadron of tipairua rushed towards the sands. When they reached the shallows, Tutapu and his warriors leapt from their canoes and waded through the surf to engage Tangiia's warriors. Stinging jellyfish, sent by an unknown god, attacked Tutapu's warriors, hindering their rush to the beach.

The drummer, left on board, had instructions to give seven rapid beats on the drum, once the fighting started. At that moment however, Ua, the Rain God, brought forth a deluge. Lingadua, the One-armed God of Drums, had not forgotten what he imagined was an insult from King Tutapu of Raiatea and Borabora, and it was he who had persuaded Ua to drench the island.

The sodden drum skin was muted by the rain, sound would not carry far, and Ragnu leading the rest of the flotilla did not hear the seven-beat signal. Hau Maringi came down cloaked in mist, to hide Tutapu's warriors until they made the beach-head, but Ua's rain drove away the mist, dispelling it.

When Tutapu looked back, through the dark driving rain, Kuku Lau, the Goddess of Mirages, made him see the shadowy silhouettes of his flotilla, bearing down on Tangiia's flanks. He believed the battle was going according to his plan.

Moko, the Lizard-God, who saw that the intervention by the gods was uneven, came to the aid of Tutapu. He sent large lizards down from the sides of the mountain, to tangle the legs of Tangiia's warriors. Those of King Tangiia's people who were not in the fight, however – the old men and women and young children – rushed forward and began pulling the lizards out of the mêlée by their tails and whirling them back into the forest.

The Great Gods – Tangaroa and Maomao – did not become involved in the actual battle. Their squabble with one another was in a state of truce and the affairs of men were but events of mild interest to them beside their own majesty.

The rain stopped and Ra swept from behind a cloud to fill the day with brilliance.

Tangiia's men, unhampered by any attack on their flanks, drove into Tutapu's troops as they emerged from the surf. The invaders began to fall, clustered together as they were and hampered by the stinging jellyfish. They fought desperately to get from the boats to the shore. The cries of dying and wounded men filled the air.

Dakuwanga swam through the ether above the island, hungrily swallowing the sau of the dead as they left their bodies on the battlefield, tearing pieces from the spirits of fallen warriors as if they were carrion. The Shark-God would be bloated with food by the end of the day. A war was the greedy Dukawanga's happiest time: a time to be glutted on rich souls.

Kupe and Karika fought either side of Tangiia, as the young king battled to reach his half-brother, surrounded by veteran warriors.

One of Tutapu's spearmen, who had made the beach without injury, rushed along the sand and was about to hurl his spear at King Tangiia, when an arrow struck him in the chest, bringing him to his knees. Seumas the bowman was sending his missiles into the enemy troops, who panicked not knowing where these small spears were coming from. With a quiver full of shafts, Seumas was able to pick his target and protect individuals on his own side without joining in the tangle of struggling warriors.

When his arrows were spent, Seumas slipped his bag-pipes from his shoulder and began playing a martial tune. His own people were now used to the terrible wailing sound they had first heard coming from the island of the giant bird. The sounds were like the screams of a god gone mad. Tutapu's troops were again thrown into a panic, thinking that Tangiia had forces of supernatural creatures fighting for him.

The word went down the line of the invaders – there were *demons* to conquer, as well as mortals – and fear swept through the attackers.

A warrior of Tutapu's forces, demented by the noise, rushed towards Seumas swinging a basalt axe, desperate to get rid of the sound that was addling his brains. When he was just over an arm's length from the Pict, his axe flailing the air, Dirk leapt at him. The man froze in horror as the mad-eyed hound buried its teeth in his side and hung there, twisting and turning like a shark gripping the belly of a whale.

The man fell to the ground where he was knocked cold by a blow from Seumas's foot. The Pict warrior did not even pause for breath as he continued his playing.

In his place on the beach, the great and magnificent Kupe, god-like in his presence and bearing, an utterly fearless champion, wielded his father's whalebone club with such calm and casual ferocity no enemy dare approach him after a while. They stood around him in a ring, their eyes revealing their admiration and fear, their bravery only growing as their numbers increased, until there were so many they could have swarmed over him like ants, yet still not one of them gave the signal, so overawed were they by Kupe's power and skill, by his charismatic composure.

Finally, a giant of a man cried, 'Are we all cowards to be afraid of Kupe? He is but a navigator, a man of the sea – he is but a *man* after all is said and done. So he slayed the giant octopus! I have killed many octopuses in my time, many monsters of the ocean. I will destroy the great Kupe with one thrust of my spear, then sever his head with my paddle club . . .'

So saying the big man stepped forward, only to be struck down by a lightning blow from the mighty Kupe, his skull cloven to the shoulders, his legs buckling under the force of the blow.

At this action they indeed tried to swarm over the splendid Kupe, only to find his club flailing amongst them, cutting them down like cane in a field, turning men to stubble, until even the most heroic amongst them, hungry for glory, turned and ran, leaving dead comrades littering the sand, and blood seeping down the strand to the wavelets of the lagoon. Finally, Kupe stood alone, amongst the corpses of his would-be killers, his teak-coloured skin shining with oil, his long hair flying.

Now that the rain had cleared, Ragnu saw that his king was in difficulties and guessed something had gone wrong with the signal they had arranged. He ordered the twenty tipairua to sail to the beach and join with the fighting. However, the wind had dropped to zero and they had to paddle the heavy canoes.

Maomao was not taking part in the battle; he had simply paused in his work to watch the outcome.

Tangaroa too, had ceased to make waves and was studying the fight with great interest, so the lagoon was quite calm.

At last Tangiia and Tutapu came face to face on the sands. Tutapu, resplendent in his helmet of red feathers fringed by grey feathers, looked fearsome. Around his neck dangled a corded, wrapped pendant, a representation of Oro. In his hands he held a club two thirds the height of a man, its honed edges bristling with whales' teeth.

A double-pointed obsidian dagger, the hilt in the centre of two blades, was stuck in the waistband of his loin cloth.

Tangiia had a short patu club and his lei-o-mano.

'At last, little brother,' cried Tutapu. 'You are within reach of my hand.'

At that moment the burly Manopa rushed out of Tangiia's ranks of warriors, shouting, 'Leave Tutapu to me!'

Before Tangiia could stop him, Manopa swung his koti-ate club at Tutapu's head. Tutapu neatly sidestepped and swept his own club sideways, low and swift. Manopa's left leg took the blow and broke at the knee. With a cry of agony, Manopa fell to the ground. Tutapu raised his mighty club above his head. He brought it down on Manopa's skull. There was the sound of a coconut cracking open. Manopa was dead.

Stepping over the body, Tutapu swung again, this time at

Tangiia's right shoulder. Tangiia was swifter, striking at his brother's wrist. The patu club reached its mark first. Slightly off-target it snapped four of Tutapu's fingers against the haft of the great club. Tutapu's blow hit Tangiia's shoulder. With a gashed and gushing upper arm he flew sideways on to the sand.

Tutapu dropped the club, his left hand now useless. He armed himself with his double-bladed stone dagger. As he leaned over Tangiia to strike him in the face with the point, Tangiia whipped out his lei-o-mano. The young king slashed down the inside of Tutapu's thigh. The flesh tore with the sharks' teeth opening a hideous wound. Blood rushed forth, unstaunched.

Tutapu had to reach down to Tangiia. This gave the younger brother an advantage. Tangiia slashed at the tendons behind his brother's right ankle. Severing these with one grating slice caused Tutapu to scream in agony and fall down beside his brother. Tutapu's body fell across Tangiia's arm, sending the lei-o-mano flying from the younger brother's grasp.

Tangiia was now unarmed.

Tutapu still had his stone dagger and rolling over he stabbed at Tangiia. The obsidian blade went through the fleshy muscle on the side of Tangiia's throat, pinning his neck to the ground. Although nothing vital had been pierced, Tangiia had effectively been nailed to the floor.

Tutapu however, had no other weapon to use, unless he withdrew the stone blade from his brother's neck. He sat on Tangiia's abdomen and leaned with his forearm across Tangiia's windpipe, trying to stem his flow of air.

The faces of the two men were very close at this point. They stared into each other's eyes. At one time they had loved each other, these two brothers, but now circumstances of power had replaced that love; not with hate, but with fear. They feared each other and so one of them had to die. It seemed like it would be Tangiia as the young man's eyes glazed over. His brain began to spin and the light started to fade.

The survival instinct in Tangiia must have been stronger than his mind. He reached up and laced the fingers of both hands behind Tutapu's neck. It was almost a gesture of filial affection. Then he pulled his brother's head sharply down towards his shoulder. It drove the second upright blade of the obsidian dagger through Tutapu's right eye.

Tutapu stiffened and then convulsed for a moment. He gave a final sigh. Then the pressure on Tangiia's throat was relieved. The two brothers were locked there, in one another's embrace, joined together by the double-bladed dagger, one blade pinning Tangiia to the earth, the other blade pointing upwards through Tutapu's eye socket into his brain.

Boy-girl came running over.

'King Tangiia!'

She lifted Tutapu from on top of Tangiia. Then she wrenched the dagger from the neck of her king. Tangiia sat up and marvelled that he was still alive. There was a feeling of exultation in his breast mingling with a deep sadness and a sense of failure and loss. He had killed his only brother. A few paces away, his good friend and basket-sharer Manopa lay dead on the earth. It was not a day to feel triumphant.

'Thank you, Boy-girl,' he croaked, his fingers on his neck-wound stemming the blood.

Boy-girl stood over her king, a spear in her hand, ready to defend him against other enemy warriors.

It was unnecessary.

A groan had gone through the invaders when they saw their king fall dead. They began running back to their tipairua canoes resting in the lapping wavelets just off the beach. A major psychological blow had been dealt them. They had believed Tutapu to be invincible, beloved of the gods, and now he was carrion. They had not the heart to fight on.

Ragnu's arrival at the shore coincided with the rush back

to the boats and he shrieked at the warriors to turn and fight.

'Tutapu is dead!' they cried, ignoring his orders. 'Our king is no more!'

Ragnu cried, 'Fight for me! Avenge your king's death.'

But the warriors had no stomach for it. The fight had not been about land, or protecting their families against an enemy, it had been about a quarrel between two brothers. Now one of those brothers was dead. There was no need for any more fighting. There was no need for any more deaths. The warriors called to Ragnu to take them away, back to their homeland.

Ragnu knew his forces were still vastly superior in numbers to the defending troops on the island, but he also knew that his men needed a reason to fight. They had not loved Tutapu enough to feel the bitter need for revenge. He was a king who could be replaced without too much sorrow wasted on him. Not a *bad* king, but not a liked one either. Just another king.

Resentfully, Ragnu turned his tipairua and headed away with his squadron of twenty vessels, back towards the reef.

Tangiia, freed from his position on the sands, called to Karika to help him.

'I must go out there!' he said.

Karika assisted Tangiia, whose shoulder wound was more painful than the pierced neck, down to Kupe's canoe. The two kings then sailed out to the tipairua. Standing a spear's throw off, Tangiia called to Ragnu.

'You will need to replenish your provisions, if you are not all to die of hunger and thirst.'

'What do you suggest?' growled Ragnu, standing at the mast of his tipairua.

'Give me Kula and your men can come ashore, unarmed, and collect as much food and water as you need. You can bury your dead too. They will need friends to put them in the earth.'

Ragnu stared around him at his disillusioned warriors, knowing that if he set sail without provisions, there would soon be a mutiny amongst his crews.

'You can have her,' he called back to Tangiia, 'but can I trust you?'

'I am Karika,' cried that man. 'I have no quarrel with you, kahuna. I will guarantee the safety of your men.'

Eventually, Ragnu nodded. 'She comes to you now,' he said.

Kula was put in a dugout canoe and she paddled towards Tangiia and Karika.

Tangiia drew his lei-o-mano, but Karika gripped his arm and said, 'Wait until you hear what she has to say.'

'I need no further proof,' said Tangiia, grimly.

'You will not do this thing,' Karika insisted. 'If I have to break your arm to stop you.'

Tangiia stared at his co-ruler and saw that Karika was very serious. The young man, full of heat and jealousy, handed the knife over to his friend, saying, 'You hold the weapon. I cannot trust myself.'

When Kula reached the side of the váa motu, she looked up with sad, dark eyes. 'You won?' she said. 'He's dead?'

'Yes, are you sorry?' answered Tangiia, bitterly.

'I'm sorry that Tutapu is dead, but happy you are alive. I went to him to try to stop him, but he wanted your death more than he wanted me.'

'You offered yourself to save me?'

'He refused to accept.'

Tangiia stared at her with hurt in his eyes. 'Can I believe you?' he whispered.

'I love you,' she said, simply. 'If you don't know that, then you're truly lost.'

Tangiia hung his head and wept.

'I'm sorry,' he said. 'You should not have gone.'

'I know that now.'

Karika helped her aboard the váa motu and she

immediately began fussing over her husband's wounds, much to his inner comfort. They sailed back to the shore, now lined with triumphant warriors, old men and women and children.

A mighty cheer went up as Tangiia and Kula stepped on shore. For Karika too, there were salutations. Boy-girl was leaping up and down in a kind of wild dance, her coloured ribbons flying in the wind. Seumas was hugging Dirk. Kikamana was already starting a sacred fire to Oro, to thank him for the victory over a superior enemy. Kieto was striding around, smiling, a young man having had his first taste of battle. Kaho was on his knees, his son Po'oi beside him, offering prayers.

The dead were then gathered in and mourning for lost loved ones began.

Not the least of those grieved over was Tutapu by his brother.

Manopa was buried with great ceremony, alongside Po, mourned by his king and friend.

After the funeral of Manopa, Kieto had a few words with Boy-girl.

'Well, Boy-girl, we have come a long way from our ancestral island. Remember we once sat on the beach and talked about Seumas – how the voyage would change him?'

They both looked towards Seumas, standing quietly on his own, physically away from the group, yet spiritually part of it, a self-possessed man, at peace within – a strong and able adventurer, resting between exploits.

Boy-girl said, 'He has conquered Seumas, as well as the ocean – he has no need to test himself, prove himself any more. His worth as a man has increased ten-fold. There is mercy and kindness in his eyes, instead of anger.' Boy-girl sighed deeply. 'It makes him that much more desirable.'

'You know that can never be,' said Kieto.

'I know, I know – just dreams,' replied Boy-girl.

Kieto said, 'I too need Seumas, but for a wider purpose – not yet, but one day in the future. The wise Kupe has prophesied my part in making our nation great. When the day comes for me to lead the Oceanians in the conquest of the Land-of-Mists, I will need Seumas as my adviser. It will be hard for him, for though he is now almost all Oceanian, a small part of him will still be Pict.'

'Perhaps you are wrong, Kieto, perhaps only a small part of him is Oceanian, and the greater part, hidden from our eyes, is Pict?'

'In that case,' said Kieto, 'we shall become enemies – but I hope he will remain my brother, not my enemy.'

Boy-girl nodded. 'We must both wish for that end, Kieto.'

Ragnu's men and some women were allowed to come ashore to gather provisions for their voyage back to Raiatea. Tutapu's cousin Haari would be waiting there for news of the expedition. Ragnu said he intended to confirm Haari as king. Tangiia, recalling Haari's disposition and common sense, thought the man would make an excellent ruler. Haari was not young, being a man in his early sixties, but so much the better. The fire might have gone from his veins, but he was a wise and stable man.

The enemy was watched night and day, until they were preparing to leave, in case Ragnu tried a sneak attack. They still had the warriors to overwhelm the island, but those warriors were obviously not in the mood for further fighting, for Ragnu's force stayed out beyond the reef.

The day of the flotilla's departure, a dugout with two people on board detached itself from a tipairua.

It was paddled towards the shore.

On being informed by Kieto that Dorcha was in the small canoe, Seumas went down to the shore. He stood waiting for her to arrive. Dirk was by his side and could sense his master's nervousness, because he whined softly and kept looking up at Seumas as if hoping for a change in his master's mood.

As he waited Seumas thought over the past years spent in Oceania with its various peoples. In the beginning he had despised the Oceanians, for their arrogance, for their apparent feminine ways, for many things. In the beginning he had resented most dreadfully his capture and forced exile. Since that time however, he had revised his opinion of the Raiateans, had made many deep friendships and strong ties. He had come to regard their mild manners and gentleness in the normal course of day-to-day living as more manly than the rough manners and aggressive nature of his own people, for he knew that when the time came for fierceness and courage, they were no more lacking than one of his Pict cousins. They borrowed the better nature of women for their daily dealings with one another and brought forth the pugnacious manliness within them for their battles.

He certainly missed the wild shores and rugged landscape of his homeland, it was true, but he had also come to love the cobalt-blue seascapes and jewel-green islands of Oceania. His whole existence was now plagued by ambivalent feelings. Yet he knew his life had been thus far an *interesting* one. He had seen things no Albannach had seen, except one other, who had shared those years with him, if not by his side, within his sight and hearing. He had experienced things of which no other Pict had dreamed. He was a man full of great stories, part of them, entwined within their multitudinous meshes. In truth, he would not have changed those experiences for a long and common life in the mountains and glens of his homeland, much as he loved his croft in the purple heathered hills of Albainn; much as he loved his clan and their fierce and glorious ways; much as he missed the white winters when the deer ran swiftly over the powdered landscape and the wolf bayed over a kill.

He thought back to his childhood, amongst the aromatic pines, running through different forests than those of Oceania. A barefoot Pict boy with an iron dagger, bow and a quiver of arrows. A hard little boy, inured to the freezing winds, careless of cliffs and their dangers, wolf-eyed, bitter-lipped, ruddy-cheeked. These were distant memories, of times when he wore ermine and foxskin coats; followed spoor over iron-hard earth, of hare and grouse. He remembered the time when he peeked through a chink in a neighbour's croft wall at a young woman changing her clothes and discovered another iron dagger between his legs – he recalled vividly how he was stunned by the sight of the dark furry creature between *her* legs and how the sight of it made his heart beat rapidly and his skin prickle with shock. And memories of stalking martens under a hard-edged, cold, stark moon; of wrestling in the rushing burns with his cousins; of being beaten by his father for crying tears when his pet ptarmigan was killed and roasted during a famine.

Such far-off memories, almost unbelievable.

Now he waited to learn the outcome of his fate in love.

When the canoe reached the shore, Dorcha stepped out and on to the beach.

Seumas said gruffly, using Gaelic because there was a stranger present, '*Thoir dhomh freagairt, caileag?*'

'What do I want? Wouldn't you like to know, *gille?*'

She called him *boy*, because he had discourteously called her *girl* and not *woman*.

'It's about time you learned some manners,' she said, haughtily, standing before him and lifting her chin.

'*Ciod e tha ort?*' he retorted, asking what ailed her.

She visibly softened and replied, this time in Gaelic, for she suddenly became shy, '*Tha gradh agam ort-sa.*'

Seumas stared at her, unable to believe his ears. What she had said, literally translated, was, 'Love is at me, on you.' In plain Oceanian, 'I love you.' Suspicion still lurked in his brain though. He wondered if she were playing tricks with him, a cruel joke.

'What do you mean, you love me?'

'It's been a long voyage. I set out looking for you because I thought I missed tormenting you. When we arrived here and I saw you standing on the beach with that damn dog by your side, I realised that what I missed, was simply *you*, yourself.'

The man with Dorcha was looking at them with wide eyes. Seumas noticed he was a filthy individual, with scabs and sores, an arm in a splint, and either his body or his ragged loin cloth smelled like stagnant swamp water. The man beached the canoe and began walking away from them, towards the huts. He moved swiftly, glancing behind him every so often.

Seumas was too overwhelmed by Dorcha's words to take any notice of the man's strange behaviour.

'Me?' he said to Dorcha. 'What about your dead husband?'

Her face went hard. 'I can never forgive you for that – but I love you anyway. It happens.'

'By heaven, I could take you now, on the sands,' he groaned, fearful that such a promise would be whisked away from him by some heartless god.

'You will not – you will wait until a respectable time.'

He said, 'You – you won't change your mind? You will become my wife? I – I need you, Dorcha, with me – always. I mean, for ever.'

'I shall grow ugly,' she said. 'If all you want is my body, you will be disappointed in me one day.'

He stared into her dark pupils, set in the pale face below the wild tangle of black hair. Already there were crow's feet at the corners of her eyes and mouth, yet her long face had such stately beauty in it he could not imagine a time when he would not see her as he saw her now. There was an inner glow to Dorcha that a thousand years could not dim.

'Never. It's *you* I love. There will always be beauty behind the signs of age – because there is beauty *in* you. That doesn't mean I can't wait to make love to you.'

'I shall become your wife,' she confirmed, smiling.

He took her in his arms and hugged her close, kissing the salt from her face, much to the consternation of Dirk. His heart was full. She was his at last.

She whispered in his ear, 'This is a heavenly island, isn't it? What are they going to call it?'

'They are calling it *Rarotonga*,' he told her. 'And you're right, it will be our paradise.'

'Ours,' she said, smiling, and she took his hand and led him towards the rainforest.

Boy-girl, standing in the shadows, sadly watched them go.

Tangiia and Kula were in intimate embrace when a man threw himself into the doorway of their hut, landing on his knees.

'My lord!' cried the man dramatically, whose foul breath filled the hut almost immediately. 'Hear me!'

Kula drew back, revolted by the stench billowing from the man's body. Tangiia, startled by this intrusion, snatched up a patu club in haste, thinking there was an attack. He studied the creature blocking his doorway with distaste.

The man had blackened teeth and was covered in dirt of some indefinable nature. Tangiia would not have been surprised to learn that the grime had been acquired while the man slept, by choice, with pigs and chickens on the tipairua. Unkempt, matted locks hung from the man's scalp, which itself appeared to be flaking in large scales. The man's nose was running with mucus into some lip sores, around which there were black rims.

'Is it Ragnu?' asked Tangiia. 'Is he coming again?'

'No, my lord,' cried the man. 'He has left on the tide –

but those two mountain goblins. I heard them on the beach. They speak with the tongues of foul demons.'

Tangiia relaxed, leaning on his club.

'What two goblins? Seumas is here alone.'

'Ahh,' smiled the man, greasily, revealing the gaps between his rotten teeth, 'the goblin woman has come too.'

'Dorcha is here?'

'The very same.'

'To kill Seumas?'

'They speak of love,' said the man earnestly, 'in that vile language they use. I mean, sometimes they speak with real words, other times they hiss and screech at each other in the ugly words of fiends and monsters of darkness.'

Tangiia glanced quickly at Kula, giving her an expression of mild surprise. 'Love?'

'Yes, my lord,' said the man, 'I thought you ought to know, considering that if they fornicate, there will soon be horrid little demons all over this lovely island – I hear they can spawn a thousand at a time, these profane creatures.'

'Talking of odious creatures,' said Kula. 'Who are you?'

The man smiled greasily. 'I am proud to be called Polahiki, O queen – a humble fisherman of no certain abode.' His face turned to a grim mask. 'I was wrongly captured by that brigand Tutapu, who called himself a king, but was nothing but a ship rat without fleas –'

'My brother, you mean?' said Tangiia.

Polahiki smiled uncertainly. 'A very fine brother, I'm sure, but a terrible king.'

'Wrong again, mongrel,' said Tangiia. 'He was a fine king, but a terrible brother.'

'That's what I meant,' Polahiki said hastily. 'I get my words mixed up sometimes – it's because I've been tortured, by – by that very fine king we mentioned.' He held up his splinted arm and showed Tangiia some crooked fingers.

Tangiia called for a priest, who came at the run and

showed by his expression that he was horrified to find Polahiki in the doorway of the king's house.

Tangiia said, 'Take this creature and give him a bath.'

Polahiki looked panic-stricken. 'My lord?'

Tangiia narrowed his eyes. 'Let me show you that my brother's tortures were nothing beside mine. You will be scrubbed with hairy gourds until you shine. Your head will be shaved. Your lice will be slaughtered by the hundred thousand. That loin cloth will be burned. You will be, in short, horribly cleansed. Take him away. I don't want to see him until I recognise skin. And pull out the rest of those teeth. If we can't do anything about his flatulence, we can certainly make a difference at the other orifice. Not another word. Go.'

When Polahiki had been dragged from their sight, Kula turned to him smiling. 'You will make a good king,' she said. 'And Rarotonga a good home for our people.'

'Karika and I will rule as well as we can,' replied Tangiia. 'Now, where were we . . .?'

Kula stepped out of her skirt.

'Here?' she said, laughing.

'Exactly,' he replied.

Glossary

Adaro: Malevolent sea-spirit in the shape of a fish-man.

Ahu: Sacrificial platform, sometimes of stone or planks, sometimes of raised bark cloth.

Balepa: Corpse still wrapped in its burial mat which flies above villages at night.

Fanakenga star: Zenith star.

Fangu: Magic spell for various general uses.

Kabu: Soul with a visible shape, though not necessarily human form.

Kahuna: Priest, wise man, versed in the arts of black magic.

Karakia: Magic chant to thwart evil.

Kava: Intoxicating drink made by chewing the root of a *Piper methysticum* shrub and mixing the subsequent paste with water.

Kaveinga: Paths of stars which follow each other up from one spot on the horizon. Polynesian sailors used these natural paths as a navigational aid.

Kopu: Morning Star.

Kotiate club: Hand club shaped like a stunted paddle with a bite out of one side.

Lei-o-mano: Dagger made of hardwood rimmed with sharks' teeth.

Lipsipsip: Dwarves who live in old trees and ancient rocks.

Marae: Courtyard in front of a temple or king's house, a sacred place where sacrificial victims are prepared.

Mana: Magical or supernatural powers, the grace and favour of the divinities, conferred by them.

Manu's Body: Sirius.

Ngaro: The food of the dead.

Nokonoko, or aito: Ironwood tree, used for making weapons.

Pahi: Large, double-hulled ocean-going canoe with a flat deck between the hulls, able to carry seventy or more passengers and ten crew for a month-long voyage without touching land.

Patu club: Hand club shaped like a stunted paddle.

Sau: Spiritual puissance of a man or woman.

Tapa: Bark-cloth made from the inner bark of the paper mulberry tree.

Tapu: Taboo, i.e. sacred or forbidden.

Tapu-tapu atia: Most Sacred, Most Feared.

Tapua: Goblin-like creature with a white skin.

Te lapa: Underwater streaks of light from active volcanoes beneath the surface of the sea.

Te Reinga: Land of the Dead.

Tipairu: Race of fairies who love dancing and who descend on moonlit nights to take part in celebrations, always disappearing back into the forest at dawn.

Tipairua: Double-hulled ocean-going canoe similar to the pahi but closely resembling a war canoe.

Tohua: Marquesan temple.

Umu: Earth oven lined with stones to retain the heat.

Váa: Outriggerless canoe.

Vis: Blood-drinking succubus.

Wahaika club: Hand club shaped like a violin.

17·11·04

7-12-00